The Einstein of the Volga

Jurek Vlascki carefully unfolded the newspaper. He held in his hand a dozen gleaming horseshoe nails, light to the touch and sharp as the claws of a great, wild cat. He picked up the sheet of paper the nails had been wrapped in. It was closely covered with writing, and he held it up to the light to read the small letters. He read it twice, trying to make sense out of it. He turned the nails over and over in his hand, studying the broad, flat heads and trying to imagine how he would do it.

Of course, they knew he could. They remembered the early days when miniaturization belonged to the Japanese until his own work had made Russian technology the leader in the field. In his laboratory in Moscow, Jurek had developed the most sophisticated system of miniaturized detonation in the world.

He laid the nails out on the table. The light glinting from the polished surfaces was hypnotic. Again he read the encoded instructions. An explosive, concealed in the heads of the horseshoe nails. It must be impervious to the blows of a hammer and be detonated by a signal only a few hundred yards away.

Jurek scratched his head. He was tired and his eyes blurred. He longed to scrap the project, say he couldn't do it, that it was impossible. Yet he knew it wasn't impossible, and the bastards in the Kremlin knew it too. He knew he could do it; there was no escape from his destiny.

THE KREMLIN CONTRACT

N.C. WEYL

ZEBRA BOOKS
KENSINGTON PUBLISHING CORP.

To W.L.W., who was, for so many years, the beloved critic on my hearth.

Special thanks to Stephen Spruill for the kindness, expertise, and encouragement that guided me through the treacherous waters of writing a first novel.

ZEBRA BOOKS

are published by

Kensington Publishing Corp.
475 Park Avenue South
New York, NY 10016

First printing: June, 1989

Printed in the United States of America

"He went out and hanged himself from a tree, from the Judas tree that blooms today on the mountainside, its blossoms red with the blood of the tyrant. Betrayed by a friend, the tyrant will fall."

Prologue

April 1989

A lazy surf lapped the black stones of the beach. The sun was hot for April, but a small onshore breeze stirred the water and moved the leaves of the trees that clung to the side of the otherwise rocky cliff. Sun and breeze together played gently on the naked shoulders of the three men who sat beside each other on one of the narrow wooden benches, smoking. Except for these three, who might have been tired businessmen from Moscow, the beach was deserted.

On the cliff, high above them, the white walls of an ancient castle gleamed, pale under the noonday sun. Built a hundred years ago, it had been the scene of brilliant parties; Nicholas had been a frequent guest, and Alexandra had walked the shaded paths with her children, the girls in freshly ironed summer dresses and the little boy bouncing ahead, the ribbons of his flat sailor hat streaming behind him. Across the bay could be seen the palace of Lavidia, guarded by its six stone lions. The lions were in pairs beside the white steps leading up from the beach. The first two were asleep, the next two had just raised their heads in startled wakefulness, and the two at the top were rampant, jealously defending the palace doors. Behind these doors, the frail, crippled President had met with Churchill and "Uncle Joe," and there, in the flush of shared victory, he had signed away freedom for millions of Europeans.

Now the palace above them bustled with activity. It was like any seaside resort, and a constant stream of men, the powerful and the power-hungry, were sent here to rest from the arduous pursuit of world domination in the Kremlin. There was a spa where heavy-handed women doctors gave treatment for disorders ranging from spastic colons to irritable prostate glands. Enemas, massages, and cupping were high on the list of cures. After seven days of such treatment came a welcome week of relaxation. Purged to exhaustion, the "patients" descended each morning to the foot of the cliff, where they spent the sun-filled hours in idle conversation or bathed in the quiet waters of the bay. At noon they climbed the narrow path to the top, where, on the veranda, a hearty lunch awaited them: meats and fish, fresh vegetables, and good home-baked bread, all washed down with beer and vodka.

One of the three got up from his wooden bench and rubbed his ample behind. He was dark and bearded, a Georgian, slow moving and heavy; he looked like a big, brown bear emerging from his den after a winter in hibernation as he stood there squinting into the sun. The hair on his chest went right up over his shoulders and down his back. He pulled deeply on his pipe and grunted. The eyes of the other two followed his. Across the black beach, past the line of surf, he was staring at the horizon. He grunted again, as if to settle a decision and turned suddenly to glare at his friends.

"Well," he began, and paused. "Well; we don't have

8

much choice, do we?"

The small man on his right shifted a bony rear on the hard slats of the bench. "Vasely Ilyitch," he began. "I don't like it —"

"You don't have to like it, idiot," the Georgian snapped. "Nobody gives a shit if you like it or not. None of us likes it, but we have to live with it, play with the cards we are dealt. Of course, it isn't the way it was before. Even in Gorbachev's time it was different . . ." His voice trailed off. When Sharovsky had become chairman of the party after Gorbachev's untimely, and perhaps suspect, death, it had been seen that the agenda he followed was moving away from the influence of the KGB; now, members of the Kometet felt their power eroded. Sharovsky was playing games with the leaders of the West, and what he was doing threatened to jettison the work so nearly completed; to withdraw the support of the Central Committee from the KGB, at this time, could cause the collapse of the whole network just before its moment of triumph.

Now there was a meeting planned in New York, at the UN, where Sharovsky would meet with the American President, Edwin Townsend. There, entirely on his own, he could commit the Soviets to a policy of cooperation with the West, a policy that would negate twenty-five years of planned disaster for the free world. Since the spate of highjackings and bombings in the early and mid-eighties, leaders of every dissatisfied Arab and third-world country had been supplied and trained in terrorism, so that travel from the West was almost nonexistent, and embassies were armed camps in many capitals. Even in Washington, government buildings were under heavy security, and there had been two hotel bombings as well as one attack on the Senate Offices within the last six months.

Townsend had been to Moscow two years ago, and talked with Sharovsky, then a member of the Central Committee. He had been a special envoy of Reagan, and in the preceding four years he had been quietly visiting heads of state throughout the Middle East, Africa, and Eastern Europe. His approach was straightforward and his influence disturbingly persuasive. Clearly, he had been successful on his visit to the Kremlin. There was Sharovsky, ready to go to New York and throw the whole thing away in the outmoded name of détente, just when panic and fear throughout the free world had brought the leaders of almost every Western nation to a point of cooperation. Every leader except the damned American!

Vasely Ilyitch chewed on his pipe. The third man spoke. "If it doesn't work we're up shit creek," he said. "What makes you think we can trust the boy— what's his name, Clements—?"

"It's the only way, Anyasha," the Georgian growled. "As long as Sharovsky is determined to cave in to Townsend, it's our only choice—get rid of him, and do it before Sharovsky can talk to him!"

"Get rid of him, yes, I agree. I even agree with using Jurek. He can make the thing all right, and the man in the State is safe." The thin man paused. "I can't see letting this kid deliver it. What do we know about him, what makes you think he will do it? Whatever he did, it was a long time ago—"

"Stop sniveling like an old babushka, you fool. It's all taken care of over there. Like you say, the man we have in State is solid, he knows the whole thing, and he's running the kid. Orlov will be there, too, a backup. They won't even let the kid know what he's doing. Besides, you say it was a long time ago, the thing in Prague. Yes, it was, but even so, he can't

10

afford to see it in *The Washington Post*."

Anyasha shrugged. Sweat glistened on his skinny back and ran hotly down his sides. The sun was high overhead. He finished the last swallow of warm beer and chucked the bottle into the trash container. "Let's go on up," he said, "and get some lunch."

Vasely Ilyitch remained standing. He scratched his crotch with a hairy paw, then knocked the ashes out of his pipe. His tiny blue eyes looked right past the two other men and sought the horizon. This time he wasn't seeing the circling gulls and the blue sky. He saw a flag-draped caisson and a stately, riderless horse leading a solemn procession down Pennsylvania Avenue. He imagined the fragmented remains inside the casket. He even imagined himself conveying to the grieving widow the sincere sympathy of the Russian people for the regrettable accident that had so mysteriously taken the life of their beloved President.

It was good to contemplate.

Chapter One

Seven hours to the west, the first rays of the sun were slanting through the old trees along Chopawamsic Creek where it runs into the Potomac River south of Washington, wandering through the Marine Base at Quantico. The April morning was still cool, and long shadows fell across the stable yard. Inside the barn, on both sides of the aisle, horses were contentedly breakfasting, munching armloads of fresh hay and cleaning up feed boxes filled with oats. Muzzles splashed in buckets of water and hooves thudded, idly stomping flies from their legs.

Three horses were standing in the aisle. Cross-tied, they stood patiently while two young Marines bustled about with brushes, combs, sponges, and towels. "Move it, you guys, we got to git these hosses done." M/Sgt. Jimmy Watson came out of the tackroom. Even in Marine fatigues, he still looked as though he was about to enter the chute of a dusty rodeo arena to spend thirty seconds on the back of a mean-spirited, double-cinched plains pony. His pale eyes reflected the Montana sky, and his face was a piece of well-cured leather. You missed the chaps and the heeled boots and the wide-brimmed hat.

The sergeant was a horseman, and he ran this barn

the way he had learned to do on the ranch, even if he had to do it with a bunch of tenderfoot kids who didn't know a fetlock from a pastern when they got here. He taught them what they needed to know, until they could take care of the barn and the horses without his help, but none of them was ever allowed to take care of the Grey Ghost while Jimmy Watson was there. Now he took the brush right out of the hand of the young Marine who was gingerly brushing the neck of the big grey horse. "Leave me take care of him, Albert," he said. "You guys don't know this old boy like I do." He took a chew out of his pocket and ran his hand gently down the strong grey back, feeling the hardness of muscle beneath the silky skin.

Jimmy Watson loved the horse and he loved his assignment here. He knew he was lucky to have it. When, like President Reagan before him, Ed Townsend had brought a horse to the barn at Quantico, he had put in a request for Jimmy's transfer to the base so that he could take care of it for him. It was the first time since he'd left the ranch that Jimmy had had a chance to do anything with horses, and it was just like coming home again to be in a barn, and have the good, clean smell of horses in his nostrils and hear the friendly snuffle of their breathing as he walked down the aisle. Even on the days when the President didn't come out, Jim would get the big grey gelding up and go over every inch of his spotless body, sponging, brushing, looking for the slightest blemish or cut. The flowing mane would shine like silk, and the Ghost's tail reached almost to the ground when he'd finished with it.

Jimmy approved of the kind of horse the President owned. It looked like a western horse and it was treated like one. There was the beautiful mane, silver and flowing, not like the rest of the horses on the

14

base, who all looked to Jim like little girls' show horses with their manes pulled so short they were no use for anything. The good Lord made manes to keep a horse warm in winter and swish flies off in summer, but here on the finicky East Coast they didn't know what a real man's horse was like. And Townsend rode his horse in a western saddle, like a man should.

Riding the Ghost was pure pleasure, too. Two or three times a week the President came out for an early-morning ride, but in busy times he might not get there for eight or ten days. Then Jimmy would take the Ghost out to give him his exercise. Townsend liked his horse to be fit, and he could tell when he had been left idle. The woods behind the stable was laced with paths where Jim could ride for hours, along the creek, in the clearing under the power line, or over to the river, enjoying the feeling of a good horse under him and almost believing he could feel the western wind on his face and hear it whistling through the mesquite.

"Don't worry, Sarge, we won't hurt your pet," one of the Marines spoke from under the tall chestnut horse. He was sponging cool water up and down the horse's legs. The other Marine was picking up, one at a time, the feet of the small palomino tied by the next stall. With a hoof-pick, he was dislodging the night's accumulation of manure and sawdust. "When's Bud coming?" he asked. "Got a loose shoe here." He held the hoof up for Jimmy to see.

"He'll git him Friday, when he does Ghost," Jimmy said. He put his brushes away and turned to speak to the horse. "How's my boy today?" His voice was conversational and the Ghost responded by wrinkling his velvety nose and nuzzling the pocket of Jim's fatigues. He knew where the carrots came from, and he was not above stealing one if he got the chance.

15

"Hold on there, hoss," Jimmy said. He reached in his pocket and laid several chunks of carrot on the flat of his hand, where the Ghost delicately scooped them into his mouth. For a moment, the wet crunching sound of his big teeth, the swish of water in the buckets, and the slidy noise of a sweat scraper were the only sounds in the barn. Leaning over, Jimmy took a soft brush from the tack box and began cleaning invisible dust and dirt from the already spotless hide of the big grey horse.

"Let's git these hosses ready, boys. Ain't got all day." The call from the White House had come an hour earlier. They never let them know the night before, so the boys had to be at work by four o'clock to feed in time for a six-thirty ride. They were sleepily checking the girths and adjusting bits on the two other horses, while Jimmy led the Ghost out into the yard. The big horse followed him elegantly, almost daintily, down the aisle.

Right behind him came the unassuming little palomino mare, led by one of the Marines. "She don't feel like she's going nowhere today, Boss," he said. She looked almost asleep, automatically picking up her feet and putting them down.

"That's good," Jimmy said. "That's why we got her. That fat-ass Secret Service, he ain't learned which end goes first yet." Jimmy spat in the dust, precisely and with meaning. They all knew poor Johnny Grimes couldn't ride worth a damn and spent long hours alone with the animal he feared, while Townsend and George rode unattended and unencumbered through the silent forest. George Clements nearly always rode with Townsend. Jim liked George and he was glad the Boss had someone to go with him; it worried him when Townsend rode alone.

He led the grey horse out into the brightening day.

16

Dust particles hung in the air and made the shafts of sunlight crossing the yard look like bars of solid gold. The sun caught on the silver of the western saddle and little lights blinked with the motion of the horse. Jimmy stood looking at the horse and admiring his handiwork. He stood in the sun, warming himself, waiting for them to bring the other two horses out.

Along with the palomino, the boys brought out a black-and-white paint mustang, Jimmy's own horse. Riding the Grey Ghost, Jimmy would lead these two animals to the meeting place, where he would turn the President's horse over to him, give Johnny Grimes the palomino, and ride back to the barn on his mustang. Knowledge of the rendezvous spot was closely guarded. Outside of Jimmy, Townsend's aide, Clements, was the only other person who had word of each day's meeting place. Clements was radioed in his car on the way to the base.

Holding the two horses' lead shanks in one hand, the sergeant put his foot in the stirrup. He paused, half on and half off. "Joe, you stay with Mr. Clement's horse till he comes. Albert, you kin git on with the stalls—I'll be back in a little." He pulled himself onto the tall horse and trotted out of the yard, leading the others and whistling to himself, old songs he remembered from the plains.

The sun was finding its way through the leaves overhead, casting long slanting fingers on the spongy ground of the path. A light breeze from the east was turning the new leaves of the maples inside out, silvery. Except for the distant sounds of a waking military base and the planes coming in low to land at National, Jimmy could imagine himself to be the first man who ever rode through these woods, making his way downhill towards Chopawamsic Creek more than three hundred years ago.

"Come on, you old cow, move it!" Jimmy gave the palomino's lead rope an encouraging tug. "It's just around the next turn." It was a different meeting place every time. In the cool quiet of the forest path it didn't seem possible that danger was close, and that guarding against disaster was a priority. Still, they insisted that the poor tenderfoot cop had to be here. Jimmy felt sorry for him; nothing was going to happen with George Clements there, anyhow. The kid could just as well be home in bed.

He rounded a corner and stopped. A tall man stepped out on the shadowy footpath, his face broken by a wide grin. "God, I'm glad to see you, Jimmy! It's been too long."

"Glad to see you, too, sir. We been missing you. Busy times, I reckon."

There was a lingering memory of the young cowhand in his slightly graceless leap from the saddle. His leathery face broke into a wide grin as he handed the reins to Townsend. He remembered the days on the ranch when he was a boy and Townsend had hired his father to run the ranch. The President seemed to echo his thoughts when he spoke. "What would we do without you, Jim, Ghost and I? We've been a long road together, haven't we, since the Bar T?" He took the reins from Jimmy's hand and clapped him on the shoulder. "Thanks for everything, Jimmy!"

In an easy vault he was on the horse's back. The look of the plains had stayed with him through the years in Washington. Under a big western hat, clear blue eyes looked out from a network of tiny wrinkles; he seemed to be scanning a far horizon. The weathered skin of his face was witness to his nearly sixty years, but the mischievous smile and graceful, athletic leap into the saddle spoke of a much younger man.

Then there was the tenderfoot. His eyes seemed

18

shifty in his white face. It was only fear that gave him that look, but it somehow brought to mind the big city, organized crime, and the days of Al Capone. His pudgy legs were encased in what looked to be perpetually new breeches, and his ill-fitting jacket didn't really conceal the bulge under his left arm. He smiled weakly at Jimmy and nervously patted the palomino's nose. He jumped back when the little mare moved. Consumed with pity, Jimmy held the reins and steadied the stirrup for him to mount. The man gave him a pleading look and heaved his heavy frame onto the saddle, which his body somehow didn't seem to fit. He shifted his weight uneasily and took the reins in his damp paw. "Thanks, Jim," he murmured. "Thanks a lot."

Jimmy waited a minute, at ease on his paint horse, while Edwin Townsend tried to console Johnny Grimes. "You can take your time, son," he said. "I want to work up a little sweat today, so I'll meet you on the way back. Just stay on the path, OK? No, you don't have to come. I'm meeting George at the bridge. Perfectly safe, and I won't tell a soul. Promise. Don't worry, son." His eyes twinkled, a schoolboy playing hooky. Before Johnny could say a word, Jimmy watched the President turn his horse and trot down the path, disappearing into the shadowy woods.

In a small swirl of dust, a silvery Porsche pulled up at the barn. The man who jumped out was stuffing a white shirt into his breeches as he dashed across the yard. "Got Chester ready, Joe?" he called as he ran.

The Marine nodded as he started for the stable. "Just a sec, Mr. Clements; he's all ready—"

"Thanks, Joe." George Clements shivered a little in

19

the dampness. He wished the sun could reach through the trees and warm him up. He took a deep breath of the morning air and pulled his belt in another notch while he waited. Joe led the horse out of the barn and George grinned at him as he took the reins. "Thanks, buddy. See you later." He ran a practiced hand under the girth, swung easily into the saddle, and trotted across the yard. Little puffs of dust rose from the ground under the horse's feet and blew across the lot.

The tension seemed to go out of George's body as he settled into the rhythm of the horse's trot. As they moved along the shaded path, he felt himself filled with an unaccustomed happiness; perhaps it was simple gratitude for the gift of being alive on a beautiful day, but, for whatever reason, George felt as though he was beginning a new chapter of life, one in which the blank pages could be filled with satisfaction and even with joy. Maybe, he thought, maybe this is reality and the past was a dream. Maybe I can live now, without remembering—

As he rode into the forest, moving shadows dappled the path beneath his feet and he could hear the small sounds of waking birds all around him; he told himself that if he remembered anything at all, this was the kind of day for happy memories, and he felt, again, that strange lifting of the sadness that had haunted most of his days for so long. He took in a deep breath and the air smelled clean; it smelled of pine trees and forest mulch and of the tidal flats that lay below him where the creek widened and ran into the river. On a morning like this the long-ago darkness seemed to vanish like the shadows under the trees—

He heard hoofbeats drumming along on the path ahead of him, and Chester's ears went forward to listen. He heard the laugh before they met, and then Townsend's voice. "Hey, George, aren't you glad I got you out of the sack this morning? What a day to be here!" The man's enthusiasm was infectious, and the grin on his face when he rode up cleared the last gloomy cobweb from George's mind. He grinned back.

"Good morning, Uncle Prez. It's always worth it, isn't it? However much you want to roll over and snooze at four-thirty, when you get here you forget all about it —" He looked at the tall man sitting erect on his horse, who stood motionless, bathed in a pool of light. He thought, This is what they mean, "tall in the saddle"; Townsend sat easy on the horse as though they belonged together. His face was tanned and lined from the weather, and George was comforted by the warmth and genuine affection he saw in the older man's smile.

He thought how different from Townsend he looked on his horse, and tried to believe the difference was only in appearance. His years of riding in competition showed in the stringy muscles outlined under his tight breeches and in the sharp angle of his ankle, above the toe that rested lightly in the metal stirrup. "Where's Johnny?" he asked. "Has he actually trusted me to take care of you today?" George laughed. He knew that Johnny, of the hard eyes and lightning reflexes, was a total loss with horses. When it came to riding, he had all the coordination of a Saint Bernard puppy.

"He thought he'd take it easy today," Townsend said. "I'll pick him up on the way back. Too fine a morning to dawdle along with him, and I can't afford to have him break his neck. We can talk state secrets, or whatever we want to."

George smiled. "Nope, not today. We won't even

21

think state secrets or budgets, or terrorists. I won't even mention your lunch with the representative from—"

It was the wrong thing to have said. Damn. For a minute the President's face lost its easy grin, and George was reminded of an eagle he had once seen in a run-down Wildlife Museum along a western highway. The eagle was chained to a heavy log; it could move its wings, but the chain was short and it couldn't fly. George remembered how he had gone close, a little afraid of the fierce beak and beating wings, and he had seen in its eye a look that he had understood. Though the eagle's body was captive and chained to the log, his spirit was still free, circling high above, ruling the sky. The same look was on Townsend's face, but only for a moment, and then it was gone. The old eagle was free again, and Townsend mused aloud.

"Oh, that doesn't bother me, son. I know I've got Sharovsky in my pocket, and he knows he has to come along with us. We can forget the rest of them. If the Soviets agree, and they will, then we've got it. The unaligned people, if that's what they really are, have given me commitments and the Soviets know it. Sharovsky knows they'll be with us, and he knows they'll stick by what they've said. The hell with the KGB boys, they're out, as far as he's concerned. And I really believe he trusts me. George, I think we're going to make it this time." He paused, his eyes on the horizon, where the wide Potomac showed silver through the trees. "Hell, we have to, son, we have to. And while I live, we will."

Why did I bring it up? I never meant to start him on this. The reason I'm here is to get him away from everything, and now I've blown it. Seeing the set of Townsend's jaw and the blue vein beating on the side

22

of his neck, George could have kicked himself. Time like this was too precious; it had been over two weeks since the President had been out with him for a ride. He was supposed to get him to relax. Doctor's orders.

"Let's forget it for today, OK?" George moved Chester up close beside the President. "Driving out here I was thinking about the time Dad brought me over to your ranch and your hands fixed me up with that cow pony. Remember?" He grinned.

Townsend turned towards him with a smile. "Do I remember? I'll say I do. I should have fired those boys. How old were you then? About six? Close to scared your dad and me to death when we saw you up on that son of a coyote they let you ride—" A faraway look was in his eyes, the look of the wide plains and towering skies of the West. "Sure," he said, "sure I remember."

George remembered, too. He was standing at the fence of a dusty corral. His head was about level with the silver buckle on the man's belt. His father and the man were talking, and laughing a lot, talking about what they called the old days. His father would reach down and ruffle George's hair, or just rest a hand on his shoulder while they talked.

It was hot, standing by the fence, and even the few chickens that scratched the dry ground under the single plane tree were dispirited. The rooster's tail dragged in the dust, and the hens seemed annoyed by the half-grown chicken that was following them around. George chucked a pebble at the rooster, and he jumped a little, but it wasn't worth looking for another stone. George chewed a long stem of grass. He held it in the corner of his mouth, hanging off his lip, pretending it was a cigarette.

The man his father was talking to was tall, and it was hard to see his whole face. George wished they would look at him. He felt as though he was invisible, and the shimmering heat waves made him think he was floating. He coughed, just a little cough, and the tall man looked down and smiled. It was a nice smile and a nice face when you could see it. The smile seemed to cover his whole face, and little lines crinkled around his eyes. "How'd you like to go with some of the boys and see my ponies? Your dad and I have a lot of talking to do and I bet you'd liefer ride than talk, wouldn't you?"

Wouldn't he? He was an experienced horseman. Months ago, on his seventh birthday, Dad had given him just about the best little pony a boy ever had. Old Spot was just the right size for a boy to be able to comb and groom and saddle up, or, better still, leap on bareback and ride the range just like the ranch hands did. There wasn't a thing he couldn't do with a pony now that he had Spot. Would he like to ride? "Sure, sir, I'd like it a lot." He wanted to spit casually in the dust to show how experienced he was, but something in Dad's expression caused him to swallow and just smile.

Mr. Townsend clanged on a big iron bell that hung by the fence. An answering "Yeooh" came from the barn, and three cowhands ambled across the dusty corral. "Sam, this is George Clements, and I want you boys to show him our layout here while his dad and I catch up on about ten years of talking. Show him the new paint pony and let him look at anything else he wants to. Just bring him up for dinner by noontime—"

He sauntered off with the three young men, walking the way they did, with a little swagger, his thumbs hooked in his suspenders, his boots kicking up the dust. It was a long way across the corral to the shade of the barn. A big fly, shiny as metal, buzzed around him and he wished he had a drink. Just a nice tin cup full of cold water, but he didn't want to ask them. Of course he knew all the hands on his father's place and spent a lot of time with them, they would have been glad to get him a drink, but this was the first time he'd ever been to the Bar-T and he didn't want these guys to think he was a sissy. *They* weren't complaining about being thirsty. He guessed he could just keep quiet about it.

They took him into the barn and showed him the paint pony. They showed him a few others, too. They asked him about his ranch and if he had a pony and if he could ride. He hadn't meant to brag, but when he got started he just couldn't help telling these men how great his own pony was, and all the things he could do with him. Maybe he exaggerated a little; they seemed so interested in what he was saying. The youngest of the hands was laughing and said something about the little mustang. The other two didn't agree with what he was saying at first, but then they sort of grinned and said OK.

"Like to ride one of our ponies, George?" the young redheaded man said, then the one named Sam said, "Maybe we oughtn't let him, Red—"

"Oh, shoot, Sam, let's let the boy have some fun. You want to show us how you can ride, don't you, kid?"

"Sure, I do," he said, and they took him out behind the barn. In a small corral he saw a horse, standing in the shade munching alfalfa. The little mustang was black all over, and his coat gleamed like coal. He had one moon eye and a long silky mane.

"Ain't he purty?" the one called Red said. He edged over to the little horse's side and put a rope on his neck. The animal stiffened, but didn't try to escape. The three men had his saddle on in no time and led him over to George.

"He sure is a pretty horse," George said, looking him in the moon eye. "Is it really OK with Mr. Townsend if I ride him?"

The men held the horse still and helped George get a leg over his back. George took the reins in his hand and the pony trotted swiftly out into the corral. He was a lot bigger than Spot, and his trot was a lot faster. George swelled with confidence as they circled the hot arena. The mustang picked up speed at the far corner and broke into a gallop. They sped past the laughing cowboys so quickly that George couldn't hear what they were saying. He reined in to slow the animal down. Nothing happened. He pulled as hard as he could, and still nothing happened.

It was a little scary to realize that the horse was in control and he was merely a passenger; the horse was making all the decisions, something his father had warned him against allowing a horse to do. They veered across the ring and ran straight at the fence. George sat back and hauled on the left rain. Just in time the pony whirled and shot back into the center of the corral. George barely had time to catch his breath before the pony pulled his muscles together and released himself like a coiled steel spring. The wind from the desert burned like fire, and for endless minutes the pony bucked and wheeled and reared. George's face was cold, but sweat ran into his eyes and down his neck. The sun wheeled overhead, and George could see its fierce eye as it spun crazily past him.

He could hear the men yelling and he caught glimpses of them running. A man would be in front of him one minute and nowhere to be seen the next. He heard, from a distance, his father's voice, and the tall man calling. The pony wheeled and ran straight for the fence again.

As the frantic hooves pounded the dirt of the corral, time held still. George saw the glistening black neck, flecked with sweat, straining and tensing in front of him. He felt the powerful muscles gather under him to fling the animal forward and up, over the fence. He buried his hands in the coarse black mane and closed his eyes. He heard a voice inside his head saying, "Now I lay me down to sleep—" It was the only prayer he knew.

They flew. The pony had wings and soared over the four-board fence as if it wasn't there. He didn't break his stride; he raced across the rough desert ground, dodging tumbleweed and mesquite, racing the very wind. George was surprised to find himself still in the saddle, hunched over the pony's neck, hands clinging to the mane. The hot desert wind was in his face now, drying the sweat and tears. He and the mustang were flying, they would never stop until they reached the far blue mountains. They dodged boulders and trees, they jumped ditches, and his heart pounded in his chest. He *was* the wind, the sky, and the sun. All power was his, and he knew what life was for. It was to dare, to strive, and to win.

The pony slowed, breathing in and out with short, rasping gulps. Sweat ran from his sides and his head hung down. George patted the heaving side, his hand slick with his sweat and the pony's. They stood for a long minute while the world came back to normal around them. Wherever George looked, the ground seemed to be racing away, out from under him. It made him dizzy, but he straightened in the saddle and picked up the reins again. The air was perfectly still, and there was no sound beyond the hard, dry scraping of the locusts in the mesquite trees.

"Good boy," George said. His voice came from far

27

away. He reined the pony around and they walked back to the ranch. Mr. Townsend and his father and the three cowboys were running towards him, so he kicked the tired pony into a gentle lope. His father ran to him and took the pony's bridle in his hand. His voice was husky when he spoke. "That was some ride, son." George had laughed, couldn't stop laughing, and Dad laughed with him. Oh, yes, he remembered that day, the day they visited the Bar T Ranch.

"You know, for years I thought that mustang was the horse you rode every day, and I just wanted to be as good as you." That's right, George thought, that's what he used to want to be. To be as good as Ed Townsend, as good as the man who rode beside him today, holding the destiny of the world in his hands, as surely as he held the reins of the grey horse which trotted serenely along the shaded path.

Townsend laughed, and George could relax. "Feel up to a little gallop?" The President threw the words over his shoulder as he spurred the Ghost ahead. George gave Chester a nudge and raced after him. A tiny breeze from the west rustled in the branches, and the warmth of the sun was on his back.

Chapter Two

Prague, May 1973

Aubrey Clements, looking through the small panes of his bedroom window, could see his son, George, talking to poor old Harrison. George was, as usual, smiling disarmingly, doubtless trying to pull the wool over the old boy's eyes and get away with some kind of murder again. The sky over the city was grey, casting a dingy light over the garden and the streets beyond. The only brightness the ambassador saw in the scene below his window was the pale gold of his son's hair, ruffled by the wind that swept across from the river.

The dark sky over Prague matched the ambassador's mood that morning. After two months in the embassy, he felt only frustration and failure in the job he had so coveted and accepted with such enthusiasm when the appointment was announced. He had looked forward to working in one of the Eastern Bloc nations; it had been a persistent dream of his for years. When he was elected to the House in 1972, Ed Townsend was serving in the Senate, and they had been appointed together to a joint commission for studying Eastern European affairs. They had made three fact-finding tours of Eastern Europe, and during this time their shared interest had strengthened a friendship begun twenty years earlier, when they had traveled together from Wyoming to New Hampshire to begin their freshman year at Dartmouth.

Now he was learning that merely to study these governments in theory was in no way to prepare for living with them. The system was unapproachable; reason and good will were useless in the face of the monotonous, impenetrable mind-set of his counterparts. He began to see the appointment as one of the most difficult and frustrating jobs he could imagine, and he was assailed by a feeling of complete helplessness in the face of what he had come to think of as his adversaries.

Looking down from his window he could see the top of Harrison's bald pate nodding in agreement to something George was saying. The boy flung the bright hair from his eyes, and in the motion, Clements could see a smile flash across the tanned face; the smile looked genuine and reassured him that it hadn't been a mistake to bring the boy with them. Originally they had planned to leave George at school in America, where he was a second-year student at Choate. It was the third school in as many years where he had been accepted, as much on account of his unfailing charm as on the basis of his unequivocally good test scores. They were hoping it wouldn't be the third one to throw him out when his high spirits, as inevitably happened, came into conflict with the school's standards of conformity.

In the end, Helen had convinced him that they would feel better to have George here with them in Prague, thus avoiding the constant fear of receiving word from yet another headmaster that perhaps George would be happier in another environment. It was also true, as Helen had pointed out, that the experience of living in a foreign country would be, in itself, an education. In the long run, it seemed to be working out pretty well. Old Willard Harrison, nearing the end of a career not noticeably marked by achievement, was in Prague, shuffling papers at the embassy, waiting out his retirement, and he fell happily into the job of tutoring George every morning in exchange for relief from some of his more routine duties.

As usual, Aubrey thought, Helen was right. She had always thought if George had gone to day school and stayed home with them in Virginia, things might have been better. Horses seemed to be in the boy's blood, and if he could have spent more time on the farm, school might have been less of a burden to him. Perhaps his troubles at school had simply stemmed from a desire to be sent home; clearly that was where he was happiest. Of course, Aubrey was forced to admit to himself that without the Institute of Equestrian Arts, the situation here might not have been any better for George than exile at Choate. The riding school had been an answer to a prayer, George's prayer, at any rate. The boy spent every afternoon there, getting instruction from an old Czech major, on whose gruff, military discipline he seemed to thrive.

The ambassador sighed. Mothers knew best, he supposed. Helen had taught George to love horses, and fox hunting, and steeplechasing, and Aubrey could see that the discipline of prep school was a pretty dull substitute for the freedom of the Virginia hills. Yes, the Institute and Major Hrdlcka were devoutly to be thanked. He straightened his tie and closed his briefcase. The car would be downstairs waiting for him.

31

* * *

In the garden, George was still smiling disarmingly at his tutor. "Look, Mr. Harrison," he was saying, "it's going to rain, it's going to rain by lunchtime. If I have to translate the whole chapter and do that math I won't get to the Institute before it starts and Major P. said I could do the outside course today, but he won't let me if it rains. Please, Mr. Harrison, just this once. I won't tell Dad, promise I won't. I'll do it this afternoon and leave it in your box, OK?"

Willard Harrison shrugged his tired shoulders. He thought of the thirty years he had served in the Department, thirty years of hard and unrewarding work; he wanted to laugh to think of where it had brought him. He was negotiating with a child over when the schoolwork should be done! Hell, he had been in Prague in the fifties when Clements was still down on the Wyoming ranch, studying how to get to Washington. Now he was spending his days on high-school math and third-year Latin, while men not dry behind the ears were running the Department. At the very least, he should keep the boy from winning the negotiation. He smiled a wry smile at the thought and, not for the first time, decided that if the boy were his, he would be in a good military academy where that accursed smile would be of no more use to him than an extra foot.

"George, I believe that is the third 'just this once' you've pulled on me in a week's time. You know the horses are supposed to come after the lessons and you know it isn't just my idea to have it that way. Your father definitely said—"

"Oh, Mr. Harrison, he'll never know. He'll be at the embassy in fifteen minutes. I'll wait till he goes, and you can, too. Then you can go to Brzenski's and I can

32

go to the Institute and neither one of us will say a word." Willard knew when he was beat. George had seen him one afternoon in the little bar on Pflenka Street. By what miserable chance the boy had happened in, he would never know; he had been certain that no one knew of his trips to Brzenski's. It had been the one place where he felt an escape from the failure of his life; it was a dark corner where he and Klowoski lost themselves in endless chess games and long draughts of beer. Klowoski was a Czech, a professor at the university. They had met on the Charles Bridge, where each had been watching the slow progress of the Moldau on its way to the sea, each absorbed in thoughts, and each longing for companionship.

So, they had begun a quiet friendship, a meeting in the dark little bar, where they found hours of relief from whatever burdens they each bore. Now, he knew his secret was in the hands of this tedious boy, and the comfortable security of its dark recesses was at risk. Of course, as far as he knew, no one at the embassy was the wiser for George's knowledge. For all his colleagues knew, if they missed him at all, they just supposed he was having a particularly harrowing day with his pupil and couldn't get back to the office. He certainly couldn't afford to disabuse anyone of that notion.

"Well, George, I know I can trust you with the translation, and if you have trouble with the math, we can start a little early tomorrow—"

"Gee, sir, thank you. You're the greatest! Hope you win, and Klowoski has to buy you ten beers!" The boy was like quicksilver, his straight blond hair blew across his forehead in the wind, and he flashed Harrison a disconcertingly genuine smile. When he smiled like that Harrison would try to resist the feeling that

33

George really liked him. He wasn't used to being liked, and he was accustomed to denying himself the luxury of hope. It generated too much pain when, inevitably, he knew he had deceived himself.

They sat on one of the stone benches with carved lions' feet that bordered the little formal part of the garden. "Look, sir, if you just give me a clue about these coordinates while we wait for the old man to leave, it'll make your conscience feel better and maybe I can really do the math this P.M." Harrison perched his glasses on his nose and picked up the book. As the ambassador stepped into the porte cochere to get into the waiting car, he waved a casual hand in their direction, clearly pleased at the sight of his son engaged in serious conversation with old Harrison.

"OK, sir, let's go. I think I've got it," George lied. "See you later, alligator," and he bounded up the steps of the Residence. Harrison's sigh gave way to a small smile. He picked up the abandoned books and lugged them to the door. From the top of the stairs, George saw him turn and head casually towards Pflenka Street.

George slammed the door to his room, peeling off his grey flannels even as he ran. Riding clothes were laid out on his bed and clean boots stood side by side on the rug. He reflected, as he flung pants and blue button-down shirt on the chair, that living in the Ambassador's Residence had its advantages. Every day his boots arrived, freshly polished, firmly treed, with gleaming spurs laid by their side. No more of Mom hollering at you about not appearing in the hunt field looking like a farmer with mud on your boots and your coat wrinkled and hairy. He could get used to

34

this way of life pretty easily. He hummed as he pulled the tight white breeches over long, bony legs. He seemed to be growing every day.

If he could get used to the perks, he could never get used to the surveillance. He knew that. When he had first discovered the bug in his bathroom he used to go in and say rude things to it, but after a few weeks this exercise palled, and he began to believe no one ever listened to it anyhow. What did he know that anyone wanted to listen to?

The bug wasn't the worst; there were bugs all over the house, after all. Dad had surprised the "gardener" climbing in his third-floor bedroom window one day. The man had coolly explained that he had left his clippers on the windowsill, and, grinning widely, apologizing profusely, he had backed down the ladder. "Clippers on the third-floor windowsill?" Mom had asked. "They must take us for world-class idiots." They never found where he had hidden it, but after that she and Dad took a lot of long walks in the park. It was the only place they could say anything to each other.

What was the worst about this crazy country was that you didn't go anywhere without someone with you. At home, George had been driving the Jeep on the farm since he was twelve, and here he was fifteen years old and being driven around like a baby, or, Mom had said, like a diplomat, in a chauffeured limo. Leon was assigned to take him wherever he needed to go, but the air of distinction this arrangement at first engendered had long given way to irritation at the man's dense refusal to understand the simplest directions.

Leon's command of English seemed adequate enough, but he functioned as though programmed from some giant computer that George didn't know how to reprogram. If it was time to go riding, they went to the Institute. If it was time to go to the library, they went to the library. If George wanted to stop at the drugstore, he might as well have been riding with a deaf mute. Any change in Leon's program was impossible.

Leon apparently felt an obligation to instruct his passenger in the history and geography of the city, so at first the daily trips were like guided tours of Prague, but after a while George knew as much as Leon about the two or three routes they ever took. He tried other avenues of communication. He asked Leon what he knew about horses, how the soccer team was doing, where he lived, and if he had a family. The responses to these gambits were uneven at best. On soccer Leon was voluble, but about horses he knew little more than a memory from childhood, when his grandfather had kept an old workhorse on the farm in the valley. Of his private life he would say nothing.

George pulled on his boots, listened at the top of the stairs to be sure Mom had left the house, and then rang for Leon. If he rang from his room, and went down the three flights of wide stairs as fast as he could, he would arrive at the door just as Leon drove up. Leon must have nothing to do but wait, in total readiness, for the phone to ring; he appeared as by magic whenever you called.

Today was no different. There was Leon, his unsmiling countenance half hidden by bristling mustache and dark beard. It was hard to tell if the greasy cap he wore was the vestige of a uniform or a proletarian statement of derision. With exaggerated courtesy he got out and opened the door for George, who smiled widely, and tried "Good morning" in Czech. Leon, as always, ignored this effort, pretending,

George knew, that it was so inexpertly done as to be unintelligible.

"Pardon?" Leon inquired, establishing his linguistic superiority with a single word.

"I said, 'Good morning,' " George said, still flashing his radiant smile. *And you know it, you bastard, just as well as I do.*

"Ah, yesss, goot morning, sir!" Leon beamed. He had won that one and could resume his attack. "It is the horssses this morning? So soon? The lessons for today are over?"

"The lessons for today are over, Leon. You're right. It is the horses; let's go, OK?" *The lessons for today are my business, you son of a bitch. You're getting good American bucks to drive me, buddy, so let's drive, OK?* Everyone who worked at the embassy and at the Residence had to be chosen by the Czech government; they didn't even allow the Americans to bring a janitor. Mom had to try to run the house and plan parties with help that couldn't speak enough English to boil an egg, she said, and her three-month course in conversational Czech had failed to render her exactly fluent, either. After a few weeks of eating cold hunks of bread with breakfast, she had asked the cook for toast. He repeated the word three or four times, questioningly, but finally disappeared to the kitchen and returned bearing champagne glasses and a bottle of Moët.

Someday, George thought, this will all be very funny and make wonderful conversation at parties when we go home. He settled into the cracked leather of the backseat and thought about home; he thought of vacations and parties and of the guys at school and weekend dances. He thought of holding a girl in his arms while the music got slower and slower and promising to write every week and trying to get alone

37

with her after the dance. It was lonesome here, when you thought about it and every day was just like the day before; he was alone all the time and someone was always watching. Nothing he did was unknown to them and his days were filled with an unsettling boredom that lent a monotonous greyness to every hour of every day, just like the dull winter sky and the ugly sameness of the cheap clothes and empty storefronts. He'd lose his f—ing mind if it weren't for the horses.

The solid and elegant facade of the Institute rose above them as Leon glided to a stop. Again the unspoken sarcasm of his manner as he jumped out to open the door. He made a somehow insolent little bow as George stepped out. "Thanks, Leon," George said. "I don't know what I'd do without you. You can come back about two. I'll be here."

"I wait," muttered Leon. "Is my job always to wait."

"It's OK, Leon. I promise you, I won't be done till then and I won't go anywhere. There must be something you want to do for the next four hours; have a couple beers, go to the soccer game—I don't know, you must want to do something. I won't even know if you're here—" He realized he might as well have spoken to the stone wall of the Institute. Leon couldn't hear what he was forbidden to hear. He would wait till hell froze over.

Well, he'll just have to wait, George thought as he went under the heavy stone arch and into the courtyard. Inside, the air smelled divinely of horses. George breathed deeply to fill his lungs with the smell of fresh hay mixed with the smell of clean horses and the steamy odor of wet bedding and warm manure. It made him forget Harrison and Leon and lessons, and led him by his nose through the heavy columns, past the great hall, and into the stable area.

38

The stalls were freshly made up twice a day, not with the lavish amounts of straw you would find in a racing stable at home, but with economical rationings of sawdust, scrupulously raked and picked out. Heavy oak doors, their top halves open, lined both sides of a wide, cobbled aisle. Here and there, students worked on horses cross-tied outside a stall, and at the far end the farrier was tending to the feet of a huge bay Holsteiner.

Prinz Heinrich showed not the least surprise when George opened his stall and walked in. His big head came down to sniff George's pockets, looking for apples, carrots, or maybe sugar lumps. "Hi, fella," George whispered. "I brought you an apple. Would I forget you, boy? Would I do that?"

The Prinz gratefully received four quarters of a smallish, wormy apple and nuzzled for more. "That's it, fella. That's all I could get for you today." It was something else to live in a country where no matter what you could afford to buy, a few rotten apples were all you could get at the market some days. The Prinz expressed no surprise at this news. He was a Czech, after all, and probably used to deprivation. Actually, he was a Danish Warmblood, one of a number of different European breeds the major kept for his students.

George knew he was lucky to have the Prinz. Horses at the Institute were assigned on the basis of the major's opinion of your horsemanship. Dad had brought him here the first week they were in Prague, to talk to Major Hrdlcka and see what arrangements could be made. It had looked like it would be pretty tame circling around that ring with some old guy yelling at you. Pretty far from the hills of Virginia where first he had learned foxhunting, and then, on Dad's big thoroughbred, had done the steeplechase circuit last spring. After those glorious afternoons galloping cross-country, jumping the big rough timber at Casanova, or flying over the stone wall in-and-out on the Oatlands drive, he just couldn't imagine plodding around an indoor arena on some school plug.

The major had reserved judgment on taking George for a student until he saw him ride. The horse he had given him to try out on was no school horse in any sense of the word as George understood it. He was above sixteen hands and very solid, a Hanovarian eventer. He had walked the horse around the tanbark ring. His stride was tremendous, and he ate up ground at the walk, George judged, at about six miles an hour. Holding the reins lightly, George had felt the power generated by the muscular hindquarters as it surged forward through the horse's body like an electrical current until it vibrated through the bit and into his hands.

"Trot!" Major Hrdlcka had barked. A slight pressure of George's legs transferred the message to the horse and the animal smoothly changed his stride to a floating two-beat trot. George had thought he was built a little like a draft horse, and expected the feet to fall like hammers in the familiar bone-jarring trot of the straight-shouldered animal. Around the arena they had floated, hooves thudding the tanbark, one, two, one, two, and George had forgotten that he meant to be bored to tears riding here, and the major had smiled under his bristling mustache, for here he saw what too rarely came to him, a real horseman. The boy's hands were perfect, his long legs contacted the horse's sides eloquently; he knew how to ride.

"*Da,*" he had said to the ambassador. "We find him something to ride. Every day he will come. We make something of the boy. You see. He will work, *da?*"

40

"If it's horses, he will work, *da*," the ambassador had echoed.

The horses at the Institute clearly were not school horses. Here the Czech Olympic horses boarded and here their three-day team trained. George discovered that the horse he had ridden and been so excited over was merely one of a group of retirees from the team, and after a few weeks on him the major had called George aside one day.

They had walked down the aisle of the barn, stopping here and there to talk to a horse or pat an inquisitive nose. The major spoke to the horses as though they were his children. Near the end of the aisle he had stopped and leaned over a stall door. "Come here, George," he'd said. "Look him. You like?"

Liquid brown eyes in a wide forehead, a tiny white star in the middle, and a lustrous dark bay coat. The brass plate on his halter said 'Prinz Heinrich.' He must have been seventeen hands, and the muscles of his neck stood out under the gleaming coat. "Hi, fella," George had whispered. "Hey, boy, how's it going?"

"He just come," the major had said. "Bred in the mountains, be some horse, right rider. You been good boy, George, tomorrow you ride him. We see how it does."

"He's beautiful, sir. I mean, I never saw a horse I liked this much. Is he for the team?" He couldn't bear to think that he might get to ride this horse and come to know him and love him and then have him taken away. "Boy, this horse is for who can ride him. You try."

He'd tried like he'd never tried before at anything. He'd spent hours in the arena, walking, extending the walk, sitting trots, slow canters, changing leads. On

41

Prinz nothing was a bore. He lived for the day he could take him out and work cross-country. That had been months ago. He'd had him over the stadium course, where he jumped with the same effortless grace and control that marked his flat work. He would be awesome, George thought, when he got him outside.

Now he rubbed the big horse's neck and felt the velvet of his muzzle. A glance out the window showed the still-leaden sky, with clouds scudding along before a gusty west wind. It could rain any minute and the major would keep them in the ring. "Be right back, boy," he whispered and let himself out into the aisle. He hurried to the office where he would sign in and get permission and instructions. It was hardly like home, where he almost lived in the barn and rode whenever and wherever he wanted to.

"Major Hrdlcka, sir, I'm early. Is it OK to take Prinz out a while before dressage. You said yester-day—"

"*Ja,* boy. Go easy the first. He vants as bad as you gallop that course. Be easy with him, let him look the jump good, first—ah, you know how I mean. Go, boy, go vith your horse. Ve see you one hour."

It was still grey and quiet outside. Here in the park behind the Institute you would think you were way out in the country. Little walking paths led back to the wooded course of jumps, threading their way among trees and bushes. It was public park here, and benches squatted by the path in open areas to catch the sun on clear days. George walked the Prinz down the tanbark path, holding the reins so lightly he could scarcely feel the horse's mouth, and there was no sound but the soft thud of hooves as they went along.

Here and there a single person sat on a bench, eating lunch and reading, or couples sat together, rather sadly, George thought, as though the contemplation of love brought them no joy. Prinz passed without seeming to see them, his entire effort concentrated on the perfection with which he moved through the stillness of the forest.

As the path wound farther into the woods George picked up a quiet trot. The first part of the practice course was set at 1.25 meters and not much challenge for a horse of Prinz's size and ability. Just a warm-up at the trot. George collected his reins and rounded the corner towards the first fence. He judged the number of strides before take-off; three strides before the fence he would signal the jump. Prinz moved steadily ahead and there were five strides between him and the fence when his body tensed under George.

There was the sudden sound of hooves beating the earth as another horse raced along the path behind them. George leaned his weight back in the saddle and pulled up on the reins, turning the horse off into the bushes. He thought he'd better let the idiot galloping behind him have the path; he didn't want to be jumped on by a runaway horse just when he and Prinz were doing their first cross-country. He turned in time to see, coming hell-bent around the corner, a small grey horse, looking neither right nor left and galloping towards the jump.

A streak of grey shot past him and flew over the jump. He didn't have time to see who or what was riding it; Prinz was rearing and plunging in frustration. For a brief moment George thought he wasn't going to be able to control him, and, in that moment, there flashed before his eyes a picture of the big horse crashing into the fence, falling, unable to rise, a leg twisted and broken beneath him. He felt the lash of Major Hrdlcka's anger and saw the pleading look in the eyes of the dying horse. He was shaking with fear and rage when, at last, he was able to bring the Prinz under control. Then he heard a laughing voice calling him. "Hey, American," the girl's voice echoed through the trees. "Hey, we jumping today?" The mocking voice became faint as horse and rider disappeared into the trees, and George sat alone in the dust by the fence.

"What the hell is your trouble, idiot?" George hollered into thin air. Prinz moved nervously, and George headed him at the jump. To his immense relief, the horse sailed over the heavy wooden barrier and moved off without a break in his stride as he hit the ground. His hooves pounded heavily on the level tanbark of the path. Around the corner was the second fence, a tricky double oxer. George reined in a little and rated the horse into the fence. He knew he was going faster then he ought to; the major's words of caution burned in his ears as the Prinz flew over the jump and galloped on into a thick grove of trees. George almost forgot his fury at the fool on the little grey.

They tore along the path, around a sharp curve to the left among the trees. He had meant to catch up with the girl and give her hell, but he hadn't meant to crash into her at a full gallop. Prinz came to a surprisingly sudden halt, just barely sliding into the little mare who stood squarely in the path, facing them. "Jesus!" George yelled. "You fool—" and then his voice died in his throat.

He was looking into a pair of laughing green eyes, set at a slight slant in a small pointed face. A wide grin showed small, even teeth, and smooth black hair was perfectly tied back under the crash helmet she wore. The girl laughed. "Hey, American, you can ride, no? Chase little Eleni with your big horse—you pretty smart!"

Her voice was small and very clear, like the sound of the bells, high and far away in the tower of St. Wenceslaus. George sat back in the saddle and tried to think of something to say. His anger had gone, and the feeling that took its place was something he couldn't quite identify. The girl kept looking at him with those green eyes, and he thought if he didn't say something pretty soon, they might still be sitting there in silence when night fell. Time and the world seemed to have stopped, and they were wrapped in the grey, foggy air, the only two people left on earth.

"Hey, I'm sorry," a voice, not recognizable as his own, croaked.

Miraculously she answered. "No, no, not you should be sorry," she said. Her smile was gone, and her face looked small and pinched, as though she hadn't had enough to eat, or had undergone hours of torture. "Me," she said. "I make you mad. Dumb idiot!"

George found himself longing for the impudent smile to come back. He had been an inexcusable boor! It was terrible to see the suffering he had caused; he must have been insane to come up yelling and screaming like that. He felt like a fool. "No, no, no, it was fun, really. I wasn't mad, honest I wasn't." He wondered what sort of animal she must think he was; someone who went around swearing at people and calling them names? She just sat there, looking at him, sad, and a little puzzled.

Then Prinz snorted and leaned towards the grey mare. She arched her neck prettily and blew through her nostrils. My horse has better manners then I have, George thought miserably. He tried a tentative grin. "I'm George Clements," he said. "I'm happy to meet you. Eleni?"

"Eleni." The lopsided smile came back, and the

45

eyes regarded him steadily; he thought they held a challenge. "I see you in class, riding. Every day."

"How have I missed seeing you?" He thought he knew all the Czechs who rode in his class, and he hadn't seen anything remotely like this.

"I been working," Eleni said. "Three months I work, clean stalls, braid manes, anything. Get money for ride on team. Now I ride every day, just work at night. Major let me work, pay for him to teach. Is good, no? Maybe I make team, who knows?" She ended her sentences with a little upward lilt, a kind of musical sound, very endearing, combined with the fractured syntax and the mischievous smile.

"Where did you learn to speak English? You're real good at it," George lied. "I bet you will make the team, sure you will." He wanted more than anything in the world that this strange girl should make the team, if that was what she wanted. He couldn't imagine why he cared; he'd never seen her before in his life, and he probably never would again, except circling the dusty arena under the watchful eye of the major.

"I try," she said. "I try hard." Her serious little face was turned towards George, and what he saw in her eyes tore at him like an open wound. She looked like a hungry child who has seen, through a window, a table set for a banquet to which she has not been invited.

"Let's ride together today. Can you ride with me for a while?" He felt himself pleading with her and he didn't know whether what he wanted was to comfort the hurt and fear that had been written on her face or, selfishly, to warm himself by the fire that he saw in the depths of her green eyes. She didn't move or reply for a long moment. The thought came to him that she was a mirage and would vanish in the mist. Only the green eyes held his, solemn and sacred.

46

Then, in an instant, her face broke into a grin, and a tinkling laugh swelled up from inside her. "Catch me again," she flung over her shoulder. The mare wheeled where she stood, and, taking off from a standstill, disappeared down the path into the misty wood. Before he caught her again, the dark sky began to release big, heavy drops of rain.

Chapter Three

Washington, D.C., October 1987

It was after seven o'clock, and on this rainy October evening it had already been dark for hours. Peering through the gloom outside his window in the Senate Office Building, George could see a world of moving and changing points of light in the blackness, gleaming on the wet pavement and winking through the trees on the Capitol grounds. The big drops hitting his window picked up the reflection of these lights and became tiny worlds of their own as they clung momentarily to the glass pane before losing themselves in the general wetness of the night. God, what a rotten time to be stuck with a deadline! He wouldn't get home before nine, even if he left now.

He leaned back in his chair and picked up the sheaf of yellow-lined paper from his desk. He'd read it over and if it sounded all right he would leave it on Jean's desk for word processing in the morning. Ed Townsend would be back from the Middle East by noon and was going to need time to go over the speech before his prime-time appearance that night. George wondered how Uncle Ed kept going on the schedule he had set for himself. He seemed to feel that it was his entire responsibility to overcome the damage done by the public misunderstanding of the 1986 Iran-Contra affair, and as one conservative senator who had received no bad press during that time, he was able to wield a certain influence on both sides of the aisle in smoothing over the issues.

The telex had come in about five-thirty and George had spent almost two hours beating it into readable form. He added a few commas and scratched out a line or two and decided it would have to do. He scribbled a note to Jean, apologies for his handwriting, and left the manuscript on her desk under two Godiva chocolate truffles.

Creeping through traffic on Constitution Avenue, he thought the weather was even worse than it looked from inside. A gusty wind whipped the rain in sheets between the buildings and carried the sound of thunder through the air. Flashes of lightning reflected from the surface of the river as he crossed Roosevelt Bridge into Virginia, and even with traffic thinning out on the parkway he couldn't make any time; the rain was blinding and the road was awash with its downpour. Warm and dry in the bucket seat of his Porsche, he thought of poor Joey, who had had to do the chores alone tonight. He'd called her at five, when the telex had come. "I've already put them in," she said. "You can't believe the way it's coming down, so I just fed them while I was out."

Now, sloshing through the gloom, watching the white line in the road, the memory of her voice on the phone stirred his desire and made him ache to be home and in her arms. God, he thought, how I love that woman! He never ceased to wonder at the good fortune that had brought her to him, and even now, after eight years, he felt the same longing he had felt that first time, the first time he saw her, a slim girl leading a massive brown horse through the windswept grass under a bright New England sky.

It had been his third year at Harvard, and he had gone over to Ledyard to see General Edwards as soon as he got back to school. The summer in the country with his parents had reawakened his need to be with horses, and he had an introduction to the general, proposing that he could be put to use exercising some of the Equestrian Team horses on the weekends. George had stood there, hanging over the rail, soaking up the sounds and smells he had tried so hard to forget, and he had known that he was home once more. Watching someone school a nice grey gelding over the fences in the ring, he found he could think of that other grey horse and its small, arrogant rider without feeling the familiar pain. The September sun had been warm on his back and the steady beat of hooves on the grassy turf had almost put him to sleep.

The general had been cordial; he said he could always use a good rider. George started riding for him the next weekend, working on some of the young prospects and exercising the team's alternate horses. George was at Ledyard every Saturday and Sunday afternoon, and the general seemed satisfied with his riding. He'd almost forgotten the leggy blonde of that first afternoon; in the beginning the riding absorbed him completely. His mind was hard at work, concentrating on remembering what he had done right with the very green horse he was hooking on to the hot-walker when he saw her. She went past him to the other side of the walker, leading a tired, sweaty horse.

"Hi," she said as she slid past him. "Can you hold it till I get him put on?" She was tall and her hair was the color of clean straw. It hung long and straight and thick, and was as wet with sweat as the horse she was snapping on to the walker. Her mouth was too wide when she smiled and freckles ran all over her nose and across her cheeks. "Thanks," she said. "Now we can cool ourselves out—" She sank down in the shade of the trees by the barn to watch the horses plod their way around and around on the mechanical walker, their muscles gradually untensing and their racing heartbeats returning to normal.

"Great invention," George said, nodding towards the walker. He sat down in the grass beside her. "I'm George Clements," he said. "I saw you the first day I was here—"

She held out her hand. "I'm Joey Newsome," she said. "I'm here every day, but I'm doing two horses, and I go to school so it's a big hurry all the time—" Her hand was hard and strong, but the structure of its narrow bones seemed almost vulnerable in his grasp. He kept on holding it for a minute and then dropped it quickly, surprised at the emotion he felt. She didn't seem to notice his awkwardness; the wide smile was still there, and, looking, he could see deep into her eyes. They were grey and still and very honest; he felt he had known her all his life.

"Me, too," he said. "School all week."

They had talked then like old friends and it seemed perfectly natural to ask her if she wanted to go with him to pick up some hamburgers. "Sure," she said. "I'd like that." It was the first, unheralded day of the happiest years he had ever known.

At the end of classes in June, George went home to Virginia. He stayed there a week, and then, after driving all day, he appeared at General Edwards's door at eleven-thirty at night. "I'm sorry to bother you, sir. I didn't know it was so late, but Joey told me you needed another working student—" he said.

It was all right. The general wasn't mad, and made

51

a pretty good job of sounding pleased that George was there. He sent him over to share a room with one of the team members and the next morning he was at the barn by five-thirty, where he and three other riders got the horses out for early exercise before the heat of the day set in. He looked for Joey, and his heart sank in his chest like a stone as the morning passed and still she wasn't there. He hadn't told her he was coming—hadn't known it himself forty-eight hours ago—and now he was afraid she had left for some reason and wouldn't be there all summer. On the way back to the barn, one of the other guys stopped him. "Relax, Georgie-boy. She's got the day off—you'll see her tomorrow."

He grinned back, relieved. He hummed as he tacked up his next horse, and all through the hot, sweaty day the thought of seeing Joey again hovered happily in the back of his mind. The heat was oppressive for June, and he worked without letup till nightfall. His tired muscles cried out for a hot shower and he felt as though he could sleep for about a week. He didn't even think about eating; he was full of Gatorade and Granola bars.

Then, as he dragged his aching body across the yard towards his room, he was arrested by a shout from the street. An ancient Jeep was stopped at the curb. "Want to come get some pizza?" Joey's voice sounded fresh and clear through the stagnant air. "Babs and I are starving—"

Bouncing along in the back of the Jeep, his long legs crammed into the tiny space between the two seats, George realized he was ravenously hungry, and the pain in his body was only a healthy reminder of work well done. Joey chattered on, and she and Babs laughed at him when he yelped as the springless rear end of the Jeep banged over the speed bump by the gate. There was a little breeze now that the sun was setting, and the somewhat reckless speed of the open vehicle added to the cooling effect of approaching night. By the time they got to Mario's, George leaped grandly out the rear window and, with exaggerated courtesy, held the door for Joey to descend. She laughed and he took her in his arms in a crushing bear hug. "Hey, you've only been away a week," she said. "Unhand me!"

"But I thought it was going to be all summer," he said. "I thought I wouldn't see you till fall—" Then he pulled Babs out of the Jeep, and arm in arm they went in to sit over a checkered tablecloth and eat two giant everything pizzas and consume a pitcher of beer. George would have sat there all night, but Joey said, "Babs, we've got to take him home. He's falling asleep on us."

The days settled into a routine of hard work. All day they rode horses and washed them and cooled them out and cleaned tack. Their bodies hardened and they lost weight. Almost every night he and Joey and Babs would pile into the Jeep and head for someplace to eat. By midsummer Babs began to see that she was an unnecessary addition on these occasions, and found excuses not to join them. "I can't face another pizza," she said one night. "You guys go on."

"Sure you don't want to?" Joey asked. "We can go somewhere else." To George's complete satisfaction, Babs murmured something about being too beat to want anything, and he rewarded her wise decision with one of his radiant, eat-your-heart-out smiles. Before she could change her mind on the basis of this engaging effort, he hustled Joey into the Jeep and roared off down the road. "Should we feel bad about her?" Joey asked. George laughed out loud, leaned over and gave her a kiss, missing her mouth and

53

ending up with her nose in his teeth, while the Jeep veered crazily across the white line.

"Don't get us killed," Joey giggled, "just when you've found out you love me."

She leaned against his arm. "Golly, we stink," she said. The sun had set, but the heat of the day still lingered in the shadowy evening air. They had piled straight into the Jeep, starved after the long hot day's work; their shirts and breeches clung to them with sweat.

"Turn right," she commanded, "at the next road. I'm not going to eat with a man as dirty as you. Or a woman as dirty as me."

The gravel road dead-ended at the edge of the river. Joey jumped out of the car and ran. "Look," she called. "The ole swimming hole." She grabbed a branch hanging over the water and swung on it, laughing like a boy playing hooky on the first warm day of spring.

"Last one in is a blue pig!" She jumped down to the bank and pulled her T-shirt over her head. "Boys change behind the bushes," she said, and pointed an imperious finger towards a clump of swamp willows.

The water was deep and cool. In the fading light George watched her white body cut through the water. He ducked under and caught her feet, pulling her down with him. When she came up she spouted water like a whale in his face and swam to the bank. They lay in the deep grass, exhausted and cool, and laughed at each other's bodies; their arms and faces were deeply tanned and their bodies as white as snakes' bellies.

"Let's run away to a desert island and ride naked on the beach all day," she whispered. They laughed until they hurt and they rolled like puppies in the soft grass. He sat up, waves of laughter still shaking him.

"I love you," he gasped, and they held each other, laughing until they cried. He knew he could never let her go; they would spend their lives together, until, old and feeble, they would hold each other and laugh again, remembering this night. It was dark when they dressed and walked to the Jeep. The night was cold, then, and they snapped the plastic windows in place. Inside the car, Joey sat close beside him, and she fitted against him like the missing part of a puzzle. "I'm starved," she said. "Does it always make you hungry?"

Two days after he graduated they were married and they had gone to their desert island. They stayed at a hotel, and there wasn't anywhere to ride naked on the beach. Joey wanted to go home to the farm. "We'll be together in our own house," she said. "That's where I want to be—" And he took her home to the house in Lincoln. They were together all the time, waking and sleeping, riding and eating, working and playing. George loved to watch her moving through the old stone house. Its thick walls were cool in summer, and they slept by the open windows, where the air from the mountains floated over them, wild-smelling and clean.

Now, straining to see the road through the rain streaming down his windshield, George thought of Joey, waking at dawn to slip from the bed and stand by the window, looking out over the valley. He loved to watch her then, when she thought he was still asleep, and he would thank God in heaven for the wonder of her love. She would move, catlike, across the room, careful not to wake him, and sneak downstairs to make coffee. Lying motionless in bed, he would wait for her and listen to the little sounds she made in the kitchen. She would let the old hound in and soothe him in his infirmity with kind, silly words that she made up just for him. He envied the old dog even this little bit of her love and then was ashamed of himself for it. There was so much love in Joey that the more she used it the more there was.

They would both go to the barn before breakfast, to bring the horses up and feed them. While the horses ate, they'd run to the house and sit together in the sunny kitchen, eating a farm hand's breakfast. The house was George's now. Helen lived alone in Georgetown, where she had bought a narrow brick house after Aubrey's accident. They had been in Australia, clear around the world, and a runaway lorry had crashed into his car, flattening it and pinning him inside. He was dead when they got him to the hospital. She had been all alone there, then; she flew home with Aubrey's body and George met her at Dulles. Aubrey was buried two days later at Arlington, and Helen had decided the farm was too much for her alone. It had been a turning point in George's life, he now saw. His father's death had left a legacy of responsibility, and on the long drive back to Cambridge, he had had time to look at his own life and feel the cutting edge of his own mortality.

So the farm was theirs and Joey had loved everything about it. Like many of the houses around Lincoln, the old stone cottage had been built two centuries ago by Quakers who settled there in the foothills and put up the long brick meeting house beside the road to North Fork. The stony fields yielded building material for both houses and barns, and the men who laid them up with mud-mortared joints were building for posterity. The house sat in a valley, protected from the winds that howl down over the ridge in winter, and close enough to the stream that its swift-running waters made music for them to listen to through the open windows of summer. Eighteenth-century farmers built their barns conveniently close to their houses, and Joey would run barefoot in the summer nights to see the horses safely bedded and check the newest litter of kittens before she came to bed.

He remembered how when she had first seen the barn she decided they should keep Helen's hunter there, along with the horse she brought with her from Ledyard. Helen came out some weekends and rode with Joey. When fall came, she could hunt, and it would help her forget, Joey said, to be doing what she loved so well. Then, on those weekends, Helen and Joey began disappearing on mysterious errands, leaving George alone, and a little resentful. They wouldn't tell George what they were doing, and as he puttered around the family farm by himself he speculated that he might be the only man in the world whose wife got along with her mother-in-law so well that they made him feel like a fifth leg on a cow. Then, one day, they came home with the horse. Joey opened the door of the trailer and George watched as she gently backed a huge grey Hanovarian out onto the grass. Helen led it over to him. "Your graduation present, dear," she said.

"I've ridden every three-day horse in a hundred miles," Joey sighed. "We've got a good one."

The rain seemed to be lessening, but the wind buffeted his car and flashes of lightning threw lurid shadows across the road. He wished he was home, and his foot automatically pressed the accelerator. The commute was a bitch, all right; on a night like this he almost longed to give up the job with Ed Townsend and set up as a country lawyer in Lincoln. Then he and Joey could have long, lazy evenings together and he would be home for lunch every day and it would seem like that first wonderful year, the year when they had used Dad's little legacy to live on, and had loved like carefree children while they worked to turn the Hanovarian into an Olympic three-day horse.

Looking back now, it seemed like one long honeymoon. The horse had been as good as Joey had thought, and they spent their days riding and traveling to every major event in the East, and their nights they spent in each other's arms, and their love grew stronger every day in the sharing of it. It was as though they were one person, so close their thoughts became. After Lexington, in 1979, George was shortlisted for the Olympics. Joey was overjoyed; she was happier than if she had made it herself. There were months of preparation, the trip back to Ledyard, and the weeks there of schooling and instruction, the fear of injury as time grew short. Then Afghanistan was invaded and Carter canceled participation by our teams in Moscow. "OK," said Joey, her chin squared and her freckles glowing. "That gives me time to get ready, too," and they laughed at the world, for there was nothing in it that could hurt them.

Then there were the happy years when life had settled into a pattern; George had begun the daily commute to Washington where he was reading law at American University. Then Ed Townsend had asked him to join his staff. As a senator from Wyoming, he had been commissioned by the President to a special task force to study terrorism and the growing hostage threat. At first George was assigned to researching background material, but, as he became more interested and involved, Townsend had discovered his talent for words, and George had begun helping with speeches and with the press.

In the quiet summer evenings they would ride out over the hills and watch night fall, first in long

58

shadows across the valleys, and then as a velvet blackness that crept up the side of the mountain, till the only light they had came from the stars that filled the sky over the hills; then they would walk the horses home in silence and together climb the narrow pine staircase and fall in bed, laughing over nothing and over everything.

He thought how radiantly happy Joey was then. She was at home every day, working the horses and keeping the farm going. She hired the grandson of old Norman, who lived in the tenant house across the road, and taught him how to do the horses. Little Ben helped with the mowing and fencing, and he would have followed Miz Joey to the ends of the earth. She taught the Pony Club kids, and they ran over the farm like rabbits. Sometimes when he came home, George would find a dozen ponies grazing in his front field, while a dozen kids sat cleaning tack under the big maple in the yard. Joey would shoo the children out, and a half hour later they would be alone on the porch, watching the sun go down over the Ridge.

Joey joined the Garden Club; Ben spaded a plot for cut flowers, and she told George she was going to be a prominent clubwoman. Every morning, after George left for the city, Joey schooled Red Devil alone in the ring behind the barn in the cool of summer mornings, or later in the year, tracking through frosty grass in the grey light of early winter. Then she would ride George's horse until sweat gleamed on its flanks and the sun was overhead. And while she rode, she prayed for a baby.

He remembered her eyes, wide and frightened, one night. She had been sitting on the steps when he came home that night, and she didn't run to meet him when he drove up. He sat beside her and, leaning her head on his shoulder, she told him. "Dr. Coleman says maybe I never will," she said. He had explained it to her carefully; conceiving was often difficult for very athletic women, and sometimes even giving up an activity didn't reverse the problem. "I've done it to myself," she said, and sat there on the steps in the gathering dark, her head bent over her knees so he couldn't see the tears he knew were running down her face.

He had taken her up in his arms and held her close. "We'll just have to keep trying, I guess," he had whispered into the top of her head as she buried her face against him.

Then she had laughed. "Waste no time," she said, and pulled him down the steps into the soft damp grass, where they held each other and laughed and cried and made wonderful love together under the blanket of stars overhead. And the winter had passed quickly. During the coldest weeks of February they left to spend a carefree week sailing the British Virgins.

The air was silken and warm, and Washington was in another planet. The first night they lay at anchor, rocking gently against the dock. George woke in the morning alone in the cabin and listened to the slosh of water against the hull. He wondered why he was alone and sat up to see if he could find Joey. Peering out the porthole he saw her bent over the side, holding back the golden hair as she retched soundlessly into the water. "Oh, Joey, you can't be seasick! Not now!" He wrapped a towel around his bare middle and climbed the wooden ladder to the deck.

Joey turned a wan face up to him. Her skin was light grey, tinged with green, but her smile was outstanding. "I'm not seasick, you dope. Don't you know a pregnant woman when you see her?" Oh, God, even now, seven months later, he was laughing to himself, remembering her face that morning and thinking of his own speechless helplessness when he realized what she had said. They gave up the boat and stayed at the hotel. They swam and walked and ate and Joey managed to only be sick in the morning.

He wished the rain would stop and he wished he were home. It wasn't like Joey to be frightened in a storm, but there was a malevolence in the air tonight and he found himself peering ahead into the dark to see the lights of Leesburg glowing under the mountain.

Joey covered her ears when the thunder crashed right over the house. It was so close the dishes rattled in the sideboard and the lights went out as lightning flashed its cold blue glare over everything. She was glad she'd put the horses in early and closed their stalls. They'd be terrified anyhow. Her eyes widened as she looked out towards the barn. An orange light was flickering through the window of the loft! She ran out into the rain and saw the loft full of hay burst into bright flames. She could hear, over the noise of the rain and the howling wind, the horses screaming in their stalls.

Her body was heavy now and clumsy as she ran, stumbling and slipping, lashed by the cold rain, towards the blazing barn. The loft was an inferno where the roof shielded the flames that were roaring through the dry hay and the flickering light of the fire lit her way to the stalls under the bank. She threw open the door where Helen's hunter was pawing frantically and snorting in terror. He ran into the night, bucking and kicking. Her own Devil charged past her when she opened his door. "Good boy," she breathed. "Run!" She went to the door of the Hanovarian's stall and opened it. The mare was rearing and screaming back in the corner; her eyes were white and rolling back in her head.

Now brands of burning hay were falling through the floorboards and landing around them in the stall. "Come on, girl." Her voice was quiet and firm. "Come on, come along, baby—" She lunged towards the terrified animal and grabbed the halter. Twice the mare reared, pulling her off the ground. She would hold on until the animal heard her voice and quieted down enough to pay attention to her. With one hand she pulled her windbreaker off her shoulder and, switching hands, she got if off. She stretched up to cover the mare's eyes with it and prayed that it would stop its senseless thrashing around and be led out to safety.

With a final lunge, the horse pinned Joey to the wall and then stood frozen in fear. Joey tried to move. She held the jacket over the mare's eyes, and trying not to think of her own pain, she stroked the animal's neck and spoke quietly to it. Her voice was drowned now by the roar of the fire. She felt the horse tremble, and prayed it would move to free her. Suddenly, it reared again and crashed down. The forefeet struck Joey's head.

When George turned the corner south of Lincoln he could see a glow of flashing lights off the road ahead, over the hill. At first it didn't occur to him that it could be at his farm. He just thought, damn, some poor guy has had his barn struck by lightning. It had been some storm! He hoped they had gotten the animals out—Whose place was it anyhow? Then a coldness gripped him and his mind went out of focus. He whirled through the gate and raced up the lane and then he couldn't think where he was. This didn't have anything to do with him—some farmer's disaster. Why was he here? Then he stood, numb and helpless, while black smoke rose from the shell of the barn and the rain hissed as it fell on the smoldering timbers.

He realized someone was at his side, crying, pulling at his arm. It was little Ben, who had run across the road when his grandfather saw the flames. His eyeballs were white and tears streamed down his face. "Oh, Mister George, Mister George, she been k-kilt. Miz Joey, she dead, Mister George!" George held the sobbing boy against him and stared into the night. The old hound crouched, whimpering, at his feet.

Helen came out that night and she stayed with him through the lovely weeks of autumn. The leaves turned and flamed and fell and George didn't see them. He sat with the old hound under the tree by the spring house and maybe they comforted each other as they sat. Some days he worked in the foundations of the barn, and finally, with Ben helping him, he built stalls and got them roofed over before winter. He saddled Joey's horse one day and rode out alone. Then every day he rode up the mountain and raced like a man possessed over the frozen ground. At night he sat silent by the window. Helen held back her tears and fixed his favorite food and he tried to eat to make her happy, but everything tasted like tears he shed alone in bed each night, and he couldn't swallow.

Healing came at last. He went back to the city and threw himself into the maelstrom of politics. He ate what Helen fixed for him, and after dinner he would play a game of Russian Bank or Scrabble with her until time for bed. Ed Townsend announced his candidacy, and George traveled the country with him, tireless and watchful. The days were so full that most nights he sank into the strange hotel bed wherever he was, and slept. Some nights there was hardly time for sleep, and the whirlwind of the campaign became the celebration of victory and the strangely anticlimactic move into the White House. George was closer than ever to Townsend, and worked long hours in his office. He was White House staff and something more. Uncle Ed needed him, and relied on him, almost like a father with a favorite son.

It was an endlessly engrossing life in Washington, but George kept the farm in Lincoln and went there every weekend. Some evenings, as the days grew long, he would saddle Helen's hunter and ride alone to stand and look at the mountains until the sun dropped behind them. And some nights he would ride over to Lincoln and stand under the old pine trees in the Quaker burying ground near the spot where Joey lay, her radiant life now still and her only child unborn.

Chapter Four

Middleburg, Virginia, April 1989

The Blue Ridge Mountains slant across the state of Virginia from north to south. The low ridges to the east of the Shenandoah River shelter the rocky valleys where settlers first cleared the forests and began to divide the land with the loose stone walls that still mark the two-hundred-year-old boundaries. The mountains of the ridge bear names older than the walls themselves: Catoctin and Leathercoat and Bull Run and Mt. Weather, and the old roads west across the Shenandoah are remembered in the names of the gaps that still landmark the area, and of the fords that once crossed the river at the bottom of the ridge.

Ashby Gap is almost impassable today, where it runs down the west side of Mt. Weather to Shephard's Ford, and an old logging road follows the trail down Duke Hollow two miles to the south. In the land between these two ancient trails, all through the valley to the east, lie some of the earliest settlements, farms carved from the rolling hills, where the log houses built by the first settlers are now lovingly preserved in the shadows of great stone houses that witness the prosperity of later generations, whose labor brought fruitfulness from the rocky, inhospitable land under the mountains.

At the turn of the century, nearby Middleburg, lying on the road to Paris Mountain Gap, now U.S. Route 50, was roused from its drowsy country ways by an invasion from the North. The fact that this was the best country in the world for fox-hunting was discovered by the rich and famous of New York society, and the old houses were bought and refurbished, and new, grander ones were built. The forgotten little settlements between Middleburg and the mountains were no longer forgotten; the hills rang then, not only with the sound of the huntsman's horn at daybreak, but with the sound of house parties and hunt breakfasts, lasting long into the night. Yet, even today, there is enough peace left in the rolling hills under the mountains that men will brave the hour-long commute to Washington for the sake of enjoying the beauty of early mornings and the quiet that descends when the sun sinks over the blue hills to the west. Another generation is living in the old stone houses, and they are filled with the sounds of life and living.

Against the foot of Mt. Weather, the sun sneaked in the open window of Carter Bedford's room and the breeze tickled his feet. He rolled quietly out of bed and tiptoed across the room to listen at the door to the hall. No one else was awake. Certainly not old Cis; he'd heard her come in at two-thirty. Mom would be furious. Satisfied, he crept silently back to look out the window, rubbing his eyes. He heard a small commotion under the covers at the foot of his bed; the dogs were awake! "Good guys," he whispered. "You can stay here, and be good dogs —" They rolled over and allowed their stomachs to be scratched. He covered them up and grabbed a handful of clothes off the chair.

He pulled on breeches and a T-shirt that said "Middleburg Pony Club—1988 Regional Champions" on it, found two socks under his bed, and crept soundlessly to the door. With the skill of a second-story man he turned the knob and let himself out into the hall, where he paused to listen. There wasn't a sound behind the closed door to his parents' room, and he knew Cis wouldn't be awake for hours. Briefly, he regarded the bathroom door, remembered its creaking hinge, and padded down the hall. Satisfied with his escape thus far, he crept down the back stairs.

In the kitchen, hunger gnawed at his belly, but there was no way he could get anything to eat without making a noise. Stealing into the boot room, he picked up a dusty pair of black boots, gently closed the screen door, and slid out onto the dewy grass. It made his socks wet and he pulled them off before proceeding down the path between the boxwoods. He hung the socks on a bush and paused behind the hedge to pee soundlessly into the grass. So far it was perfect. No one knew he was up.

On the way to the barn Carter luxuriated in bare feet and cool, wet grass. He ran a little extra loop around the big oak and headed for the barn. A noise behind him brought him to a sudden halt. The screen door slammed twice, and two little dogs shot across the lawn towards him. Albert and Emma, the Jack Russell terriers, had somehow got out of his room and followed him. "Be quiet, you guys," Carter hissed at them. They flung themselves at him for an affectionate moment, and then raced off on business of their own. Carter crouched behind the box hedge and watched the house through the shiny leaves. He cursed the terriers silently, practicing words he someday hoped to dare to use in public. When no one appeared at the door in a reasonable length of time, he edged out into the open.

A quick scamper across the grass, and he vaulted the white fence into the stable yard. He pulled on the boots, his wet feet sticking to the old leather linings. A row of hunt caps and riding helmets hung on the wall. Carter ignored them studiously, while he picked up his saddle and bridle and started for the stalls.

Halfway out the door he paused. Riding alone without telling anyone was bad enough; maybe he'd better wear the stupid hat. Even members of the Team had to wear safety headgear now, and Dad would ground him for sure if he got caught riding without it. The event was only weeks away and he couldn't afford the risk of losing even a few days of training. Carter went back and pulled his helmet off the hook. He felt unreasonably righteous as he buckled the hateful strap under his chin.

It was quiet in the barn, the peaceful silence of animals at rest in the last few minutes before full day. The Russells raced through the door, chasing their own imaginations and, as they scrambled down the aisle, Carter could hear the small sounds of waking beasts; a snort here and a cough there, hooves stamping the soft straw bedding. He would hurry to get out before Bob came to begin the morning barn work.

He put down his tack and climbed to the loft. He threw a bale of hay down and jumped on top of it. He pulled out his Barlow knife and cut the strings. He loved the fresh grassy smell when the tightly packed bale fell open. Even in winter you could smell summer in a bale of hay, and now its fragrance blended with the scent of spring blowing into the barn from the orchard across the lane. Carter buried his face in the armload he was carrying down the aisle. He gave each of the four horses a section of hay to keep them quiet and then he tied the bale back up the way he'd learned at Pony Club camp. He pulled a wizened apple from his pocket, cut it in quarters and offered it to the grey pony in the end stall.

"Here, Beau, I saved you this from dinner and it's more breakfast than I've had. Be a good boy and be quiet. We're going for a ride." He threw the saddle over the stall door and brought a brush and a hoof pick from the tackroom. Pushing the pony to the side of the stall, he gave him an energetic scouring with the brush, lifted up each foot, and gave it a quick scratch with the pick. Beau thoughtfully chewed the apple and stood still.

"Gotta hurry before Bob gets here," Carter told his pony. Expertly, he pulled the bridle over Beau's ears and slapped the saddle on his back. Beau was resigned to unceremonious treatment and endured it stoically; Carter yanked the girth tight and hurried him out of the stall. He was a pony of exceptional qualities, patient and courageous, and possessed of energy almost equal to Carter's. Carter loved him.

The sun was beginning to show over the tops of the trees by the time Beau and Carter disappeared into the woods. It was shining into Adrian Bedford's eye as the wind ruffled the white curtains at her window. Henry was still asleep, bless him. He needed his sleep, God knew, and Adrian was glad he hadn't waited up with her to see what time that boy had brought Cissy home. Adrian remembered hearing a car on the gravel sometime after two o'clock, far too late for Henry's rather Victorian taste.

Heavens, it must have been only a couple of hours ago, and here she was awake, worrying. She wasn't quite sure why she worried about Cis. It had really been fun having her home from school this year. It had certainly made her coming out easier, having her here for the season and, except for the everlasting parties, she had spent most of her time working with Chelsea. Really, her head was on pretty straight for nineteen years old.

The last year at Foxcroft they had gotten Chelsea for her, and Miss Marian had been so encouraging about what Cis could do with the horse that even Henry had agreed to the year off before college. Adrian didn't like to push the children in competition, but they both felt that when they had invested that much money in a horse and let the child stay out of school a year to ride it, then they really should see that she worked at it. And she had been very good about it. Of course, she was thrilled that Bruce had been over to help her, and he had been very encouraging. The horse might be an Olympic prospect, he had said.

And now that they were having the event at Oak Hill she was going to have a chance to see what she could do in real competition. Adrian sighed as the thought of the event entered her mind. It was only three weeks off, and so much was left to do. She must have been out of her mind to think their little Pony Club could sponsor an International Level Three-Day. She certainly wouldn't get back to sleep if she began thinking about that, or about what they would do if the Team actually did want Chelsea. It would be still another reorganization of their lives. Well, she could worry about that when it happened. Meantime, she did wish Cissy would go a little easy on the partying.

That started her remembering the parties of other springtimes, remembering the late nights and the long lazy days of twenty years ago. She remembered a little too well, actually, and that was what made her nervous. Boys coming home from school, arriving at the parties in new sports cars that were their graduation presents, or in their father's Jags; girls in pale summer dresses, floating out into the warm nights. Floating, as Adrian remembered, into some boy's car; too many of them piling into it, calling to each other, "Meet you at the Sleepy Fox," or "Are we going to your house to swim, Jenny?"

Then, finding the bottle under the seat, passing it around to everyone, including the driver, and laughing as they sped through the night to the next party. Or as they sped through the night, down the back road, to park and watch the sun come up on the banks of the Shenandoah. Adrian thought she would be more comfortable about it if she didn't remember so well how it was, and she rolled over, careful not to wake Henry. She was so accustomed to his big, warm shape next to her that it reassured her to lie there in the early light and watch him sleep. His chest, rising and falling regularly, had a soothing effect. She simply wouldn't think about what Cis did or where she went on these long summer nights.

She didn't think about it after a few minutes, but she still wasn't asleep. The sun really was up now, but the breeze coming in over the mountain was still cool. As soundlessly as Carter had done a few minutes before, Adrian slipped out of bed. Henry growled and moved, but he didn't wake up. Adrian pulled on a pair of jeans and a T-shirt and, carrying her socks, she slid out of the room, and down the back stairs. She paused in the kitchen to take a hard-boiled egg out of the fridge, debated whether to put salt on it or not, decided in favor of salt, and ate it. She gulped down a glass of orange juice, and quietly slipped out through the bootroom.

71

She shivered as her bare feet swished through the grass and, making no stop behind the boxwood, she ran to the barn. Heavens, it was good to have the horses. What did people in the city do when they were too worried to sleep? She'd just get Carol out and have a little run through the woods, all alone, and the whole day would start out better. She knew it was her own fault that she always had too much to do. She just seemed to get involved in things. As if Pony Clubbing the children wasn't enough, she had volunteered, mind you, volunteered to head the committee at Oak Hill. And then there was Henry; he was in some kind of swivet at the office that he couldn't tell her about. She knew without being told. There was that little muscle under his eye.

Well, a good gallop would clear her head, and she could get it all together by breakfast time. She walked down the aisle with her tack, and almost didn't notice the empty stall. She stopped and looked over the half-door. The pony was definitely not there. That child would certainly be the death of her yet. He knew he wasn't supposed to ride out alone. None of them was supposed to, and it was a good rule. He was probably jumping fences and very likely without his headgear on, too.

Poor Carol received as hasty treatment as Beau, but lacked the temperament to enjoy it. Adrian's horse was a big, kind bay mare, a Thoroughbred and the mother of a lovely filly that was in training with Mike Plumb. She was a real lady and used to being treated like one. "Sorry, dear," Adrian said, "I know this isn't what you like." She threw the saddle on, tightened the girth, and started off. The horse trotted briskly out into the growing daylight, and Adrian breathed in big gulps of the cool morning air.

She sat her horse comfortably, and there was a

trace of the old fox-hunter's slouch in the relaxed line of her back, but her head was up and her blue eyes scanned the horizon as, imperceptibly, she urged Carol into a trot. At the edge of the yard they popped over a bar-way into the field. Startled, three grouse whirred up in front of her and flew off, and in the brush along the fence row she heard the clear call of the red-winged blackbird. By the edge of the woods the dogwood made a frothy white background for the tiny red blossoms of the Judas trees. It was a good day to forget worries, and Adrian hummed as she put the mare into a gentle canter.

Then, as she approached the forest, she listened sharply. She could hear, clearly coming through the woods, the thunder of little hooves. Ye Gods, it was Carter, and he was galloping over the cross-country course! "Nothing is too good for my little girl," Henry said when he had the course built for Cissy. It was a course clearly not meant for ten-year-old boys and thirteen-hand ponies. The sound came nearer and then she saw him barreling along through the trees, straight for the big oxer.

Adrian froze in the saddle. She wanted to yell at him to stop, and put her hand over her mouth to keep herself quiet. If he was going to make it at all he'd better not be distracted when he did it. She caught the look on his face as he rated the pony. It was sheer joy.

Then he raised his head to look at the horizon as Beau jumped, and on the horizon he saw his mother. His expression changed to one of utter horror, but his hand never moved and he flew with his pony over the jump to a perfect landing. He galloped up to Adrian. "Hi, Mom," he said in a feeble attempt at a normal greeting, as though to make the whole situation vanish by ignoring it.

She was so mad at him, and so cold with fear, that

she didn't speak for a minute. "Mom," he said, "why are you out riding alone? You know Dad hates it when we do." He managed a strained little smile, testing the waters.

Testing quite needlessly, Adrian thought. There isn't a thing I can do with this man-child of mine. He will have to grow up as best he can. I am a hopeless mother. I set bad examples, I allow my children to be disobedient, and I even plan to deceive my husband about it. "Carter," she finally said, "if I ever catch you and that pony doing a thing like that again —" Oh, it was useless. He was grinning at her. And he *had* gotten over the fence. Beautifully.

"Ride down the creek trail with me," she said. "We can see the Virginia blue bells and give the horses a drink." Carter nodded.

"Want to race?" he said.

"Fat chance you and Beau have against Carol." Adrian laughed and booted Carol into a slow gallop. Carter and the pony shot past her and she took care to stay a length or two behind him as they chased down the leafy path through carpets of blue flowers and out into the sunlight. The valley was glowing with gold and the creek reflected a thousand little lights, moving and changing.

"We won, Mom, we won! Beau can beat anyone, Mom, can't he?"

They let the horses splash into the clear running water. Minnows were darting in the shallows over the rocks where Beau buried his muzzle and began snuffling in the great gulps of water. "Just let him have twelve swallows, Carter. He's really breathing. You're going to work that pony into the ground before May if you aren't careful."

"Mom, he's so fit! We're going to go Training, Jessy said he could do it. She said so yesterday after

74

we jumped. You saw him this morning, Mom, too, didn't you? Watch his recovery—he isn't breathing half what he was a minute ago."

"Carter, you bribed Jessy to say that. You just walk the course this afternoon and look at it. The water jump is miles wide and the tiger trap is horrible. I don't know what the TD is thinking about, the way he's built some of that stuff. You can go Pre-Training and have a really good round—"

"Mom, that's for babies! Jessy said—"

"Well, I'll talk to Jessy," Adrian said. You bet I will talk to her. I pay her to coach these kids, not to get them killed. He doesn't need any help in thinking of ways to destroy himself, she thought, and a familiar chill ran down her back as she sat in the sun watching the water dividing and coming together around the rocks in the stream. Danger for those she loved was a commmonplace in her life, but one she did not suffer gladly.

"We'll ask Dad about it at breakfast, then," she said.

"Good. You lose then. Dad doesn't want me to be chicken. He'll want me to do it. He always says be the best you can at anything you do." Smug, Carter grinned up at her.

Bob was at the barn, feeding and turning out when they got back. "Them two miss their breakfast half the time," he said. "Don't you never sleep, Miz Bedford?"

Henry was at breakfast when they came in. "Sorry, darling. It was just so divine out this morning. Carter and I had a race to the creek and we had to walk them in." Adrian leaned over his shoulder and kissed his ear. Henry turned and smiled. "Forgiven dear. I never

75

heard you go. Carter, go tell Berenice your mother and you are here. I guess you couldn't eat a stack of these hotcakes, could you?"

The kitchen door opened and Berenice ambled in. Her smile was as warm as the morning sun. "I heard my hungry boy comin' in," she said. Carter loved Berenice. She lived down the road in the tenant house where she had lived all her life and raised her family. Her husband had been dead for years and she had supported herself and Bob, by hiring out, until he was old enough to work. Now Bob did the barn and Berenice did the house.

When he was little, Carter used to spend hours in the kitchen with Berenice. He would sit on her lap while she told him stories of her childhood, of farming twenty acres of this stony Piedmont land. She was the youngest of nine children, and had stopped going to school along about third grade, when she was big enough to help at home. Berenice was skinny and small, but the muscles of her arms were hard and stringy. She could do any kind of work, and she could make bread that Carter dreamed about. If he was going to go to heaven, he knew it would smell like Berenice's kitchen when you came home from school and she had been baking bread. She would give you the crust, with butter melting on it, and there was nothing in the world to want beyond that unless you were a fool.

Carter watched his parents. Dad was worried about something. It sort of twitched under his left eye when something was wrong at work. He wished Dad did something normal like a stockbroker or a lawyer or anything that other people's fathers did. They didn't have the whole world to worry about, and they had more time to enjoy their families, to watch their sons ride to glory, winning events with ponies who far outperformed even the most expensive and athletic horses in the whole state. Ponies who were even better than their sister's expensive and athletic horses.

This line of thinking brought Cissy to mind. "Where's old Cis?" he said. "Still in the sack, I bet. I heard her come in last night." A quick look to judge the effect of the last statement yielded little satisfaction. Mom was drinking coffee and Dad was behind the paper again.

"Who was she out with? Old Peyton?" Peyton Andrews was a leftover beau from last year. He was home from Washington and Lee for spring break and had been hanging around enough to merit Carter's fullest scorn, reserved for anyone fool enough to moon around after Cis, when there were so many clearly superior ways to spend valuable vacation time.

He wasn't having a lot of luck with this line of conversation. "I saw them in the car. Dad, you should have seen what they — "

Henry's voice came from behind the paper. "That's enough, Carter. I have to listen to enough spies at work, I don't need one in my family. I'm sure your sister's business is hers and not yours." It wasn't the response Carter had hoped for.

Resigned for the moment, Carter applied himself singlemindedly to the business of eating. "Henry, have you seen Beau and Carter lately?" Adrian spoke from behind a steaming pile of hotcakes. "He wants to go Training and he says Jessy told him he could? What do you think?"

"Well, we pay Jessy enough to tell them how to ride. Don't you think we should trust her judgment?" Ah, the efficient executive, Adrian thought. If you want something done, get the best person you can find to do it and then let them do it. But this was Carter, this was their own son, and his safety they

77

were talking about. It wasn't something trivial like the security of the nation; it was important, it was Carter. Adrian laughed at herself; she was using an old ploy she often tried when there was a worry she couldn't deal with. Just put it in a ridiculous perspective, and then try to laugh at it. Sometimes it helped.

She smiled. "I guess you're right, dear. You usually are. I s'pose we ought to let him try it. But, Carter, you pay attention, hear? You may not ever go on that course alone, ever again. Promise? Right now?"

"OK, Mom. Sure. Gee, Berenice, have you got any more cakes?"

Henry put down the paper. "Well, time to be off to the wars, I guess." He picked up a tangerine and put it in his pocket. "Sustenance for the journey," he said.

"You're tired, Henry. Can't you take a few days—"

"God, I wish I could. Maybe after New York. I don't know. There were three more bombings last night; forty-three dead. It's too close to home." Adrian wished a wish something akin to Carter's; if only Henry did something normal like other men, something safe and dull. He kept making these counts of the dead, as though the terrorist attacks were his doing, when the fact was he probably did as much as any man in the world to stop them.

When Townsend was elected he had appointed Henry to this job, probably on the basis of the work they had done together in the years before. Henry had become obsessed, she thought, with the problem of terrorism, as through the last few years it had been an increasing frustration to the free world. Travel abroad, for Americans especially, was almost an impossibility. All the security on the airports, all the threats of retaliation over the years had done nothing to stem the growing tide.

Now Townsend thought he could do something

about it at last. Over those years when he had traveled from nation to nation, reasoning, bargaining, he had laid a foundation for negotiation that he was now in a position to realize. After four months in office he had set up a conference at the UN in May where it was expected that the Soviets would have to back out of their position of support for terrorist movements. He really had them in a corner, and Sharovsky seemed willing to cooperate. She only wished someone besides Henry had the responsibility for the security of the operation.

"It isn't fair, Henry," Adrian said. "The damned conference is right after the three-day at Oak Hill. Your poor children will have to ride with nobody but old Mom to watch, and God knows they must be sick of that. You'll be downtown every minute of the weekend, I bet."

"Honey, we should have the whole thing wrapped up a week before. I can be as free as the wind on Sunday. Plan your picnic, ask your friends. Tell the kids they better win—I'm going to be there." Henry smiled. "If we can't cover every option by the fifth we shouldn't have our job." If he knew something he didn't like, Adrian couldn't tell it. The muscle under his eye was quiet, and loving him very much, Adrian made herself believe him.

"Want me to wake Cis up?" Carter said, having eaten his second stack of cakes and asked Berenice for more.

"I guess you'd better, hon. We've got to be at Oak Hill by eleven, and you've both got dressage this morning." Carter was up the stairs like a deer. A door banged, a blood-curdling shriek rent the air, followed by a short string of obscenities and Carter descended the stairs with unwonted dignity. He addressed his new plate of cakes with undiminished hunger. "She's up," he remarked. "She really is out of bed. I guess she doesn't like cold water down her back too much when she's asleep."

"Mother, you have *got* to do something about that child, if that's what he is! Mother, he is a monster! I was getting up! I know I have a lesson! How can you let that little deranged animal—? Cissy stopped in midsentence. "Oh, hi, Dad. Didn't know you were still here."

"Evidently not. Do you often address your mother in that manner when I am not here?" He unsuccessfully hid a small smile.

"I'm sorry, Mom. He is a beast. He threw ice water on me—"

"She was asleep. She was sleeping *naked*. She thinks that's sexy."

Henry got up. "It breaks my heart to leave you people. The relative calm of the White House will refresh my nerves." Adrian got up and kissed him. He gave Cissy a hug and ruffled Carter's hair. "Be good to your mother, infants. I'll see you tonight, thank God!"

Adrian watched her children with amusement. She supposed she should be harder on them, but they were so dear to her, and they were so funny. If you can't enjoy them, what good are they, anyway? she thought. "You guys go out and get ready before Jessy gets here," she said. "I'll make a few calls and we'll go over there at eleven."

The phone rang and Adrian went to the kitchen to pick it up. Berenice had answered it and handed her the receiver. "It's some man about the poles," she said. "You want to talk to him?" Adrian nodded and took the phone.

"Yes," she said. "Didn't they tell you where to leave them?" She explained to the man that the poles were for jumps on the cross-country course and he would have to wait till someone got there who knew which jumps they were for, and he explained that he was a busy man and he would just dump them where he was. She explained that they had hired him to deliver them where they were needed and he had bloody well better not dump them where he was.

"All right, I can be there in ten minutes. Yes, it would be very kind of you to wait. Yes, I understand you are in a hurry. Bye." Adrian sighed. "Berenice," she said. "Please tell Cissy she'll have to bring Carter and come on over in the Jeep when they're through. I've got to go right now—"

"Miz Bedford, I don't know how you go the way you do. I'll tell 'em, and I'll send a nice lunch with 'em for y'all to eat. They's that ham from yesterday an' the bread'll be done time they go."

It had seemed like such a good idea last year when they started on it. Pony Club was looking for a way to raise money for the kids to go to the National Rally and thought of enlarging their event. Adrian, God forgive her, had suggested that they could have a really good event if they had a good course. The Oak Hill Military Reservation had closed down and was for sale. If it could be bought, they could build a first-rate course on it, and starting then, they could schedule a major event for spring of 1989.

Now she was chairman of the project. It had been some year. Adrian was inclined to agree with Berenice's estimate of the probability of anyone surviving a schedule like hers. They had got the property, the government had cleared out the old installation and combed the ground in the bombing range area, it had been graded and seeded last summer, the USCTA had sent a technical delegate, Bruce had designed a course, and just four weeks from now the first Oak

Hill International Combined Training Event would be a reality.

She forced her mind to remember the quiet of the early-morning hours and promised herself that once this was over she would never volunteer for anything again. Outside, clouds were beginning to build up. It was going to rain again.

Chapter Five

Washington, D.C., April 1989

His mouth was dry and he realized his hands were shaking. The old man sighed. He had thought they would leave him alone; after three years of living in peace it had been a surprise to find they wanted him again. The quiet life he lived in the slightly seedy neighborhood above Georgetown had begun to seem natural to him, natural and beautiful, as though it was the way a life should be lived. Now he found himself resenting them, resenting them in a way he would never have imagined before, nor dared to imagine.

Jurek had been nearly sixty years old when they sent him to Washington. He had arrived with some notice from the press and from the people at Langley. He was a dissident, a defector from Moscow, and his reception had exceeded the wildest dreams of the poor peasant boy from Russia.

True, by the time he came to America, the poor peasant was well concealed under the veneer of a scientific education and years of accomplishment in his field. His work in electronic and nuclear miniaturization had revolutionized Soviet capabilities during the late seventies. And it was then, at the height of his usefulness, that his orders had come.

It hadn't been easy when he'd gotton here. It didn't happen like the stories from his childhood, boatloads of poor kulaks sailing past the statue of the lady, with the hope of freedom and happiness in their hearts. Not for him to survive long days in the stinking hold of a ship, nor to stand at the rail, tears in his eyes, realizing a dream of freedom.

It was no dream of freedom for Jurek. It was an assignment from his masters in the Kremlin. He spent weeks, shut up in rooms with recording devices, with men asking questions, endless questions, probing into his life. He'd spent the weeks telling them lies, repeating carefully learned, and cunningly false, details of his former life. He gave them the reasons he had been told to give them; he explained why he had left Russia. He told them how he hoped he could serve his new country, and he gave them his reason for betraying his old one.

They kept him there until he'd convinced them. When they finally believed him he was treated like a hero. They found him a home and they found him a place to work, and he told himself that it was good. Even while the American press idolized him and photographed him and interviewed him, he was being congratulated by Moscow for the beauty of his deceit and the success of his mission. His first assignment arrived two months after he had settled into the yellow row house in Burlieth.

Yes, he had told himself that it was good. Yet sometimes in the night the old man wept, and he remembered the little boy in the village. And the tears burned his eyes when he realized what that little boy had become. He would close his eyes and see the dirt road, see himself walking the three miles to school, books in a bag on his back; walking alone because he was reading one of the books, and not listening to the others when they laughed at him and called him "the scientist."

He supposed he had been lucky to grow up in Russia. At least that is what they had always told him. The Soviets rewarded excellence in their citizens, and even in the back country where his father farmed, an exceptional student was noticed in school.

For generations his family had lived in a hovel, the men bent from back-breaking labor, the children toiling in the fields from the time they could walk, and the women, old at thirty-five, chained to the never-ending work of feeding and clothing and bearing too many children. But when his teacher saw little Jurek helping a great hulk of an upperclassman with his math assignment, no time was wasted before he was given tests and brought before the Office of Education.

They pushed his bright little mind then as fast as it could soak up information. He was ten when they sent him to Moscow, to the Institute of Science at the university. The strange little boy in the big city couldn't understand why he was there. The problems they gave him seemed so simple and the work he did so easy that he wondered why he couldn't be back home in the village instead of living this frightening existence among strangers.

But he studied there, alone and sorrowing, until he knew all they could teach him. He was given a fellowship for independent study. He never once went back to Keivla, to the miserable peasant existence that he remembered with increasing warmth as his life narrowed day by day into a routine of nothing but study and work and loneliness. The work was exciting, the discoveries he made fulfilled a need deep inside him, but at night his room was empty and his heart longed for home.

He was twenty years old when he received the Order of the Red Star for his work in miniaturized explosives, and his life radically changed. Overnight he was a hero and a wonderful eight-room apartment was his. He was invited to glittering parties and toasted by important men. In a few years he had a beautiful dacha outside Moscow, and a beautiful wife, a young actress in the state theater. He vacationed at the Black Sea, and a long dark limousine took him to the laboratory every day.

His mind was steadily at work, and other honors came his way. Natasha made great successes in the theater, and took a lover. Their children were sent to school in Leningrad and the fine apartment was lonely. His work was his solace, and he grew old before he realized how swiftly his life was passing by. He had been pleased when the American assignment was discussed, and, though he had no choice in the matter, he was happy to go.

Life here was different. By day he worked at a job they had given him at the Bureau of Standards. The work was nothing, it was no challenge to his mind, nor did it interfere with the job he was sent here to do.

In the quiet yellow brick row house in Burleith, above Georgetown, the old Russian worked in his basement at night. Until the early-morning hours a light burned unseen in the sealed-off room under the house he shared with the family of a Treasury Department clerk. The house had once been a single family dwelling, but in the 1940's it had been converted into a duplex. The upstairs family shared the front hall and tiny backyard with Jurek. The whole first floor and basement were rented as one unit, and the old man had converted the basement into a workshop.

It was no ordinary workshop. Completely fitted for his scientific studies and experiments, it was well insulated and soundproofed. No one else in the house could have any idea what went on down there on quiet winter nights. For two years he had worked on a complicated device that in the end was never used. The assignment was abruptly terminated, and Jurek heard no more of it. He could only assume that somewhere security had broken, someone was exposed, and the work was canceled.

He had continued, then, his charade of work at the Bureau of Standards. Each day he walked to Wisconsin Avenue to catch the bus, sat working in his cubicle till five o'clock, and then made his way back across northwest Washington, a part of the indistinguishable mass of people hurrying to get home, stopping along the way to pick up something for supper and enjoying the last light of day as he walked from the bus the two blocks to 37th Street.

He would walk up the eight cement steps to the front porch and take the letters addressed to Occupant and Resident out of his mailbox. Then, before he could put his key in the lock he would hear Boris running from the kitchen to greet him. There would be a small, welcoming "woof" and the scratching of little feet on the door. The landlord had not noticed the claw marks, and, in any event, he was fond of Boris. He asked about him whenever Jurek had occasion to talk with him.

Two nights before, when Jurek opened the door, he greeted Boris as usual. "Yes, my friend," he said, "now is time to play." He picked the little dog up and felt a moment of warmth and affection. He smiled at his foolishness as he held the animal in his arms. An old man, he thought, far from home, with four

87

pounds of white fuzzy dog his only companion; a fuzzy dog, old, too, a little stiff in the joints and smelling terribly when he breathed. Nevertheless, Jurek kissed the top of his head and gave his ear a good scratch before he put him down.

It was warm and the days were getting longer. Each evening the old man and the tiny dog would walk down 37th Street and over to the park.

Glover-Archbold Park cuts a swath of wildness through the otherwise overcrowded area above Georgetown. The paths through its valley could be trails in a wilderness, once out of sight of Reservoir Road. Age-old trees shade them in summer; now the tiny leaves of spring were just beginning to bud. It was not an evening to expect trouble.

Jurek kept Boris on a leash, even in the deep, wooded part of the park. His fear of losing him was almost irrational. The little dog trotted obediently at his side, and the old man respected his desire to stop at interesting bushes and investigate exotic smells. Their walk was erratic, marked by many side trips and pauses. As Boris investigated a particularly titilating smell by the path, Jurek noticed a girl walking towards them.

It was spring, and as he watched the beautiful girl the old man's heart ached for his lost youth and lost loves. She walked with the swinging, athletic stride of these American girls. Dressed in one of the absurd jogging suits, this one pale lavender with a white stripe down each leg, she seemed to be catching her breath after a long run. Her cheeks glowed with health and vitality. She stopped when she was beside Jurek and bent over to look at Boris.

"What a darling dog!" She smiled at him, a mouthful of white teeth, like a toothpaste commercial. Jurek smiled back. He nodded and mumbled, *"Da, da,* a good dog." His command of English often left him at the most crucial times, betraying him for what he was. He had, of course, learned it in school, and before they sent him to America he had spent hours with records, hearing and practicing the American idiom, but it seemed as though the longer he was here the worse his command of the language became.

She didn't notice his awkwardness. "May I pick him up?" Without waiting for an answer she had Boris cuddled in her arms, where he happily curled up, resting his head on the lavender shoulder.

"Oh, *da,* he be happy you play with him. Poor Boris, all day alone." Jurek watched, charmed by the young woman's grace and beauty, as she stroked the rough, white head and fondled the shaggy ears.

"You're lucky to have such a sweet dog," she said, turning to him as she put Boris down. She ruffled the hair around his neck; then she straightened up, flashed another blazing white smile at Jurek, and said, "Well, thanks for letting me see your doggy. I'd better be jogging on, I guess. It'll be dark before you know it."

As she turned to leave, she stopped. "Oh, listen, you'd better check him for ticks. I thought I felt one just by his collar." And she was gone.

It was almost dark when he and Boris got home. The pleasing episode with the girl hovered in the old man's mind. He felt a surge of gratitude for the beauty of the world around him, where pretty girls stopped in the park and children played on the street. It was very far from Moscow, far from the treachery and fear he had known for so many years. His heart was light as he took Boris down the alley and into the backyard. The chain-link fence clanked as he closed the gate, and out of the dusk a small voice cried, "Hey, Mr. Bronski, you're late!"

The children were on his back step, sitting together in the near dark. My children, the old man thought, and he smiled. "Billy and Janet, is it? You want play with Boris, no?" Janet was four, and a plump, rosy contrast to her brother Bill. At seven, he was turning into a beanpole. They were the upstairs family, and shared the backyard with him. They shared Boris, too. Their parents wouldn't let them have a dog, and they waited every night to see Jurek bring Boris back from his walk.

He left Boris in the yard with the children and went in to get his dinner ready. Americans are clever, he thought, as he pulled the box out of the freezer. He could put it in the oven and have a whole dinner cooked in a half hour; clever, indeed, but cold. In Russia, there would have been, instead of a frozen box, an old woman in the kitchen, and the smell of fresh, hot bread, and beef and cabbage boiling for his dinner.

The knock on the door made him jump. It was only Janet, and he was annoyed at his own nerves. How long he had been here, and nothing had happened. Why should he jump like a guilty conspirator at a knock on the door? It had been years—

"Mr. Bronski, Boris and I want a cookie. We waited a long time. Can we have a cookie now? Can we?" How simple life can be, Jurek thought. A cookie for a child, and the sound of small voices, laughing in the yard. And he had sat in the last fading light, with Janet's small, warm body pressed against him, and watched while Billy made Boris balance a cooky on his nose. They had all laughed together, and Janet had hugged the old man and put a wet, crumby kiss on his cheek. "I love you, Mr. Bronski," she had said. "I love Boris, but I love you most."

When it was dark and the children had gone up-

90

stairs, Jurek and Boris went in to eat their dinner. They ate swiftly, and with little conversation, as became two old bachelors, and, after, Jurek remembered what the girl had said about a tick on Boris's neck. He lifted the fat little animal to his lap.

Then he set him on the table, pushing his dish aside. He felt carefully all around the collar. Nothing. Maybe it had fallen off. He turned the collar around, and something struck his finger. A small roll of paper was held to the collar by a fine wire. It took Jurek by surprise. He resented the paper; it was hateful to him.

How like them, to lead him on with a lovely illusion, a pretty girl on a quiet forest path, and then to leave him with this! Oh, he knew what it was all right. They wanted him again, they would never leave him alone. They couldn't let an old man live out his days in peace, even after all he had done and all he had risked. He cursed the knowledge that made them follow him to the ends of the world and wished, not for the first time, that he had been born with the dull mind of a peasant, a mind that could never give them what they wanted.

He didn't look at the paper in his hand. He thought he could just light a match to it and watch it burn, without ever knowing what they wanted. It would be gone and he would be free.

Even as he thought this, he knew it wasn't true. He, Jurek Vlascki, would never be free. He was their creature and they would find him no matter where he went (where could he go?) and then they would kill him. Here, there was no sending a man to Siberia. Instead, accidents happened.

"So, Boris, we have a letter. I read it to you, my friend." Slowly, he unrolled the paper and held it to the light over the kitchen table, while Boris snuffled wetly against his trouser leg. It was from Orlov, set-

91

ting up a meeting for him, telling him how he must make a contact; he was going back to work for them.

So it was that on the next night Boris missed his walk. The children saw the old man start off alone, in the direction of Wisconsin Avenue, and though they waited till after dark on the back steps, he did not come home, not till long after they were in bed. Billy was awake when he came and he heard him climb the front steps and open the door. His steps were slow and painful.

He was tired. He had walked over to Wisconsin Avenue, and gone the half block to Bob's Ice Cream Store. As usual, it was jammed with people. On the sidewalk a young man and his girl were laughing as the girl tried to eat a triple-dip cone that was melting faster than she could lick the dripping ice cream, and he was mopping her up with a handful of paper napkins. A middle-aged woman in running shoes and city clothes was serenely lapping up a single dip of chocolate, and a mother of three sticky-faced and sticky-pawed children was talking unconcernedly with another young woman as they sat on tall stools by the counter.

Jurek edged his way forward. He waited till the clock said exactly 7:05. "Please, a double dip, I want. One Rocky Road and one Devil's Delight." He would, in other circumstances, have laughed at the absurd names, but now he said them grimly; he might have been ordering his own coffin instead of an ice-cream cone with a ridiculous name. Without a smile, he paid the gangling black boy behind the counter and turned to leave, the disgusting concoction already melting and running over his hand. He brushed past a thin man standing at the end of the counter, jostling him with his free elbow as he went out. It wasn't necessary. The man had heard him give his order and was ready to follow him out onto the street. He pushed past the three sticky children, and could feel the tall, thin stranger behind him. "Can you tell me where 37th Street is? I'm looking for my uncle's house," a quiet, almost apologetic voice murmured.

"*Da,* I tell you." Jurek didn't even look up. "I show you," he said. I'll show you, he thought, even though you know as well as I do, you bastard. Your damned embassy is just up the street. It must be a new man; he'd never seen him before. The embassy was at the top of the hill, on Mt. Alto, the most strategic location in the city for an unfriendly foreign embassy. From the site of the abandoned Veteran's Hospital the Soviets could monitor all communications emanating from within the city. They were on higher ground than the Agency at Langley, across the river. Were the Americans so trusting that they didn't know how the very framework of the building on the hill could intercept telephone messages from anywhere in the city? They didn't suspect the reasons the Soviets had for choosing the site? Jurek felt an unwonted surge of love for the people of this new country, and he longed to share their innocence.

Forcing his mind back to reality, he shrugged in the direction of Georgetown, and the man fell in step beside him as he hurried down Wisconsin to White-haven where they turned off and headed for 37th Street. They walked together in silence down the narrow sidewalk until they came to Reservoir Road. Jurek gestured gruffly to the right and turned the corner without looking at this companion. Lights were going on in the rooms of Georgetown Hospital across the street as Jurek half pulled the thin man along the sidewalk and past the entrance to the French Embassy. The massive white building crouched like a fortress behind its heavily barred gates, and they hurried by without looking up. A block farther on Jurek turned suddenly into the dark, wooded cover of the park. He was walking very fast and breathing heavily. The younger man had to hurry to keep up with him.

In the park it was fully dark. "All right, old man. We talk here." The familiarity, the insulting assumption; you are ours to do with as we will. Resentment welled up in Jurek. This boy wasn't even born when I was at the university; he was a puking infant when I was exploring the essence of matter and a snot-nosed kid in school when I was showing them the uses they could make of what I had found. The old man was sick with disgust at himself and at the cowardice that had brought him here; for he knew that it was only the familiar habit of fear that held him, and he longed for the freedom he would never know.

The man motioned him to a bench, faintly visible under the dark trees. This was work to be done in the dark, surely, and Jurek sighed as he sat heavily, obediently, on the seat. "Comrade Vlascki," the quiet voice began, ameliorating his earlier rudeness. "Vlascki, you have the honor to serve your country. Your homeland has need of you again; has need of your great knowledge, your skill—" The voice was soft now, oily and caressing.

Jurek waved an impatient hand. It was always the same. The pompous posturing, the appeal to patriotism. He wondered what he owed them, what debt to the country that had owned him and used him for all of his sixty years. Surely he had paid them in full. "Come to the point, boy. The rest I know. I grew old knowing. What do they want? Just tell me that—"

Expressionless in the dark, the young man mumbled a few words, pushed a folded newspaper into Jurek's hands, and stood up. "Read the paper, then, old man," he whispered, the pretense of courtesy now vanished. Without any sign of farewell, he turned and stalked off towards the street, leaving Jurek alone on the bench. He sat there for some minutes in the dark, until the sound of footsteps faded away. Then he tucked the paper under his arm and started the slow journey home.

I'm too old to be curious, he thought. I can wait till hell freezes over to know what I will find in this paper. Going up 37th Street he passed the lighted windows of small row houses, some, like his, converted into multi-family dwellings, where students from Georgetown University lived in groups of five or six, sharing the rent money and housekeeping chores, and some still owned by old couples who had begun their married lives on this quiet street and raised their families in these same narrow houses. It was a friendly mix of neighbors, and on this night Jurek yearned to be part of it, to escape from his past. He longed, as never before, to really be the "Mr. Bronski" of little Janet's innocent belief.

The four long blocks uphill left him with a dull pain in his chest and rasping breath, but he hurried up the steps; he could hear Boris running to the door. Ah, Boris, my friend, perhaps not much sleep for us tonight. Your old master is at work once more.

He went through the kitchen, a wriggling old dog under one arm and the folded newspaper under the other. He unlocked the door to the basement stairs and felt his way down in the dark. Once in the workroom he locked the heavy door behind him and felt for the light switch. The room sprang into dazzling brightness. Under the glare Jurek blinked and squinted. Boris jumped down and ran little circles around the floor, finally coming up with a rubber mouse, which he presented proudly to his master.

95

"No, my friend, we play later. Juri must do some work and you must be a good dog." He put the little dog on the table and gave him a handful of biscuits from a can on the shelf. Then he carefully unfolded the newspaper.

He held in his hand a dozen gleaming horseshoe nails, light to the touch and sharp as the claws of a great, wild cat. He thought he hadn't seen a horse since he left his father's farm so many years ago. He remembered the old grey animal that stood so patiently in the shed and waited for the thin flake of hay that Jurek brought it each morning. And he remembered the terror in its great, dark eye when at last it fell to its knees under the weight of the cart, and he felt again the sharp, searing report of the gun that brought its miserable life to an end.

He picked up the sheet of yellow paper the nails had been wrapped in. It was closely covered with writing, and he held it up to the light to read the small letters. He read it twice, trying to make sense out of it. He turned the nails over and over in his hand, studying the broad, flat heads and trying to imagine how he would do it.

Of course, they knew he could; they remembered the early days when miniaturization belonged to the Japanese until his own work had made Russian technology the leader in the field. In his laboratory in Moscow, in the late seventies, Jurek had developed the most spohisticated system of miniaturized detonation in the world.

He sighed and bent to ruffle the white fur on Boris's head. The little dog responded with a lazy wag of his tail and snuffled slightly in his sleep. "Stay with me, my friend," Jurek said. "Tonight we work." Boris grunted and rolled over. He snored in little snorts and the regular sound of his breathing comforted the old

96

man as he worked.

He laid the nails out on the table. The light glinting from the polished surfaces was hypnotic. Again he read the encoded instructions. A preposterous idea! An explosive, a powerful explosive, concealed in the heads of the horseshoe nails. It must be impervious to the blows of a hammer (They intended to put these nails in a horse's hooves!) and be detonated only by a signal a few hundred yards away, at most.

Jurek scratched his head. He was tired and his eyes blurred. He longed to scrap the whole project, say he couldn't do it, that it was impossible. Yet, he knew it wasn't impossible, and the bastards on Mt. Alto and in the Kremlin knew as well as he did that it wasn't impossible. He despised again the craven fear that kept him here, as much a captive of the system he hated as if he were behind the barbed wire of a prison camp.

He knew he would do it; there was no escape from his destiny. Here, in this airless little room, hiding beneath houses where children laughed and played, here in this ugly little room was where he belonged, he and Boris alone. He began scratching figures and numbers on a pad of paper. The little dog stirred in his sleep and cried out, dreaming of wolves chasing a fuzzy, white dog across the frozen tundra.

The sun was rising over the city when Jurek tenderly lifted the little animal in his arms and took him upstairs. It was time for breakfast.

Chapter Six

Prague, September 1976

The dull grey light that filtered through the high windows above the gallery did nothing to raise George's spirits. There was something fundamentally wrong with the whole day; Prinz even knew it and showed how he felt in the sullen way he responded to George's most reasonable requests. The major was watching as George cut the far corner and made a sloppy change of diagonal as he started down the side of the ring. George felt the eyes following him, burning into his back, but still he couldn't concentrate. He could only wonder where Eleni was. She'd been riding with his group every day for the last month and he had come to expect to see her bombing around the track in front of him. He rounded the near corner and caught the major's eye; he decided he'd better get his mind on what he was doing or the old boy would yell at him again. The fat Czech girl on the Holsteiner always enjoyed hearing the American get hell. She was here today and he was damned if he'd give her the satisfaction of hearing—

"No, boy, not like that! Vith the seat, boy, vith the seat ve move the horse. Not vith the leg, vith the seat!" The major's voice brought George back to earth and left him feeling like an idiot. The worst thing was, the major was always right. If you did what he said, the horse did what you wanted. Sweat broke out on his face and he forced his eyes to look straight ahead as he let his weight sink down in the middle. The fat Czech trotted past, and he could see her derisive grin. Plenty of weight in *her* seat; no wonder her horse moved so well.

As the horse moved around the edge of the arena, obedient now to his and the major's will, George's thoughts assumed a life of their own, and he found himself thinking of Eleni again. He was almost glad she wasn't there to see him humiliated by his own stupidity. Of course if she were there, he wouldn't have been worrying about why she wasn't. And it was probably silly to think she cared about him at all. She certainly couldn't feel the same way about him that he did about her. He tried to compare her to girls he had known at school—girls whose fathers gave them ski weekends, and Caribbean vacations at Spring Break; girls whose big ambition was the Dartmouth Winter Weekend, who floated from party to party in pale dresses, giggling in the backseats of boys' cars, or waving sunburned arms from behind the wheel of sleek little convertibles, their own graduation presents.

Beside Eleni they were as empty and lifeless as the crumpled party dresses they left on the floor for someone else to pick up the next day. Eleni, so tiny and so helpless looking, was alone in Prague; she had been here for three years. Her family lived in a village, far away, eking a marginal existence from the communal farm. Her first passion had been for the heavy horses that worked the land, and as a baby she had cried to be put on their backs as they were led to

99

and from the fields. In school she gravitated towards the equestrian team as naturally as water seeks its own level. As captain of the winning junior team three years earlier, she had been chosen for training at the Institute in Prague, and here she would stay as long as she made satisfactory progress under the watchful eye of Major Hrdlcka.

Circling the arena, George's body responded automatically to the major's commands; but while one part of him rode the horse, another part of him kept thinking of Eleni and willing her to appear. Lately, he had found that much as he valued the time he spent with the major, the thing he really wanted for every day was the end of the class. As soon as the old boy pulled out his big gold watch, he could feel his heartbeat speed up, and he would look across the hall to catch Eleni's eye and smile at her. Then the major would click his heels, clear his throat and growl something in Czech. As an afterthought he would sometimes nod at George and say, "Is enough today, boy—vas good, *da?*"

Then he and Eleni would ride together out under the heavy arch leading from the hall. They would walk side by side, letting the horses relax while the sweat dried on their steaming flanks. They would walk quietly for a few minutes through the paths in Slovenska Park, but sometimes when they were far from the school they would follow each other over the outside course or race through the cool wet air, laughing and breathless. Then they were like children, playing Fox and Hounds through the tangled paths, and once they had crashed into each other and fallen together on the ground, helpless with laughter.

George had got up first, and pulled Eleni to her feet. She felt very small and breakable when he held her in his arms. The laughter had died in his throat

100

and for an instant the taste of fear filled his mouth. She'd hidden her face against his chest and her body was shaking; he'd thought she was crying and he was afraid even to ask if she was hurt. Then she had looked up at him and she was laughing. "Oh, God, you're OK!" was all he could say, and Eleni had nodded her head, but her laughter had stopped when she saw his face. She'd smiled and pulled away from him a little to look at him. Her green eyes had held his for a long moment and he found her hand was still in his, friendly and warm. "Sure, Georgi," she had said, "You OK, too?"

The moment was over, and they had ridden back to the barn in silence, untacked their horses and said goodbye. George knew she would spend the rest of the day mucking stalls and cleaning the tack that he would use tomorrow, and he was always filled with a helpless guilt when he watched her stubborn little back disappear down the aisle of the barn. They never talked of the hours they spent apart; the times they were together were magic times, and separate from anything else in their lives.

For George, the make-believe time was becoming the only real time. He ate meals with his parents, had lessons with old Harrison and studied in his room at night. But after his lights were out, alone in his room, George dreamed a whole other life, where he lived in a bare attic room, or in a palace of unequaled splendor, or on a lonely mountaintop with a tiny green-eyed girl. He loved the girl with all his heart, as she loved him with hers.

He would dream himself into a restless sleep, a sleep interrupted by fantastic imaginings where two sweaty bodies wrestled with their passions and knew ecstasies he couldn't believe existed. He would wake, hot and damp, embarrassingly clutching his pillow, or

101

worse, his blanket; no longer the friendly blue satin-bound companion of nursery days, but a deceitful object, replacing, with its limp uselessness, the warm and living creature that sleep had given him to hold in his arms.

Then there were moments of half-awake terror, believing, but not believing, that this was the way you stunted your growth, or lost your virility or became an idiot. He would lie sleepless, then, for hours, and watch the square of light on his wall grow pale as daylight slowly replaced the light from the streetlamp that shone in through the window. Then, an hour before breakfast, just when sleep had finally come, the agony of the alarm would jangle beside the bed, waking him, startled, from his first sound sleep of the night.

At breakfast he wondered if his father, or worse, his mother, suspected how he had been spending his nights. "Eat your eggs, dear. You need the protein." Oh, God, he must look awful! After breakfast he would study his face in the mirror. He came to hate the mirror in his bathroom. It knew too much about him. It showed him the dark circles under his eyes, a sure sign of his depravity. He would stand under the cold shower and let the water stream over his face and he would rub the rough towel over his skin till it was red. It didn't make him look any better.

Old Harrison didn't say anything about the way he looked. Maybe it wasn't evident to everyone, after all. And he had been better about his homework, so the old boy wouldn't have anything to complain to Dad about. With a supreme effort of will, he would force himself to forget Eleni for three hours every morning, and then he would feel guilty for not thinking of her. He wondered if she knew how he suffered.

"Hey, Georgi, wake up!" He was still trotting

around the arena and the major was, for a change, smiling. Eleni was beside him, the little mare matching the Prinz's easy stride.

"Now the young lady joins us, ve get to vork. Vere you been so late, lady? Make yourself pretty for Georgi, no?" George thanked God the major wasn't pissed at her; he could probably make trouble if he wanted to. Eleni was smiling, too. Her face was scrubbed till it glowed and her smooth dark hair was pulled back, flawlessly knotted at her neck. She wore a white shirt and pale blue choker, the gold safety pin absolutely horizontal at her throat. George decided he'd better stop looking at the way her breeches fitted her perfect little ass, at least until the lesson was over.

The major meant vork when he said vork. An hour later, his shirt drenched with sweat and his legs aching, George turned to leave the arena. He could see Eleni reflected in the many mirrors that lined the walls of the ancient hall. She floated by, her image repeated endlessly from mirror to mirror. The great hall had been built in a happier, more relaxed time. Above the arena, crystal chandeliers twinkled and cast shadows on the carved capitals of the columns that held the vaulted ceiling. A gallery curved all the way around above the mirrors, where once royal spectators had watched officers high schooling their mounts and had applauded the Grand Prix jumpers of that earlier day. Watching Eleni, George couldn't imagine that any sight of the previous century had been more lovely, or more perfectly suited to the elegance of the old hall. He watched her and he was sick with desire.

Later, on the path, Eleni rode close beside him. Their knees touched now and then, and the clean, soapy smell of Eleni herself enveloped him. They were silent, listening to the horses' footfalls on the damp turf. A fog had settled over Prague, and George could feel the magic of the old city soaking into him. The very air was alive with it, and the trees were ghosts, looming from nowhere beside the path. Branches reached down through the mist above them, and sounds from the city were muffled and faint. They were alone in a pocket of velvet fog. George would have given his life to stay there forever.

He was startled by the sound of Eleni's voice. It was very clear and so small it was almost a whisper. "Georgi?" He leaned close, and felt her shoulder against his arm. "Georgi, we have fun riding here, no?"

"We have fun riding here, yes," he grinned at her, watching for her odd, sloping little smile. Her face stayed grave, almost frightened. She looked like a lost child, her lower lip caught in her teeth, her eyes wide and pleading. "Yes, we have fun, Eleni. There isn't anything I do that's more fun than being with you." His voice broke before he could finish this declaration, and he could feel his face getting red. Still, she looked at him, more in sorrow, he thought, then fear.

He reached across to put his hand on hers, and was surprised to find it was as warm as his, though the damp air was cool and penetrating, forcing its way through his sweater and chilling him to the bone. "Eleni, is something wrong? Why were you late today? Are you in trouble or something?" He sounded to himself like the Inquisition, and cursed himself for an idiot. Eleni shook her head and turned away.

"Look at me, Eleni. Tell me."

"Not here," she said. "By the lake. Come, I race you!" She wheeled the mare where she stood, and, in a thunder of hooves, she was lost in the fog.

She let George beat her to the lake, and she still wasn't laughing. Her green eyes were dark, and deep as the water in the still forest lake. "Georgi," she began again, and stopped. She caught her breath in her throat and swallowed. "Georgi, no more we can ride here together. They know and they watch." She looked down and laced her fingers back and forth in the little mare's mane.

"What do you mean, we can't?" He pulled her around, almost roughly, to look at her face. The horses were steaming in the thick air, and their breath came in little puffs of white from their dilating nostrils. It was very quiet, except for George's voice, harsh and angry. Eleni put her finger to his mouth.

"Be quiet, Georgi, they listen. I told you—"

"What the hell do you mean? I don't understand what you're talking about. Don't you want to come here with me anymore?" A cold dagger was in his heart. He could see an actual dagger sticking out of his chest, from wherever his heart really was. A trickle of blood ran down his shirt. It was better than life without Eleni, rejected by Eleni.

"No, Georgi, don't say that. I want come, always I want." Then she pointed to the edge of the lake, where they could see, through a break in the mist, a man sitting on a bench, his face hidden by a newspaper. An old guy, reading the paper on his lunch hour, a brown bag on the seat beside him. "Three of them we have passed. They watch me, Georgi, always. They want for me never meet with American, never have fun together, never to love. They know and they tell."

"I don't believe it. You just imagine it, Eleni. That old grandfather can't hurt us. He isn't even looking at us. What do they care what you do, anyhow? Look, we go to class together every day—"

"So does Major Hrdlcka, Georgi. You think he doesn't listen, doesn't know?"

Then something tightened around George's chest. He couldn't really breathe for a minute. Oh, God, it was awful to think of the major spying on them; it was a betrayal, worse than the guy with the newspaper. Sure, they had to watch Dad and Mom and the embassy, he guessed. They had a right to do that. But what did the damn spooks want from him and Eleni? Even Communists must fall in love sometimes, couldn't they understand that?

"What if they do see us? We aren't doing anything. Is love against the law here?" As soon as it was out of his mouth he realized he had said the word "love" out loud, to Eleni. He'd said it so many times to himself and to her in his dreams that it had seemed perfectly natural to say it. She probably thought he was a fool, blurting it out like that, sitting here on a horse, in front of an old fart of a spy. "I mean," he finished, weakly, "what can they do about us anyway?"

"What you say, Georgi? Love?" Her eyes were wide with surprise. She turned to him. "Can we love, Georgi, can we?"

Oh, God, George thought, I don't know what the next line is. Help me think, for God's sake. "I guess we can't here," he said. It was the mouthing of a certified cretin. She would never want to see him again, not if she had a brain in her head. He wished he could disappear into the ground. He wished Prinz would bolt and dump him on the ground, wounded grievously, but not permanently, and Eleni would jump down (forgetting that he was an idiot) and hold his head in her lap—her lap! She would be kind to him if he were hurt. She would put her cool hand on his flaming forehead, she would tear her blouse in strips to bind his wounds, he would bury his face—

His face was burning. She must be able to see how he felt. She could read his thoughts and she hated him for them.

"Georgi," she said, quiet, and close to him, "we find a way. I tell you." She wasn't mad at him, she didn't hate him. "I tell you a story. We walk the path here, you listen what I tell. OK?"

The movement of the horses was almost stealthy as they trod the spongy path through drifts of fog. As they moved along, enveloped in the soft white air, Eleni told George the legend of the Golem of Prague. "Hundreds years ago," she began softly, "the Jews had a Golem. Not a real man. Something they made." She laughed, and the sound, echoing over the water, struck George as the most beautiful music in the world. He rode beside her in a trance, seeing nothing clearly beyond her face, now solemn again, and wistful.

She told how the Jews, in their synagogue, had made a creature able to do everything a man could do, and more, but it was a machine. It could go all over Prague, to places denied the Jews themselves, and work its magic in whatever ways it was commanded. For six days the wonderful Golem was free, but on the seventh day, the high Sabbath, the rabbi took the "shem" from its mouth, and it was lifeless for twenty-four hours to honor the Holy Day.

Then one Sabbath, the rabbi forgot to deactivate the Golem and it ran wild all over Prague, creating such devastation that the city fathers demanded its death. Of course, the rabbi refused to harm his Golem, and only threats of violence against the whole Jewish community brought about apparent submission. The rabbi said he would kill the Golem and free the city from his mischief.

All kinds of stories came down regarding the death and final disposition of the poor Golem. His bones and fingers and toes and heaven knew what other parts were said to be kept in hiding; some said his whole body was preserved and kept in a sealed-off part of the attic of the Old Synagogue. Nobody, not even the Jews, knew the real story, but everyone had heard of some mischief that only the Golem could have done, and only a fool, Eleni said, would not believe that the Golem himself was still hiding somewhere in Prague, laughing his high, wild laugh, creating small havoc wherever he could.

The most likely place for him to hide was the Old Jewish Cemetery. This holy place was older then anything in Prague, as old as the Golem himself. Naturally he would like to hang out there. The cemetery itself was one of the most frequented tourist sights in Prague. Through centuries of persecution, the Jews were only allowed this one small plot of land to bury their dead, and after hundreds of years, the bodies were in some places buried twelve deep, and the marker stones were packed in so tightly that only narrow paths gave access through the plot. Stones were jumbled together, leaning on each other crazily. It was a fitting home for the Golem.

Eleni's eyes were bright as she told the story. Among the fog-shrouded trees, George could almost feel the ancient, mysterious force. All of the history of the city was entwined with magic, and for a wild moment, the Golem was real to George, a logical extension of the very air of Prague. He could have been behind the next tree, around the next bend in the path.

"You know Old Cemetery, Georgi? You been there? All Americans go there. Sightsee, you call it?"

"Sure, Leon shows me everything. He's regular tour guide."

Eleni leaned close and drew up her reins. They stopped in the middle of the path, conspirators together. She whispered. "Golem will help us," she said. "Be our friend—"

"What do you mean, he'll help us? Eleni, we can't even see each other—you just said so. What can the stupid Golux—"

"Golem, Georgi. Say it right or he get mad. Golem." She laughed again. "You not speak so good, Georgi, like me." In the faint misty light her eyes were deep green pools, sparkling with a light of their own. George's heart sank inside him. He could feel it, all hollow, as though it had shrunk and disappeared. He couldn't imagine living in Prague without Eleni, without hearing her clear little voice, carefully speaking to him in "American," in those endearingly crooked phrases. The world was empty, as empty as the impenetrable air around them.

"Not so sad, Georgi! Listen. Listen what I tell. What you think Golem does? In cemetery Golem keeps notes people write, people have secrets, they give to Golem and he keep them, give to their friend." She told him that always, through the centuries, when people needed to exchange messages, unknown to others, they left a note with the Golem, under the stones of the cemetery and he would see that the right person, and no one else, got the message. Secrets of every kind had been transmitted there, for generations. Lovers had arranged meetings, religious refugees had been rescued, and during the war spies had contacted each other with important dispatches.

"See, Georgi, I tell you to find me where I live, come see me. I tell Golem, no?"

It would be easy, she said. He would just tell Leon he wanted to walk in the cemetery, and that would make the old boy happy. He'd think George had taken his tour-guiding seriously. Eleni told him exactly how to find the pile of stones where he should look and she would signal him in class on the day she would leave a message. If it worked, then they could leave other messages for each other, whenever they couldn't be together, and no one would ever know. She touched his arm and he thought that his desire for her would explode his head if she came any closer. She leaned up and whispered in his ear, and the throbbing of his blood seemed to him loud enough for her to hear. "Remember, Georgi, no one knows. No one finds out. I go back alone, no one sees us, OK?"

She was gone. Vanished into the mist like a magical creature and George was alone. He could feel the hair rising on the back of his neck, and in the pit of his stomach there was a great hollow space. His head felt as if it would burst with the sudden influx of joy. Only seconds ago it had seemed he would never see Eleni again, and now her words echoed through the thick white air, "—find me where I live—" She really had said that. The fog rose a little, and he could see the branches above him and a brightness in the sky overhead. He could have flown back to the Institute.

He sat silent in the backseat of the limo. It was Friday, a week after the ride in the mist. He had only seen Eleni across the arena or at the other end of the barn, working. He had been sick with worry. She had only been leading him on, there wasn't any Golem; it was all a story to make him look like a fool. Almost he hadn't come for his lesson today, and now his heart stopped to think that he might have not been there and not heard her whispered words as she met him circling the hall this morning. She was riding on the opposite rein, coming towards him as they warmed up for the lesson.

110

She didn't smile, but the corners of her mouth were just barely turned up and her eyes were bright. "Hello, 'Leni." George had managed a grin while his heart stopped beating. She went past and then turned the little mare smartly and reversed direction. Gradually she overtook the Prinz and then fitted her stride with his and they rode together down the far side of the arena. The major was watching, and must have seen her turn to him. "Under tall crooked stone," she said, "against wall, in far corner." Then with a little flick of the mare's tail she turned and circled the opposite direction. The major made no comment and the lesson went on; went on for centuries, as far as George could see.

At last, in the limo, he sat silent, his mouth so dry he was afraid he couldn't speak. The words went round and round in his head, "Under tall crooked stone, against wall, in far corner—" Whether his voice would work or not he was going to have to say something to Leon if he expected to be taken to the cemetery. If he didn't speak soon they would be home and it would be a big scene to get him to start out again. Then again, Leon was just as apt to pretend he couldn't understand and go right straight home. He watched miserably as the old buildings crowded against the narrow sides of the street. Traffic was pretty thick, and Leon was taking his time.

At last George cleared his throat and swallowed hard. "Leon," his voice came out rather weakly. "Leon," he tried again, "remember that old cemetery?" He was surprised at how casual it sounded. "The Jewish one you showed me that time? Let's go there today. I've wanted to see it ever since you told me about it. Just wait and let me walk around in it; it sounds really neat." Perhaps he was a little too enthusiastic about a trip to some old tombstones. He held

111

his breath, waiting to see what Leon would say.

At first, he just grunted something in Czech. Then, as though pleased that George had remembered, he actually smiled and said, *"Da,* we go then." He took the next right turn, and, crossing the river, reentered the old city. Here the streets were even narrower and paved with cobbles. Tourists were crowding the sidewalks, herded carefully along by Intourist guides, obediently viewing all the approved sights. Slowly Leon threaded his way along until he pulled off beside the high stone wall. "Cemetery," he said through the little window behind his seat and he cut the motor.

"You just stay here, Leon. Better stay with the car, the way you're parked, OK?" It was good there wasn't a real place to park. Leon might have wanted to come in with him and continue his earlier lecture. Fortunately he did not seem disposed to communication, and had already lit a cigarette to solace himself during the wait.

He nodded and said, "I be right here. Take your time."

Through the narrow gate George could see nothing at first but a seemingly endless pile of stone, crazily piled on each other. He couldn't even see a path at first. Despair seized him. He was here on a fool's errand; if there was a note here he'd never find it. The stones all were crooked and they all looked the same. In the few spaces he could see between the stones the earth was covered with pebbles, small white stones about the size of marbles, with some bigger rough stones mixed in. It was hopeless. In spite of his panic, he grinned when he thought of the Golem. This was just the place for a crazy robot to live, a much better place for a Golem than for a sensible person who was looking for a hidden message.

112

Sweat soaked the back of his shirt, even here in the chilly damp beneath the trees. He felt the weight of all the years the old city had lived; it seemed distilled in the very atmosphere of the ancient burying ground. Time stood still here, and the sense of urgency passed. A narrow, twisted path became visible, bending around the dead white stones. He followed it until it divided and branched off in three directions. He met a couple coming the other way, middle-aged Americans, clutching guidebooks and bristling with photographic equipment. He ducked off to let them pass, and then picked his way over a few larger stones towards the far corner of the lot. "In far corner," that was what she had said.

That must mean diagonally from where the gate was, so he kept on in that direction. The sweat ran down inside his shirt now, and his hands were cold. Again, he had to climb some of the stones to continue towards the corner. Some of them were so old they were perfectly smooth; all signs of the life they witnessed had been obliterated by time. Some had inscriptions he couldn't read, carved in Hebrew. Others had only the Star of David scratched on their surface. The sorrow of the people who for centuries had brought their dead to this tiny patch of ground rose like a palpable miasma here under the ancient trees. George wanted to get out and breathe in the sunlight. He scrambled over another stone, scraping his hand as he stumbled forward.

Jesus, all the stones were crooked, leaning on each other, jammed in together. He'd never find the right one. They all looked the same. Maybe she just told him all this stuff to get rid of him; he was an idiot to believe her. God, he'd even begun to believe in the Golem! Well, if there was a Golem he was probably the kind of thing that would hide your note where

113

you couldn't find it and be laughing at you from somewhere instead of helping you find it. It was undoubtedly the Golem who had made him trip over that stone; it was the kind of thing he would do.

Then George saw that his hand was bleeding and he stopped to get out his handkerchief. He leaned against a huge stone that rested at an angle in the corner of the wall. He knotted the handkerchief around the bleeding finger before he noticed what he was leaning against. It was the crooked stone! The space under the stone next to the wall was filled with the white pebbles. "Under the little stones" was where the Golem was supposed to put things for you.

He looked around the cemetery. He was alone. On his knees he began, almost frantically, to dig in the pebbles. They were mostly smooth as beach gravel, and pleasant to touch. They ran through his fingers easily, leaving a dry white dust; the dust of ages, George thought. His fingers found something that wasn't a stone; it was a crumpled piece of paper, jammed deep in the corner of the wall. His hands shook, and he held it for a minute, just looking at it, a tightly wadded ball of paper. He straightened up, and heard a scraping noise across the square. He closed his hand over the ball of paper just before he saw Leon peering over the stones at him.

"Got to move car. Better come."

Maybe you've got to move, buddy, George thought, or maybe you just thought you'd like to see what I was doing. "Sure, I'm coming. Be right there," he called. He jammed his hands in his pockets and started for the gate. Leon was all smiles now.

"You like old cemetery, no?" he asked.

"It's neat, Leon. Maybe we can come again. I'm really interested in the history of this place — maybe I can use it for a term paper or something." And maybe

I've got my own reasons for coming here, Leon, and they are none of your fucking business.

The limo crept through the streets at a snail's pace. The drive home was endless. The paper burned in his pocket, but clearly he could not risk Leon seeing him read it. His face felt like fire and he hoped he could get up to his room without meeting anyone in the house. With exaggerated courtesy, Leon deposited him at the door of the Residence, and he streaked up the stairs. He slammed the door of his room and pulled the curtains, remembering the gardener on the windowsill.

He threw himself on his bed, luxuriating for a moment in anticipation. He took the ball of paper out of his pocket and set it on his stomach, there to observe it anxiously for some moments, unable to make himself open it. It could be the wrong piece of paper, a note from a drug dealer instructing his supplier, or a letter to an unfaithful wife from some fat Czech official. It wasn't from Eleni at all. She wouldn't tell him where she lived. His heart was beating like a hummingbird's wings; he could feel it fluttering in his chest, and the rise and fall of the wad of paper on his chest matched its anguished beating.

Then he was in such a hurry to read it that the cheap paper tore as he tried to smooth it out. He pieced it together and began to read the tiny, neat writing. No name. No "Dear Georgi," no signature. It just said, "From phone booth, alone, call 378-0967. Call before you ride Monday. Ring 3 times. Hang up. Ring again. Not say my name. I answer. I tell you where to come."

He read it three times. It was from her, unbelievably, it really was from Eleni. "Phone booth alone," she said. How in hell could he do that? Make Leon stop on the way to the Institute, say he'd got to call home, he'd forgotten something? He was beginning to feel like the Pink Panther. It was clearly a corrupting influence to live in a society that functioned on surveillance and distrust. Corruption bred corruption. For a perfectly honest, normal guy to make a date with a gorgeous girl he had to sneak around like a world-class spy. On reflection, he began to rather enjoy it.

And it worked. Leon didn't blink an eye when he told him about the phone. He dialed the number and heard it ring three times. His hand shook as he hung the phone up. Then he rang again and waited. He waited an eternity. She wasn't there; it was a fake number. An irate Czech would answer and swear at him; it was the number of her boyfriend, who would find him and kill him.

He was about to hang up when he heard a click. "Allo?" A pause, and George couldn't speak. "Allo, allo. Is you?"

Chapter Seven

Middleburg, Virginia, April 1989

The rain had just begun and the first big drops made a pattern where they fell on the brick walk. Carter pretended he was dodging between them as he ran to the barn. He and Cissy had a dressage lesson after Mr. Fleming was through, and he knew they'd have it even if it rained buckets. There were only twenty-two days left before the event, and Dad said there wouldn't be any excuses for not doing well. If you wanted to ride in it you would darned well ride the best you knew how. Never compete if you don't have a chance to win. Jessy would come, hell or high water, and he and Beau would jog from A to H, and canter from H to M, around the dressage ring through a foot of mud, if necessary.

Bud Fleming was already there. He had his anvil set up under the porch roof of the barn, out of the rain. Carter loved Bud. He'd been their farrier ever since his first pony, a lifetime ago. They'd been through a lot together, he and Bud. Like the first time they'd tried to trim the feet of that rotten little Shetland. Mom wouldn't let Carter hold her, she said he wasn't big enough. He was four and a half, clearly old enough to help, he thought. The pony came about up to Mom's waist. She was named Strawberry, and she was a sweet, docile animal, a pony that took care of her rider and could be trusted with the smallest child.

But she was a different animal when it was time to take care of her feet. As soon as Bud had picked up one of her legs that day, all hell had broken loose. She's strained forward against Mom and Carter, and they'd held her with all their strength, braced against her force. Then, sudden as a snake, the pony had shot backward, dumping them both on the ground. Bud's trimming knife had shot across the yard, Mom said a word Carter had never heard before, and Bud had laughed to hear it. It had taken hours to finish all four feet and Carter had gotten a lecture on teaching ponies to behave.

Beau would be a different proposition entirely. Every day since Beau had been on the farm, Carter had gone to his stall and walked all around him, patting his rump and scratching his ears and leaning down to pick up his feet, one by one, until he was so used to it that now he would stand like a statue for the farrier and offer his feet even before he was asked. Carter was pretty proud of his pony.

"Hi, Mr. Fleming," he called as he ducked under the rail. Bud straightened up and waved. B.D., his ancient lab, was sniffing around the barnyard, a short piece of rope hanging from her neck. "Sorry, B.D., you won't have the Russells to play with," Carter said. He looked at Bud. "Mom shut them up because you were coming. She says they get sick every time from eating the hoof parings. They never get sick outdoors, always in my bed—I don't care, though, so why does she? They aren't in her bed."

B.D., short for Black Dog, received this informa-

118

tion calmly. She stretched out under the oak tree and settled for cleaning her toenails, doubtless overjoyed at being relieved of the tiresome task of entertaining two energetic Jack Russell terriers. Bud grinned and rolled up his sleeves. "Hey, buddy, you wouldn't keep an old friend waiting on a morning like this, would you? Let's get the pony out here. It's nine o'clock already—I bet you just got out of the sack."

"You're kidding, Mr. Fleming. We've done the creek trail already and had breakfast, too." He ran a grimy hand across his chin to remove the evidence. "Old Cis is just getting up, though. Let's do Beau first, can we?" Cissy had come in some time after midnight and Carter's breakfast had been enlivened by his father's remarks on the life-style of today's young women in general, and his own daughter in particular.

The big drops of rain were turning into a fine mist, and over the mountain the sky was lightening again. Bud gave a practiced glance to the west and allowed, "I thought we were getting a real toad-drowner there for a while, but looks like it'll fizzle out. How you coming with Beau?"

"Jessy said she's sure we can go Training, and Mom argued a while about it, but Dad said Jessy knows what I can do and what Beau can do and she ought to let me do it, so I'm going to." He offered a filthy hand full of yogurt-covered raisins. Bud took a couple and quickly put them in his mouth, wisely not looking at them. They were supposed to be white and Carter was glad that Bud appeared not to notice the changes wrought in them by a few days in the pocket of his jeans.

Beau stood under the roof, swishing flies with his tail, suffering shoes to be pulled and new ones fitted and hammered on. "You're running this pony into the

119

ground, kid." Bud held up the shoe he had just pulled. "Look at that. Thin as paper, and it was loose, too. You wanta watch that, don't let 'em get that way again. He'll hang one on a fence and dump you someday."

"I was waiting so it wouldn't be too long before the event," Carter said. "These have got to last till then, don't they? You can't change them in three weeks, can you? Even if he grows hooves fast?"

Bud studied the hoof he was holding. "Sooner don't," he said. "Put the holes too close. But this pony's got good feet. We probably could" His big hand rested briefly on Carter's head, ruffling the straight hair. "You call me any day if they give you trouble, OK?" Carter nodded his head, threw the hair out of his eyes, and searched his pockets again for raisins. Nothing turned up except a wizened quarter of an apple, which Beau gratefully nuzzled up. "I love you, Beau," Carter whispered in the pony's ear. Beau munched the apple in silence.

The silence was momentary. "You little beast!" Cissy screamed, racing down from the house. "You know I have to be at the ring at ten. How did you get Mr. Fleming first?"

"I got out of the sack before noon, dummy, that's how! I wasn't sitting in old Peyton's car half the night —"

Cissy paused. "Oh, hi, Mr. Fleming. Sorry about the Brat, here. He always weasels in if he can. You don't mind stopping and doing Chelsea, do you?" Her smile was very convincing; irresistible, it might have been called.

"Oh, no you don't, Cis! No you don't. I got here first, and I'm getting done first! Aren't I, Mr. Fleming? Aren't I?"

"Well," Bud said, "I think I can get 'em both done

by then. We're almost through with Beau." Cissy turned the dazzling smile on him again. "If you can get them both done, why don't you just do Chelsea first, then?"

Jessy' faint if you were on time, anyhow, Cis." Carter grinned. He knew he'd won. Mr. Fleming was his friend, however much old Cis tried her fatal charms on him. Besides, it was only fair. If a person got up, exercised his horse, made his bed, and got to the barn in time, he deserved to be first. Cissy started, with great dignity, back to the house. She wouldn't dare say anything to Mom; it was her own fault, and she wouldn't get any sympathy. "I wish you could always come on Saturday, then I could be here every time and help you." Carter was holding eight nails in his hand, the nails that would go in the left hind shoe. Even in the dull light their faceted surfaces glinted like silver. He liked holding them in his hand.

"Well, I guess I could. I can come almost any day you want," Bud said. He reached in his pocket and took out a hunk of tobacco. After he bit off a chew and arranged it in his mouth he went on. "Any day but Friday," he said. "Every other week that's the day I go to Quantico and I don't get home till late." He leaned down and picked up another hoof.

"Why do you have to go so often? Have they got a lot of horses?"

"They got about forty down there, so I do six or seven a time. They keep a schedule." He bit off a chew of tobacco, tucked it in his cheek, and went on. "Yeah, they got a bunch down there and it's a good job to have; I can count on it, like, all year round." He chewed thoughtfully while he trimmed the hoof.

"Whose horses are they, Mr. Fleming? Who rides them?"

"Well, kid, one of 'em belongs to the President, to

121

President Townsend. You know that?"

"Gee, Mr. Fleming, do you do the President's shoes, too?" Eyes filled with awe, under the scraggly mop of hair.

"Sure, I do. His feet's just like any horse, just like Beau's."

"I don't believe it. You ever see the President? I have. Dad works for him. He goes to the White House a lot. You ever see him ride?"

"Nope, never see him at all. No one at the barn does. You oughta know the President doesn't go anywhere without a bunch of Secret Service. When he comes to ride, no one even knows where he starts from. They just take the horse out in the woods and meet him."

"If they don't know where he is, how can they meet him?"

Bud was silent, his mouth full of nails, pounding them into the last shoe. When he finished he said, "Oh, you know. They bring him in a helicopter, stick him in a Jeep, and drive him someplace in the woods. Then they radio to Watson at the barn to bring the horse. He knows then, but nobody else. All secret, hush-hush like. Nobody but Watson gits to even touch that horse of his — Watson and me, when I shoe him, that is." Carter kept watching him, so he went on. "Watson brings two horses, one for him and one for the Secret Service guy. There's another guy rides with him most days. He comes to the barn and rides out to meet Townsend wherever it is. I guess he knows, too. That's all that knows, though. The rest of the guys at the barn never know nothin' about where he is." Uneasy lies the head that wears the crown, Carter had heard. He guessed that was what it meant. He was glad *he* wasn't the President.

"I bet my dad knows about it," Carter bragged.

"Only he doesn't tell us, like you do."

"I guess all these bombings have got 'em worried," said Bud. "You never know these days what all them crazies are up to. We oughta kept all them Iranians and things out when we could of."

"Dad says it's not that easy, Mr. Fleming. He says it's big countries behind it, not just the guys that do it. I think he thinks the Russians help them, or want them to do it. Look how it's always Americans that get blown up, not Russians." Carter was glad he listened so much at dinner; he learned a lot of things that way and the authoritative sound of his remarks was gratifying to him on occasions like this when he could impress someone like Bud with his knowledge.

"Dad has a lot to do about the conference in New York next month," he continued. "At the UN. Mom thinks he's worried about it, but I dunno. I think old Sharovsky is gonna talk to the President, I think—"

This gem of wisdom was interrupted by Adrian. "Hi, Bud. None too soon for that pony, was it? Carter will have him worn down to ten hands before he's through!" Bud laughed. He straightened his back and dried the sweat off his hands on his leather apron. Even on this grey day the heat was beginning to settle in. The rain had definitely stopped, but the air was holding all the moisture like a sponge.

"He tells me he's going to ride the big time next month, ain't you, Carter?" He stooped over and picked up his thermos. He drank straight from the bottle, long gulps of cool water. The sweat ran down his back and soaked his T-shirt.

"Goodness, Bud, how hot you are already, and the day's just begun." Adrian sympathized. "Have you got a lot more to do today?"

Cissy came out of the barn leading Chelsea. "Brat, I'm sorry. You were right and I shouldn't have

123

yelled."

Magnanimous now, he moved away. "Thanks, Mr. Fleming, thanks a lot."

"I guess you'll be glad when your event's over," Bud said to Adrian. "Take a lot of your time getting ready, don't it?"

Adrian sighed. "I'd never have started if I'd known what it would be like. I've lugged enough timber and lopped enough branches in the last two weeks to qualify as a lumberjack!"

"Mom's getting good with the chain saw, too, Mr. Fleming. You should see her. She can even start it herself now. I can use it, too, but she won't let me. Shit, I'm ten — I mean, gosh, I'm ten years old and I could be a big help."

"You'd be a real help in the emergency room with your leg cut off, Brat," Cissy cheerfully volunteered.

"Well, Bud, you can see I have lots of help. Half the county really is working at it. I guess everyone sees how much it will bring into the county, having a top-level event here. I think it's pretty good for our little Pony Club to have pulled it off." She sighed again. "If we ever do, if we ever get it finished. Suppose we will, Bud?"

Bud was bent over, a leg clutched between his knees. "Mrs. Bedford, if anyone I know can do it, you can. You and Carter sure can." Under the horse's belly, Carter was watching where Bud bent to trim off a curly strip of hoof. Cissy stood motionless, holding the lead rope, and the hum of the flies was the only sound in the barn. Then Bud laid a shoe on the anvil and the clang of his hammer on the metal rang and echoed in the valley.

Adrian started back to the house. The sun had

124

begun to come out, but low clouds still hung over the hills. She turned and looked back towards the barn. She saw a pretty picture, framed by the trunks of the old oak trees; the farrier, hammer raised over the anvil; a symbol of strength. Beside him, the sleek flanks of the chestnut gelding, gleaming like copper in the pale light. The sturdy grey pony munched quietly where Carter stood by him, his hand, idle and loving, scratching behind an ear. And Cissy, standing straight and tall, her shining head bent to whisper something to Carter; as she watched, Adrian's heart ached with gratitude for the loveliness she saw, and for the knowledge that it belonged to her. A cloud moved across the sky, blotting out the faint efforts of the sun, and a cold shadow covered the ground. Adrian hugged her arms around herself and shivered. She felt the presence of terror, like the absence of sunlight; Henry had left early, right after the phone call in the middle of breakfast. Please God, she prayed, keep them safe, and she ran up the brick walk to the house.

Chapter Eight

Prague, March 1976

He stood in the phone booth without moving. He was afraid to look at Leon; the fire that was burning in his guts might be visible, even through the dirty glass door of the booth. His whole body felt transparent, and he could still hear Eleni's voice as though she were standing beside him. He pretended to make another phone call, and held the receiver to his ear while he edged around to get a look at Leon. The old boy was affecting to watch two pretty girls crossing the street, and George put the phone back on the hook when it began to make a rasping phone-off-the-hook snarl.

He simply had to get back to the car; Leon was watching him now. With what seemed to him a nonchalant smile, he sauntered to the curb. He said, "It's OK, Leon, I don't have to go back. Mom will mail the letters for me." For a spur-of-the-moment lie it was pretty good, he thought, but then Leon's courteous little bow and its accompanying smirk made George certain that he knew exactly what had happened in the phone booth. He probably knew that George had just made a date with the most beautiful girl in Prague. He forced himself to smile at the oily little man. "Thanks, Leon, thanks for stopping—it really helped me out." He heard himself babbling aimlessly and forced himself to shut up. There were little drops of sweat on his upper lip.

Smoothly Leon shifted gears, and as the car pulled away from the curb George slid down into the back seat. Then they were in heavy traffic; it would be stop-and-start from here to the Institute. He had time to think. There had to be a way for him to get out Friday night, somehow without Leon, and he couldn't think of a way he could possibly do it. In almost a year in the city he'd never been able to escape without him. He had turned sixteen last month. If he was at home he would be driving himself now, maybe even in his own car.

Eleni's words pulsed through his head as he watched the throngs of people moving along the sidewalks. For a few blocks the pedestrians were moving faster than the traffic; for minutes at a time the car was stopped and George studied the old facades that crowded against the walkways. He wondered what it would be like to be walking alone down one of these streets at night, going up to a doorway in one of the narrow brick houses and finding Eleni waiting there. She had invited him to meet her at a house in the Old City where she said she met with a group of friends every Friday night. It was near where she lived, and she would be waiting there for him; they could drink some beer, she told him, and dance, "Have fun," she had said. "Good times, there—you come?"

He couldn't remember answering her, his heart had been beating so fast, but he must have said something because she had laughed and told him it would be wonderful—"wunnerful," she said—because her friends all wanted to meet him, her American, and she was so proud of him she couldn't wait to see their faces when he got there. These friends, she told him, were mostly students, and they were working for international peace; in fact, the house was a meeting place for a sort of club, the Dzcerny Vlasck, that was organized by the students to promote understanding between East and West. Of course, a club meeting wasn't exactly going to her house, but it was a start, and his imagination raced wildly ahead to see himself hurrying through the dark streets with Eleni, taking her home from the meeting, climbing the steps to her apartment—

Hell, he hadn't even figured out how he would get to the meeting! He tried to believe a conversation with his parents where they would say, "Of course, dear. What a wonderful opportunity! You can get to know people here and learn the language." They would be enchanted with the idea. It sounded great until he came to the place where they would say, "Leon can take you there," and he knew it would never work. Old Leon would queer the whole thing, Dad would say it would ruin our foreign policy—Oh, God, it was hopeless!

Then his despairing gaze was arrested by a small blue-and-white sign on the patterned brick facade outside his window. They were still only a few blocks from the residence and the car was completely stopped in traffic. He couldn't believe he'd never seen this sign before. He must have passed it a hundred times. It was the Way Out! The sign said, in English, "Language School—Czech for the English Speaking." Old Harrison was always telling Dad that George should be learning the language of the land, not from him, but from a Czech. He said George should take an intensive course, immerse himself in it until he was fluent; it was one of the advantages of living in a foreign country. He had heard it a million times. Dad would be overjoyed when George, on his own initiative, asked to take a crash course, wouldn't he?

He could hardly contain his excitement until he was home. He raced up the stairs and carried the phone book upstairs to his room. It took some deciphering, but finally he found "Schools, language." There were only seven listed. It was easy to find it because of the address and he dialed the number. It rang a long time and he began to think maybe it wasn't a real school; then he thought, If they ever do answer they will speak in Czech and I won't be able to talk to them. It rang three more times before a voice answered.

It sounded more like Queen Elizabeth than a Czech tutor. George quickly elicited the information that the Czerny School had night classes, and that although a term had just started, if he had a little knowledge of the language he could enroll and be able to catch up with the others. It was perfect. The school existed, Mom and Dad could check it out, and without attending one class, he could probably learn enough of the language from Eleni and her friends to convince them he had actually gone there.

129

It really wasn't a lie to say he was going to learn Czech. He wondered why he wasn't able to say to his parents that he wanted to spend the evening with some Czech friends; it seemed such a simple solution, but he was beginning to find out that in this country, nothing was simple. It was easier to let them believe in the Czerny School; the only problem would be getting there alone.

It was close enough to ask if he could go on his bike, but could he actually do it without being followed? It was still hours till dinnertime, and his head whirled and throbbed with solutions and non-solutions. They could just say no to the whole thing. He was wasting his time figuring out how to get there. They might easily tell him to forget it and study more with Harrison. He lay on his bed and watched as the sun sank below the roofs across the street. He spent an extra five minutes on his hair and washing his face. He rehearsed a thousand times what he would say to Dad.

Then Dad wasn't even home for dinner, so he and Mom just had dinner in the library. What a good omen!

Mom was in a good mood. It was nice to sit here with her while the dark night was beyond the curtains and the fire crackled and spat just like a fire at home. George talked to her about the lessons with Major Hrdlcka, and made her smile at the way the old boy got after him when he made a mistake. He imitated the major's gruff voice and stood with his legs bowed and his belly sticking out, the way the old cavalryman stood. *"Da,* boy, ve get it right, yet!"* he growled, and Helen laughed out loud. She pulled him back to the couch and put her hand on

130

his knee while he talked. She said she was glad he was getting some fun out of being here.

He shrugged. "It's not bad," he allowed. "I really guess I appreciate what it means to me, Mom. Not many guys get a chance like this, to live in another country." He gave her his best sincere smile. It had gotten him a lot in the past, and he prayed for its success tonight.

It was a good start. Helen took her hand back and brushed the hair off her forehead. "Well, I just hope it will be a good experience for you. Sometimes I don't know—" Her voice trailed off.

"Talking about the experience, Mom, there's something I was wondering—maybe we can talk to Dad about it—I think I'd get a lot more out of being here if I was better at the language. You know, to talk to the people at the Institute, and when we have dinners I have to go to. I could get along better with the people and all—" he thought of how well he could get along with Eleni—"if I could learn a little more Czech. I could say something besides, 'Good morning. Where is the bus stop?' I thought maybe I could take classes at one of those schools, you know, where they teach foreigners their language."

He couldn't stop. "I saw a place today, Mom. It's right near here, and they have night classes. I called and they said I could get in. Would Dad like that if I tried it?" He looked up at Helen and knew he had it made.

"It's so close, I could go on my bike. I wouldn't have to take up Leon's time, would I, just to go five blocks?"

"I'll ask Dad what he thinks. I should think he'd

131

like the idea." Of course he would like the idea, his idiot son actually seeking intellectual advancement, all on his own.

The ambassador was pleased. He knocked on George's door before he went to bed. "Your mother told me your idea about night school," he said. "I think it's a great idea, and it shows a lot of initiative on your part to have looked it up on your own."

George stood up and smiled. "Well, sir, I know you think I'm only interested in horses, but I've been doing a lot of thinking since we've been here, and I can see how much I'll miss if I don't take advantage of everything I can—"

"Tell you what, son," the ambassador went on. "Since you've made all the arrangements, suppose we just up your allowance enough to take care of the tuition, and you can handle the whole thing yourself." He paused. "Your mother said you wanted to go on your bike. Is it just over on Glerzcy Street? If it's all right with her, I'd like it if you did that. I don't like to keep Leon at night if I don't have to."

"Sure, Dad, or I could even walk. I'd be home by nine or so. I won't be late."

The deception had been too easy, the lie too painless. George was shocked at the ease with which he had brought it off. Deceit should be more difficult. He almost knocked on their door to tell them what he had done and ask them to forgive him. He lay in bed feeling lonely and alienated; cut off from his family and the security of their trust. He turned the light back on and read until sleep overcame his conscience with dreams of an improbably lustful

132

future where he and Eleni floated on clouds of love forever together—

He had one more message from the Golem that week. Leon grudgingly agreed to another look at the cemetery; George told him he definitely was studying for a paper on its history. When he got home he spread out the crumpled wad of paper, and, lying on his stomach on his bed, he read it. "Club is here," it said, and there was a crude map of the streets of the old city. On one of the streets ran two horses, one small and sleek, and it was being chased by a fiery steed with flames coming out of its nostrils. The little horse seemed to be smiling over its shoulder as it ran. It had the same smile that Eleni flashed at him when they rode under the major's watchful eye, a smile that said more than the few words she spoke to him if they saw each other on the way to class.

Pedaling over the rough cobbles on the way to Glerzcy Street that night, George kept looking back. He wasn't sure about two old guys in a Volvo. The only thing he was certain about was that they weren't ours. He conscientiously cycled to the Language School and paused once more to check the street. He saw no sign of the Volvo, and decided even if they were there, the report they sent wouldn't go to the embassy. He'd never seen them before.

He wished it hadn't got dark so soon. He'd memorized the map, but the signs were hard to see, and among the twisted streets one block might have been two, or two might have been one. The city must have been laid out by wandering goats a thousand years ago; tonight it was thronging with

133

people and noises. He began to sweat. What if he couldn't find her?

It was past eight when he leaned his bike against the steps of number 73, a narrow brick building jammed between two larger houses. It was three stories high and little windows were set into the steep roof. It didn't look like a club. There wasn't a sign, and behind the door he couldn't hear a sound over the clamor of the street.

Light as bird's wing, something touched his sleeve and he jumped. "Hey, Georgi, you find it!" There was that smile again and the huge, slanted eyes looking up at him in the yellow glow of the street-lamp. He would have kissed her, he was so glad to see her, but she laughed and pulled him through the door. At the end of the hall voices and laughter poured from a dimly lighted room.

Smoke and the smell of beer wafted down the hall. The room was crowded and hot and no one seemed to notice when Eleni pushed him through the door. A scratchy tape was playing American rock, but no one was listening. Everyone was talking to everyone else, and it was impossible for George to understand a word. Eleni pulled him to the back of the room and a girl in a dirty apron gave them each a bottle of dark beer from a tub that had a lot of water and a few almost melted ice cubes in it.

She spoke in Czech to a couple standing near the beer tub. Whatever she said ended with "Georgi," and she made a sweeping gesture in his direction. The girl smiled and the man held out his hand, rattling a string of unintelligible words to George. Close beside him, her sweet breath in his face, Eleni

134

murmured, "My friends Marzca and Uri. They glad you come."

Before the evening was over, George had met almost everyone there. Eleni seemed to know them all. He was surprised when Uri took her hand and pulled her to the front of the room, where a sort of podium stood under a bare light bulb. She spoke for about five minutes, an impassioned speech. Her face was very white and the shadows cast from the harsh light showed him how thin she really was. He wanted to hold her in his arms and carry her to a safe place.

The room burst into applause when she finished, and Uri put his arm on her shoulder and began talking. She ducked away from him with a smile and came to sit on the floor beside George. Then they were in a dark corner of the floor, oblivious to the insistent voice of Uri, or the low rhythm of music from the stereo. Eleni was warm beside him, and leaned against him as they drank another warm beer.

At last he said, "Eleni, you've got to help me. I told my parents I was taking a class in Czech — I've got to learn enough so they'll believe me." It wasn't what he wanted to say at all. He wanted to tell her how beautiful she was and how he thought about her all the time. Instead he said, "I don't even know what's going on here. I didn't understand anything you said — "

"My poor Georgi," she said. She smiled. "Only I told them about you. Tell them you are good friend, make them glad. Is World Peace meeting here on Friday. Is good to have American to help." She put her hand on his and looked up at him.

135

"You help, no?" He would have helped her murder her grandmother if she had asked him at that moment. His flesh burned where she touched him.

"I teach you Czech," she said. "I help you." She giggled, a throaty little sound, like water just beginning to boil.

"But, where, Eleni —?" He was almost shouting now, to be heard. The speeches were over and the music blared. People were dancing, jammed together in the little room. There was hardly space to stand and George was sure they were going to be stepped on where they sat. They certainly weren't going to get any studying done here.

Eleni wrinkled her nose and wiggled it like a rabbit. "I know," she said. "You come my house next time. Be quiet, we make a glass tea. I talk in Czech, you learn. No?" It was like something in a dream. He felt himself carried along like a raft through the rapids, unguided and powerless to stop, towards a destination he couldn't see or even imagine.

"How can I find you? I almost got lost coming here."

"I show you now," she whispered in his ear. "Not far."

"I've got to get home pretty soon," George blurted. "They think I'm at that class."

She took his hand and pulled him to his feet. "Come," she said, and they were in the long hall, the noise and light fading behind them. She told him to leave his bike; they could get there on foot in just a few minutes. He checked the lock and hurried after her. They darted through dark alleys, until, behind a tall house of patterned brick, she led him up a narrow wooden stair. She stopped at

136

the third floor and pointed to a blue wooden door. "My home," she said simply. "You come in?"

"Not tonight. Golly, Eleni, I want to, but I've really got to go —" His voice was hoarse and embarrassing.

She didn't laugh. "OK. I show you back to clubhouse. Then you know next Friday how to come. Will be good place for learn Czech." She smiled and he could see the flash of her perfect white teeth by the light of the streetlamp below.

George stood there, helpless, on the landing. I would kill to be here next week, he thought. He took her hand in his and they stood on the rotten wooden platform. They stood for a minute that seemed a lifetime. He could stay there forever, he could live in Prague, with Eleni and the Golem, never go back to the Residence, never go back to the States, never go to bloody Harvard and be happy forever.

"Georgi, come." The voice held a little command, the way she would speak to her horse. And George obeyed, like the horse, not from fear, but from love.

He unchained his bike and rode the streets of Prague, which were paved with gold. It was just 9:05 when he opened the library door and, in a surprisingly casual voice, said, "Hello, revered parents. Your one and only son, returned from a far country and speaking in tongues." He could go on the stage if this kept up.

"How was it, son?" Dad looked up from his book. His son's face was glowing with health and innocence. Helen was writing a letter. She got up and came over to him. "You're all grown up; out at night alone in a strange city. I'm glad you're back."

137

"Good grief, Helen, the boy rode his bike five blocks and back. He's sixteen years old, for God's sake!" He all but winked at George and Mom laughed. It was OK. He had done it; the world was his and he had made it. He wondered why, instead of a glow of triumph, he felt only a vague hollow space in his middle.

"G'night, Mom," he said, and backed out of the room without really looking at her.

It was a long week. Old Harrison drove him crazy. He kept pouncing on him with Czech phrases (to see if he had really taken the class?) and the major jumped on him for everything. He knew his mind wasn't on what he was doing, not even on his riding. For the first time in his life the sound of hooves thudding on tanbark didn't excite him. He thought only of Eleni.

He tried to imagine what Friday night would be like. None of the lurid locker-room talk he could remember seemed to be relevant to his present situation. Instead, he felt noble and gentle, and his imagination could encompass only vague scenes of beauty and love. His whole body was heavy with the burden of his love. The days dragged endlessly on; the future was very far away. In the fevered dreams of those nights, he never foresaw the dark and twisted path he would walk with his Eleni. He only saw a light that filled his whole being with joy.

He didn't recognize a bite of food he ate for dinner on Friday. He excused himself before coffee, gave his mother a quick peck on the cheek, waved an airy hand at his father and said, "G'night, sir. I hope I learn more this week than last." The double entendre of this escaped him for a moment, but in the hall he burst out laughing.

He found the dark staircase without a hitch, but as he climbed the steps, his hands were cold, and the beating of his heart was so loud he was sure it could be heard through the flimsy walls and the blue door at the top of the steps. What if she wasn't there? He chided himself for this lack of faith. He'd called her after class and told her he was coming.

"I'll be there," he'd said. "They won't even know what time I get home. There's some kind of party and they'll never miss me." Actually, they had seemed rather glad he was going out. The bigger parties were a bore for him, and Helen was glad he had something else to do. She had enough on her mind, entertaining a houseful of diplomats and their fat wives.

His hands were shaking now, too. God, why did he feel like this? At home, after horse shows, after parties in the country, he'd certainly never been afraid of the girls who were always there in their neat, tight breeches or soft summer dresses. Modestly, he reflected, he'd had a good deal of experience for a man of sixteen.

But never like this. The girls at home were silly, fluffy things compared to Eleni. She was eighteen and lived alone, in an apartment of her own, in a city far from her parents. The government paid for her apartment, and they would take care of her as long as they saw her as an Olympic prospect. But only so long; if she wasn't able to do the job they gave her with the horse she was riding, someone else would have her apartment, and someone else would have her horse. She was an adult, with adult responsibilities. And yet she was as small as a child, and there was laughter in her eyes and warmth in her heart. George would never love again as he loved in that moment, standing in terror at her door.

He couldn't knock. She would think he was crazy when she saw how he was shaking. He'd never really lied to her about it, but he had let her think he was at least eighteen. He was reasonably tall for sixteen and his body was good. His voice hardly ever let him down anymore, though now his throat was so dry he was afraid he couldn't speak at all. It might be better if she wasn't there. Disappointment was easier to bear than humiliation.

He couldn't stand there forever. Two tentative knocks, a pause, and three more, quickly. Barely audible, from inside, almost a whisper, "Is you?"

He always forgot how small she was until he stood next to her. She was wearing an old jersey and pair of forbidden American jeans. In place of the perfectly polished black boots she wore at the Institute, her feet were shoved into ancient fuzzy slippers. The sweater was old and much washed so that it hung limply from her spare shoulders. Only the smile and the eyes were the same as the elusive girl on the grey mare; her hair, in the mornings so neatly pinned up, now hung, dark and loose, halfway to her waist.

She closed the door softly. "You are here, Georgi," she whispered as though announcing the Second Coming. "I am happy," she said, and took his hand in her small, firm one and led him across the room. A kerosene stove warmed one corner and a curtain partly covered what might have been the kitchen area. A bright scarf was flung over the worn back of an old couch and two candles sputtered in wine bottles on the table. "Hey, it's a party, Eleni. You've fixed your house up for a party. I thought we were going to study."

His voice sounded scratchy and there was no place to put his hands. He felt like at his first cotillion and he could hear Miss Osterman saying, "It is important to make a little polite conversation with a young lady before asking her to—"

Eleni was very close to him. He could smell the clean scent of her hair and see that she was wearing nothing under the thin jersey. She pulled him to the table. "We have a glass tea before we work. Make us feel good, no?"

"Sure, Eleni, that'd be swell," George heard himself say. His voice was husky now and he had stopped shaking. She sat across the table from him and, from a dented samovar, drew two steaming cups of tea. With the same grace and economy of movement he knew from the riding hall, Eleni offered him one of the cups she had poured. Aunt Lucy, serving at the DAR tea party, could not have moved with more elegance than this slight, childlike woman.

They warmed their hands on the thick china mugs and sipped the tea slowly. George couldn't think of a thing to say. He didn't want to talk about the language lessons while Eleni was smiling so perfectly at him over the tea cups. It didn't seem polite. He looked into the deep green of her eyes and it didn't matter what they said, or if they said anything. He tried not to look down to where, with each breath, her firm little breasts rose and fell beneath the rough material of her sweater. He hardly knew her, he didn't even know her last name, and here he was thinking — well, thinking about her like that.

"Georgi, not you must worry. Here we have happy time, only us, together. We laugh, talk — later, maybe lessons." She stopped talking. Then slowly, in a very small voice, she said, "Is not time for worry. Maybe is time for love?" The queer little question at the end of the sentence seemed the most endearing sound he had ever heard. It was what he had come here for, wasn't it? He had known it would happen when she said she would teach him at her house. He had certainly known it when his hand was shaking, trying to knock on the door. He just wasn't prepared for *how* it would happen.

The trouble, he realized, was that he hadn't the least idea what to do now. A lot of good it did to listen to guys talking about it; he bet none of the fellows who used to tell what they did and who they did it to had ever done it to anyone. None of them knew a thing about it. He felt betrayed by his peers and by his past. What the hell was he supposed to do? She would find out, there would be some way she could tell and she would think he was a fool. Christ, she'd probably done this before — no, he recoiled in horror from the thought. She wasn't that kind of —

Eleni reached across the table and put her hand on his. Then she slid around beside him and knelt on the floor. She laid her head in his lap and he thought she was crying. "Is lonely for me, Georgi. So far from home, all alone. Afraid sometimes and no one to care —"

142

He had never seen her like this. Her voice came in choking sobs and all that remained of the smart-ass confidence he knew was the hard little body pressed so close against his thigh. "Maybe you love me, Georgi; maybe take care of Eleni?"

Her eyes were liquid, filled with tears that didn't fall. His heart was full and he whispered hoarsely, "Don't cry, please don't cry. I'll always be here; I'll never leave you alone." He thought he believed it. Yet even as he spoke, another, cynical part of him was thinking that it was going to be easier than he had thought. She had become so helpless and dependent; his strength would save her and his love would make her strong.

Gently he ran his fingers through her wonderful hair. It was getting a little awkward having her head in his lap. He was afraid she could feel what was happening to him, and he wondered if he couldn't shift her to another position. Maybe it was embarrassing to her; they had better move to the couch (a more suitable site for a seduction?). Good God, a seduction! He slid to the edge of the chair, preparing to transfer to the couch, but she clung to him as she wept, and he sort of fell on the floor beside her.

At least it had got her face out of his crotch, but it had got her whole body plastered up against him instead. Her sweater seemed to have slipped up, and his hands, no longer cold, were moving over her skin, her very warm skin, finding, to his alarm, the tight nipples on the soft flesh of her breasts.

At least she had stopped crying and muffled sounds were coming from her as she buried her face against his neck. She was laughing! Laughing, and clinging to him like a drowning person. "You're

143

laughing!" he said. "What's funny? What are you laughing for?" She was making fun of him! Christ, he was probably doing it all wrong. This wasn't what she wanted after all. He felt his face going red and hot.

A helpless giggle came from under the dark hair on his shoulder. Her voice was low and moist, coming in little gasps. "Oh, Georgi, it is happy to laugh. I laugh for love, for how good we make for each other. Is wrong to be happy?"

The laughter stopped and her face was still wet with tears when she raised her head. She looked about ten years old, a small, hungry child. The shaking had stopped and they lay motionless on the hard floor. George held her so close he could feel her flat little belly and the sharp bones of her hips pressed against him. He was permanently marked with the impression of her body against his. He knew that as long as he lived he would always feel her there whenever he was alone and filled with longing. He knew she could feel now what was happening to him and she didn't seem to care.

"No, oh, golly, no. It isn't wrong to be happy. It's good—" He felt her hand touch him, and laughter filled his throat. He rolled on top of her, covering her open mouth with his. The hardness of her teeth surprised him; her lips were so soft! Then her tongue darted, like an independent being, in and out of his mouth. He heard someone moan, and realized it was his own voice, and his fingers were digging into the flesh of her hard little behind, pressing her to him, fueling the fever in his flesh.

He hardly knew that she pulled him up; her strong arms drew him to his feet. Gently and swiftly—and expertly, a part of his mind insisted on telling him—she began to undress him as they walked toward the bed. He lay naked and alive, watching her. She pulled the jersey over her head and almost in the same motion she peeled her jeans off and left them on the floor.

He thought briefly that he should stop her and tell her he had never done anything like this before. He also remembered briefly the "man-to-man" talk he had once had with his father, a talk that he now saw bore no relation whatever to his present situation. Should he get up and help her into bed? What was he supposed to say? He considered leaping up, putting on his pants and making an end run for the door.

Before he could activate his craven scheme, ninety-six pounds of animal fury landed on him. Her arms circled his neck, her hair was all over him, and her hungry, wet mouth was on his. Her naked skin felt like silk against him and she lay very close beside him in the narrow bed. There was still laughter in her eyes, but her wild fury was gone. She lay quietly, and began to touch him. Her fingers played idle games with him. "Look, Georgi. Look at him. We must keep him warm, put him away. I show you—"

She showed him, and he wasn't embarrassed after all. He found that he did know what to do and she seemed to like what he did. After, they lay, laughing no more, content in each other's arms. George slept like a baby.

The wail of a siren in the square woke him. He sat up and wondered where he was. The familiar parallelogram of light was not on the wall of the room, he wasn't in his own bed, and nothing made sense. Then he saw, in the intermittent light from the hotel sign across the alley, Eleni lying by his side. He could see, in the lurid flashing, that she was wide-awake, smiling at him. "Was fun, no?" she whispered, and George felt it beginning all over again, very tender and very sweet.

"Stay with me, Georgi," she whispered.

"Oh, God, I can't!" He looked at his watch. "Christ, it's after eleven! Eleni, I can't stay, not even a minute. The party will be over and they'll know!" He buried his face in her hair and kissed her neck, her face, her mouth. "I love you, I love you, I love you. I want to stay forever—"

He wasn't laughing anymore. "You know I love you. After this, after what we did—" he couldn't finish. She touched his arm. "Is OK. You go now. Another time come then. Not have trouble happen—nobody knows, nobody find out."

Nobody found out, that night or ever. He raced home on his bike, slipping perilously through the narrow, cobbled streets. He could feel his heart beating, pounding in his chest, as much from fear as from exertion.

The party was just breaking up. Long black cars lined the street and light streamed from the open front door of the Residence as goodbyes were said and couples in evening dress hurried down the wide steps. He parked the bike by the side door, sauntered through the kitchen where he picked up a few tired canapes, grinned at Dmitri and the cook, and disappeared up the back stairs.

It was that easy. The Friday "classes" continued, his command of Czech improved slowly, and Dad

146

was pleased with his progress.

Most nights they went to Eleni's apartment. George was consumed by the anguish of love and the inconvenience of his increasing lust. Unlike other appetites, this one grew larger, instead of becoming sated, as he fed it. He lived for Fridays and he suffered tortures of jealousy when they went to the Peace Meeting instead of to Eleni's. He was in agony when she talked to Uri or one of the other men in the dirty, noise-filled back room. For all his study, he couldn't understand most of what they said. The phrases he practiced as he and Eleni lay pressed together and exhausted in her bed might have been another language entirely.

They would translate for him, the slow-headed American, and Eleni would whisper to him. Her nearness to him, here in the crowded room, was a torment. He longed to be alone with her. But, she told him, they had found a use for him. He could serve the cause of peace very easily. There would be bits of information that he could get quite readily, from talking to his father, or perhaps from the micro in the ambassador's office at the Residence. Nothing secret, or sensitive, just things that would help them in their work. And here, she said, was where the Golem could be used. George could ride his bike to the cemetery and leave things there under the stones where Eleni could pick them up without being seen.

It was a small price to pay for the nights with Eleni. George didn't care to look at it that way, and he tried to separate the two aspects of his Friday nights, to pretend the one had nothing to do with the other. Nothing Eleni wanted could be wrong,

147

could it?

When Uncle Ed Townsend came to visit, George wanted to tell him about Eleni. He needed to tell someone, to share his love, if not with the world, at least with one other person. He could have started with the Peace Group. Uncle Ed was on a fact-finding mission, and he might like to know that there were young Czechs who were involved in the problems of the world. The week of the visit passed, and, somehow, the right time to talk to him never came. They went to the riding school, and Townsend enjoyed watching the fine high-schooled animals perform. He complimented George on his riding, and one day went for a ride in the park with him. When George saw Eleni on the path, he turned and showed Uncle Ed the lake instead.

Townsend left, Mom and Dad went back to their usual schedule, and George and Eleni moved through the long days of winter like two children in an enchanted world.

Chapter Nine

Middleburg, Virginia, April 1989

Adrian Bedford glanced at her watch. People would be coming in less than an hour, and she wasn't dressed and Henry wasn't even home. It was par for the course, actually. Sometimes she thought they should give up entertaining entirely. It seemed as though the mere discussion of a social event brought on world crisis; anything to detain Henry at the office — a new threat on the President's life, an ultimatum from the Kremlin, or a mob of protesters lining Pennsylvania Avenue. She sighed, and laid her watch on the counter. Better get into the shower and at least be ready herself when the guests arrived.

She dashed, naked, from the bathroom to rummage through her drawer for a clean bra and pants. The reflection in the mirror was a creditable one for a woman of forty-three; no bulge at the top of the cotton bikinis, and the strong, slender thighs showed muscles instead of fat. Pleased, Adrian momentarily regarded her image. In the evening light, the blue eyes looked almost transparent in her sunburned face, and her hair, bleached straw-colored by the sun, swung easily above her shoulders. She looked at her wrist and realized her watch was still in the bathroom. No need to see it; it was late.

She'd been over at Oak Hill all afternoon. They'd been able to round up a couple of laborers and she had spent hours in the heat explaining the construction of an Irish Bank to them. In the end, she and Cissy had lugged the heavy poles over and put them in place. God, no wonder she'd lost five pounds since March! She should have been at home all day, getting things ready for tonight, but who knew when they'd get two strong men on the same day again? "Never volunteer," Henry had said when she first mentioned the idea to him. "The first rule of life, old girl. Guess who'll be doing all the work if you're the one who brings it up?" She supposed she should have listened then, and kept still, but, on the other hand, the whole thing would never have happened at all if she hadn't pushed for it. A big developer had wanted the land, and it had taken a lot of lobbying around the county to get support for the idea. Well, work or no work, thank heaven they had done it. Who wanted Levittown two miles away?

She opened her closet and looked through the row of dresses. She was pulling a white cotton sun dress over her head when Henry opened the door. "Smile, you're on Candid Camera!" he said as she struggled to get into the dress. "You look fine to me the way you are now—" Lines of tiredness showed in his face, lines that were only partially obscured by the grin that broke across it when Adrian's startled face appeared from the folds of white cotton. "Oh, good, you're home, darling.

150

Thank God, no crisis tonight!"

She ran to him and leaned up to kiss his sweaty face. "You look tired, hon. Bad day?"

"No worse than a lot of them," he said. The smile faded, and Adrian saw the familiar closed-up look in his eyes, a look she had learned to read all too well in the years he had been at the White House. She wished he could bring his work home more than he did. He couldn't, really, and she knew it, but she thought it ought to help a man with too much on his mind if he could talk it over with his wife, or his someone; whatever. But there was always this wall, this separation; Henry might be two people, the one whose daily responsibility was the security of the nation, and the other one, the one she wanted to take in her arms and comfort with her love. The look passed while she thought about it, and when she raised her eyes to look up at him, his old smile was already erasing the tired lines from his face.

"What time is the invasion? I'm not really late, am I?" he asked. He sat on the edge of the bed and took off his shoes. He loosened his tie and leaned back on his elbows. "Is Cis getting ready to charm the breeches off George?"

"Don't laugh at her, Henry. She's being wonderful, she's been such a help all day — don't tease her. Anyhow, Carter's already said all there is to be said on the subject of his sister and the great George Clements. *He's* worse than she is about it. He wants to show him, tonight — tonight, mind you — that he can take his pony around Cis's jumps — can you reach this zipper, Hen? I've got to get down and do something with the flowers."

151

Henry struggled briefly with the zipper. "I'm glad I ran into the boy last week. Evidently he's been weekending on the farm for quite a while. Helen is in Georgetown—you knew Aubrey had that accident? She's been alone for several years— Is the zipper OK?" Adrian nodded. "Thanks, dear," she said. She wrinkled her nose in a smile that faded as she spoke. "I remember about Aubrey—poor Helen, all that way from home, too! Then didn't something awful happen to Geroge, too? I can't think what—"

"I believe he was married to some girl up in Massachusetts—she was a rider, too, I think. You're right, there was some kind of tragedy there—" Henry stood up and pulled off his shirt. "Well, I guess you want me dressed, don't you? I'll just shower and be down in a flash." The weary sigh was barely audible.

"Don't hurry, hon. We'll handle the mob till you get there." Adrian turned and smiled at him. She flipped her hair off her face with a shake of her head so like Carter's that Henry laughed. "Don't tell me you're the mother of those ancient young people I saw on my way up here. Let's sneak out the back and leave town—"

"Old goat," Adrian said, and thought, how I love you, Henry Bedford. She brushed his cheek with her lips and stooped to pick up her sandals. "Go get dressed, man. People will be here."

There was a tap on the door, immediately followed by Cissy. "Mom, Dad, can I come in?"

Henry stopped, discarded shirt in his hand, and looked at his daughter. He might have been seeing Adrian as he had first seen her, the time he and his

152

roommate had gone from W&L to a dance at Sweet Briar. Cissy was a little taller than her mother, but she moved with the same animal grace that had drawn him across the dance floor to take Adrian from the arms of the Hampden-Sidney quarterback and, with no thought for his personal safety, dance her right out the door and into a dark corner of the porch. "Hi, hon. Come in and let your old man have a look at you."

Cissy floated into the room and gave him an airy kiss. She whirled in front of the mirror. "Do I look OK? This old thing from last summer—"

Adrian stopped her. "You'll knock 'em dead. You look beautiful." It was hard to believe that this was the bratty little kid she had dragged to a million horse shows, and worried through pimples and braces and puppy fat, and threatened with excommunication over the mess she called her bedroom. She did look beautiful. There is beauty inherent in every young, healthy creature, and this shone from Cissy like the sun. She carried herself with that flippant assurance of an athlete that is almost arrogance, yet her cornflower-blue eyes were innocent like the eyes you sometimes see in mountain people, eyes that reflect the blue of the sky and look like windows into the very soul. They were vulnerable eyes, and Adrian thought how easily life could fill them with pain and disillusionment. She prayed it would not. Cissy's voice startled her.

"Hey, Mom, wake up! You look great. Is that my belt you're wearing? It's OK, it looks good on that dress. Want me to help downstairs?" Her mood shattered, Adrian laughed. Just this morning I could have killed the child, she thought. Now she said, "Oh, thanks, dear—we've got to do something with all those daffodils Midge brought over, and I made Carter chop down masses of apple blossoms. Come on, we better start." Padding barefoot down the stairs, sandals in one hand, she pushed her hair out of her eyes with the other. "God, I'm awful with flowers," she mumbled.

Cissy followed her mother down the stairs. "How can it be so hot and still April?" Adrian said. "People will perish on the lawn if the sun doesn't go behind the mountain before they come."

"Hopefully Carter will perish," Cissy said. "Mother, he is a menace. Tell him not to say a *word* to anyone tonight. He's being a beast! He'll say something to George Clements, I know he will. I'll die if he—"

Carter, comfortably stretched out on the hall floor beside the staircase, was privy to this conversation, and stored it in his memory for future use. Surveillance of this kind was vital for a good agent, and Carter was constantly developing his memory and honing his methods of information-gathering against the day when his President and his country should call upon him to save the world from forces too evil to imagine. This particular bit of information should enliven the evening for him.

Carter loved parties and he thought this was going to be a humdinger. He'd already been in the kitchen and seen what Berenice was doing. In fact, he'd offered to help her. He had sampled just about everything but the caviar to make sure it was all OK. It was, and he told Berenice so. She said she appreciated his help and gave him another ham biscuit, but suggested he might be of more use to them in the front of the house. That was how he happened to be under the stairs when Cissy and Adrian were coming down. He melted quickly into the closet before they got down and heard them going on back to the kitchen.

He couldn't see what Berenice thought he could do to help out here. Nobody needed him; he'd already asked about parking cars, and even though he knew perfectly well how to drive, they weren't going to let him do it. It wasn't fair. All day tomorrow he'd have to listen to Bob and Joe Binns from down the road talk about the Rollses and Jags and Mercs they had driven and discuss knowledgeably which ones they would have themselves when they were rich. He'd driven Dad's Merc all the way around the circle once, but it didn't do him any good because he could never tell anyone, just like the priest who made the hole in one on Sunday.

Mostly, though, he wanted to talk to George Clements. Dad said he worked at the White House and went riding with the President. Of course, Dad talked to the President all the time, but that was business. George was his friend. Sitting on the bottom step of the wide, curving staircase, Carter was idly scratching his initials into the polished surface of the old pine floor. H. C. B. III, Henry Carter Bedford III. He was thinking of ways to impress George Clements and scarcely noticed how deeply he was engraving the floorboard at his feet. George lived in Lincoln, just about five miles away, at least on weekends. Maybe he'd come over and ride with me sometime and see Beau jump the outside course. What did Cis mean, don't talk to him?

He looked down and saw "H. C. B. III" staring up at him. The old wood was dark with age, but where he had cut into it, the original honey color of the pine showed brightly. Spit, liberally applied with a grubby finger, helped some, but in the end he slid the little Oriental rug closer to the steps and sauntered onto the porch. The front door was open, and, drifting out into the heavy air, Carter could hear an evening bird singing, and the shrill cry of spring peepers came up from the bottom pasture. The porch was deserted; it contained only the expectant emptiness of a place waiting to be filled with people and voices and laughter. The bar was set up, and no one was near it. Casually, Carter dumped a half inch of Jack Daniel's into a glass and quickly swallowed the burning liquid. After all, he knew he wouldn't get anything but a Coke or lemonade later.

Fortified, he wandered back to the kitchen to see if Cissy had found the small grass snake he had left among the apple blossoms. It served her right. Mom didn't make *her* get out of the pool and go climb around in the old trees all afternoon to get a bunch of lousy flowers for the party. Her fingernails would be dirty, too, if she'd been crawling around up there like he had. Apple trees aren't any good for climbing, except the big branches in the middle, where, if they are old trees, you can sit comfortably and read or spy or eat sandwiches. If you have to get out on the little limbs where the flowers are, you get all scratched and the sticky stuff is black and gets all over you.

He waited a long time in the kitchen with

Berenice, who wouldn't give him anything more to eat. In fact she was so busy by now that she wouldn't even talk to him. Two girls were helping her, and it was diverting to hear her giving them hell, but that wasn't what he came for. The snake must have betrayed his trust and gone somewhere else, because all he could hear from the pantry was Mom and Cissy talking quietly. Not a sound equal to a snake being discovered by either one of them. He really didn't want Mom to find it. She was awfully nice to him sometimes (at least as long as she didn't look under the rug by the stairs this would be true), and he didn't want to scare her. She was brave, for a mother, in most ways, but not with snakes.

Berenice left off persecuting her two helpers. "Miz Bedford, you leave them flars for me to put out. They's a car in the drive already, Mr. Bowman and them, I think." Berenice was always there when you needed her, and as she went past him carrying two vases to the sink, she barely turned to say, "It's yore lucky day, boy. I never put that snake in yore bed for tonight, I just throwed him out." Berenice knew everything.

When Henry came down, the lawn was filling with people. Cissy was surrounded by a circle of admiring young men and Carter, God be praised, appeared to be making polite conversation with Mrs. Rogers. At least the old girl was smiling at him. As he drew near, Henry could hear Mrs. Rogers saying, "Well, thank you, dear, that's very nice of you, but actually I seldom drink my whiskey straight. Maybe your father will get me some with a touch of branch water in it." Henry said he would be delighted to, and left Carter to entertain the old lady while he went to the bar.

Carter and Mrs. Rogers were deeply engaged in controversy over the relative merits of gag snaffles or dropped nosebands for slowing down overcharged ponies when he interrupted them. "A lovely boy you have, Henry," she murmured as Carter melted into the crowd, his social obligations satisfactorily discharged. Henry smiled, rejoicing in the belief that his son had a long and happy future ahead of him. The way he charmed old ladies at age ten, God help the girls when he was twenty. Mrs. Rogers still had a twinkle in her eye, and Henry was happy to spend some time with her. On every side he could hear little cries of recognition and shrieks of, "Darling, too divine to see you —" or, "Teeny's not coming, she's in Newport —"; all the encoded vocabulary of a country party. He reflected that, while conversation in general seemed to be a lost art these days, it still flourished in the parlors of Upperville when this grande dame of the Virginia hunt country was around. He and Mrs. Rogers made logical disposition of the affairs of the day.

He saw Cissy detach herself from her group and wander towards the circle. A silver Porsche was pulling to a stop under the big oak trees that lined the drive. How did that girl know that George Clement drove a Porsche? There is a homing instinct in girls of her age, he decided, that gravitates towards romantic alliance. They are drawn by a force beyond our ken, or their control. He excused

158

himself and started over to greet George.

The sun had fully set, but the mountainside was still bathed in a pale, shadowless light. In the valley, mist floated belly high on the Angus which grazed in the deep grass. Over the clamor of the party, and blending with it, the sounds of little night creatures rose from the ground. Cissy saw him, and waited for him. "You'll introduce me, won't you, Dad?" she asked.

"Sure, hon. I wouldn't want him to miss you."

"You won't have to stay and talk or anything. I'll show him around. There must be hundreds of people you want to see. Aren't there, Dad?"

"Don't worry, Cis. I won't show him baby pictures or tell about—"

"You're funny, Dad, you know that? But I love you."

George got out of the car in an unnecessarily agile leap, Henry thought. The girl is already impressed with you, son, so just take it easy. Just take it easy on my daughter, she's the only one I have. He smiled at himself, the protective father. Cissy probably knew a lot more than he cared to know about, and needed his protection about as much as she needed a crutch.

"George," he called. "Delighted you could come." The young man offered a firm handshake and turned to Cissy. "This is our daughter, Caroline, George. You'd better call her Cissy. We all do."

Cissy gave George her hand, in a straightforward, almost boyish gesture. George took it in his and smiled a dazzling white toothpaste ad. He held the hand a little longer than seemed necessary to Henry, who tried to blame it on his years in Europe. Don't, please, devastate my daughter right here and now in my front yard, he found himself thinking. She's only a child. He felt that at any moment George might bow and kiss her hand, her arm, her throat; might carry her off bodily and ravish her behind the box hedge.

The danger passed; the sounds of the party in full swing behind him brought him back to earth, he murmured something about seeing to the other guests, and left them to talk about the weather or horses or rock concerts—whatever young people talked about these days. It seemed to Henry that the young were very serious, the new young professionals. They carried the weight of the world on their smartly clad shoulders in a way that he couldn't remember himself and Adrian doing. Cissy's beaux were all stockbrokers, electronics engineers, or lobbyists, and they were locked irretrievably into their blazers and power ties.

Cissy watched in horror as her father, obedient to her wishes, turned his back and abandoned her with George. For once she was at a loss for words. The charming flow of aimless chatter that she regularly bestowed on any young man within hearing had deserted her. She could only think of Mom saying, "For God's sake, Cis, if you get a decent man to talk to, talk about something besides horses!"

This decent man rescued her. "Your dad asked me to help with your mother's event. I'm really excited about it." *He* was talking about horses.

"So are we excited," Cissy said. "But it's hard for Mother—it turned out to be so much more work than anyone ever thought. We need every able-bod-

160

ied man we can find. How lucky that Daddy mentioned it to you!" She turned to him with a smile that would melt ice at the North Pole.

Melted, he returned the smile. "No wonder you're excited. Your dad tells me you have a super horse and you're having a go at Intermediate."

"Well, I'm going to try. Chelsea can do it, I know. We'll just have to see if I can."

They were still standing in the same spot. The Porsche had been driven off to park in the field, and the light had faded from the sky. Under the oaks it was dark, except for shafts of light coming across the lawn from lanterns up by the house. George had to stand very close to see Cissy's face in the flickering light; only her white dress stood out against the dark night. A breeze blew past them, and Cissy shivered after the heat of the day. "Good heavens," she said. "Here I am keeping you from getting a drink. Let's go get you something." She took his hand, and started to pull him towards the house.

They almost fell over Carter. If they hadn't stumbled on him Cissy would have pretended he wasn't there and dealt with him later, but there was no ignoring him now. Under her breath she hissed, "You weasel!" before she turned to smile sweetly at George and introduce him. "Carter, this is Mr. Clements. George, my brother, Carter. Now, be good enough to fetch him a drink, please, little brother. What will you have, George?"

"Oh, I'll go with him and see if there's any J&B. Then maybe he'll come down to the barn with us and show us his pony when you show me Chelsea." As they threaded their way up to the bar, he chided

161

himself for a coward. He was afraid to find himself alone with this girl; he couldn't do it, not yet. Nothing had touched him like this since Joey. Nothing had pierced the armor he had worn ever since that night, how long ago?, when, in the dark and the wind and the rain, he felt his life end, because there was no way he could go on without her. Of course he had gone on, but part of him had stayed buried with Joey and now he feared the pain again as though it were yesterday. Please, kid, come to the barn with us. Help me.

With Carter between them, they eased out of the crowd and Cissy let Carter lead the way to the barn. The grass was wet with early dew and their feet left paths across the lawn. Carter kept up a steady discourse, alternating astonishing bits of information with breathless questions. Cissy would cheerfully have drowned him if she didn't love him so much. George answered him, seriously, and even promised to come over and ride with him some weekend.

The barn was friendly terrain, and, pulled along the aisle by a little boy's grimy hand, the panic lessened. The quiet sounds of animals at rest, and the cool air moving through the barn, slowed the beating of his heart. Even Carter wound down, and the three of them walked like old friends, talking a little and sharing the peace of the country night with each other. Cissy stood close by him at the door to Chelsea's stall, and he could smell the scent of flowers in her hair when she leaned over to open the latch. "Hold my shoes," she said, and handed him a ridiculous pair of sandals. "I'm going to bring him out so you can see him."

162

Carefully she led the big horse out of the stall, and stood stroking its neck. George would never remember what they talked about, or how long he stayed there, holding the shoes in his hand, forgetting the existence of any world beyond the one he was in. Carter had left them alone at last, feeling, perhaps for the first time in his life, that his presence was superfluous. George didn't see him go; the murmur of Cissy's voice was all he heard, and its cadences flowed through him like the waters of a clear mountain spring and healed the wounds that had torn at his heart for so long.

He didn't know how long they stood there, the girl in her pretty dress, barefooted on the cold earth floor, and the horse breathing quietly beside them. Then Cissy led the horse back to its stall. She took George's hand and led him down the aisle to the open door at the end of the barn. She walked barefooted on the dirt floor until she stood in the wet grass outside the door. "Oh, golly," she said. "You'd better give me my shoes; it's freezing out here." She sat on the sloping lid of a tack box and put her feet into the narrow straps of the sandals and stood up beside him. The light from the barn shone out over the field and cast long shadows over the clipped grass. "I'm keeping you from your guests," George said, and hoped she hadn't heard him.

"I'm sick of the old party," she said. "I had parties all winter." She leaned on the fence and looked up at the lights by the house. Sounds came softly through the damp air, and while they talked they watched the stars come out and listened to crickets in the stalls calling each other through the night. Later, lights began to shine in the field and cars

163

were pulling out to go home. Adrian and Henry were standing in the drive saying goodbyes, and they saw George and Cissy coming up from the barn.

They walked together, not even touching hands, but Adrian knew, as she watched them, that something had changed for them both. Cissy was talking quietly, looking up at George; the way she looked at him was light years different from the way she flirted with her other beaux. Henry saw it, too, and remembered how George had looked when he got out of the car. Somehow, it didn't bother him now, the way it had then.

Driving home that night, with the sun roof open to the foggy night, he began to hum to himself. Then he laughed; he laughed as he hadn't laughed in years. He was free, and life was ahead of him, complete and shining. And he prayed, with the faith of a child, to the neglected Episcopalian God of his childhood; he prayed, please, God, please, don't let it happen again! "Each man kills the thing he loves." Oh, God, I've lived with that so long. Help me, oh, dear God, help me—

The Porsche hummed down Route 50, and the wind on his face was clean. The terror that had held him so long was over at last.

164

Chapter Ten

Prague, Summer 1975

The terror had started that night in Prague. It had begun as an ordinary Friday. Then when he got to the Institute, the major had him ride a new horse, and it was a bitch. He worked the damn animal for an hour without a sign of improvement, and, as the hour passed, he worried increasingly because Eleni wasn't there and the hall seemed empty without her. The major finally let him stop and sent the horse back to its stall, listing its sins, which were many, as George led it down the aisle. While he was cooling the horse out, the major watched, companionably. "You seen Eleni?" he asked suddenly, so suddenly it made George jump.

The old man scratched his ear, and rubbed the back of his hand across his mustache. "Maybe she got sick, something like that?" he said. "You seen her, boy?"

"Major, sir, you know I only see her here," George lied. It could be some kind of investigation; Eleni believed the major watched them, even reported to someone. His hands were cold and his heart was a lump of ice. "No, sir, I haven't seen her since class yesterday." The old soldier was watching him; his little eyes were deeply set in a network of brown wrinkled skin and looked out at him, unblinking, perhaps knowing everything. George felt the hair rise on the back of his neck — a goose walked over your grave, his mother would say. He stood there a long time, holding the horse and steadying it while the old major remained silent and motionless beside him.

Then the major's face broke into a smile. "Don't vorry, boy," he said. "She come back for her horse if she don't come back for you!" He seemed inordinately pleased by his remark, and deep rumbles of laughter came up from his chest; no longer a sinister agent of evil, he became merely a jolly old uncle, slapping his thigh, laughing over a tremendous joke. George smiled, too. "You're right," he said. "She'll be here tomorrow." He wished he believed it.

He shoved the horse hastily into its stall and reached up to take off the halter. "Bite me, you sonabitch, and you'll get it," he whispered as the horse bared its teeth in final farewell. He shot the bolt on the door and headed for the street, glad to be rid of the horse and relieved to be away from the major's inquisition. When he got to the street he realized he was early, and Leon wasn't there. He evidently did find things to do while George rode; certainly he wasn't sitting there patient, martyred, a slave to the ruling class, as George was meant to believe.

He paced along the curb, staring into the gutter where dirty water flowed down the hill. Bits of

166

paper, cigarette butts, and unidentifiable objects floated along, and a smell of old drains assailed George's nostrils. For a Friday, this was turning into a very bad day. Just this morning he had waked with the expectation of Eleni, of happy hours in her room, in her bed, warm and tumbled from their love—now it had all turned into some kind of shit.

Damn. Leon still wasn't in sight. He looked up and down the street. Nothing. Only a man on the opposite side waiting for a bus. He wore a dark suit and a shapeless hat pulled too far down on his head. The bus came, and when it moved off, George saw that the man was still there and he was starting to walk across the street. The grey stones were wet and glistening between the puddles even though the rain had stopped, and the man walked carefully, trying not to splash water on his shoes or his legs. His eyes were lowered, watching the street in front of him; he was jaywalking without watching traffic, and he came in a straight line to where George was standing on the curb.

He stood beside George for a minute, then felt in his pockets and brought out a crumpled pack of cigarettes. He tapped one into his hand and moved quite close to George. "Match?" he asked hoarsely, very close, now, to George's face. He was shorter than George and he didn't look up when he spoke. It was impossible to see his features. He smelled horribly of cologne mixed with the stale smell of cooking and dirt and unclean clothes.

"Sure, I think I've got one." It was an effort not to recoil from the odious smell. He found some matches in his windbreaker pocket and lit one, holding it towards the man. The wind blew it out. He leaned over and lit another and together they cupped their hands to shield the flame. As the man drew the flame into his cigarette, George felt something pressed into the palm of his hand. He would have given it back, but the dirty little man had not waited even to thank him; he had turned his back and started to walk away. He had taken the matches, too. George watched his receding form as it disappeared into the gloom.

Leon almost ran into him as he drew the car up to the curb. George jumped in before Leon could do his manservant act and sank into the backseat. "You got friend?" Leon asked. "Someone you know?"

None of your business, buddy boy, George thought, and smiled a cheeky smile. "He's my contact with the KGB, Leon. Didn't you know I'm an agent?"

Leon attempted a laugh. "Funny joke you make," he muttered and lapsed into the sullen silence he affected so often of late.

Furtively, George opened the hand that still held the crumpled paper. He saw Eleni's handwriting, and almost cried with relief. She was all right! The sky brightened and the sun almost showed between the clouds, and he was ready to believe the whole universe rejoiced with him. The note was crumpled and written on a piece of newspaper, but no matter. It said, "Come early, I cook dinner. Leave bike at club, walk." He wanted to apologize to Leon for teasing him, he wanted to tell him he was a great guy, he wanted the whole world to be as happy as he was. He stuffed the paper into the pocket of his breeches and sat back in the deep leather and closed his eyes.

Leave the bike and walk she had said. He wondered why. And why the man in the dark suit instead of Golem? Maybe the cemetery was being watched; maybe Leon had ratted on him. It had been so easy all year; all the times he had gone to Eleni's, he had almost forgotten the shadowy figures he had spent so much effort eluding the first year in Prague, the old men on benches, the cars across the street, and the footsteps following through the park. Why should he leave his bike and walk? He finally decided someone in the group must have seen his bike at her house and was jealous; she didn't want trouble from an old beau. That was all. Nothing was really wrong, nothing that wouldn't be forgotten tonight, when after dinner they lay on the rug before the fire, whispering dreams and planning the impossible future.

He was in luck. Mom and Dad were going to be out; there was a reception at the embassy. He could get away an hour early, an extra hour with Eleni! and no one would be the wiser. He told the cook he would just eat a sandwich because he had to be at school early, and he sat at the kitchen table with Jerzy and the maid and practiced speaking to them in Czech. They laughed at him and made jokes and it was very jolly, and he hated the ease with which he told them lies. Outside, it was dark and a blustery wind whipped dust and leaves in little swirls across the walk. He pedaled through the darkening streets, across the bridge, and, threading his way through the evening traffic, he stopped in front of the clubhouse. No light was showing, and he pushed the bike through the gate beside the house. There was a narrow passage between the buildings, and here he leaned the bike against a wall and locked the wheel.

Back on the street, he dodged past a group of young people with his head down, looking at the sidewalk. If any of them knew him, they didn't speak, and he hurried along, staying close to the buildings that crowded right up to the edge of the sidewalk. He ducked into the alley where he had first followed Eleni and made his way through a maze of streets and alleys until he came out behind the tall house where she lived. He remembered the first time he had come here, how his hands had trembled and his legs gone weak, and he found that even now, a year later, the same excitement gripped him as he climbed the creaking stairs to her door.

He waited a minute on the top step, and smiled. He felt like a husband coming home to have a nice, hot dinner and then go to bed with a real wife, one he knew in every mood and every way, and would love forever. It was a good feeling.

As soon as she opened the door, he knew the good feeling was wrong. Her eyes were shadowed, the mischievous light extinguished. Her mouth smiled, showing her straight little teeth, and the tip of her tongue was caught between them. But the rest of her face was stiff, almost a mask, and there were deep hollows under her eyes. When he looked into them, the thing he saw was fear.

"What's the matter, Eleni? What's wrong?" He held her shoulders, and felt the sharpness of the bones beneath her sweater. Very gently, he kissed the top of her head.

She threw her head back, almost defiant, and he could see tears shining in the corners of her eyes. "Nothing wrong, Georgi," and her voice almost broke. She smiled up at him. "We have nice dinner, see how good I cook." She pulled the back of her hand across her face and sniffed. He followed her to the kitchen and took her in his arms. Her breath was little sobs; he could feel each gasp against his chest, but when he let her go she smiled again and said, "We drink—look, I got wine!" and she whirled around with a jug in her hand. George carried it to the fire and she brought two glasses.

When they had filled the glasses Eleni held hers up. She raised it in a toast. "We drink to remember all the good times, Georgi, all the love and the happy times." Her hand was shaking now and her voice was very small. "We drink to forget, to forget how nothing is for always—" Her glass clinked on his and she lowered her head over it as she drank, to hide the fear in her eyes. Her hair was loose, and it fell, dark and straight, over her shoulders. It made her seem very small, and more dear to George than ever before.

"Eleni, what do you mean, 'nothing is for always'? I'll always love you, nothing can change that." His voice shook. He took her face in his hands and made her look at him. It was wet with tears. The smile was gone and tears streamed from

171

her eyes; the very substance of the deep green pools seemed to be overflowing and running down her cheeks. George was terrified; he had never seen her like this. "What are you telling me?" he choked.

"I love for always," she whispered. "You know that, Georgi. But tonight is last time for us. They know." She stopped and closed her eyes. The tears kept running down her face. When she opened her eyes, they were very wide, and dark with pain. "They know," she repeated. "And they kill us. As easy as I step on a little bug, they kill us." He could hardly hear her, and hearing, he could scarcely believe. Holding her to him, he thought that no power in earth or heaven would make him give her up. Then, tenderly and gravely, they made love, while the fire burned low. Now Eleni's hair was wet with George's tears; tears he didn't know he was crying. Finally he believed her, he knew this was the last time; this sweet and wonderful time was the last.

They made wild, desperate love, sleeping, and waking again to hold each other and to weep. At last, George got out of bed. Slowly, while Eleni watched, he got dressed. She sat in bed, with her knees drawn up to her chin, her eyes gravely following him as he moved around the room. "I'll find away, Elli, I'll find us a way. We could get married, then you'd be a American and they couldn't get you. I'm seventeen, we could be married in a year. We can wait — Oh, Elli, don't cry!" Tears ran down his cheeks as he talked and he knew what he was saying wasn't true. They

172

couldn't save themselves; there was no way out.

They didn't want the dinner. Eleni wrapped the sheet around herself and came to George. She clung to him as he stood by the door and he thought his heart would break. He wondered if you could hear the sound of a heart breaking and listened in silence, until he tore himself away and almost angrily opened the door. The night air was cold, and seemed evil; he hated Prague, hated the very streets and rivers, as though they were responsible for his pain.

"I love you always," she whispered, close to him. She slipped something in his pocket. "Read it in your room, alone, and remember me," she said. "Help me."

It was the last time he heard her voice. Numb and cold, he made his way back to his bike, and, bumping over the stony streets, he pedaled slowly towards the Residence. He knew it was the last time forever; had known it all the time he was speaking his brave words, burying his face in her hair and comforting her while she cried. The car was still out when he got home and he pulled the bike under the bush by the back door. He scorned to stop in the kitchen to eat; hunger seemed out of place in a man with a broken heart. Miserable, he climbed the back stairs and thanked God he didn't have to see anyone until morning. Surely, his face would reveal the depths of his sorrow; perhaps he was marked for life with the pain of first love denied. He would just have to see if time truly heals all wounds, and he would have to do it alone. There was no one he could tell.

He threw himself on his bed and stared at the ceiling. He kept himself from looking at what she had put in his pocket for as long as he could. The anticipation of it was sweet, and he imagined the words of everlasting love she would have written for him. It was all he had of her, all he would have for the rest of his life, the long, lonesome years he would live with only a memory. A tired old man, alone with his memories, he would take out the piece of paper and read the words written on it with tears in his eyes, and he would warm the chill in his bones with its message of love.

He spread the crumpled paper out on his pillow. It was not a declaration of undying love at all; it was a cry for help. In her neat, small hand, he read a tale of terror. Her friends were false, they were enemies. They said she had lied and she was afraid. She had told them George would get information they needed from the embassy and she had been afraid to ask him after she learned that Peace Group had another meaning. George must forgive her for lying to him, she had been afraid, and now her fear would be realized if he didn't help her. The clear little words sprang from the page, telling him exactly what he must do. The packet delivered to his father tomorrow morning would contain a secret paper, a paper which he must borrow. He could make a micro copy and leave it with the Golem, returning the papers exactly as they were. If he loved her and wanted to save her, he would find a way.

It was impossible! How could he get something, borrow it, from his father's desk? What was it?

Oh, Jesus, what can I do? He put the paper back in his pocket where it burned like a live coal. He took it out and read it again. Memorize it, you idiot, he said and his mind was a blank. He spread the paper on the tank of the john and took a shower. Through the rush of water he could still feel its presence, reproaching him for a coward. He tore it in little bits and watched it swirl around in the bowl and vanish. He thought he might forget it and frantically wished for it back, but, when he was brushing his teeth he realized he was repeating the words over and over to himself; the message was one he would remember to his dying day. How in God's name did they think he could do it?

He dreamed in agony of his capture by the CIA; they found him carrying off plans for a new nuclear submarine, an Eastern offensive, the latest ICBM. God alone, and Eleni's friends, knew what the packet contained. How in bloody hell did they know? Who were they? His fitful sleep was interrupted by a screech of tires in the street, and when he slept again it was to dream of Eleni, tortured and bleeding, screaming out to him, her dark hair matted with blood and her face swollen with bruises. He woke at daybreak and watched the oily light creep into his room. With it came the realization that whatever it was, and whatever it meant, he had to find a way to do it. He couldn't let Eleni die.

Breakfast was pieces of cardboard. He couldn't swallow anything, and hid behind the paper while he burned his throat with black coffee and his head ached and throbbed. There must be a way to get to Dad's office, but his brain went numb when he tried to think of a reason to be there instead of with Harrison or at the riding hall in the middle of the day.

Dad came in and sat down. Helen poured him a cup of coffee. He murmured, "Thanks, dear. Maybe it'll wake me up." The morning was grey and dark; it suited George's mood exactly. He only looked at his father to mutter, "Good morning, Dad," and let his gaze wander to the window, where he could see the wind whipping the branches of the trees and blowing rain flat across the garden. His father's voice startled him. "How'd you like a day off from school, son?" he asked. "And a day off from horses, if you can manage that. It looks like we're stuck with a senator on junket today — I clean forgot him till I saw this." He pulled a letter out of his pocket. "It's been here for days," he said. "Helen, I'm sorry, it isn't much notice. Can you do your famous tour guide thing for them?"

Helen shrugged and smiled. "I guess you could say I volunteered — hardly time to back out now. Who are they, and how many? I'll have to talk to the kitchen if we have to feed them." George knew she always played tennis on Saturday (so did Aubrey know it) and he knew how much she would miss it. Yet, without even mentioning it, she had scratched the tennis game and agreed to baby-sit the senator's family. It was all right for her; a game is a game, but how could he waste time with the senator's damn kids today?

"It's Senator Garcia from New Mexico, with, I

176

think, wife and three little Garcias. He's here on Arms Control and I'll have to set him up with the right people after lunch. I guess we will have to feed them; they get here about eleven. The kids are yours, George, and I can't tell you how I'd appreciate it if you'd help your mother out. Three boys, I think."

"Gee, Dad, I really had something I needed to do today, if I—"

"I'm sorry, son. I hate to ask you; it isn't really your job, but it would sure help your mother. We can't simply turn them loose in the city just because I forgot they were coming. You can think of something—"

"Sure, Dad," he said. Even the gray light filtered through the window hurt his head. There had to be a way out. He'd wrestled all night with the miserable problem and now, to add to his troubles, he was going to be stuck with a bunch of rotten kids—

Helen smiled at him, a fellow victim of the system. "We can do an embassy tour after lunch," she said. "Then you can show the boys around while I deal with their mother." George had done this with visiting kids before and he thought it must be about Endsville for them. Well, maybe he knew enough more about the city now that he could walk them around till they dropped. He'd show them the horses and then go past the cemetery and tell them about the Golem. The Golem! The word appeared in flames on the back of his eyeballs, and he knew what he was going to do. After the embassy, they'd go to the cemetery, and he would show the brats how to leave a message for the Golem. They weren't brats, they were a gift from God!

The problem of getting into Dad's office was even solved. He was halfway there! Surely the unprecedented good luck was a sign; he felt it like a message from beyond, telling him everything was going to be all right. There was no way he could even imagine being left alone with some "Eyes Only" thing on the ambassador's desk, or imagine that it would be lying there in plain sight. But, then, he had never dreamed that there would be a way he could even get into the embassy without a whole lot of shit, and here these wonderful Garcias came along, an answer to prayer—he had actually prayed during the night—and, with them beside him, he could stroll right into the office. He'd cross the next bridge when he came to it.

Lunch lasted forever. The visiting brats were fairly decent; only the middle one was truly obnoxious. The oldest one was fourteen and seemed to have pretty good sense, and the little one was small enough to listen to stories, so George pumped him full of the Golem, until he was wide-eyed and raring to go see the spooky cemetery. "Will we see him?" he asked. "Will he hurt us?" The middle brother affected scorn for the whole idea and made rude remarks about the Jews whose cemetery it was, and had to be silenced by his father. By the time he was eating his frozen strawberries and fake whipped cream, sweat was running down George's back and he felt as though everyone at the table must see what a nervous wreck he was.

178

They walked down the blue-carpeted hall at the embassy and a small, tight knot formed in his stomach. The little Garcia held his hand and he somehow made conversation with the fourteen-year-old. Following his mother and Mrs. Garcia, they went to Dad's office. The door was open and, when they went in, the amazon who served as receptionist effused all over Helen and the senator's wife. George flashed a smile at her. She was easy prey—George was not above using his fatal charms on older women. The amazon was charmed and said he was sweet and so good to take care of the boys. "You'll have a wonderful time with George," she told them.

"Kate's out to lunch," she said, waving a fat hand towards the ambassador's office. "If you want to go in, though, of course you can." "No, that's all right," Mom said. "We've got a lot more to see."

Mrs. Garcia said, "Of course, dear, we're just excited to see whatever you can show us, aren't we, boys?" The boys studiously ignored their mother and spread out into the room on a search-and-destroy mission. And all the while a clock was ticking inside of George, telling him that somewhere in the city Eleni was waiting, trusting him with her life. Somewhere they were waiting for her to bring them what he alone could get for her. How in hell was he going to find it, or even know what it was? The door to the private office was open enough for him to see the corner of Dad's desk. Beyond the desk he could see the model of *Challenger* that a visiting space person had given

179

him. It was worth a try.

"Hey, Mom, why don't you go on? I want to show the guys Dad's model." Helen looked relieved and agreed that she and Mrs. Garcia would take the car and see the sights in comfort, while George and the boys might walk through the old city. "Just be sure and be back by five. We're all having dinner at home."

George caught up with the little Garcia just before he pulled an ormolu clock off the mantel. "Come on, guys," he said in a the brisk, businesslike voice of a scout master. "Wait till you see this thing. You can open it up and look inside and they have guys sitting in there just the way they'll be shooting through space in a few years. The man that gave it to Dad is going on the first one—" The amazon simpered at him and bent over her work. He pushed open the door and went around behind the desk, making himself a little sick with his falsely enthusiastic voice and hearty manner, when inside he was jelly, and most of his mind was engaged in anything but the fucking model.

The boys were impressed by the *Challenger*. He let them take it over near the window and for the moment, at least, they were absorbed in looking and feeling, and discussing the future of men in space. He looked at the desk. It was a mess. Nothing on it looked like anything; he'd have to try the drawers, and the amazon could see him if she just raised her head. He could see her profile through the door. She seemed to be filing her fingernails with obsessive attention, but when the drawer made a tiny squeak, she swiveled her chair a little, just

180

enough to make his hand freeze where it was.

He wondered how they did these things so easily in books. Fictional spies (spies! is that what he was? a spy?) got all the breaks. The amazon would have to go and take a leak at this very moment if he had been writing the scenario, but there she sat, her bladder content, while his hands went clammy and his eyes blurred.

He jumped and whirled around at the sound of a crash behind him. "You jerk!" the oldest boy hissed. "You've busted it." *Challenger* lay on the floor, little men and tiny pieces of equipment scattered all over the rug. The Amazon heard it and rushed into the room, an aura of Estée Lauder encircling her. The little boy clung to George and wept. "I didn't mean to," he sobbed. "Billy hit me and it fell. It just fell—it did." He was soaking George's khakis with tears and slobbering like a puppy. The receptionist was on the floor with the other two boys, trying to pick up the pieces.

"Hey, you need a handkerchief," George said, trying to unglue the child from his leg.

"H-h-haven't got one," a muffled voice replied.

They were standing right by the desk. "Let's find some Kleenex, buddy," George said. He pulled out the top drawer and looked in. It was right in front of him, a brown envelope. Bold letters leaped up from the envelope: "Eyes Only" it said. He scarcely saw his hand reach in and pick it up. It slid easily into the inside pocket of his blazer and the drawer closed without a sound. "Excuse me, Mrs. Collingsworth. I think we need some Kleenex here." The snuffling was louder and wetter with every minute. The poor woman struggled to her feet and sought to rearrange her bouffant hair. She looked wildly around the room, focusing finally on the wailing child. The ambassador's office had never been so completely out of her control.

"Oh, dear," she said. "Oh, dear. Don't cry, honey." Then she produced, with some dignity, a handkerchief from the depths of her silken bosom. George mopped the soggy, slimy little face and apologized to the amazon for the trouble. She wouldn't take her handkerchief back ("You may need it again, dear"). She took another look at the mess on the floor, shrugged her shoulders, and told them she thought she'd just better call the janitor; they were not to worry their heads about it for one more minute. Then she herded them all out of the office and told them to have a nice afternoon.

George walked on air down the blue-carpeted hall. It hardly seemed the same hall where he had, not a half hour earlier, followed his mother blindly, filled with apprehension and indecision. The paper in his pocket was a palpable presence, the means of saving Eleni. Good God! He almost stopped in his tracks. He hadn't copied it! There hadn't been time; the amazon had railroaded them out so fast he couldn't have done it even if he had seen the micro machine. There was nothing to do but keep on walking, and by the time they were out in the street he knew there was no going back, either. He couldn't very well have asked the amazon to let him use the copier. "It's just for this top secret stuff I have to steal, Mrs. Collingsworth." Great.

It, the only copy? was in his pocket and it was

never going to go back. "Oh, by the way, Mrs. C., this envelope fell into my pocket while you were on the floor—" Or, more bizarre, he could climb in the window at midnight and replace it before it was missed. Who was he kidding? He couldn't take it back anyway. That was the whole point; Eleni had to have it this afternoon. He was practically pulling the little boy along the street, hoping against hope to get to the cemetery before she did.

As they shoved their way through the crowded streets, he heard himself talking, but it was like the voice of another person, telling the boys about the Golem; how he went all over Prague creating havoc if anyone made him mad, but how he would come to your rescue if you needed him. A small voice, hoarse and moist, spoke at his side, "Did he make us break it, George? Is he mad at us?"

They rounded a corner, and two blocks away, George could see the narrow gate leading into the cemetery. It was open and he could see the old headstones, crazily leaning together like so many old drunks, holding each other up. A guide was ushering a gaggle of tourists into the street. She was holding up a yellow sign and trying to count heads before her followers blended into the shoppers and sightseers crowding the sidewalk. Leaning against the crumbling old wall, a few feet beyond the guide, was a red bicycle. It had been left there, unattended and half sliding into the walk. Someone had been in a hurry. Then George realized why it looked familiar to him—it was hers! Eleni was here.

He practically shoved the boys through the gate

183

and dragged them over the stones. The place seemed lonely and deserted now. Voices and street sounds assailed them from over the fence, but when the last straggler made his way through the gate a somber quiet seemed to fall over them. "Come on, guys," he said. "I'll show you how to leave a note for the Golem." The sound of his voice in the eerie silence startled him. Was Eleni in here? He didn't dare call her name, and, while he continued talking to the boys and answering a million questions, his eyes darted around the corners of the cemetery, looking for a slight figure who would be hiding, waiting, afraid.

He made a big deal of finding the right stone, the big one in the corner — "his very favorite one," he said — and he let them help dig out the little stones to make a place to hide the envelope. He folded it over four times and they covered it with a heap of pebbles. Then he stood up and straightened his back and breathed again. His eyes swept the walled area. Where was Eleni? Had she seen him? The only thing in sight was a new group of tourists coming through the gate, and nothing else moved among the twisted headstones.

He ruffled the small boy's hair, the same way Uncle Ed Townsend had done to him when he was little. "Let's get some ice cream, fellows," he said. "That's one thing they know how to do here." So they walked across the bridge, dribbling melted ice cream as they went, until they came to the Institute, where George showed them the horses and they were wildly excited to watch a couple of Grand Prix jumpers in the hall. For George, the place was haunted by Eleni; showing the boys her horse brought a lump in his throat, a lump that he couldn't swallow. He knew, then, that she was gone forever; finally he knew. Look as he would down the aisle between the stalls, or in the great hall, or in the tack room among the soft, gleaming pieces of clean leather, he was never going to see her dear, funny face again. The old bike leaning on the fence was going to be his last memory.

"What's the matter, George?" the middle kid said. "You look stoned out of your mind. Where'd you get it?"

"Shut up," his big brother said. "We could just leave you here and you'd be arrested for a spy." He turned to George. "Forget him; he really sucks sometimes. Hey, are you OK, though? You looked kinda funny—"

She waited a long time behind the trees in the corner of the cemetery before she crept along the inside of the wall and stopped in the corner by the crooked stone. She leaned nonchalantly against the stone and took a cigarette out of her jeans pocket. When it was lit she drew on it once or twice and crushed it out against the wall. Nobody was in the cemetery with her. Her head barely turned as the slanted green eyes searched every corner of the walled area; then she knelt and felt behind her in the pebbles.

Her fingers touched the envelope and a chill crept over her. It wasn't a micro-copy; he had taken the whole thing! In one swift motion she shoved it under her sweater and was on her feet, running for the gate. It was late, and Uri would be at her apartment for the pickup in less than an hour. Pedaling through the streets of the old town, bumping and lurching over the cobbles, she pictured the scene at the embassy when, inevitably, they would find the document missing. She was cold and shaking and the fear that gripped her fed her imagination; she saw George in prison, being questioned, threatened, and branded a traitor. As she hid her bike in the angle beneath the stairs tears were streaming down her face. She wiped them away with the sleeve of her sweater and ran up the stairs. It had started to rain and she slipped on the old wood of the stairs as she ran.

She sat at the table with the envelope in front of her and stared blankly ahead of her, across the room. She began to see George's tall, lean figure in the shadows, and to catch the reflection from his pale hair as he came towards her. The light was growing dim, and she cried out to him to forgive her. Then slowly she walked over to the stove and opened its door. The ring of the oil fire was burning low, and she turned it up. When every shred of the paper was consumed, she closed the stove and lit the bulb over the table. "Uri," she wrote, "he couldn't get it. I'll try tomorrow. Don't look for me tonight."

She almost fell down the stairs, running, her breath searing her throat and tears running down her cheeks. It was raining in sheets when she pulled her bike out and began to pedal down the alley. The wind blew the rain and it lashed at her when she rounded the corner. She looked back, and the rain in her face almost blinded her, but not so much that she couldn't see Uri get out of his car and start up the three flights to her door. He must not have seen her, because he opened the door and went in. She skidded out into the street then and headed across the city, breathless with terror, racing through the night. What the Americans would do to her didn't matter; it would be better than telling Uri, and she would be safe there. She would tell George how she had burned the papers and he would know that he was safe, too —

Later in the afternoon the boys were deposited with their mother, who was having tea with Helen. The littlest one was glued to him like a leech. "I wanta stay with George," he wailed, and there were several sticky minutes before he was pried loose and George could excuse himself and go up to his room. Somehow he would have to find out if she had gotten it. He went down the back stairs and out into the yard. He crossed the tennis court and walked behind the fence, maybe looking for lost balls. He hoped no one had seen him duck through the bushes and he loped the two blocks to the phone booth. After he rang her number he waited an eternity for her to pick it up. There was a click and a man's voice answered.

"I have to talk to Eleni," George said. He felt as though his head was bursting, his eyeballs filled with blood. What was happening to him? Only yesterday his life had been so simple, so good; it had been Friday, the best day of all, and only yesterday Eleni had been his to hold in his arms forever. Now there was this voice on the phone.

"I tell her what you want."

"I want to talk to her.

"I tell her what you want," the voice said, heavy and dull. There was no pleading with that voice, no arguing.

"Tell her to ask the Golem, if she hasn't already," he said, and he clicked the phone off with his finger. He stood, stupidly holding the receiver in front of his face, looking at it as though it would bring her back to him, would materialize her, warm and alive, right here beside him. He rested it on his neck and closed his eyes. At last he banged it back on the hook and walked out into the street. Unseeing, he went back, through the hedge, across the tennis court, and up the back stairs.

Jesus, his dinner jacket was lying on the bed, all ready for him to put on and be presentable in. He'd have to sit through a whole evening, being polite, smiling at Mrs. Garcia, listening to a damn opera, pretending the world wasn't going to pieces around him. Struggling with his tie, he was surprised that his face looked exactly the way it always had; it was impossible that he hadn't changed at all. He was like the picture of Dorian Gray; on the outside he and his tuxedo looked just like they had at so many dances and proms at home, while his insides were nothing anymore but pain and fear. He felt as though he was dressing for a funeral.

Dinner was endless torture. The senator and his

188

wife were there, and another couple. The boys had been left at the guest house, but George was expected to go to the opera after dinner. It was part of his education, Mom said. She would never know what an education he had gotten today, in subjects she would never dream of.

It was raining when they went out. The limo moved slowly over the glistening cobbles, and lights reflected on the wet pavement like Christmas candles. The rain was falling in big, round drops, lashed by sudden gusts of wind. The whooshing of the windshield wipers was oppressive to George and he sat, silent, on the jump seat, looking backward as they moved through the iron gates and out into the street. Senator and Mrs. Garcia and Helen were facing him, and his father was on the other jump seat. He was thankful for the dark that hid his face, and in the crowded car there was enough conversation that his silence wasn't noticed.

The limo was stopped just outside the gate; traffic in the street was at a complete standstill and they waited in the dark with the rain drumming on the top of the car and wet leaves blowing to stick against the windows, making little plopping noises when they hit. Then, weaving through the stopped traffic, skidding as it snaked its way over the shiny cobbled pavement, they saw a slight figure on a bicycle heading towards them, straight for the gate of the Residence. There was no way for it to get through; it jumped the curb onto the sidewalk next to the wall. Then, behind the bike the traffic seemed to open up to make way for a dark car that was speeding after it, chasing it, running it

189

down.

"Look out!" George heard himself yell. The bike swerved in front of them, and in the headlights, he saw the white face and streaming black hair of the rider. The tires of the dark car screeched and it narrowly avoided hitting the embassy car. George was frozen where he sat, his mind wasn't working, was hardly registering what he saw. The car leaped the curb, following the bicycle. There was a sharp, searing noise as it smashed into the bike, crushing it against the solid stone of the wall before it swerved back into the street and was lost in the now slowly breaking-up traffic jam.

Then the high, wild rise and fall of the sirens came and flashing lights swept across the darkness. George jerked the door open and ran through the rain. Uniformed men were cordoning off the corner of the street; he couldn't get to her. He saw them lean over the twisted little body lying on the pavement. They lifted it up and laid it on the sidewalk. One of them took off his coat and covered it over against the rain.

Then George felt his father's arm on his shoulder. "Come on, son." The voice was kind. "Come on, it hasn't got anything to do with us." His father held his shoulders while he was sick in the gutter and then led him back to the car.

Chapter Eleven

Middleburg, Virginia, April 1989

The stars over the Ridge were very bright and fireflies winked in the deep grass like reflections of the sky above. There was no moon and the valleys were filled with a low mist that left trees and telephone poles hanging in the air. Speeding along Route 50, the car open to the night, George could smell the new-mown hay that lay in the fields and the honeysuckle that bloomed along the fence rows. Passing through Aldie he saw a few lighted windows, glowing yellow above the mist.

It was two o'clock and he had just taken Cissy home. They'd sat in the Sleepy Fox in Middleburg until the one remaining waiter began turning out the lights, and they'd talked of everything and of nothing. Then, on the way back to the farm, there wasn't anything left to say. Cissy had sat very close to him as he drove, and he could still feel the warmth of her body where it had pressed against him. When he'd stopped in the driveway, she didn't move; she was sound asleep. Then he held her in his arms and buried his face in her hair. It smelled like the fresh-cut grass in the fields where they had worked all day, and he felt a forgotten kind of happiness welling up inside him, and they kissed each other, a sleepy kiss, and Cissy's body was soft and warm in his arms.

"Go to bed, my love," he whispered and, against his chest, he could feel her laughing.

"It's hardly worth it," she said. "I have to get up at five — I think I'll just stay here with you."

"Good," he murmured into her hair. "Stay."

"Oh, shoot, I wish I could." She pulled away and sat up. "Carter would love it," she said. "Want to bet he's glued to the window now, with his other eye on the clock?"

"Good luck," George whispered. "I love you." And she was gone, a wraith of light, running across the dark lawn and into the house.

A half hour later entering his apartment, he saw the blinking red eye of the answering machine, insistent, demanding attention. He glared at it fiercely, resenting its intrusion on his blissful mood; it hadn't any business reminding him of that other world, the world of principalities and powers where he lived every day. He pressed the rewind button, and then heard the mechanical voice declaring itself to be Bill Henderson and asking to be called first thing in the morning, something about meeting for lunch. For a minute he couldn't think who Bill Henderson was, and when he remembered, he couldn't see why he felt a sense of foreboding in the memory.

There wasn't anything ominous in an old friend from college, however forgotten he was, wanting to meet for lunch. It was probably some alumni thing; most likely Bill was class agent and needed to get money from George for the annual drive. Now he remembered Bill, it was the kind of thing he would be doing. He thought of the first time he had seen Bill Henderson, and it started a whole train of memories. When he closed his eyes, he saw Harvard Yard as it had looked on those first fall afternoons, and felt the loneliness and the pain that had followed him from Prague to Boston, as if it were his portion for life.

When he arrived in Cambridge, the terror of that night in Prague was as fresh as the moment it happened. He could sit in class, not hearing a word of the lecture, and see, instead, the night in the square, the hideous night when he had stood in the rain with his father, unable to take his eyes from what he couldn't bear to see, the broken little body lifted from the sidewalk by other arms and covered with another's coat, while he stood in craven silence and let them take her away. He would feel hollow inside, and taste the panic in his mouth, taste the sour bile that he vomited in the gutter while his father held him and comforted him.

He didn't have a clear memory of the last days in Prague. He had moved like an automaton and had done what they told him to do. Mom said he didn't seem happy—the understatement of the century!—and they concluded he would be better off among his contemporaries in America. After three years of studying under old Harrison, he had been accepted at Harvard, and a flurry of preparation had begun. Hours of extra tutoring, new clothes fitted, and name tapes sewed in; he scarcely noticed it all. Day after day only one thing occupied his mind—what had happened, and where had it gone wrong?

Of course the papers were missed at the embassy, and he waited in fear. His father didn't say anything about it for a few days; then, at dinner, he told how the thing had vanished from his desk. George's ears burned, but he kept on studying his salad and eating it, just as though his entire fate were not hanging on the next words his father spoke.

"How could it get off your desk, dear?" Helen had asked. "Or out of your drawer?"

"Good question," Aubrey said. Mrs. Collingsworth and Kate had both submitted, nervously, to interrogation. Suspicion centered on the janitor. Mrs. Collingsworth had admitted that she had been on the phone almost the whole time he was in the office, so she hadn't been able to watch his every move. Kate wasn't back from lunch, so she was alone, and she hadn't known, only Kate had known, about the paper in the drawer. Of course, she said, in an aggrieved whine, if she had known what was in the drawer she never would have taken her eyes off the man for a minute. And it had been an upsetting day, with the visitors and the children, and the broken *Challenger,* and the tears. In the end, the poor amazon was so undone that she burst into tears herself, and required a great deal of assurance that nobody held her to blame in the least. The janitor was returned to the Czechs, who, taking umbrage at the implied accusations, delayed his replacement for a full three weeks.

That seemed to be the end of it. It was that simple. George had almost jumped up at the table and yelled, "I did it, I did it! I took the damn thing, and she was killed because I did it." Let them put him in prison, let them shoot him for a spy. It was incomprehensible to him that he should be free and Eleni dead. In the end, of course, he didn't say anything, and they put him on the plane and he flew to Boston.

For weeks he walked the campus in a private hell. It was on a cold, blustery New England afternoon, just after Thanksgiving, that he met Bill Henderson. He was hurrying across to the library, his head down against the wind that was whipping across the square. There was the taste of snow on the wind, and dry leaves blew past him, and the wind blew through him. A jogger went by, dogged, in the early dusk, trying to finish his laps before dark. Two girls hurried past into the wind, their hair blown back from their faces, their voices lost in the cold air.

"Hey, Clements, wait up!" The voice behind him was a little breathless. He turned to see a cheerful grin under a pair of thick, steel-rimmed glasses. He knew the grin and the glasses belonged to a guy who was in Government 101 with him, and he was embarrassed not to remember his name. In spite of the embarrassment, he was warmed by the sound of a voice, cheerful and friendly, calling his name.

"Sure," he said. "You going to the library?"

Henderson caught up, panting. A teddy bear body went with the cheerful voice and George

195

slowed down so he could catch his breath.

"Well, actually, no. Not the library. My room. Warmer there, and refreshment before what passes for dinner in this far country." As his breathing returned to normal, his speech slowed and the soft cadences of the South became apparent. "Thought maybe you'd want to come along up."

Whatever George had to do in the library was suddenly of no importance. A friend and a drink were worth more than any book on a day like this; the Reading Room seemed a poor substitute for life. God, how alone he had been!

Henderson's room seemed to be the watering hole for half the campus. It looked as though everyone in Cambridge knew Henderson; in a few minutes the room was packed with bodies. Glasses were filled from a supply of Jack Daniel's stored under the bed and a lidless styrofoam cooler was rapidly being emptied of beer cans. In the midst of the uproar, George sat unconcerned, cross-legged on the bed, nursing a warm beer. The beer seemed to fill the emptiness he'd had inside himself for so long, and by the time he was well into his fourth one, he began to see life stretching ahead of him, and saw that in that life he was free. The other life, the one he had been living, belonged to someone he once knew and remembered with affection, but only dimly.

Now he wondered how long it had been since he'd even thought of Bill Henderson. He owed him so much; it was Bill's friendship that first year that had brought him back to life. He'd made him part of the circle of his friends, and with him, George had begun to live the happy days—the halcyon days, weren't they called?—of college. Bill's friends were mostly government majors, and they spent their time saving the world, drinking a lot of beer and trying to deplete Bill's endless supply of whiskey. Sometimes they got together in a discussion group that met at Elliot's house. Bruce Elliot taught political science. He'd been one of the leaders of student protest in the sixties and early seventies, first as a graduate student and later as a teacher. Burn the draft card, all that stuff.

Now Bruce and his lank-haired wife, Gretchen, opened their house and encouraged the boys to come for long evenings of talk, sometimes aided by a discreet joint passed from hand to hand. Henderson introduced him to Bruce and Gretchen as though George were some kind of prize he had won. "He lived in Prague almost three years," Bill told Gretchen. "He knew a lot of people there." Gretchen kissed him on both cheeks and pulled him into the kitchen where half a dozen people were gathered. She must have been in her late thirties, but the sad and neglected look of the flower child clung to her like a sleazy garment. She wore a shapeless dress, printed with pale flowers, and her hair hung straight down her back. Home-baked bread was rising on the back of the stove under a sign that said "Animals are to love, not eat."

"What a great time to be in Prague," she said. "Here, we are so isolated from anything real. You must talk to me." She stood too close to him when she talked and her grey eyes penetrated his.

George's throat choked up for a minute. "Oh,"

197

he said, "we didn't get to do much outside the embassy. Just dinners and stuff my father had to do. I guess we got to know some people, but not the way you think, maybe—"

"Don't let him give you that, Gretchen. I'll bet you knew plenty of Czechs, man. You must have done something besides hold your father's hand and ride your fucking horse! You must have known some girls—"

"Oh, sure I did. Yeah, I knew some Czechs pretty well. That's all there were at riding school." Shut up, Henderson. I don't remember those things. Christ, I don't remember.

Gretchen pulled him over to the table and sat down with him. "Talk to me; Bill runs off at the mouth like that all the time." She knew how he felt, and she'd only met him five minutes before! She pushed her hair behind her ears, impatiently, twisting it into a loose knot in her neck. "I really want to know," she said. "Tell me how they live— how much does the government help them? Without this repressive conservatism—?" She leaned forward and put her hand on his. Her excitement was contagious, and he sat with her for a long time, weaving a fabric of lies that satisfied her ideology; he answered her questions with the answers she wanted. A make-believe life in Prague gradually became the real one for him, and he could talk about it endlessly, and painlessly. He could even tell about Eleni and the work he did for the Peace Group as though he were speaking of people he knew slightly. It was what they wanted to hear, and in gratitude for their friendship, he told them. Gretchen listened to him and fed him hot fresh bread and vodka.

The nights at the Elliots' continued through his second year at Harvard. He had become their resident expert on the satellite nations of Eastern Europe. Sometimes he was guilt-ridden to see how even Bruce and Gretchen took what he told them for Gospel truth, but consoled himself that there was a basis of truth in all his stories, and besides, it made them so happy to hear of the clever deceptions the Czech government employed to abuse the fascist Amerikan position in Eastern Europe. It was good to be part of something, to have friends and warmth and never be alone. All through his second year he and Bill went regularly to the Monday evenings at the Elliots'.

Maybe it was the memory of those nights in Gretchen's kitchen that was putting him off. It had been so long ago and, in the light of today, so carefully forgotten, that it struck him as an insult to be reminded of it. Damn Henderson for calling him; damn him for bringing it all back. Nothing he could say at lunch would be worth the pain of reliving those shameful years. He lay on his back and stared at the ceiling until light began to creep across it and the sounds of the street announced the beginning of another day.

He put off calling Bill until after lunch, and was vaguely annoyed to hear the same hearty cheerfulness he had remembered from ten years before. Bill picked him up at noon on Tuesday and they drove across Chain Bridge into Virginia. Bill had suggested the Auberge in Great Falls; they could talk

199

on the way out and catch up on old times. Bill was, if anything, rounder than before, and the same cherubic smile lit his face. His friendly, short-sighted eyes still peered through thick lenses, though horn rims had replaced the wire frames of Harvard days. Gentrification had set in. He was married and had three children, all, George supposed, looking like him. He was at the State Department, a deputy on the Russian desk.

He must have known about Joey, because he didn't ask. George relaxed back into the soft leather of the convertible's seat, and talked about the Bedfords, about Carter and Cissy, any harmless thing he could think of. The car hurried along the winding road, and glimpses of houses hidden in the trees flashed past. It was warm, and George squinted in the sun, now directly over their heads.

Lunch was good, and expensive, and Bill picked up the tab. On the way back, the car idled along, and the scenery unfolded slowly. Bill was watching George from the corner of his eye.

"George, I've been asked to do this," he began. "There's something they want you to do. I've been working directly with the Secretary on it, and we seem to have come up with the only solution. It has to be absolutely in the dark. That's why we're here, not in my office."

"What's up, then?" George asked. He looked across at Henderson's friendly profile and the two chins beneath it.

"Normally we wouldn't do it quite this way, but this isn't normal. The Soviets have got their wind up about something and we've got to arrange a

200

meeting. They're going to blow it when we meet with them in New York if we don't." He turned his owlish eyes on George, briefly, and then looked back to the road. "They have some idea that Sharovsky will come to an agreement if he can meet with Townsend before New York. Now, they want absolute secrecy; a 'walk-in-the-woods' scenario is what they have in their dirty little minds. Townsend and you, Sharovsky and an aide. A lot hangs on this, George—"

"Why me, for Christ sake?"

"Listen, buddy, listen to old Bill. What the Russkies want is like this. We get Townsend to a safe place. They give us guarantees, we choose the place, we have a man there, no leaks, no problems. They're willing to bring their man down from New York, secretly, and get him to the rendezvous alone. They've got to be running scared to risk it, and on our turf, too. See, that's why you—they're willing to meet in the woods at Quantico."

So they even know about that, George thought. We are all in glass houses, and none of us can throw a stone. "He'll never do it, Bill, not there. That place is almost sacred to him. You better think again."

"He'll do it, and he'll do it there. He wants this thing to work more than he wants anything, more, I guess, than life itself. Believe me, the best minds have had this one. Where else is he ever alone? We don't even know where he is when you guys are out there; and let me tell you, buddy, it scares the shit out of us. It even scares them at Langley. The man is an unguided missile security-wise and you know

201

it. Let me fill you in—"

He went on explaining as the car loafed along towards the city. He pulled off by the bridge at Difficult Run and turned to George.

"It's up to you, friend. This thing was dumped on me, and I've been in touch with them right along. They'll buy our plan, it's safe, and it'll work." He told George how he had met with his Soviet counterparts and they had worked out the plan. They had insisted there would be no summit on terrorism without this one-on-one conference first. They were going a long way to make it work; Sharovsky was being smuggled onto a private yacht in the Potomac and he would be brought downriver to a spot off the Marine base. They would await a signal to bring the chairman ashore.

"Bill, I don't think he'll do it. I don't like it much, either. I guess I just don't want to be the one to take him there. Let's say you never asked me." He felt as though he were pleading with Bill, and wondered why it mattered so much to him.

Henderson's round little face momentarily took on a cold, steely look. "You don't seem to understand me, son." The soft southern drawl suddenly struck George as sinister. "You are going to do it. Maybe you don't realize what they know about you, boy. They know what happened in Prague, they know about the Elliots. Just how you think it's going to look if you get funny with us, anyhow? You've got to keep your nose clean, son. Ah would hate for anything, say, damaging, to happen—" He was smiling when he finished, as one friend giving a confidence to another might smile, and then George knew the reason for the fear that had flashed through the dark when Henderson's voice had appeared on his phone tape. Bill Henderson was his past, and his past held the power to change the present and the future for him, in ways that, until now, he couldn't have imagined. He closed his eyes and leaned his head on the back of the seat. Obviously, he wasn't going to be given any choice in the matter, and his opinion certainly wasn't being asked for, either. Well, what the hell, if he couldn't do anything about it and if both State and the Agency thought it was all right, he probably shouldn't make waves. His imagination was just getting out of hand, he decided. He did wonder how Townsend felt about it, though, about the place, about the security, the whole thing.

"What does he think about the Quantico idea?"

"Oh, he won't know the time or the place until it is time. That's where you come in, George, my lad." The teddy bear was back, and the edge was gone from his voice. "You're riding with him, alone—we know about Johnny, by the way—you've left him at the helicopter and you're alone. You get as near the river as you can, in a well-covered spot, and then you tell him this is it. Of course, he's been briefed on it, he knows it will happen sooner or later. He knows, as a matter of security, that it has to be done this way. He doesn't even know we've told you—he wants it quiet as much as we do. Hail-far"—at moments of stress, the sound of Alabama intensified—"boy, you know what the sonabitchin' press would do with a leak. No talk, son, no talk with no one. You get him there, you pick the place and then you tell him—"

"I pick the place? What about them? I suppose the Russians just automatically appear? How the hell—?"

"Relax, boy, relax. You're getting yourself all worked up. We're dealing with that now, some system to signal them. They've got some ideas at the Agency, a homing-in thing, I think. You'll be briefed on everything you need to know. Maybe not a minute before you need to know, but, trust me, son, they'll tell you what to do." He started the engine and pulled out onto the Pike; settled back in his seat, he looked the picture of perfect contentment. "George, I can't tell you how good I feel about you doing this. It was a real big one for us, and we was between a rock and a hard place on it, all right." The comforting down-home phrase went with the innocent smile that lit his pudgy face, and behind thick glasses his honest eyes twinkled.

The clear air swept George's apprehensions along with it, and when they parted in Georgetown, it was almost with the back-slapping camaraderie of old school friends.

Only later, in his room, the chill crept over him.

Henderson was breathing hard as he walked along the path around the Tidal Basin. Pedal boats were out in force, looking like giant water bugs lazily skimming the quiet surface of the water. He had parked five blocks away, and the exertion of carrying his roly-poly body that distance had almost winded him. He was looking for a big man, alone on a bench, and wished to hell Orlov had picked one closer to the street. Drops of sweat stood out on his upper lip and he mopped his face with a tired Kleenex. At last he saw what he was looking for, and hurried the few yards to sink gratefully down on the bench.

The other man didn't look up. He was intent upon watching the boats, and the glimmering light falling through the Japanese cherry trees above him reflected from his bald head. A heavy, curved pipe protruded from the depths of a black beard, and he puffed on it dreamily.

At last he spoke, still regarding the scene in front of him. "So," he growled, "how is our boy?"

Henderson tried to smile. "Well," he said, "I think it's going to work —"

There was an eruption from the bearlike chest under the beard. "You think? What is this think? You told us you knew him — what you give us? Some story? I told Vasely Ilytch, I said to him, what if the fucking Americans can't do it, if they back out? Don't give me this think, idiot. Tell me what means you think it works?" His face was livid, making the dark eyes, buried deep in folds of skin, look black as coals. The drops of sweat were back on Henderson's lip.

"He's not ours anymore. I must have misread what I knew —" He was babbling and he couldn't stop. "But, listen, listen, it's going to be all right. When I saw how it was, I mean after we'd talked a while I knew it was over for him, and I'd have to spring the alternative." It was beginning to come easier now. "Listen, he doesn't know where I come

205

from, he really doesn't. I didn't tell him what he's doing. He doesn't even guess. I gave him the secret meeting story—"

Orlov interrupted. "You mean you have failed. You mean you have given us lies, mistakes—could be fatal mistakes." He looked at Henderson. "Could be very bad for those who made mistakes—"

"No, no, that isn't it," Henderson stammered. "We—we were prepared for this, and it's OK, listen, the fool believes it. He don't know tiddlysquat about an explosion. He's a babe in the woods." He laughed weakly at his humor and Orlov continued to stare at him.

"So, tell me," the big bear grunted. His interest encouraged Henderson to go on. He explained how he had been able to talk George around to agreeing, and how they would keep the details from him till the last minute so that nothing could arouse his suspicions.

"Shit, man, there isn't another way in hell we can deliver it—"

Orlov grunted again. He seemed to have accepted the arrangements, and Henderson's breath came easier. Orlov's little eyes now reflected the light coldly; blue-grey like burnished steel. For an unbearable minute he regarded Henderson in silence. When at last he spoke his voice was an almost inaudible growl. "What of the watch, then?"

Warm relief flooded Henderson and he smiled. Orlov wouldn't catch him on this. He'd taken great care over the table at the Auberge to remark on the watch and get George to show it to him and tell

206

him about it. "A-OK," he said. "Perfect. He still has it, the one I remembered. Rolex, about '73—the one his dad gave him before Prague. A stopwatch." He breathed easier. "No problem getting one?"

Orlov shrugged. He nodded, and a small smile flickered across his face. "We deliver it after Jurek finishes then—"

He went on. "As for your boy," he said, "we have ways to make him behave. He steps out of line once—"

Henderson wished his confidence in George was as real as he had made it seem. "He won't—" he began, and then his voice trailed off into the soft air. The huge man had disappeared as silently as a shadow and he was alone.

Chapter Twelve

Quantico, Spring 1989

Master Sergeant Jimmy Watson took a last look down the aisle of the barn. No wisp of straw marred the clean-swept floor and the low sun sent fingers of light through the windows and over the stall doors. Dust filtered through its rays, drawing lines like laser beams in the still air. On either side of the aisle, horses were munching their feed and nosing through the piles of loose hay in the corners of their stalls. Jimmy paused, savoring the peculiar, almost holy peace he always felt in the barn at evening, when the animals rested from their work and men had gone home for the night. Here, alone with the horses, he was grateful for their unchanging needs in a world where nothing else held still; where everything else shifted and changed from day to day, life in the barn was timeless.

Satisfied, he pulled the baseball cap down over his forehead and walked across to his car. The old Chevy complained to a start, and Jimmy rolled all the windows down to catch the slight breeze that came through the trees, up from the river. It was hot for April, and he thought he'd better get the air in the old car working before it became real summer. He cursed the muggy climate along the Potomac and longed for the open plains of home. He loafed along to the main gate and waved himself out. Half way to the Interstate he turned off and drove through streets lined with mobile homes, until at a corner of Old Route One, he pulled off and parked beside the Iwo Jima. Might as well have a couple beers to settle the dust in his gullet before he went home. It would give Emma time to finish looking at her soaps, and that would make her happy. Sometimes he wondered if she didn't prefer the fool men in the stories to her real flesh-and-blood husband.

Inside it was dark and cool. He snaked his way through the tables till he found an empty one in the corner. He didn't feel like conversation; he'd had enough of that today from the two boys assigned to him at the barn. It seemed to him as though they were making Marines out of children barely off their mother's milk, and they could talk more foolishness in an hour than a man needed to hear in a lifetime. He leaned his head on his hands and studied the scarred top of the table. The ancient dark varnish was marked by a generation of lonesome recruits; initials and dates and girls' names cut into its surface. He waited for Ernie to bring the foaming glass to the table.

The room was crowded and noisy, and, absorbed in his contemplation, Jimmy didn't hear the screech of the chair beside him as someone pulled it out. He looked up and saw a man in civvies getting ready to sit down next to him. Jimmy rec-

ognized him; some kind of salesman, he remembered, that Ernie had introduced him to a couple
of weeks ago.

"How's it going, Sergeant?" the man asked.
"Mind if I join you?"

He wiped the sweat from his ruddy face with a
very white handkerchief. "Sure, come on," Jimmy
said. "Just settin' here waitin' for Ernie to make up
his mind to git over here with my beer." Oh, shit, a
man couldn't have ten minutes alone anymore; now
he was going to have to talk to this bozo instead of
just sitting there letting the cool beer trickle down
inside him while his mind focused on nothing and
his body forgot the heat of the day and the tired
muscles and the aching joints.

The man was going to talk all right. He didn't
sit there a second without starting right off. "A
fine man, Ernie," he said. "We've been having a bit
of a chat, hoping, I might say, that we should see
you. He's bringing us each a beer—on me, this
time, Sergeant, I won't have it any other way." He
smiled, showing yellow teeth, highlighted with
quantities of gold. "He tells me you are the man-
ager of the barn back there on the base," he went
on. "So it seems we are in the same line of work.
How fortunate that we have run into one another,
as though we were fated to meet!"

He seemed enormously pleased with this pronouncement, a pronouncement Jimmy viewed with
about as much excitement as a cat does kittens.
Out of respect for the promised free beer, he made
an effort. "So, what line you in?" he asked. "You
in hosses? You sell 'em, maybe? We pick up some

now and then—"

He was interrupted by Ernie putting two foamy glasses on the table between them. Wiping his hands on his apron, Ernie went away, satisfied with the social arrangements in his establishment. "No, Sergeant, I am not a horse dealer." Jimmy couldn't tell where the man was from, but from the way he talked he sure wasn't from around Virginia. He wasn't even American. English maybe.

"Where you hail from, mister? Ain't from around here, I kin tell that."

"Right you are! Allow me to introduce myself. The name is Bancroft, Ian Bancroft, and I represent the Newcastle Farrier Supply Firm, Ltd., of Newcastle, England. Suppliers to Her Majesty the Queen, God bless her." He held out his hand. "Ernie was kind enough to inform me of your profession, and it occurred to me that we two are in the way of being able to bring some advantage to one another." The hand he offered was soft and white, and the golden smile was sincere.

"Jimmy Watson, First Sergeant, Mr. Bancroft. Pleased to meet you." Jimmy shook the pale hand, and said, "Well, now, what kin I do for you, Mr. Bancroft, and what is it you can do for me?" He wasn't born yesterday, and he wanted to hear what the limey had to say for himself. Mr. Bancroft was looking him straight in the eye with one of his eyes. The other turned to the outside, so that it was disconcerting to try to read his intentions. The straight eye looked perfectly honest, but from the looks of the other one, he could have been up to anything. Jimmy told himself the man could no

211

more help the wandering eye than a dog can help scratching, and he would hear him out if he had a decent proposition to make.

"Have another beer, Sergeant. This weather creates a terrible thirst in a man." He signaled to Ernie, and turned his good eye back towards Jimmy. "My proposition is like this, Sergeant. Our firm, Newcastle Farrier Supply, is contemplating entering the market on this side of the Atlantic. And where better than the state of Virginia to begin, where horses and horsemanship have held a position of prominence in society for centuries?" He paused to note the effect of this introduction, but not long enough for Jimmy to get a word in. He went right on. "In seeking to introduce our product we will require responsible contacts, men, for instance, who might, upon receipt of a sample carton of nails, make use of these nails over a period of time, and get them in the hands of local farriers. We are assured that once our nails are in use they will prove so satisfactory as to virtually sell themselves. It occurs you are in a position of responsibility and could give us a bit of help along this line."

He sat back in his chair and took a long swallow of beer. "Well, now, I don't hardly see what you mean. What do you want from me?"

"Sergeant, this is a mutually beneficial proposition. Should you be of assistance, as well you might, in cornering a portion of the farrier supply market, my firm would show its gratitude in a very tangible way." He spoke these words as though they tasted good to him; he almost licked his chops before he went on. "Should your farrier try our nails, and finding them superior to his present brand, as I have no doubt he would, and then place his order with us, a substantial percentage of the profits would be yours. As the market expands through the state and up and down the East Coast, you'd enjoy a nice steady commission on all sales of nails, anvils, tools, whatever we sell; you would be, in effect, a partner. All this for simply taking this sample box and urging your farrier to try it. A chap in your place stands a good chance of making some gold on this—" He was toying with a handful of nails that he had taken from a fancily decorated box. "Yes, sir, a nice steady income."

Maybe it was a flash-in-the-pan idea, but it could be the chance Jimmy'd been waiting for; the pot of gold to make retirement easy for him and Emma. He took the box of nails, and when Bud Fleming came a few days later, he told him about the deal. Bud said, sure, he was glad to have them; his supplier had been slow lately, and more than once he had to go into D.C. to pick up nails. He was willing to give them a try and see how they did. They looked like any other nails, and if Jimmy stood to make a buck or two off selling them, he said it didn't bother him any. He shod four horses on the base and put the box in his truck.

Jimmy called the number Bancroft had given him. He was supposed to let him know what luck he'd had, but all he could do was leave a message on one of those answering machines. When Bud told him he wanted to order a supply of nails and a trimming knife, Jimmy left a message again and waited for Bancroft's answer. Two days went by and he hadn't heard from Bancroft, so Jimmy began stopping at the Iwo Jima on his way home, hoping to see the man again. Emma was able to see the end of *As the World Turns* almost every evening for two weeks. Jimmy could hardly wait to see Bancroft and get started on their lucrative proposition. He asked Ernie, but he hadn't seen him either. Maybe he'd given up and gone back to England. By the middle of the second week, Jimmy had about decided he'd never see Mr. Bancroft again, and he almost didn't stop in at the bar on his way home. Then he remembered Emma was going to the movies with her girlfriend, and he thought he'd just stop and pick up a sandwich with his beer; the hell with Mr. Bancroft, he could stay in England!

"Your friend's been looking for you," Ernie greeted him as soon as he came in the door. "He's been a couple times and ast."

"I been lookin' for him, too, buddy. He says he has this great deal and then he splits. What the hell, it don't pay to listen to nobody—" Jimmy sat down with two other non-coms and ordered a beer.

He drank the beer slowly and it was flat. He was sick of listening to the guys he was sitting with bull-shitting about their women, and he pushed his chair back to get up. He almost bumped into Mr. Bancroft, hurrying through the gloom and smoke with his big sample case under his arm. "By Jove," Bancroft cried, "just the chap I'm looking for! How did the nails suit? Top drawer, aren't they?"

Jimmy's mood was nothing to match the little salesman's enthusiasm, but he let himself be hustled off to a table in the corner, willing, out of sheer curiosity, to hear what the man had to say this time.

"Have a drink, my friend, and hear the good news!" He waylaid the one tired waitress and ordered whiskey and water for them both. "Newcastle is on the roll! They have commissioned me to pursue the market here and in Maryland as well as the Carolinas. Tell me, have you put the nails in the hands of your farrier? Has he ventured an opinion?"

When the flood of words stopped, Jimmy looked him in his steady eye and said, "Sure, I give him the nails. He used 'em and said they was fine. I been wonderin' where you had got to because he said go ahead and get some from you. He needs a trimming knife, too." Their drinks came and Mr. Bancroft made a formal gesture with his glass, raised it in a toast, and clinked it against Jimmy's. "To our venture!" he said. "To the future of Newcastle in America!" He swallowed half the drink and sat back, exhaling a deep breath like a sigh.

"I knew I had picked a good chap to place my faith in, Sergeant. I can always judge a man by his conversation and I knew you were a right one as soon as I met you. We'll bloody write up his order tonight, and when it comes you can deliver it yourself. That way you can see we are on the up and up. My word, I am encouraged. It will be a matter only of months, I feel sure, until the name of Newcastle Farrier Supply has become a household word on this side of the Atlantic, and you and I, my friend, will be the first to profit from the venture." His enthusiasm was warming. He ordered them another drink, and then another.

The bar was getting crowded and noisy. It was hard to talk, and Mr. Bancroft moved closer. "It came to my knowledge, in conversation with Ernie, that you have the honor of caring for the horse that is kept for Mr. Townsend to ride. You must value the trust he places in you." His tone was almost caressing, and Jimmy felt a nostalgic warmth glowing inside himself.

"Oh, he don't trust nobody like he trusts me," he said. "He was my daddy's boss when I was a little kid, and he don't let nobody even touch that hoss but me." Jimmy's eyes were rimmed with red, and a slow, satisfying burp interrupted his account. He sat back and smiled, content with the world.

Bancroft continued as though Jimmy had never spoken. It took a lot to disrupt the avalanche of his words. "The reason I mention this fact, old chap, is that because of this confidence you will be in a position to add greatly to the success of our marketing operations, and thus to increase the profitability of our scheme." He pulled one of the fancy boxes of nails out of his sample case and laid it on the table. "You have seen, I am sure, the inscription on these boxes from Newcastle Supply?" He held the box up for Jimmy to see. It was hard for Jimmy to focus on it, and he held it unsteadily in his hand, close to his eyes. It sure was a pretty box.

Bancroft leaned closer and pointed a pale finger

at the top of the box, where a handsome picture of a lady on a white horse was printed over a sort of a shield with animals standing beside it, all done in gold. "Notice," Bancroft said, "the device of the Royal Family, their crest, emblazoned on the box! Suppliers to Her Majesty the Queen! Newcastle provides the nails that hold the royal shoes; the highest honor in the land for a commercial firm. And a great stimulus for sales!" he added in a confiding tone.

Jimmy turned his glazed eyes on Bancroft, who sat smiling beside him. It was pretty impressive; Jimmy had never imagined a box of horseshoe nails having such a glamorous history. Mr. Bancroft was still talking, and Jimmy made an effort to think clearly and hear what he was saying. "Now, what I want to ask you is this, Sergeant. Can you imagine this same box with the inscription changed to read 'Suppliers to the President of the United States of America'? Can you imagine the pride we would feel at Newcastle if we could put *that* on our boxes? And it is all up to you to make it possible." He paused to let this information take hold on Jimmy's consciousness.

"Up to me?" Jimmy hiccupped.

"Yes, indeed, my friend, you are the one man in the world who can facilitate the project. Hear me out, and you will see how easy it will be for you. While you wait for his order to be shipped, take these thirty-two nails, especially made in England, to your farrier and ask him to use them when he shoes the President's horse; he is already familiar with the quality of our product and will be happy to use them. Then, with these nails in place, Newcastle Farrier Supply will be able to claim with accuracy and truth, 'by appointment to the President.' You can see that every detail of our operation is scrupulously honest, not to mention the power of snob appeal to sell a product so advertised!" Jimmy gazed into the honest brown eye, and nodded his head.

Bancroft carefully put a handful of nails on the table in front of him. "Now, Sergeant," he said, "time is of the essence in these matters. Strike while the iron is hot! When will your farrier next change this animal's shoes?"

"Hell, I'd have to see the schedule for any hoss if it wasn't Ghost, but I kin tell you right now when he gets his feet done—Friday a week Bud'll do him. Yup, on Friday the third—" He picked up the nails and wrapped them in a paper napkin, carefully, with the deliberate motions of a man unaware of his state of inebriation. He pulled out his wallet and stuffed them in with the bills. Bancroft shuffled his papers and frowned.

"Oh, dear me. Let me see my schedule here," he said. "You couldn't possibly move that up could you? You see, we need to go to press with the advertisement and get the design for the new boxes by next week. It would set the whole program back immeasurably—" He leaned over and almost whispered. "In these matters, you see, a whole scheme may fail because of a delay. A rival firm could seize the market, Sergeant, and we would be out in the cold. You do see the importance—?"

Jimmy swallowed the last of his drink and set

the glass down. "Well, it ain't gonna hurt to move him up a week. Bud'll be there Friday, anyhow. Sure, I guess we can do it." He slid the wallet into his back pocket and rose unsteadily to his feet.

"Don't forget the order blank, Sergeant," Mr. Bancroft said. "That's where the money starts. By God, I think we're on our way! I toast our venture and your good health!" He raised his empty glass in salute as Jimmy began pushing his way to the door. "I shall ring you Friday night to make sure it is done before we get on with the scheme—" His voice barely penetrated the haze inside Jimmy Watson's head.

Emma was home from the movie and dozing in front of the TV when he got home. He burst unsteadily into the room. "Wake up, honey. Take a look at Mr. Rockefeller!" He told her all about Bancroft and his good fortune in meeting up with him. Emma received the news of their future affluence with restrained enthusiasm. It was not the first time Jimmy had come home with a scheme guaranteed to retire him from the service and set them up with their own place, stocked with a few horses and many head of cattle. For him, the good life was always just around the corner, and Emma had followed him down the road to the end of the rainbow too many times to feel either surprise or excitement over this new Utopia. Her mind was on the dinner that had been simmering in the Crockpot all afternoon, and on the hour after dinner which she expected to share with "The Colbys."

"Jimmy, honey, I know you're gonna make us rich some day, I always have known it. But let's set

219

down to supper and put a little something in your belly on top of all them drinks. Lord, see you set there and let that man fill you up with likker like that!" Jimmy could feel the nails making his wallet fat in his pocket and his belief in their power to change his life was undiminished by Emma's ignorance.

When he brought the Ghost out of his stall two days later, Bud Fleming looked up. "Not s'posed to do him today, Jimmy, not till next week" Bud consulted his notebook. "Nope, not till May three."

"I know," Jim said. "I just don't like the way his feet look. Been so dry, all this hard ground, and I been working him a lot. The boss'll be out this weekend and I don't aim for nothing to be wrong. Take a look." It was true, the shoes showed some wear, but Jimmy held his breath to see what Bud would say. He wasn't sure he wanted to let Bud in on the whole scheme.

"Well, he's growed a good lot of hoof here; I reckon it won't hurt, if that's what you want." Bud put the horse's foot back on the ground and straightened his back. "Sure, we can do it today," he said, and Jimmy breathed easy again. Jimmy took the nails out of his wallet and kept them in his free hand while he held the Ghost with the other. Bud went to the truck and took out four size two shoes. Leaning over, he took one of the forefeet up and began rasping the nailheads to loosen the shoe.

"They're still on pretty good," he said, but he went right on working at them. The Ghost stood still while the shoe was twisted and pulled off. "It's gonna tear up a little hoof, and be a little close, but he's got good feet—" Bud was talking more to himself than to Jimmy. "Leave me get the rest of 'em off." As he moved around the horse from foot to foot, Jimmy was studying the handful of nails that spelled his fortune. Even in the sober light of day, Bancroft's scheme sounded good. He rolled the nails around in his hand, and they felt good, like dice before a lucky throw. He decided he'd better tell Bud about it, after all.

"Bud, remember them nails I brought you? I got in with this guy that sells 'em, and we got a deal going that oughta be a pretty good thing. Listen, you and me are gonna be in on the start of it. This company is gonna open up the market here and we can like be partners with him for selling the stuff." He told him all about Newcastle Supply, and by the time Bud was ready to nail the new shoes in place, he had worked around to the presidential appointment part. "He give me these nails," he said, "and if we use 'em on the Ghost, they'll put it on the box, like about the Queen, it'll be in all their ads and his picture will be on the box—"

Bud took eight of the nails from him, and, holding seven in his teeth, he drove the eighth one into the hoof he was holding between his knees. Then he started around the shoe. He drove a nail on each side, and then three more on the outside rim. He hesitated after he had put two more on the inner side and decided to leave the last hole empty. It was a little close to the old nail hole and he just

221

didn't like to put a nail in it and risk splitting the hoof. Better just go with seven nails this time.

He dropped the eighth nail in the pocket of his apron and picked up another foot. It was the same way, and so were all the others when he got to them. Too bad they had to change the shoes so soon, but he guessed business was business. He went on shoeing, nevertheless, leaving one nail out of each hoof, and when he was finished he put the last foot down and straightened up to look at Jimmy. "Well, there's your horse. He'll be OK, but I'd do a little Hooflex if I was you. It's a lot of weight on them feet, and like you say, the ground's like iron unless we git some rain." He stretched to get the crick out of his back, and Jimmy went to get them a soda out of the machine.

"We'll take it easy this week," he said. "The Boss'll be in New York next week, meeting with them Russkies" Bud bit off a chew and leaned on the pickup. "What you think they'll do up there?" I ain't got a lot of patience with how they run this thing. Heard the news coming in. In France, Paris, France, I guess they said, they blew up a whole block this morning—they took and blew up a school, a MacDonald's, a whole block of apartments. How in hell do you talk to people like that?" He chewed angrily and spat on the dusty ground.

"The Boss kin talk to 'em all right," Jimmy said. "Shit, he ast for the meeting, he's gonna run it and the Commies'll do what he says." His faith was absolute. "He's been to all them African places and he's talked to them Jews and even them Ayrabs.

222

The Boss kin git 'em in line, you wait."

Bud yawned. "Well, I sure hope you're right. The news this morning don't sound like they've got everything down so pat." He took a few swallows of his soda and walked over to the anvil. "Let's see the rest of 'em, Jim. I gotta get on here."

He was done early, hurrying through two more horses. "Jim, I'll have to leave those others a week. Got to see a kid about a pony."

He was going to have to go to the Bedfords'. He'd had a phone call from Carter early in the morning, before his alarm clock had gone off. "Bud, you've got to help me. Beau's shoes have got so thin, they're getting loose like you said. Dad says I can't ride this weekend if you can't come. Bud, please—I've got to ride, I've just got to. I don't know how they got this bad, Bud, but, please, Bud, can you come this afternoon?" The voice on the phone had been a little shaky when it finished, and he felt so sorry for the kid he decided to cut his time at the base and just go by on his way home. It was hard for a little kid to have worked like Carter had to go in the big event and then have a loose shoe keep him home.

Traffic was heavy on Route 50 all the way to Gilbert's Corner. He cut off before Aldie and got to the Bedfords' lane by about four. He was met at the gate by Carter and Beau. "Gosh, I'm glad you're here, Bud. Beau and I've been waiting ever since lunch—"

"Well, git him off the road and bring him up to the barn. We'll git him fixed up for you—" The truck rattled up the drive, trailing a cloud of dust.

223

He waited in the yard for Carter to bring the pony up. It was cool under the trees, and the sun already looked low over the mountains. He whistled softly as he buckled his apron around his waist. He remembered the four nails in the pocket. They jingled as he leaned over to tie the legs of the apron. He guessed he'd just put them in the pony's feet and tell Carter where he'd got them. The kid would like that. He thought the pony was Secretariat, anyhow.

He pulled the worn shoes off and rasped the little hooves smooth. His hammer clanged on the anvil as he fitted the shoes, and the echo of its sound came back to them from the hillside like the ringing of church bells across the fields. "Looky here, boy, what I got." He showed Carter the four nails. "Hold onto those for me till I'm ready. They're something special for a special pony." He picked up a foot and Beau turned to view him gravely with one big brown eye.

Carter held the sharp, shiny nails in his grimy hand. He pushed them around with his finger. "They don't look special," he said warily. "What about them, Bud. What are they?"

Bud explained how Jimmy had got them and how he had shod the Ghost with the rest of them. "Boy, when this pony has those presidential nails in his feet, nothin' gonna beat him!

Carter reflected on this. A slow smile crept over his face. "I knew something nice was going to happen, Bud. All day I just felt it. I bet you're right — this is what he needs to be unbeatable!" He showed the nails in his hand to Beau. "No, you can't eat them, pony. They're your good luck nails." He closed his hand and felt them in his palm, cool and prickly. "Let's put them in his right front, Bud—that's the lead he jumps on."

In the house Adrian heard, through the open door, the small steady taps of the farrier's hammer as he drove the nails. "Thank God he came," she said to Cissy. "What would we have done with Carter if he hadn't?"

"You'd have let him go," Cissy said. "You can't ever tell him no."

"Oh, Cis, no I wouldn't. Did you see those shoes? They were like Reynolds Wrap! No, just thank God Bud came—"

She stood by the door and watched the little boy lead the pony to the barn. It would have broken her heart to disappoint him after all the work he had put in. She ran down the path to catch Bud and thank him before he left.

"That's OK, Mrs. Bedford. It didn't bother me none to do it. We sure don't want nothin' to happen to them two, do we?"

Chapter Thirteen

Washington, May 2, 1989

Jurek carefully placed the works back in the stainless steel case. It was an old Rolex with a stop watch, the kind they use to time sporting events. It had been delivered to him in the cafeteria at lunch time, in one of the square styrofoam boxes they put sandwiches in. He thought they must be short of help, because it was the man from the ice-cream store, the same one who brought him the nails.

He had finished with the nails in three long nights of work. It was daybreak of the third night when he had held the thirty-two deadly nails in his hand and showed them to Boris. "Look, Boris," he said, "see how we have hidden death? Can you see where Juri has hidden it, under the silver head of the little nail? Here it lies, waiting for the signal, waiting for the signal to kill. Who do they kill, Boris? Why?" He sifted the nails through his fingers and dropped them on the table. "See, Boris, they are harmless, waiting for their command—"

Boris yawned. It was nearly six o'clock and he had watched his master all through the night, lying awake on the old red rug, occasionally rising to

226

stretch his legs and then carefully circling and pawing to make a safe bed from which to resume his vigil. Jurek smiled at Boris and gave him a biscuit. "We give them away, no, Boris? Before we blow one up ourselves." The little dog made an arthritic try at sitting up to beg. "Poor doggy," Jurek said. "No time for sleep and no time for play. Tonight we go for a walk, maybe see Billy and Janet, *da?*"

Weeks had passed since that morning, when he had stiffly climbed the stairs to his kitchen and fallen asleep over a glass of tea. Later in the day, he walked in the cemetery at Montrose Park, and, sitting on a stone bench under the budding oak trees, he laid a small package on the seat next to him. When a woman sat beside him, reading *The Wall Street Journal,* he got up, and apparently forgetting the package, walked slowly towards the street. He was glad to be rid of it, and had almost forgotten that his job was only half done until he recognized the man in the cafeteria line. He was not surprised to find two sandwich boxes on his tray after he was jostled against the wall on his way to the table.

As soon as he came home from work, he took some brown bread and cheese, picked Boris up under one arm, and started down the stairs. I am too old, he thought, to work all day and then stay up all night. He ate his bread and cheese before he opened the box, as though it would go away if he could put it off a little longer. Boris sighed deeply and settled himself once more on the worn red rug at Jurek's feet. The old man took the tissue paper out of the box and unwrapped it. He laid the

227

watch that was inside it carefully on the table, under the light. He attached the jeweler's loupe over his thick glasses and leaned close as he opened the back of the watch.

He lifted the tiny parts out with a pointed forceps and laid them methodically on a clean piece of paper. He picked up the toothed gear that controlled the timer. Holding it close to the light he studied it for a long time, then with infinite care he filed away three of the sharp teeth on its circumference. Where the teeth had been, he filed a deep notch. Boris dozed off and snored, with his mouth open. Jurek checked and rechecked the fit of the gear wheel. When he was satisfied, he picked up the case of the watch again.

He examined the surface where the gear was seated. He drilled a hole at about six o'clock on the edge of the circular indentation. He fitted the gear back in place and turned it several times. Satisfied, he leaned over and picked Boris up. The little dog made resentful noises against Jurek's chest and a string of saliva dribbled down onto the old man's sweater. "We must take care, my friend," he said, and carried Boris up the stairs to the kitchen, where he left him half asleep on the chair by the window.

Downstairs, he closed the door carefully and walked to the corner of the room. He used two keys to open the door of a small lead-lined safe and extracted a tiny ampule. With great care, he laid the ampule down by the watch and closed the lead door to the safe. He locked the door with both keys and slowly went back to the bench, where he stopped and looked a long time at the ampule before he put the loupe back over his glasses and picked up the watch.

He took the gear out, and studied the hole he had drilled. Then he opened the ampule. With a tweezer more delicate than a hummingbird's beak, he transferred a speck of the material from the vial into the hole in the watch. His hand was steady, and he moved slowly, with the elaborate care of a father carrying his newborn baby for the first time. His breathing was very quiet, and it was the only sound in the room. Upstairs, Boris cried in his sleep. Then, swiftly, the old man put all the parts back in place and closed the back of the watch. He held it to his ear and heard its steady tick. It could run harmlessly like this forever, and be used by its new owner just as he had been disposed to use his own, identical, watch.

It could run harmlessly until, and only until, it was close enough to its thirty-two targets, and then the simplest act would set off the powerful force that would—Jurek scratched his head. What were they going to do with it? Who was going to be the recipient of his wonderful work? He couldn't imagine all this rush to blow up a horse. Perhaps they really were mad, as he had often thought. He stood at his kitchen door and heard the city waking up. The air was clear and he breathed it into his tired body. It seemed to him the breath of freedom. The old man straightened his back and said aloud, "Enough!"

The sound of his voice startled him and he looked around to be sure no one had heard him.

Then he sat down with Boris on the top step and thought, when this is over, this time I will *really* defect. I live now in a free country and I will ask asylum. I have worked for madmen long enough. He carried the watch back into the kitchen and put it far from him across the table. It disgusted him. He thought of how he had studied to discover the deepest secrets of energy and matter, of how his mind had glowed and expanded in the learning, and now, it revolted him to think of how he had used his knowledge. At the best, what he had done would blow up a horse. What the worst could be, he refused to imagine.

He decided he would give them the watch; he was too tired now to risk disobedience. But, after, he would put an end to the cowardice that had kept him captive all these years, and he would go, at last, to the other side. Leaning down, he picked up Boris and whirled him in the air above his head. "We drink to it, my good dog, we drink to freedom!" He poured out a glass of his precious vodka, and drank it with tears running down his cheeks.

George couldn't stay in the apartment any longer. It was after eleven on Friday night and he was too restless to sleep, too tired to work. He had talked a long time to Cissy on the phone, and when he put the receiver back he felt as though a lovely light had been turned off and the world was dark for him, and full of fear. He wandered down 30th Street to M, pushing his way through the throngs of young people that crowded the sidewalks, cruising the streets of Georgetown looking for excitement, or relief from boredom.

He hardly saw or heard the bustle around him. He tried not to admit to himself that he was afraid, and he couldn't identify a real reason why he should be. The UN trip couldn't be it. The conference was only four days away, and the arrangements had been confirmed weeks before. He had been overjoyed to find he was going to go with the President as a part of the special staff; during the three days in New York he would be constantly at his side. He had looked forward to it ever since the idea had surfaced, and he knew he should be elated at the opportunity to see history being made before his very eyes.

He thought Henry Bedford didn't feel too good about it either, not necessarily from anything he'd said, but George thought he recognized the symptoms of a man uneasy about his work. But then, why shouldn't Henry worry? All the security for the thing was in his hands, and even if it did go off without a hitch, the safety of the whole operation was a big load for one man to carry. The UN Building had been surrounded for weeks in a net of security and the number of airport marshals had been doubled, but a blast in the New York subway two days ago had everyone on edge. The streets fairly bristled with cops, and surveillance for ten blocks around the actual building was in the hands of the Agency. Still Henry worried.

Of course, he knew it wasn't New York that was keeping him awake. It was the thing with Bill Henderson. After all, Henry had New York sewed up tight. It was he, George Clements, alone, with the help of two horses, who was being dumped on for the Soviets' damn "walk-in-the-woods." And he might as well admit it to himself; he didn't like the idea. Something in him still resisted it, still made him feel there had to be another way. Why dump the damn thing on him? For that matter, why play the Russian's game at all? Let them talk at the UN, for Christ sake, not at Quantico.

He'd told Henderson he was worried about it and that he didn't like the responsibility, but Bill, all puppy-dog friendliness and honest face, had poured reassurance all over him, like honey, in his soft southern voice. "Son," he had said, "you know how hard we have worked at this, and even your pea-pickin' brain has got to see yourself as the only person that can be there. Ah never said they chose you for your pretty blue eyes; you are doing it because you *can,* boy, because you are the only one who can. You're the one who's there with him, and he trusts you, you know that." He had explained security again, and cautioned George that nothing must leak either before or after the meeting with Sharovsky.

It was silly to feel the way he did. Bill's job at State was one that he had certainly earned by being not only brilliant, but safe. Both the Secretary and the Agency had evidently sent him to George. Even so, he had felt resentment at Bill's offhand treatment of his perfectly reasonable desire to be taken a little more into the picture. They were sitting on a bench in Montrose Park, near the cemetery wall.

232

Bill had wanted to meet, to go over things, he had said, but George didn't know any more after he listened to him than before. He at least wanted to know how he was supposed to signal the Russians. "What do I do, stand on the bank and wave an American flag at them? Send up fireworks? Come on, buddy—"

Henderson had interrupted him then, and his voice had a little edge to it. "I told you, George, you're going to know when you need to know. This isn't tiddley-winks we're playing; it is a very sophisticated operation. Some of the best people are working on the mechanics. Hell, I don't even know yet, exactly. Just take it easy, buddy. There isn't any backing out; you can forget that. It means too much." It sounded like a threat, and George didn't remember saying anything that sounded like he was wimping out. He tried to convince himself that the footsteps he kept hearing behind him were only echoes from the past. He wished the hell it were over.

There was a cold wind blowing off the Potomac and the hair on the back of his neck stood up. He stepped off the sidewalk to let a group of students past, carrying a sign and singing. "Stop the terror," they chanted, "Stop the killing." The sign said "USSR for Peace—what about Townsend?" George shrugged and stepped back on the sidewalk. Forgive them, for they know not what—

He turned and went back up 30th Street, the wind behind him. He was cold, and wished he had worn a sweater. Hurrying up the hill he thought he would call Henry, even if it was late. Bill had warned him off from discussing it with anyone, saying it was a totally separate operation handled through the Agency and no consults were in order. Everyone concerned had been briefed, and absolute quiet was supposed to surround the operation. Still, Henry should know something, National Security couldn't be in the dark about anything like this. Of course it was possible he couldn't talk, but George thought he wouldn't be quite as alone if even one other person knew how he felt. He quickened his steps. He would call Henry as soon as he got home.

He unlocked the heavy Victorian door on the ground floor. His apartment was the whole second floor of an old house near the top of 30th Street, one of several in the block that had been converted twenty-five years or so ago when an apartment in Georgetown had become the *sin qua non* of existence for the army of graduates streaming into the city from the universities of the Northeast. The seat of power on the hill attracted them to Washington and Georgetown was the mecca to which they turned. Like a lot of other old houses, this had been divided into multiple living spaces, and its big, airy rooms gave an aura of permanence to George's life when he was in the city.

It was quiet in the carpeted hallway. Evidently the three girls who shared the first floor were not at home. The light they always left on in the back was still burning. The open staircase led to an upstairs hall, and George took the steps two at a time. The call to Henry was only a straw to grasp at, but he hurried to unlock the door at the top of the stairs. He was in such a hurry, he didn't notice that the door opened before the key had clicked in the lock. He reached for the light switch, but before he could touch it his mouth was covered by a heavy, gloved hand, and something hard pressed the back of his neck. In anger, he tried to lash out at his assailants, but his arms were pinned to his sides.

The gun was still against his head as he was pushed into the living room, where a shaft of light from the streetlamp illuminated one end of the couch and a section of the bookshelves that lined the wall. Everything else was dark except for the occasional sweep of light from headlights turning the corner at the top of the hill. Gradually, George's eyes accustomed themselves to the dark and he saw that there were two of them. At least he could still feel the one behind him, with the gun at his head, and he could see another one in front of him, a nylon-covered head on thick shoulders looming out of the night.

They shoved him down on a straight chair, and Nylon-face was behind him, tying his wrists together at the back of the chair. Then they gagged him, freeing the hand that held his mouth, and they tied his ankles to the legs of the chair. Very thorough thugs, he thought—if they knew how little I care about anything in this place, if they'd just let me talk, I'd tell them to take anything they want. Then they'd go and I could call Henry.

The cords on his wrists were too tight, and George's resentment grew in proportion to the increasing pain. The gun was gone from his head now, and its owner stood in front of him. He wasn't wearing a mask, and George could see his narrow eyes glinting in the shifting light. He could hear him breathing, and, irrelevantly, smell the garlic from his dinner.

Then he knew. These men weren't here to rob him. He'd seen this face before, in a car parked on R Street by Montrose Park. The car had stayed parked by the curb the whole time he and Bill had sat on the bench talking, and the face, lit by the nearest streetlamp, was the same as the one he saw in front of him now. This was a message from Henderson, straight through Langley. One old boy to another. He really thought I was backing out and that's why I'm here, trussed up like a goddamn turkey.

He glared at the bearded face close to his, and tried to make a sensible sound through the gag. He could only grunt. He tried to twist loose, and the Beard laid a hand on him. "Don't try," he said, not unpleasantly. Over the garlic, he smelled of expensive cologne; in other circumstances George would have laughed. Nylon-face had the gun now and had pulled up a chair at George's right. He sat straddling it, the gun resting incongruously on its delicately carved back. It was aimed at George's head. Sweat began to run down inside his clothes. His position was absurd. If they would untie him he could assure them that there was no need to threaten him. He could make it clear that he was with Henderson and the Department all the way and they could go home and have a good night's sleep.

They were not disposed to let him speak, or to untie him. There was no way for him to communicate with them and they didn't seem in a hurry to talk to him. The silence seemed to go on forever and the air was heavy with the tension of their waiting. The stillness was hypnotic, and the sudden sound of a voice behind him made George's muscles leap under their bonds. The Beard was speaking, apparently to himself, or to Nylon-face. "This man seems to think we don't mean what we say. He seems to want to make his own decisions in the matter. He must realize what he is risking, for he is not stupid." The voice stopped and, in the silence, George could hear the man shift his weight from one foot to the other. The other man nodded, and a twisted, grotesque grin showed through the transparent material of the mask.

Again, from behind him and slightly to the left, a question. "What shall we do to show him his folly? How can we educate him? He is given a simple task and thinks he has the option to refuse it." The voice had scarcely ceased when a blow to the side of his head sent George and the chair crashing to the floor. He couldn't catch his breath; the gag was suffocating him. On the floor, the dark was complete and threatening. Then, he was roughly set upright again and he could feel the breath of Nylon-face close to him, its foul smell in his nostrils. His left ear was ringing and he could feel blood running down his cheek.

His throat ached to yell at them, to tell them to get the hell out of his house and leave him alone. They were obsessed with the idea of convincing him to do what he had every intention of doing anyhow. Certainly he had made it plain to Bill that he was going to go through with it—his head was still throbbing from the blow, when he felt gentle hands washing the blood off his face and again he heard the disembodied voice of the Beard. "Don't fear that we will destroy your handsome face; it will not be seen that we have been here. We will be careful of you, since you are needed." He paused in his work and straightened his back.

"It is not personal, you understand." George understood. He understood that they were very good at their work, and he knew what they could do to him. A chill ran up his spine and he clenched his teeth on the gag in his mouth. Then the voice began again, this time from his right side. He twisted his head to look at the man, and heard him move behind the chair, where he continued to speak, this time apparently to himself. "This man lived in Prague, once. Surely he remembers it. He was a boy, and he learned to play a man's game. The game was dangerous, but the rewards were great." George tried to lunge around in the chair, and received a fist under the ribs. He almost blacked out as the air left his lungs, but the voice never stopped.

"The rewards were very great. Lucky for him we didn't know then, at Langley, what we now know, how in return for the slightest, most unnecessary betrayal of his country, he was rewarded by the sweet and beautiful body of Eleni." There was a pause, and an obscene giggle before the voice went on. "The lovely Eleni, given to him by the KGB,

238

and taken from him most cruelly, to end her life in sudden violence. For what reason? Because of the boy's inept and childish—"

George couldn't breathe. The air had left the room and the blood in his head pounded like thunder. He could hardly hear the droning voice as it continued its infuriating monologue. "Now this fine patriot has grown to manhood and serves his country. He is a friend and companion of Edwin Townsend. Can he imagine to what use our enemies could put this story? How would Mr. Townsend like to hear what they could tell him? How sad for him to learn that he has trusted and loved a man who once betrayed not only his country but his own father, all for a roll in the hay?" The voice droned on, while the man with the nylon-face lounged in the chair in front of him, where George was forced to look at the hideous grin and once thought he saw one of the distorted little eyes close in a lascivious wink.

He closed his eyes to avoid that face, and then he saw the street in Prague, in the dark and the rain, and he saw the black car screeching across the cobbles, chasing the girl on the bike. He saw the crash and watched while the black car disappeared into the wet darkness when its work was done. He wondered who had kept this knowledge all these years, kept it to themselves in their secret corridors. The voice began again. George's head dropped to his chest and a rough hand seized him by the hair and jerked it up. His eyes were used to the dark now, but focusing badly.

Once the phone rang, but no one moved to answer it. George's heart quickened to think that someone outside was trying to communicate, but when the answering machine switched on, the caller hung up without leaving a message. George slumped in his chair again. The room was ominously silent now, and the faint hope was gone.

The Beard didn't like it. The softness left his voice, and cold fear filled the room. Beard was losing control, and George sensed the danger. He grabbed George's shoulders and Nylon-face clicked the safety on his gun. He pressed the barrel against George's forehead. He felt his wrists being untied and Beard knelt to unfasten his feet. He wanted to spring up and beat the hell out of them, gun or no gun; then he felt the numbness in his arms, and knew he was helpless to fight. The arms that jerked him to his feet were like iron.

A karate chop dropped him to the floor and everything was darkness and pain. They didn't leave a part of him untouched, and the blows came so swiftly there was no defense or protection. He thought he would choke on the gag, then he thought he would kill them for what they had said—

The darkness moved, and he was under water and his lungs were filled with it. Bright flashes broke the darkness, but they were only pain. The brightness was beautiful, but it hurt; his head was exploding and there was fire behind his eyes. Then he was floating and there was no more pain. There was nothing, and he was happy. He was soaring through a cool whiteness and he was alone. Then beside him, and all around him, tiny flowers rained

240

down, and Cissy walked with him on a beautiful mountaintop.

They sat under a weeping willow by a clear brook, and her hands were cool when they touched him. Her hands moved all over his body and cooled the tired ache of his muscles and she kissed him gently on the mouth. Then she leaned over the stream and dipped a silver pitcher in its silver water. She dumped the water on his face.

Awake, he opened his eyes to pain, red, glaring pain, and a bright light shone on his face, while water dripped from his head and ran into his nose. He was on the floor of his apartment, struggling for breath, and around him a familiar voice was talking, its words floating through the blazing light that seared his eyes. He tried to move and found that nothing worked.

Nylon-face peered at him. "He can hear you. He's back," he said. And the voice floated nearer. "So many accidents happen in the country," it said. "So many young people meet with unfortunate accidents on the highway. But, of course, Miss Bedford is an equestrienne of some note, and we all know, regrettably, that riders often meet with accidents when competing. Things happen, mistakes of judgment, failure of equipment; there are many ways for such a girl to meet disaster. What a misfortune if something like this occurred, that we could easily prevent—" The face was close to his, and then it was gone. He couldn't see, there was a heavy cloud in front of his face.

The two policemen carried her body gently. As they laid it on the stretcher they straightened the queer angle of her leg and covered the red mask that had been her face. The rain washed over the broken little body, and under the sodden sheet the slanted green eyes stared, unseeing. He could see them, through the material that covered them, and they followed him when Dad led him back to the car. "Come on, son," his father said. "It hasn't anything to do with us." The bitter vomit rose in his throat and he choked on it. He pulled away from his father and ran back to throw himself on the stretcher, the torrent of his tears forever mixing with the rain.

Then the rain fell on the grass and the cold electric smell of the lightning mixed with the thick black smoke that was choking him. Three men were holding him and Joey wasn't there. He couldn't think why she wasn't; Joey was always there, and now he was alone in this hell, and they wouldn't let him go, and he needed Joey. Something was wrong with the barn, the horses would be afraid, were afraid, and he was afraid and they had done something with Joey. A scream filled his head and he tore himself away from the men.

He knew what he had to do. Joey was in the barn and they wouldn't let him get her out. She was in the fire—he could see now that the barn was in flames—and he raced across the wet grass. Burning brands fell hissing around him and on him, but he didn't feel them, although he noticed his clothes were in flames. The faster he ran, the farther he was from the barn and Joey was crying, and his breath was burning, and the arms that held him now were not human arms.

He was tied to a tree and Cissy rode by on a white horse. She was smiling and he called out to her, but his voice made no sound. She didn't look at him, and he knew that he was invisible. He was a nonperson, and he couldn't save her. He couldn't stop the white horse from turning into a speeding sports car, and Cissy was standing on top of the car while it raced around a track. Her hair blew straight out behind her and the car went faster and faster. Don't, Cissy, oh, don't! his soundless voice kept repeating, and she saw him and laughed. Her laugh was golden and she flung her head back and spread her arms as though she would fly.

"Oh, George," she called back to him. "Don't worry. I'm fine—" and the car turned over and over and over and the flames spurted to the sky and George couldn't move. Then he held Cissy in his arms, and while he wept, the substance of her body melted and was nothing. His arms were empty and the pain was unbearable.

The pain was still there when he opened his eyes on the first light of day. He still lay on the floor and the familiar sights of his room swam in a grey, watery atmosphere. He raised his head and an anvil struck him between the eyes, so he gave up and lay still. He was in his apartment, that much he knew, and he was alive. Serene in this knowledge, he closed his eyes again and floated into oblivion. I can figure it out tomorrow, he said, tomorrow I will know the answer.

Oblivion didn't last, blessed though it was. He remembered two men and he could feel their stale breath in his face. His mouth tasted of vomit and he remembered the gag. It was gone, and his hands and feet were free. Beard had untied him. He remembered the Beard, then, Bill's friend. His brain wasn't working too well, and he couldn't make any sense out of what he could remember.

As long as he couldn't move, which he thought might be forever, he might as well try and think. Clearly someone thought he was going to fuck the thing up, and viewed what they had done as insurance. Christ, Henderson, I never said I wasn't going to do it. Have you ever heard of overkill? He shifted his shoulders and heard himself groan. A shaft of sunlight crept across the floor and he glared at it resentfully when it hit him in the eye. It brought reality with it and made him wonder what day it was that was breaking so brilliantly outside his window. He wondered, idly, what time it was. He couldn't see the clock on his desk, and the arm with his wristwatch was far too heavy to lift. The hell with it, he thought, I'm not going anywhere, I'm lying on the floor. That's all I'm doing today, lying on the floor. If I never move, I won't hurt. I'll fool the pain and lie here forever.

So he lay there and waited for his mind to start working. Well, if I don't know what time it is, do I know what day it is? he asked himself. It has to be one of seven, that's all there are. It wasn't Sunday, or he would have heard the bells from the Presbyterian Church on P Street. It wasn't Saturday or he would have been in the country. He was going to be in the country on Saturday—oh, my God, it *was* Saturday! Cissy and Adrian and Carter would be looking for him. He'd have to find out what time it was and call them and tell them he couldn't move and was spending the day on the floor of his apartment.

Carefully he shifted his left arm. When he could see his arm he realized how well his visitors had known their work. There wasn't a mark on it to show the pain that ran through his muscles, or to give away the secret of their cruelty. He focussed his eyes on his watch. It jumped back and forth, but finally he pinned it down and discerned that it was after half past six. The watch kept slipping around his wrist and it occurred to him that his arm ought to be swollen and the watch should be too tight, but the complexity of this thought was more than he could handle. He'd better get to the phone. One thing at a time.

He rolled onto his side and rested a minute from the effort. By the time he got on his belly he had to pause again to get his breath. He started to inch across the floor to his desk.

"Answer it, Carter, quick, dear." Adrian was pouring lemonade into the gallon thermos. Carter streaked through the kitchen in his undershorts, carrying hangers full of jackets, breeches, and clean shirts.

"Mom, I can't. Look at me!"

He turned with an apologetic grin and fell over a pile of boots on the floor. The phone went on ringing. "Just get it, Carter. I'll pick your stuff up in a minute—"

He scrambled to his feet and grabbed the phone

245

off the wall. "Hello—oh, hi, George. When are you coming?"

Adrian was still sorting clothes and trying to restore order when Carter came back. "Mom, he can't come today. He sounded funny. I mean, not like him at all, like maybe he was sick."

"Did he say he was sick?" Adrian asked.

"No, not really. He said something had come up today, but he'd be here tomorrow and we shouldn't worry. He didn't want to talk to Cis. I bet he's got another girl. Old Cis will—"

"Oh, Carter, shut *up!*" Adrian snapped. She was immediately sorry. She hated it when she caught a case of nerves from the children. Of course they were on edge before the competition, but she needed all the sense she could muster to get it all together. Sometimes she wondered how they always did it—just the mechanics of getting two horses, two riders, their saddles, bridles, coats, breeches, boots, halters, and psyches there intact, along with food for an army, gallons of drinks for themselves and feed and water for the horses. Well, thank heaven George was coming to help out tomorrow. She simply could not look for another jump judge at this point.

The future jump judge had crawled to the bathroom. Naked, he leaned on the cold edge of the washbasin and examined himself gingerly. Except for the cut above his ear, there was nothing that would show when he was dressed. He forced himself to bend down and start the hot water in the tub. He sank to the floor and stared morosely at the rising water. An hour later, crawling out of the

246

Chapter Fourteen

Washington, D.C., May 4, 1989

In his office Saturday afternoon, Henry picked up the phone, stared at it a minute, and carefully put the receiver back down. He didn't really know who to call; he wasn't even quite sure what the trouble was, if there was trouble. He had spent the whole day trying to run it down. For all he had found out he might as well have not come in at all, and he sincerely wished he hadn't. Cissy and Carter and Adrian were all at Oak Hill, and he kept wondering if the children were all right. He clung to the odd belief that if he were there the crash could not occur or, if it did, the child would emerge unharmed and ready to go on.

It pained him to remember the look on Carter's face as he sat at the table this morning. "You're coming, aren't you, Dad?" he'd said when Henry joined them for breakfast at 5:30. "You'd never be up now if you weren't, would you?" The ungodly hours that horse people kept were a commonplace occurrence at the Bedfords, but Henry had warned the children that he might sleep late and just catch them up later at Oak Hill, so his presence at such an hour had been misleading. It was the phone call, not the desire to be the first person at Oak Hill, that got him up early, and he was simply going to have to disappoint the children again. The call had wakened him around two A.M., and he was still awake to hear the first rooster crowing across the valley.

He had lain in bed staring at the ceiling, and later at the finger of light coming from the setting moon, moving slowly across the floor and up the wall. Adrian had gone right back to sleep, lying on her side with her head in that hollow between his shoulder and neck that seemed to have been made for the sole purpose of holding her head. He lay for a long time without moving, trying not to wake her up, but when, finally, his arm went to sleep and he rolled gently away from her she didn't stir. Poor girl, she had been going night and day and he would be glad when this was over for her. He didn't want to wake her with his problem.

It was his worry, after all, no need to bother her with it. It was an anonymous call, undoubtedly a false alarm, but this close to the peace talks, with Sharovsky already in New York and Townsend leaving in two days, any suspicion of a threat to the President's life had to be taken seriously. No two ways about it, he would have to be in his office as early as possible.

When Adrian's alarm went off at 5:00, he had just dropped off to sleep. "Don't get up, dear," Adrian whispered in his ear. "You know what these mornings are like. Just get up when you feel like it —"

250

What he felt like was both of them rolling over and staying in bed and making long and leisurely love. She was warm and sweet and sleep clouded her eyes. With her soft breath in his ear and her loose hair on his shoulder, in the grey light of breaking day she was dearer to him than life. He held her to him and closed his eyes. "Let's don't get up," he said. "Let's say we're the only people in the world, and just stay here."

Adrian sighed. "I knew I never should have married you. You are a sex fiend, and we have a long day ahead of us, no matter how you lust—" She pulled away and sat on the edge of the bed, pulling the sheet over her breasts. "Oh," she said. "Shit. When can we ever have some time of our own?" Henry slid across the bed and sat beside her, his arm over her shoulder. She leaned on him for a minute and he smiled in spite of himself. "My mother told me about girls like you," he said.

But while he was holding her and smiling, last night's phone call oozed back into focus and the day became simply another grey morning. The sleepless hours of the night came back to him and his body ached for sleep. He brushed Adrian's cheek with a kiss. "I'm sorry, hon. After this meeting is over maybe—"

He got up then, and showered, and by the time he got to the breakfast table the house seemed filled with children, racing through the boot room, out to the van, back to the kitchen, begging Berenice to hurry with the hotcakes. Adrian, checklist in hand, was piling things on the table and gulping a mug of coffee.

251

"Y'awl set down an' eat," Berenice commanded. "You, too, Miz Bedford, set down an' I'll carry you yore breakfas'." Order was momentarily restored, and they sat.

"Carter, I'm sorry, son, but I have to go to the office." Carter's face went blank, but only for a minute. He made a pretty good effort to smile.

"It's OK, Dad, it's only dressage today, anyhow." It was good try, and Henry appreciated it. They'd had to learn to do without him too often, and it hurt to see how they tried to cover what they felt. "I'll probably mess it up anyway and you'd be embarrassed." The admission of fallibility was, in itself, coming from Carter, an indication of how deeply he felt Henry's desertion.

It even brought Cissy to the rescue. "Look, Brat, you're going to be fine. Jessy would never have let you go Training if she didn't know you could. Beau is a real smart pony—you guys aren't going to mess up a thing." In gratitude, Carter refrained from any reference to his clandestine knowledge of her love life and allowed her to tousle his hair without even cringing.

She turned to Henry. "Dad, is it something scary? Why today? when you said everything was all set—"

Adrian put her hand on Cissy's. "It's probably nothing. Dad had a phone call last night that worries him a little, and you know how he is. We wouldn't want him any other way, would we?" She smiled at Henry and said, "Maybe by this afternoon? You'll miss seeing Cis, but Carter doesn't go till four o'clock or so."

252

"I hope so," Henry said. "Anyway, isn't the great George Clements going to be here? That ought to make up for one old father, oughtn't it?"

Adrian stood behind his chair for a minute. She leaned over and brushed his cheek with a kiss. "Hurry home, hon," she said, "We'll be looking for you." As she hustled the kids out through the kitchen door, Carter had turned around to look at him with a strangely grown-up look that haunted him now as he picked up the phone again and slowly dialed a number.

He heard the click of the phone being picked up on the other end. He switched on the scrambler. "Have you been able to trace it at all?" he asked. When he hung the phone up, minutes later, he had very little more to go on than before. The office had been working on it since morning, and had no more idea of the source of the threat than they had when they started. They had run it by Langley and the FBI, without a glimmer. Clearly, someone who knew, or thought they knew, of an assassination plot, had decided to tell, but as of now, Henry didn't even know if it was a warning from our side, or a threat from theirs.

The voice in the night had refused to answer him. It said what it wanted to say, and then hung up. At first he thought it was some religious freak, a born-again reciting biblical verse: "He went out and hanged himself from a tree, from the Judas tree that blooms today on the mountainside, its blossoms red with the blood of the tyrant." The voice was impersonal, almost mechanical, and, recalling it, Henry felt the hair rise on the back of

253

his neck.

He heard his own voice, a little strained, saying, "Who do you want to speak to?" and then waiting, the silence echoing in his ear.

"Betrayed by a friend, the tyrant will fall—" and then, click. Henry held the dead phone in his hand and then slowly reached over in the dark to hang it back up. Adrian was asleep already.

The first thing he did when he got to the office was to call and double security around the White House, where Townsend was going to spend the weekend resting up for the New York trip, and he had sent a new team to New York to comb the area again and seal it off forty-eight hours ahead of time. Best not to say anything to the White House about it yet. Let everything proceed there as if nothing had happened. After all, nothing had happened. Maybe he was too jumpy; the call was most likely some nut without a clue in the world of what he was saying. God, I'll be glad when this is over, he thought. If only we knew it was going to work; if Sharovsky would keep his word and cut off the KGB from its sources of power in the Middle East. If only it works, he thought, I could spend the day with my children when I wanted to, and fathers all over the world could spend days of peace and happiness with their families. Townsend *had* to get there, the talks had to work. He put his head down on his desk, and prayed, as he hadn't for years, to the God of his childhood, to the God who would answer the prayers of his children.

It meant so much to Ed Townsend; ever since Henry had known him it had been the driving passion of his life to find a way of ending the tensions that held the nations of the world in postures of hate and distrust. He remembered coming to Washington more than twenty years ago to work on the Hill. Straight out of Harvard—"How do you get to Washington? Go to Harvard and turn left"—he had brought his crisp Yankee efficiency to the office of Congressman Ball from his own district in New Hampshire. Ed Townsend was the new junior senator from Wyoming when Henry first met him. It was at a party in Georgetown where he was striving to drop enough names to impress the very lovely girl he had brought with him. They stood crushed in a corner, smiling at each other above the noise of a hundred overachievers hard at work building their egos; conversation was impossible. He didn't know anyone there well enough to talk to them; he wondered why he had come at all. He grabbed his date by the hand and shouted something about leaving. They struggled towards the door. He didn't realize that he still had a half full glass of red wine in his hand until he saw, appalled, its livid stain spreading over the sleeve of a man he had been pushed against.

That was how he met Ed Townsend. Ed laughed at the spilled wine and pulled Henry with him to the kitchen where they sloshed cold water on the stain and condemned all parties and Georgetown ones in particular. "You're Don Ball's AA, aren't you?" Ed said. "Aubrey Clements and I have been working on him to do a little trip with us. Wish you'd help us talk him into it." He had explained that they had an opportunity to visit some of the

255

Eastern Bloc nations to try to make headway towards an approach to Moscow; it was Ed's unshakable opinion that reason and goodwill could make a difference. It was also his conviction that without mutual knowledge and understanding, relations between the two sides could only become worse.

"If I don't do anything else with my life, son," the tall man's eyes were grave as he spoke, "I mean to make a difference." And, through the years that followed, a friendship had grown between them. Breakfasting together on the Hill Ed would talk to him about his dream of peace. "I mean real peace," he said. "Not us laying down our guns and rolling over to play dead. I mean working together with Moscow, the two big powers sharing a responsibility, making it safe, safe anywhere in the world."

Once, just back from a trip to Russia, he had told Henry how he had met one of the Committee, vacationing in Yalta. "He was on the beach, there," Ed said. "Just sitting on one of those hard little benches, smoking. I sat down with him and tried my ruptured Russian on him. You know what, Hank? He just laughed and said maybe his English wasn't perfect but it was better than my Russian." He smiled. "It was."

He had talked a long time that day with the man on the beach; reluctant to end their conversation he had suggested they meet for a drink back at the hotel. Together they had retrieved their clothes from the lockers and, still talking like long-lost friends, had climbed the steep steps up to the hotel. "Hank," Ed had told him, "I could get along

256

with a guy like him. His name's Sharovsky, Leon Sharovsky. He asked me for lunch in his suite the next day—we could get somewhere if they were all like that. He didn't give a shit that we were being watched—"

A friendship by correspondence had grown up between the two men, to the extent that friendship can survive censorship, at any rate, so that when, in a surprise move, Sharovsky became chairman of the party, Ed's hopes for resolution of the East/ West conflict were high. If Sharovsky could only distance himself from the KGB's program of terrorism, now becoming worldwide—Townsend was jubilant as he had begun his campaign for the Presidency.

He had run for office on the promise of the upcoming peace negotiations and when he was elected he had called Henry at the CIA. "Hank, you're going to have to quit the Agency. I've got to have you here—" The job at the White House was, as Carter had said, stress city, but the chance to be close to everything that was going on compensated at least in part for the weight of responsibility and back-breaking schedule. And it had begun to look as though they were going to do it. Everything from Moscow sounded good. Oh, God, the talks had to come off; Ed had worked so hard and so long for this—

The phone jangled and he jumped to answer it. It was from Fielding at State, reporting back on the feelers he had put out in the morning. He'd been in touch with their delegation, and all he could gather from there was a feeling there might be something between the KGB and Sharovsky, something that was making them nervous. Fielding said he had read this between the lines, the only place, in his view, to read anything worth reading in their communications. It certainly didn't seem to be pointing to Townsend in any way that Fielding could perceive. Mostly, he felt, there was a move in the KGB to undermine Sharovsky's influence at the meeting; perhaps the monolith in Moscow was cracking and he couldn't view that as a threat. Henry was left with the impression that his night caller was not an unfriendly. It felt more like a warning from a source that didn't wish itself known.

The message went around and around in his head. The queerly biblical sound of the message didn't point to their side, unless they were being very coy. Taking it in its biblical context, there clearly was a traitor involved. "He went out and hanged himself—" that was Judas; the question that Henry had to answer was obvious; who is Judas, who are we looking for? Damn, why didn't they turn up something at the Agency? Judas was their business, wasn't he?

In Burleith the sun shone through the lacy leaves of a big mimosa tree that covered the tiny backyard of Jurek Vlascki's house. The soft pastel flowers drifted down lazily to plaster themselves on the sidewalk and on the aluminum yard furniture where three children were playing.

"I don't want to play anymore," the little girl

258

said. "I don't like this game, anyway."

"Of course you don't, because you always lose," her big brother, not unkindly, answered. He picked up the sticky cards and turned to the other boy. "She's only four," he offered in explanation. "She can count, but she can't remember about the kings and queens."

"Why do we have to let her play, then? You're dumb, Bill—we could just make her sit on the step and shut up. Then we could play."

"I do so know about the kings and queens, and Billy isn't dumb. I'd tell Mommy if he made me sit on the old step, and then he couldn't play at all. An' you couldn't either. It's our backyard anyhow an' Mr. Bronski's an' Boris's an' not yours." The effort of this speech left Janet a little breathless, but triumphant in her command of logic.

They were really waiting to play with Boris when Mr. Bronski let him out, and waiting to see Mr. Bronski, too. Janet had a lovely licorice whip in her pocket that she was going to give her friend, because she loved him. It was odd, they hadn't seen the old man all day, and, actually, they hadn't seen him come home the night before either.

"I think something's wrong with him," Bill said. "I think something's happened to him. Look, he'd have to let Boris out by now; it's after one o'clock."

"Let's go knock again, real hard, and make him hear us," Janet said. "You come with me." She tugged at his arm.

They went up the steps to the back door and Billy beat with his fist, then Janet joined with firm

259

kicks at the bottom of the door.

A small, thin sound came from inside the basement door, and both children froze where they stood.

"It's Boris!" Janet cried. "He's hurt, I know he is!"

"No, he's just scared," Billy said. "He's all alone, I bet — I bet Mr. Bronski isn't even there!"

"He's always there. He *lives* there," Janet announced reasonably. "He wouldn't leave Boris alone; he's so little." Her voice, still firm, was getting smaller again.

They yelled at Boris for a while, and beat on the door, but all their efforts brought them were a few more feeble whines from the little dog inside.

"I want Mr. Bronski," Janet wailed.

"Stop yelling," Billy automatically commanded his sister. "Let's get Hermie Young. He delivers the paper; maybe he saw him this morning. Mr. Bronski is always out early to get his paper, Hermie told me."

When Hermie was finally produced it was after five. His information was even less reassuring than their original ignorance. Mr. Bronski hadn't picked up his paper the morning before and he hadn't been there this morning either. Janet was openly weeping, and smudging her face with the licorice whip. Boris, apparently taking heart from the uproar outside his prison, was now barking and crying continuously.

Arriving home, their parents found Billy and Janet in the yard surrounded by half the children in the neighborhood. "Come on, kids," Mr. Sherman said. "Let's all go home. He just went away for the weekend, is all. He doesn't have to tell you everything he does."

"He wouldn't leave Boris, he never would," Janet sobbed. "He wouldn't leave him all alone—"

Her mother held her close. "Honey, he must be all right. Suppose he did go away, maybe someplace he couldn't take a dog. He'd leave food and water for him and he'd be all right—"

"He isn't all right. He's crying. He's scared, Mommy."

Mr. Sherman tried all the doors. They went next door and asked the neighbors if they knew whether Mr. Bronski had gone away for the weekend. They never saw the old boy, they said, they hadn't an idea where he was. Finally, Janet was persuaded to eat her supper and go to bed. They would check on Boris in the morning. "I know he's scared," she whispered, "and so am I." She lay looking at the dark for a long time, and listening for the sound of tired old footsteps that never came.

Chapter Fifteen

May 5, 1989

He tried once more to reach Bill Henderson. Each successive ring of the phone on the other end grated on George's nerves a little more than the last one. He let it ring twenty-three times. The answering machine wasn't even there today. Where in hell had the man gone?

Sunday morning was a whole lot better than Saturday had been. He had finally drifted into a deep sleep after a day of fevered, dream-filled tossing and turning. The ache in his bones was less, and his mind was clear. He had to talk to Bill. By now his rage had quieted to a steady anger. He might have expected to be treated like this if he was on *their* side; that's how they worked, after all. But, who in the world at Langley was into this kind of tactic?

He rationalized with himself as he lay watching the increasing light outside his window. If even Townsend wasn't going to know until the last minute, obviously security was very tight; evidently the quarry would scare easily. After all, they had their man in a boat waiting for the signal, and it implied a certain degree of trust on their part to leave Sharovsky so exposed. Of course, everyone was up tight about it —

Still, his body kept reminding him of the price to be paid for even the suspicion of failure. He knew he was the vital link and he had already made one mistake. He decided to forget the call to Bill; it could only make matters worse, and, doubtless, he wouldn't find out any more than he already knew. He almost thought he would break security and check with Uncle Ed; he knew he could get a line to the White House, even today. Yet something held him back; they must have reasons for their crazy game plan, and he was just a player on the field —

Another part of his mind felt oddly hopeful. There was still today to live, and he resolved to enjoy every moment of it. He cautiously sat up and tested various muscles and joints. Everything worked pretty well, and he supposed that, camouflaged in khakis and shirt, he might offer himself as a fairly good excuse for a normal, healthy young man.

Carter Bedford made no such careful arrangements for getting out of bed. The minute his alarm went off he was awake and in motion. Barefooted and in jeans, he leaped down the back stairs and out through the boot room. The wonderful smell of Berenice's bacon and biscuits followed him out the door. Mist rose from the valley, and the dogwood and redbud trees along the creek bed picked up the first rays of the sun over the mountain.

Albert and Emma caught up with him by the box hedge. They ran between his feet and he had to jump over Albert's wildly leaping form; he almost trioped over Emma then, as she paused to examine the tunnel of a mole that cut across the lawn. He disentangled himself from the little dogs and ran across the lot to the barn, bare feet sending up puffs of dust from the dry ground. No one was in the barn yet, and the horses stood still, relaxing in their final moments of sleep, heads low, and breathing quiet. It smelled divine to Carter— the fresh hay, clean leather, the sawdust on the floor, and even the earthy manure steaming in the damp air; he took a couple of deep breaths and ran down the aisle to the last stall.

"Beau," he whispered. "Beau, I love you." He stood by the pony's head and rubbed between his ears. Beau nuzzled his hand, looking for carrots, and Carter dug into his pocket, bringing forth a wizened orange chunk. "For you, boy," he said. "You deserve more than this, you deserve the world, pony." The soft lips scooped the carrot out of his hand and contented munching sounds broke the silence of the morning.

Carter was almost as pleased with himself as he was with the pony. Jessy had been right, he and Beau had not disgraced themselves among the horses and older riders who made up the Training Division of the event. He had actually come in thirteenth out of twenty-eight competitors in dressage. For a boy of Carter's exuberance and a pony of Beau's headlong desires, the discipline of the dressage test was a real trial. The pony seemed as satisfied as Carter with the results, and, giving up on getting more carrots, he pointedly nudged Carter against the stall door.

"OK, I'll get your breakfast. You don't have to wait for Bob." He let himself out of the stall and started down the aisle to the feed room. He picked up two buckets and scooped one full and one half full. Might as well feed for old Cis, too.

Cissy drifted into the barn, still in her white cotton nightgown, and sleep in her eyes. "I was going to do it for you." She took Chelsea's bucket from her brother and gave him a quick kiss on top of his head, an act which he endured with more than his usual grace.

He stood watching Beau eat. He leaned into the manger and fluffed the hay up appetizingly. The slow, steady, and faintly moist grinding of teeth was mesmerizing. His head had dropped against the door, his eyes, though open, were unseeing.

"Wake up, little brother," Cissy said, gentle. "Wake up, we'll be late." Carter turned to look at her and she smiled. "Hurry up, boy—Mom is hollering at us." In an instant transformation, Carter was off and running for the house.

"Come on, guys," Adrian said. "Breakfast is— God, you're not dressed yet, either of you! Eat, for pity sake, and get your things on!" Cissy snatched a biscuit and shot up the stairs. Carter sat down and assembled a plate of scrambled eggs, bacon, biscuits, jelly, and ham, enough, he hoped, to last until they got to Oak Hill and unpacked the food. He dug into the steaming plateful and watched his mother across the table, swallowing a cupful of tepid coffee while, with one hand, she was making a list on the back of an envelope.

"Don't forget an apple," he said. "For Beau after we win."

"I won't," his mother said. "Don't bolt your food, dear; we've got time to eat." The food bolted, Carter dashed for the stairs, narrowly missing his father coming through the door. "Oh, good, you're here today. Hurry and eat—we're almost ready!" He grabbed the hanger full of clothes that had been laid out last night, gave the boots a quick rub, and hurtled back downstairs. Cissy was there already, helping Mom get the picnic organized and carried out to pack into the Jeep. She was really not such a bad sister; last night she'd helped him clean his tack and then told him to go to bed while she got it packed up in the trailer.

Dad and Mom looked happy, and he was glad for them. He guessed whatever Dad had to do at the office had worked out all right, and Mom was certainly glad the event was half over. Dad was smiling, and Carter saw him pat Mom on the behind as she got in the car, and she laughed and called him a hairy beast. Parents were silly sometimes.

He and Cis got the horses up, and shoved them hastily onto the trailer. Dad helped him close the heavy tailgate and finally they started off, only to be stopped by Berenice hollering after them. "Carter's boots," she panted, catching up to the car.

"Good thing yore head is fastened tight, boy," she said as Carter grinned his thanks to her. Carter sat in unnatural silence next to Cis in the back seat, and listened to Beau and Chelsea shifting uneasily as the trailer bounced over the gravel in the lane. They wore matching sheets to keep the dust off their gleaming backs.

It was cross-country day, and in the midst of his relief at the good showing he'd made in dressage, Carter was concentrating on holding back the cold-blooded fear that creeps into the mind of any three-day rider when he thinks about the big jumps and complicated course still ahead of him.

"Mom, is George going to jump-judge on my cross-country?" Carter's voice was a little hoarse with contained excitement. He wanted more than anything for George to see him and Beau take those big fences.

"He'll be judging all afternoon," Adrian said. "He'll be sure and see you. He's doing the second fence, I think—" Silence settled over the back seat; dreams of glory require concentration of a high order.

The Porsche made good time going out Route 50, and George could almost feel the soreness going out of his muscles as he distanced himself from the city. The air was clean and the mountains rose blue and purple ahead of him as he sped towards them. It was a day to forget everything and to give himself over to the familiar sounds and sights of horses in competition, and to feel the excitement of young riders, testing themselves as well as their horses, guiding them through the intricacies of dressage and then bringing them in steaming and breathless after the cross-country phase. George remembered the sensation of steeling himself for the twenty or more fences on other, long-ago, cross-country courses, and thinking that they were designed as much to test the rider's nerve as the horse's ability. His hurting body ached to be part of it again.

He parked the Porsche and worked his way on foot through the rows of trailers, trucks, and vans, trying to keep out of the way of horses who were backing off trailers, dogs who were tethered to car doors and children who darted in every direction. He was looking for the Bedfords' rig in the competitor's parking area when he almost fell over two definitely untethered dogs. They shot across his path between two vans, and in the fleeting moment he saw them, he recognized Albert and Emma, making good their escape, leashes dragging behind them. His body rebelled at giving chase and he was relieved to see Bob hot on their heels.

Over his shoulder Bob called out to him and pointed across two rows of vehicles to where the Bedfords' old Wagoneer and trailer were parked. George altered his course and started towards it; as he turned, with somewhat less than his usual alacrity, he was run down by Carter who was racing along, trying to tie his number on his own arm as he ran. "Oh, George—Mr. Clements, I mean—I'm sorry. You OK?" He was panting a little, and clutching another pinney in his teeth.

"Gotta hurry. I've got Cis's number. She's going in ten minutes and she's being sick behind the trailer—" Carter grabbed George's hand and dragged him along. "She's always sick before she does anything. That's what they learn at old Foxcroft," he further volunteered.

"Carter, have pity—" George said, and hurried along through the crowd. When Cissy emerged from behind the trailer, she was pale, and, George thought, lovelier than ever. A girl who has just lost her breakfast behind a trailer has no business looking like an angel trailing clouds of glory. She stopped when she saw George and the color came back in her face.

"Oh, you're sweet to come," she said. "You didn't have to get here so early."

The blue of her eyes was breathtaking. It exactly matched the blue Virginia sky, and George knew he would have dragged himself here on his knees for this moment. She held still for him to fasten her number on, and then turned to him with a smile. "Give me a kiss for luck," she said. She trembled slightly as he held her a moment, oblivious to Carter's intent scrutiny, and he hoped it wasn't just the chill of anticipated danger that shuddered through her body.

"You're going to be great," he said, and let her go. Carter stood close to him as they watched her jump into the saddle, effortlessly turn the big bay Thoroughbred, and walk off towards the starting box.

"Come, see Beau." George winced slightly at the tug on his arm as Carter led him towards the temporary stalls. "She isn't going for fifteen minutes, and you can't see only the first little bit. It goes in the woods then, and takes forever." Three rows of wooden stalls had been erected at the foot of the hill where the competitors parked, and through the open half-doors, nervous heads were peering out, and nervous owners stood by some of them, checking tack, conferring with coaches, or simply assuaging their fear with cigarettes, soft drinks, milk, or whatever each one placed his faith in as a pre-competitive tranquilizer.

They saw Beau, perky and eager in his stall, snuffling in frustration at being left alone. George stood at the stall door while Carter went in and lovingly inspected every inch of the little grey pony, and gave him one forbidden sugar lump. He remembered a long ago time, and a spotted pony, and the wild, open plains where he had galloped free, under another blue sky, in another life.

They wandered back for a look at the starting box, and were just in time to see Cissy steadying Chelsea to enter the roped-off area when their number was called. The timer and a judge stood by the box and, at the count of ten, Cissy carefully moved her horse to the starting edge of the box, where she held her until the final count of one, and the timer's cry of "Go!"

As Carter had said, after they galloped across the first field the path went into the woods and the spectators had twenty or twenty-five minutes to get over to the steeplechase course before they would see them again.

Adrian and Henry were watching the start, too,

and after Cissy had gone they all went back to the Jeep, where Adrian was setting out a table with picnic things. "You'd better eat now, Carter," Adrian said. "You go just after lunch, and you don't want a full tummy."

"George has to eat, too, doesn't he? He's got to be at the jump before me." Carter offered George a drumstick with one hand, as he poked around with the other, looking for the biggest thigh.

"Just take the first one you get hold of, Carter. For heaven's sake, you can't be starving after that breakfast." Adrian poured him a glass of milk and turned to George. "What'll you have to fortify yourself for the ordeal? A Coke, or some Gatorade? It can get pretty hot out there." The warming sun and the clear air, combined with the happy excitement of the day, went a long way towards making George forget yesterday and ignore what tomorrow would bring. The aching of his beaten body became irrelevant and, included in Adrian's motherly concern, he felt himself surrounded by something that was strong and good, something that would protect him from loneliness and fear.

"Oh, thanks," he said. "I'll just take the Gatorade. It ought to keep me healthy."

Carter looked up at him, a white milk mustache on his upper lip. "Can you time me with that watch? Does it have a stopwatch?"

"I'm not supposed to time, just judge the jump," George said.

"But you *could* do it, couldn't you, in case they are wrong, or something?" Carter looked at the watch. "It's a neat watch—just do it so I can see

271

how it works."

"OK, I'll do it, and we can check your time after I'm done. I've got to be there till the last of the Intermediates get through, though."

Carter took his hand and looked at the watch. "It's super," he said. "I wish I had one like it. Cis had a stopwatch, but it's not a neat one like this." He sighed deeply. Henry was glaring at him. "But, Dad, think how much better I'd do if I had one and could time myself."

"Tell you what, Carter," George said. "I'll leave it to you in my will."

Owl eyes looked at him, grave and silent. "Oh, George, you aren't going to die! I wouldn't want it then."

"I didn't say it would be soon, buddy." George laughed. Carter was strangely quiet.

Adrian broke the silence. "Oh, gosh, look at the time! They'll be at the jumps." They all raced over to see Cissy on the steeplechase course. George saw Adrian's knuckles, white, twisting the rope shank she was holding, and he saw the little jerking muscle under Henry's eye while they watched Cissy fly over the ten jumps in the field. He realized that he was holding his breath at each fence with a fear he had never felt for himself since the day of the black mustang on the Bar-T Ranch. Later they waited by the finish to listen for the sound of hoofbeats coming through the woods, and then Cissy's cornflower-blue shirt and helmet flashed out of the trees. Chelsea was running strongly with Cissy standing in the stirrups like a jockey. Sweat gleamed on the horse's sides and the sun glinted

272

from the polished metal of stirrups and spurs. Chelsea's ears were pricked forward, alert, and after the finish she ran a hundred yards before Cissy could slow her down and pull up to a stop.

She jumped to the ground and was loosening the girth in one graceful motion. Then, heads down, catching their breath as they walked, horse and rider came towards them across the grass. Cissy was laughing, and her laughter came in little warm gasps. She patted the horse's neck and handed the reins to Bob, who stood by with a bucket and sponge. "How was our time, Mom?" she asked.

"They haven't called it yet, hon. You looked fine," Adrian said. Henry put his arm around Cissy and she grinned over his shoulder at George. The loudspeaker chose that moment to call the fifteen-minute warning for cross-country. "Jump judges in place, please, and riders ready!" George looked at his watch and flashed a crooked grin at Cissy. "That means me, I guess. Man must earn his bread by the sweat of his brow."

"I'll come down and keep you company when I get Chelsea done." Cissy smiled at him over her shoulder; she was rubbing her horse's legs, one at a time, as Bob finished sponging them. She had pulled her helmet off, and wet strings of hair fell over her face when she leaned down. Sweat stained the back of her jersey, and there was a rip in her breeches just above where they fitted into the dust-covered boots; George thought he had never seen anyone so beautiful. Henry coughed and cleared his throat; Adrian patted him on the arm and gave him a thermos of Gatorade and Carter said,

"Hurry up, Mr. Clements—they called you five minutes ago!"

"Thanks, Cis," he murmured. "I'd love it."

"Don't forget you're timing me," Carter yelled after him as he trotted down the hill.

Chapter Sixteen

May 5, 1989

It was a relief to find a folding chair set up for him near the jump. Sweat was running down his back, and his hands felt clammy. His brain was too large to fit inside his skull and his eyeballs seemed to ache from the pressure of it. Behind the dark glasses he looked out from deep circles of pain; he put up a hand to shield his eyes from the sun, now directly overhead. From the chair, he could look across a rolling field to the starting box, where riders would wait for the signal to enter the course. Two or three horses were already standing near the box, one of them skittering nervously, moving to the side and then wheeling suddenly.

The sky was turning from bright blue to a glarey kind of white; the sun beat through the glare and little beads of sweat began to stand out on his upper lip. The Gatorade was cool, and he gulped it down in great swallows while he waited for the first horse to come by. He could hear the announcer's voice and see the horses lining up to start at three-minute intervals. It would be a long time before

Carter would be there; twenty or more Preliminaries had to go first before the Training Levels had their turn.

Somehow he got through the next hour and a half. Cissy came down with sandwiches and a wonderful red apple, and stayed with him through six or seven riders. She was radiant; Chelsea had finished second overall and she was happy as a child about it. "I just had to come right over and tell you," she said, as though it was the most important thing in the world for him to know it; as though her joy wasn't complete until she shared it with him. While she stayed beside him he couldn't think of the pain and he could forget the night and the fear. Then she had to go up and help Carter get ready and he was alone again.

He watched each rider as they came into the fence and mechanically he checked them off; he tried not to remember the night. He didn't hear the loudspeaker announce the beginning of Training Level, and he was surprised when he looked up at the box and saw that one of the three waiting horses was a pony. He felt his heart beating faster and a chill of fear ran through him. Looking up to the starting box where Carter waited, George felt strangely moved by the sight of the little boy, sitting straight and firm in the saddle, giving no sign of the fear that must be gnawing at his guts. His own tired muscles tensed, remembering the old, familiar feeling.

He looked at his watch and waited impatiently for the first rider to start. Carter was going second and, for some reason, he wanted it to be over; he wanted to know that Carter was back safe at the finish line. Maybe then his head would stop throbbing and the hard knot in his stomach would be gone. He was surprised that he cared so much; it wasn't a thing he had been used to for a long time, caring too much about what happened to someone. The first horse cleared his jump without incident. George watched the horse till it was out of sight and then turned to see Carter enter the box.

He and Beau looked very small as they waited inside the roped square, but the pony was still behaving well, and stood quietly during the countdown. He saw Carter gave him a boot and the pony shot forward. They left the box so quickly George almost forgot to push the button on his stopwatch to ON. The pony galloped across the grassy stretch and over the first post and rail fence. He cleared it nicely, and George felt his breath coming easier as he watched them pick up speed in the long open stretch before they came tearing down the hill towards his jump. Then he wanted to call out to Carter, "Slow down, kid! Take it easy!" They were almost flat out coming at the fence. Carter would have to rein in before the jump, and with that much speed—

Then he saw what Carter was doing. He was going for the high side of the combination! He should be taking the in-and-out option, jumping the two lower rails one at a time. Instead, without the slightest hesitation, the boy was driving the pony towards the high side of the jump. The pony, ears forward, muscles bunched, made a perfect approach. Time slowed to a crawl. Four, three, two

277

strides to the jump. Take *off!* take off, now! And the pony flew into the air. George held his breath, his eyes riveted on the top of the fence.

He had done it just right, and he had given it all he had, but, at thirteen and half hands, the pony simply wasn't big enough to clear the high barrier. He hung a toe on the rail and pecked badly as he landed. Carter, from his racing seat, was rolled off onto the ground and the pony, head up and tail in the air, galloped on into the woods.

George ran towards the fence, and saw Cissy racing from the sidelines to meet him. Carter was scrambling to his feet, holding his shoulder a little crookedly as he began to climb back over the jump. Cissy got to him first and helped him over. "Is he OK?" George panted. He had forgotten his own pain in the running, but when he stopped, his head was pounding and his breath was hot and dry in his throat. Cissy held Carter against her for a moment, but it was like holding a nest of snakes. "I'm OK, Cis. Let me loose—I've gotta get back on!" He looked over his shoulder. "Where'd he go, Cis? Where is he?"

George was looking into Cissy's great blue eyes when he remembered the stopwatch ticking away. He was thinking more about the blue eyes than about the watch, but automatically he pressed the button to stop its now needless running. His eyes were still on hers when they heard the blast, close by them in the woods. The air was shattered, and the ground shook under their feet.

He saw her eyes widen, and Carter seemed frozen in her arms as they both stared at him in

278

horror. Nothing moved, and then a woman's shriek rent the air.

"Stay there!" George yelled at Cissy. "Keep Carter there!" and he ran into the woods. The air was filled with dust, or smoke, and voices were calling and the woman was still screaming. He missed the path and the woods were dense where he fought his way through the fifty yards or so to where the woman continued to shriek. He pushed through the thick undergrowth, Virginia creeper and poison ivy wrapping around his legs and thorns tearing at his shirt, and finally came out into a ghastly clearing. The scream was beginning to be words, now, and between the harsh sobs, George could hear what she was saying.

"He just exploded! I saw him—oh, my God, I saw him!" she yelled. George stood at the edge of a cleared space where dust and smoke were rising, obscuring, at first, the large crater that had formed among the trees. The screaming woman was being held by two men; she was bleeding from the side of her face. George began to see through the hazy air, into the crater, and he saw twisted trees, blasted rocks, and bloody scraps of something that must have once been alive. Globs of something red were everywhere, and the smell of burnt flesh, sweet and horrible, filled his nostrils. Then he saw, at his feet, a bloody heap of something, and he couldn't make his eyes stop looking at it, even after he knew that the long grey hairs that looked like a scalplock were the hairs of a pony's mane.

He stood looking at the fragment of bone and hair and flesh and thought he would faint. Voices were calling through the smoke and confusion, and people were running in every direction. "Is anyone hurt?" "Who saw it happen," "Get the Rescue Squad!" People were all yelling at once now, and George could hardly remember where he was. He leaned against a tree.

"What happened?" a voice from somewhere was asking, over and over. Then he realized it was his voice, and he stopped asking. A face materialized in front of him.

"She was judging the jump over there and this loose pony came along—stepped in the ditch and then bang!" The man was pale and smudges of dirt on his cheeks and chin make him look unshaven. George focused his eyes on the face and made himself speak. "What do you mean—and then bang? What bang?" It didn't make sense, and then he remembered why he had come through the trees and brush; Cissy and Carter were waiting for him to tell them what the bang was. The pale face in front of him went on speaking. "They never should have built anything here," he said. "It was a practice bombing range, for God's sake. Shells could have been anywhere—" Then the face drifted off and he was alone.

He had to get back and tell them something, and his head was too addled to think. He started back through the woods, leaving the smoking hell behind him. The stench stayed in his nostrils and tears ran down his cheeks. Now he could hear people coming the other way, running towards the smoking crater. He didn't look at them as they pushed past him; he was struggling to keep on his feet. Everything looked grey, and his body shook. Then he was on the ground, retching, and the heavy air caught in his throat when he tried to breathe. He heard Carter screaming. "Let me go, Cis! He's hurt, Beau's hurt! Let me go!"

He pulled himself to his feet, and ran again, stumbling and almost falling more than once. He caught a branch under his left eye and didn't notice when his sunglasses fell to the ground as he ran on. At last he came to where Cissy stood by the fence, holding Carter fast in both arms, while he hit her on the back with his fists and fought to get loose. "Don't let him go, Cis—oh, my God, don't let him!" He put his arms around them both and held them tightly to him.

Cissy stared at him, and when she looked into his hollow eyes, the question died on her lips. She only breathed the syllable, "What?" and, still holding him with her eyes, she leaned her head down a little and kissed Carter's damp hair. George shook his head and opened his mouth to speak, but words didn't come. He saw the blood-streaked shred of mane that had lain at his feet and couldn't find any words to tell them about it.

Carter's head came up and his face was very white against Cissy's pale blue jersey. "What was it, George? What happened to Beau? Where—?" There was panic in the little boy's voice, but he held quiet in their arms. He snuffled on the back of his hand. "Tell me, George. He'll be all right, won't he? Won't he?" His voice got small and he choked on the words. George remembered the sight of the boy and the pony, just minutes ago, waiting

281

in the starting box, and then he found the words he had to say.

"Carter, you've got to listen to me. You've got to listen close. Your pony was the best pony there ever was, and you'll always love him more than anything you'll ever have, but—"

"I've got to see him," Carter interrupted. "Maybe I can help him. He needs me if he's hurt." He was trying to wriggle free. He was sobbing again, and his wiry, bony little body was shaking. "Let me go! George, make her let me *go!*" Cissy looked at him, wide-eyed, the question written on her face. Tears ran unnoticed down her cheeks, and her hair was wet where Carter had been crying.

George nodded in answer to her question, and she closed her eyes for a moment. "Honey," she whispered in Carter's ear, "Honey, you've got to believe George. You can't help Beau. He's had a terrible accident—"

"But he isn't dead, I know he isn't!" Carter maintained. His jaw was firm, and all that was left of his tears were streaks running down through the dirt on his cheeks. "Is he, George. Tell her he isn't!"

The Rescue Squad sirened past them. People began coming out of the woods and going over to the judges' stand. "Find Mrs. Bedford," someone was saying. "God knows how many more there are; we could all be blown to bits!"

"Get the horses all in," someone else was yelling. "Whose pony was it?" The voices mingled and George and Cissy and Carter stood, stunned, as the commotion passed them by.

282

"Where's Mom?" Carter asked. "Mom will know what happened, she'll tell me. You guys, let me go!" He tried to pull away and George held his arm tightly. "Promise me, and I'll let you go," George said. "Look right at me and promise you won't try and go back in there. It isn't safe until they find out what happened. Whatever it was, it did kill Beau. He really is dead, and you have to be big enough to handle that. It was very quick, he never knew what hit him. Just think of him running free, running free forever now. He loved to run, didn't he—" the tears were running down his face now, and he had to force himself to keep looking into the big green eyes, waiting for the promise. When it came, it was a small jerk of the head. Carter's lips were a straight line across his face and his green eyes never wavered from George's face.

He and Cissy each took a hand, and slowly they walked Carter across the field. George thought he was moving like the walking wounded, and remembered the way he had held his shoulder when he climbed over the fence. "You hurt anywhere, Carter?" he asked. "Your shoulder OK?" Over the noise of bedlam all he could hear was a snuffle and a hiccup. He leaned down and said again, "You all right?" and Carter nodded, a minimum kind of nod. He sniffed again, and threw his head back in a gesture that might have been defiant, or might simply have been to get the hair out of his eyes. He still held their hands very tightly.

They finally found Adrian, at the top of the hill, surrounded by angry and disappointed riders, who were besieging her with questions to which, at this point, there were no answers. Henry stood with her, and finally got her away from the crowd. He was fending them off as best he could, telling them, quite truly, that no one knew right now what was going to happen, and that if they would let Adrian alone she could confer with the other officials and sort things out, temporarily at least. George admired the diplomacy with which Henry extricated Adrian and got her over to the judges' stand where the USCTA representative was trying to calm a group of anguished French riders, whose voices rose in Gallic passion, and whose gestures spoke volumes of alarm.

Adrian's face was white under the shade of her straw hat, and beads of sweat stood out on her forehead. Carter broke loose from Cissy and George and started to run to his mother. She had her back turned to them and didn't see him coming. He ran until he was about fifteen feet from where she stood, and he stopped. He stood there for a minute, and George could see his chest expanding and contracting in little jerks that were almost sobs. Then he turned around and walked slowly away, not looking back once to where his mother stood. He hardly looked at George and Cissy, either, and he walked right past them. Over his shoulder, he said, "I'm getting my stuff out of the stall. I guess Mom doesn't need any more problems." When he watched Carter's unsteady progress down the hill, George thought again of soldiers, wounded in battle, starting on a long, sad retreat.

"Oh, he can't go down there alone," Cissy said,

and they followed him across the field, dodging through the disorganized crowd. Horses were neighing and screaming; those near enough to have smelled the fresh blood were frightened and were fighting to get away from it. Riders were untacking and loading their horses, and cars were edging through the mob, trying to get out. Through all of it, Carter was heading straight for the stall where Beau had been stabled. They watched while he unlatched the half-door and went in. "Let's just stay here and see what he does," George said. "Maybe he needs to be alone."

They sat together on a bale of hay and waited. They could hear him moving around in the stall, taking down buckets and screw-eyes, but they couldn't hear the silent tears that ran down his cheeks while he worked in the empty stall. Cissy leaned against George; he could feel each breath she took as it caught in her throat. They sat in silence for a long time. George couldn't think about anything except what he had seen in the clearing, and he didn't want to tell her about that, so he just sat there, holding her hand and waiting. After a while the door to the stall opened, and Carter came out, dragging a manure basket. Without looking up, he hauled it around the end of the row of stalls. Through the open door they could see a neat pile of buckets, blankets, and tack in the middle of the stall, and clean straw was banked against the wall.

Carter brought the empty basket back, and still without looking at them, he went into the stall and started picking up blankets and tack and buckets until he was holding all he could carry. He looked very small as he came out of the stall with his arms full, a bridle around his neck and a girth dragging on the ground behind him. The sight of her little brother galvanized Cissy into action. "Hey, wait, Brat, we'll bring the rest of it," Cissy called. He didn't look back and he didn't stop. In the stall, picking up the rest of Carter's things, Cissy sighed. "Oh, poor Carter." she murmured. "How can he bear it?" Then she straightened up and looked around the empty stall. She seemed so completely forlorn and lost that George wanted to take her in his arms and hold her forever. He thought he had never seen her more beautiful than she was then and, irrationally, he almost envied Carter for being the cause of her sorrow.

They found Carter sitting in the front of the trailer under the hay net. He wasn't crying anymore, but his cheeks were streaked with drying tears. George leaned over and held out his hand. "Come on," he said. "Let's help Cis get Chelsea and load her up. Then I'll drive you guys home. Your mom is going to be here a while, I think." Carter didn't answer, but he got up and came with them back to the stalls. He didn't say anything the whole time and his face was empty, as though all the feeling had been drained out of him. They walked down the hill together; Carter let each of them take one of his hands, but he never looked at them, or at anything except the grass beneath his feet.

When George and Cissy had gotten home, Carter had stayed with them until everything was done in the barn, and then he went down to the pond, where they could hear him chunking little stones in the water. Cissy sat beside George on the porch and listened to the plunks and splashes of Carter's pebbles. "If he doesn't stop, I'm going to cry," she whispered. "I wish I could just hold him and make him forget everything." George had seen her put her arm around him on the way up from the barn and he had twisted away from her and run to the pond. The ice was melting in the pitcher of tea that Berenice had brought them, and George tried to get her to drink some of it. "I can't," she said. "I really couldn't swallow it. I don't know what's wrong with me. George," she whispered. "George, what are we going to do?"

The monotonous splash-plunk went on, and there didn't seem to be another sound in the world. George felt as though the birds and the crickets and pond frogs were all in the same state of shock he was, the silence around them was so profound. He wanted to say something to comfort Cissy, but his strength seemed to have evaporated as soon as they had reached the safety of the farm. It did feel safe here, after the horror of the afternoon, and holding Cissy's hand was the best thing he could think of to do. She seemed satisfied to sit there, in silence, as though the touch of his hand was an answer, and they sat on the steps and waited for Adrian and Henry to come.

Adrian looked awful. The effort of control had drained the color from her face and she held Henry's arm as though she was afraid he would disappear. "Look," said Henry. "Just what Aunt Mary

287

ordered—a little tea to brace our nerves." Adrian smiled a wan smile and sank to the steps beside George. She accepted a glass of the tea, and drank it in one swallow. She pushed back her hair and patted Henry's arm. "Can't you do us a little better than that, hon? Get us something to drink before I faint?" Henry smiled, and stood up. "Anyone else use a drink?" he asked, and George said he'd come with him and help get them all something.

When they came out with the drinks, the plunking in the pond had stopped and George saw Carter creeping around to go in the back door. Cissy was sitting by Adrian, her arm over her mother's shoulder. "What's going to happen, Mom? What are they going to do?"

Adrian sighed. "God, I don't know yet, dear. The French team is furious and the Canadians have to find a new barn after tonight. I guess we won't know what to do till we find out if it's safe to go on. Lots of the riders are being wonderful, and people on the committee—they're really trying to help, you know, getting places for the horses, things like that." She stopped, and looked towards the barn where Bob was just turning on the lights. "Where's Carter?" she asked. "Poor baby! I saw his face when you brought him up. How is he?" She pushed hair out of her eyes again with a grimy hand. "Ask Berenice just to put out something cold for us, Cis. I'm going to see about Carter."

"Sure, Mom, don't worry about us. I think he went up to his room. He won't talk to us, not at all. Is he going to be OK?"

Adrian put her arm on Cissy's shoulder. "I'm

288

sure he will, hon. Tell Dad I'll be back for my drink in a sec. I think I'll go up and get Carter. I don't like leaving him all alone—he'll need to eat, anyhow."

George watched her straight back disappear into the hall, and something in the gallantry of her approach to disaster made him feel unworthy to be part of the warmth that was holding the family together; the closeness of the early morning was gone, and he yearned to be back in the circle of love that was their strength. He sat with Henry and Cissy in silence, as the sounds of night floated across the fields. "It doesn't seem real," Cissy whispered. "Dad, what was it?"

Henry said he was pretty sure it was something left over from the bombing practice range, something that had escaped detection by the crew that handled the cleanup when the Army left. They were going to send a group in in the morning and check the whole site. "I raised a little hell," he said. "That area was supposed to be clean when they turned it over." He sighed. "Maybe I raised more than a little hell. They'll be there by six-thirty—"

Adrian did get Carter to come down for supper, and they all sat on the screened porch with plates of cold ham and chicken and potato salad. George saw Carter slide off the swing and drift into the house. He hadn't touched his dinner, not even the big chocolate-chocolate chip cookie Berenice had slipped on his plate. Later Adrian went up to tell him good night, and soon Henry went in to make some phone calls before he went to bed. George sat quietly beside Cissy on the porch swing, and the chain creaked monotonously as it swung gently back and forth. George took Cissy's hand in his and it was cold, like the hand of someone in shock.

He took both her hands to warm them and she leaned her head on his shoulder. The loneliness left him and he was safe in her love. Now the noises of summer had begun again and the hush of the afternoon was over. Sounds hung clear in the crystal air, small voices harmonizing to make a little night music for them as they sat there, close together, to comfort each other with the warmth of their bodies. The words of the old Episcopalian marriage vows came to George's mind — "with my body I thee worship" — and he wanted to say it to Cissy, but she began to talk, her voice muffled against his chest.

"I don't know why things like this happen," she said. "I don't know how they can. Poor little Carter, poor little Brat — will he ever be OK, George? I hated the way he looked at supper. He's my little brother, and he looked so *old!*"

For answer George could only put his arms around her and hold her. She was shaking in his arms, and he could feel that she was crying, soundlessly. Her tears were soaking the front of his shirt. "Poor Cis," he said, "poor girl. Your mother is with Carter and she'll see that he's all right before he goes to sleep. Bet he's tougher than we think, he'll be fine in the morning. But how about you? No one worries about you, do they?" She began to shake with silent sobs.

The fireflies came out all across the valley, and the night bird stopped his song. Lights went out in the house and still they sat, swinging and holding each other.

Then the jangle of the telephone, and Henry called from the library, "Phone for you, George."

Damn, they knew where he was, awake or asleep, or in heaven! The call was from Henderson's office, but not from Bill himself. The hour was set for the meeting: tomorrow afternoon at five-thirty. They told him to be at Quantico at five, ready to ride.

"Does he know?" George asked.

"He will," the voice answered. "You won't see him till you meet him on the trail. You will ride with him, just like any day, and when you've decided on the place, you tell him. You stay with him during the talk. Sharovsky will have one escort as well. If it's anything else, abort."

"How?" he asked the voice, irritated. "How abort?"

"Get him out; get away, back to the helipad. OK?"

"I don't have the signal yet," George snapped. He was sick with thinking about it, and tired of the Mickey Mouse that went with it.

"Pick up an envelope at the gate when you go in. It's all you need to know." The phone in his hand went dead.

Cissy was still sitting in the swing, waiting. "Do you have to go?" she asked when he sat beside her.

Very gently he kissed her forehead, and held her to him. "Go to bed, love," he said. "Sleep, and have good dreams; dream about me, dream that I love you." And quickly, while he still could, he turned and ran to the Porsche.

When he let himself into his apartment, he didn't even switch on a light. He flung himself on the bed and lay without moving, without feeling. Hours later, sleep came at last.

Chapter Seventeen

May 6, 1989

For once, Cissy was up early. She helped Berenice put things out for breakfast. "I couldn't sleep, Berry," she said. "I just kept thinking about Carter and poor Beau, and I woke up before it was light, and I couldn't think of anything else." She picked up a biscuit and buttered it.

"Chile, Lord knows it's luck it weren't Carter 'stead of the pony that's dead. Think how your mama'd feel then." Berenice could always find an alternative worse than any situation you were in, and somehow, this morning it irritated Cissy instead of comforting her as it was meant to.

"I know, Berry, I know—but think how Carter feels! He plain disobeyed everyone and tried to make Beau jump that big fence, and I know he thinks it's his fault; he said so yesterday. Now he won't talk at all, not about that or anything else—" Cissy had looked in on Carter before she came downstairs. He was awake, and staring out the window, sitting cross-legged on his bed. She had asked him how he was and he had just waved a listless

293

hand in her direction and gone on looking out the window.

"Yore daddy's already been and gone to work," Berenice volunteered. "That man! He don't have no time his own, now, does he?"

"Oh, Berenice, what are we all going to do? Mom has to deal with the mess at Oak Hill by herself, Carter won't talk and Dad has to tear into town—" She felt like crying again, but probably wouldn't have had to, except that Berenice came over and put her strong arm around her and said, "There, now, baby, don't cry—" and she immediately burst into tears on the bony gingham shoulder beside her.

Adrian came in, pale beneath her tan, and there was dark circles under her eyes. Cissy looked at her, and was ashamed to be bawling, "wallering" as Carter called it, on Berenice's bosom. She splashed some water on her face and went to her mother, with a fairly good likeness of a smile on her face. "Have some breakfast, Mom," she said, and pulled her to the table. Adrian leaned over and gave her a kiss on the cheek and sank into a chair. She smiled a crooked sort of smile and said, "That was some day, wasn't it, Cis? Poor, poor Carter—I tried to talk to him this morning—"

"Me, too," Cissy said. "Mom, what's going to happen to him?"

"It'll take a while, hon, but he'll be all right. It just isn't any good to tell a little boy with a dead pony that he'll forget it one day, or even that life will go on and there'll be other ponies. It's just so hard to watch him and not be able to do anything—" Her voice trailed off as they heard sneakered feet slowly coming down the back stairs. He didn't even pause by the breakfast table. "Hi, Mom, hello, Cis," he murmured as he went past them, straight into the kitchen. Adrian got up and followed him.

"Honey, have some breakfast. You'll be sick."

"He isn't dead," Carter said, looking away. "My pony isn't dead. I bet he's back in the barn. He ran home after the explosion and they just couldn't find him."

Cissy stood behind her mother. "George told you, remember, Carter?" she said. "Remember, he went and found out, and he wouldn't have told you if it wasn't true. He knew, he went and looked. Don't try to believe something that isn't so—you'll just feel worse."

Carter pulled away from his mother and stood, very straight, in front of Cis. "Tell me what he said, then. Tell me what happened if you're so sure he's dead."

"Oh, Cis,—" Adrian looked over Carter's head at her daughter.

"You believed him yesterday. He said you were big enough to deal with it, and I think you are, too."

"If he's dead, we have to bury him. We have to say a prayer and put up a marker. I'm going to have a bronze thing made to put on his grave, like Dr. Rogers had, and we'll have to go get him and bury him. But he isn't dead. That's how I know, because we didn't bring him home to bury him." As though this was settled for good he walked past them into the breakfast room. Adrian couldn't bear to see the hard line of his jaw; the baby softness that had been there yesterday was gone, and there was a quiet resignation in the set of his mouth that cut through her like a knife.

He sat at the table and looked at his food. " 'Scuse me, Mom. Can I go to the barn now?" He didn't look up, and Adrian sighed. "Sure, dear, go see what Bob is doing. Maybe you can help him get things straight. If you want to, you can give Carol her exercise. Heaven knows, I won't have time to. Get Bob to go with you—he'll like that. He can take Colonel; Dad hasn't ridden him in weeks."

Carter gave a small nod and went out. Adrian picked up the phone and dialed the barn. "Bob? I'm glad you're there. Carter's on his way down— please keep him busy this morning. I've got to go to Oak Hill, and I need Cis with me. He's so upset—let him ride Carol; go with him on Colonel. I can't thank you—" She turned to Cissy. "We'd better get over there. D'you mind coming? I don't even know where we begin—" Cissy looked up. "Sure, Mom. I'll come with you. Maybe Joan and I can do something with the competitors. We'll find someplace to put those horses till you decide what to do."

She went ahead of her mother out through the screen door. The porch swing was moving idly in the breeze, creaking back and forth just as though two people were sitting in it, swinging. Cissy sank into the soft pillows and remembered the night, the fireflies and the singing bird. It had been in an-

296

other life, years ago that she had sat there with George. The light of day seemed hard and she closed her eyes to remember the sweetness of the night. Remembering, she smiled and the sun felt warm and she absorbed strength from the memory, as healing as the heat of the sun. Adrian stood in the doorway a moment and watched her daughter. The line of worry across her forehead smoothed and she smiled. "You look like the cat that swallowed the canary, Cis. Can you come back into the real world long enough to give me a hand with these files?"

Once beyond the hedge, Carter veered off towards the upper field. He wasn't going to go and ride Mom's horse, and he couldn't, couldn't ever again, go into the empty stall at the end of the aisle. He circled the barn, and saw Bob pushing the wheelbarrow out the back door. Before Bob could look up, he ducked behind the spring house, and, keeping the building between himself and the barn, he sprinted up the hill.

Safely over the crest, he turned left and followed the fence row to the corner. He was in the hay field and bees hummed around his knees as he ran through the dew-damp grass. He could just barely smell the clover that would be in full bloom in another week, and the smell of it was another hurt, for haymaking was one of the best things to do on the farm, because it meant fresh, new hay for Beau and he always took him some for dinner the first night they cut it. Thinking of Beau he hurried across the field to the corner. There he climbed the fence and hid in the bushes by the edge of the road, listening for a car. He heard the distant rumble of an engine, and risked a look up and down the road. The dust from their Jeep was settling in the distance, and, reassured, he crossed the road and climbed the fence on the other side. The hedge hid his progress across the pasture from anyone on the road; except for a few startled heifers he was unnoticed as he ran. If he went straight across this field and the next one, he would be at the Big Woods.

Oak Hill lay on the other side of the woods, almost five miles for Adrian in the car, but Carter knew all the trails through the woods, and now he began an easy jog along the shaded paths. He figured he had about two miles to go, about a half hour of steady jogging. It was cooler under the trees, and the color came back in his face as he ran. He tripped over a root and fell flat on his face. His hands burned where they skidded along the pine-needly ground. He stopped when he came to the stream and let his hands hang in the water till they were cool, and he splashed water on his face. As he sat waiting for his breathing to get back to normal, he heard, at first far away, but then coming closer and closer, a series of barks and happy yelps, and he knew he was not alone— Albert and Emma were tracking him and when they bounded out of the underbrush they pounced on him with the joy of discovery. It was useless to try to get rid of them; Carter disentangled himself from them and got up. They dodged in and out under his feet as he ran, and he took a certain comfort from their presence.

Mom and Cis would be by the road, way at the other side of the reservation; they were meeting with the officials and the other competitors. They'd be too busy to go look for Beau; too busy to stop him from looking either. It was a thing he had to know; he had to know for himself what had happened, and he guessed he would have to see for himself how to get Beau moved back to be buried on the hillside behind the barn. Cis's old pony was there, and Duncan, the best black lab that ever lived, the dog he remembered from as long ago as he had known anything. Beau deserved to be there, and nobody could keep him from bringing Beau home.

His footsteps thudded evenly for a while, and he passed through the deep forest, where big hemlocks closed off almost all the light from the sky. He was running beside a rocky creek that came down from the mountains, and he stopped with the Jack Russells to gulp down a few handsful of its clear water.

He took one more swallow and ran on, feeling the water sloshing in his belly. The forest grew lighter and he could hear engines, vehicles moving over the rough ground. He was at the back of Oak Hill.

He threw himself on the ground and inched forward. These were Army guys working here, and he would have to infiltrate carefully. He heard the trucks drive off, and the sound of their motors died in the air. It was high noon, and the sky was blazing clear; there wasn't a breath of wind. There wasn't a sound, either, except the excruciatingly loud snap of twigs and the scraping of his body over the ground. Emma and Albert skulked beside him.

He stopped to listen. Maybe they had all gone and he could go right out in the clearing and see for himself. He strained his ears and heard a murmur of voices, and a low laugh. They had left a guard.

When he inched ahead to the edge of the trees and brush, he had to scramble over some big rocks, and there were broken trees and branches on the ground. It was harder than ever to be quiet. But he could see into the clearing now, and saw that there were just two guys sitting on a log, eating sandwiches and talking. There was a lot of funny equipment around, big dishes with aerials, a long caterpillar thing with a scoop, and a couple of regular bulldozers sitting idle in the hot sun. He had a clear view of everything, and except for the equipment and the two guys in uniform, there wasn't anything else there. Beau was gone!

They had taken his pony away and not told him! Throwing caution to the winds, Carter stood up and ran, leaping over the debris and stumbling on the uneven rocky ground, straight towards the men on the log. He would make them tell him; they would have to tell him what they had done with his pony.

The dark-haired man looked up and saw him. He poked the other one in the ribs. "Look, Joe," he said, "we got company for lunch." Carter slowed to a tentative walk and then stopped in front of them. He knew he was dirty, and he felt blood oozing from a skinned place on his knee. He stood there, catching his breath while Albert and Emma ran circles around him, their noses to the ground.

The second man swallowed the bite in his mouth and picked up a can of soda. "Where'd you come from fella?" he said. "Nobody s'posed to be here, kid. You better run home, just like you run here." He took a gulp of Coke. It sounded awfully good to Carter, but he hadn't time to ask for anything; only for his pony. He caught his breath, and hoped his voice would come out sounding right.

It didn't. It was a raspy squeak at first. "Where is he?" he croaked. "Who took him away?"

"What you mean, kid—who you talking about?" The dark man was puzzled.

"My pony, my pony Beau. He was here—"

"Oh, Jesus," the man called Joe said. He turned to his friend. "Hell, Jack, it was his pony. What we gonna—?"

Jack was staring at Carter, as though he was growing wings or a second head. What was the matter with these men? Couldn't they answer a simple question?

"Son," Jack said. "Son, if I was you, I'd just run on home. We can't tell you nothing. Go ask your daddy."

"He doesn't know," Carter said. "That's why you're here. You're supposed to find out what happened, that's what you're supposed to do." He felt his face getting redder. His voice was just fine now, and he was shouting. "That's all you're supposed to

301

do; you can't take my pony away. I got to take him home—I won't leave him here."

Then he knew he was crying and he ran at Jack, and hit him as hard as he could, again and again. "Give me my pony! Where did you take him? Where is he? Where's Beau?" He felt strong hands holding him and pulling him away from Jack and all the stretch went out of him. He just felt weak and tired and he wanted to lie on the ground in the sun forever, or at least until dark. Emma and Albert were barking now, excited by Carter's sudden rage.

Joe set him on the log, and they sat down with him. They didn't seem to be mad at him for fighting them and Carter was ashamed of what he had done. "I—I'm sorry. I guess I got upset. I didn't mean to hit you. I j-just want my p-pony's body so I c-can bury him—a d-decent burial." They had to bend close to hear what he was saying.

"Well, son, we can't tell you what happened, we ain't able to say anything. That's why we're here now, to keep it quiet like. See, it's all secret, they ain't sure what happened anyhow—"

"You know, you know and you just won't tell me!" All of his strength seemed to be coming back, and something in his face must have changed Joe's mind.

"What the hell, Jack, let's tell him. He ain't gonna believe it, anyway."

Jack thought it over. "Kid, we'll tell you what these scientific types were talking about, but you promise you won't tell no one what you hear, OK? They ain't told us, but what we heard 'em say was this: Nothing in the ground blew that pony up. It was something in his shoe that done it."

Carter's eyes were wide, and the freckles stood out on the whiteness of his skin. "He blew up? What do you mean? What happened?" He held Jack's arm, and his tough little fingers dug into the flesh.

"Take it easy, kid, calm down." Jack turned to look at Joe. "My God, he didn't know at all. Look, kid, I'm sorry. You asked, you wanted us to tell you. I don't know where your pony is, I never saw him." He looked at Joe again and shook his head in warning. "Honest, we never got here in time to see him. All we seen is this shoe they found, or what was left of a shoe, anyhow. It was all blowed apart—they said it must of been some high explosive somehow got in the shoe. Jesus, I don't know what to think myself, kid. Don't cry about it, OK. Come on, have a little Coke." He offered him the half-empty can and, mechanically, Carter swallowed some of the warmish liquid.

He stood up, a little shaky, but not crying. He would never cry again, for Beau, or for anything. He pushed his sleeves up and wiped his mouth with the back of his hand. "Thanks, you guys, thanks for telling me. I guess I better go home now." He turned to go. "Oh, thanks for the Coke, too." He stumbled back across the crater, not seeing the rocks or ditches or broken branches. He saw four gleaming nails in his hand, and heard the hammer blows as they were driven into Beau's right forefoot.

It was a long walk home. Carter had plenty of time to think, and it just didn't make sense to him. He'd wanted to get his pony back, wanted to see him one more time. Now that Beau had actually disappeared, Carter began to think he had never been, maybe he'd never had a nice grey pony who could jump any fence in the world—

He remembered going at that last fence. He really had meant to jump it the way Jessy told him to, he really had, but Beau just seemed to drift naturally towards the high side and Carter had sort of let him do it. Maybe he couldn't help it, maybe Beau was too strong. He heard his heart thumping inside his chest and he remembered the sound of Beau's hoof hitting the rail. Then it hurt too much to remember the awful moments after the jump. He wanted to stop thinking but, plodding home under the hot sun, Carter's mind took him over the fence again and again.

He could see the jump, and Beau galloping towards it, just like a movie running inside his head. Then, horribly, the picture expanded, the camera panned to take in a wider scene and he saw Beau running off and then he was in Cis's arms and George was there. The sound exploded in his mind again and he saw the look of fear in Cis's eyes and felt himself go rigid.

Last night, that was as far as the picture went, but now, inexorably, it went on. He saw Beau running, running free and kicking up his heels, neatly sidestepping the dragging reins. Then the camera ran backward. Beau ran back into the clearing and

304

then the bang. In a big glare of light, everything vanished, and Carter's eyes burned. Then, out of the light, came a shining horseshoe, twisted and broken, and from it fell four gleaming nails, shooting sparks like firecrackers.

The glare hurt Carter's eyes and then he realized he was looking at the sun, straight over his head. He had stopped to rest in the shade of the big lone oak in the pasture, and only closed his eyes for a minute, but when he opened them, the sun had moved and the shade was gone. He sat up and saw big green suns wherever he looked. The Jack Russells, motionless for once, were asleep at his feet.

It was all a dream. He'd call Bud and ask him if shoes could explode. Those guys were crazy! They just didn't want him to find out what really happened. He ran to the fence and climbed over. He ran down the dusty road and up the lane. The Jeep was still gone and he found Berenice and Bob in the kitchen.

"Here he is, Mama," Bob said. He looked happy to see Carter, but Berenice seemed ready to burst into tears, something Carter had never seen, nor believed possible.

"No thanks to you he's here," she said, and ran across the kitchen to grab him as though he would vanish if she didn't have hold of him. "His mama said you watch him an' you let him git off by hisself—! Where you bin, boy? You scairt us half to death! Pore chile—" she turned on Bob again. "He coulda bin lost for all you paid attention—"

"Mama, he never come to the barn. I never seen him atall this mornin'." Bob looked miserable. As

305

skinny and tough as his mother, he always looked as though he hadn't had enough to eat for about three weeks and, today, under Berenice's withering scorn, he seemed to shrink even more. Carter felt sorry for him.

"It wasn't his fault, Berry, honest it wasn't. I don't need to be watched anyhow. I just had something I had to do, so I didn't bother him. Don't be mad, Berry, please—"

"Oh, honey, it's just you scairt us so. It don't matter—here, eat a nice hot piece of bread an' butter an drink this big glass of milk." Berenice was herself again. There wasn't much in life that she couldn't cure with a stomach full of good cooking.

Carter took the milk and gulped it down, but while Berenice was buttering the bread he said, " 'Scuse me, Berry, I guess I'm just not hungry. I think I'll just go upstairs." Instead, he went into the library and closed the door. He picked up Dad's phone, the one that didn't have any extensions in the house. Then he dialed Bud Fleming's number.

"Bud, can you come over? Now?" he asked.

Bud really didn't want to go anywhere. It was one in the afternoon and he had just got back from doing the horses at Paper Chase Farm. It had been his idea to take the afternoon off and go fishing. He'd been at Oak Hill all day Saturday and Sunday and started at seven this morning. He was looking forward to a few quiet hours by the pond and a couple of nice bass for dinner.

"Bud, I need to talk to you—can't you come? You could cut the pads off Chelsea; you said they ought to come off as soon as we could do it." There was a little silence on the line. Then, "Please, Bud?"

Poor little kid, he must feel rotten, Bud thought. He remembered the light in those green eyes, was it just two days ago? when he had reshod the pony and Carter had been talking a streak about how well they would do, and he had showed him the nails from Quantico and put them in for good luck. Some luck they brought him. First the poor kid fell off and then the pony—he didn't want to think about the pony. He had been one of the first people to get there after the explosion and he had seen what had happened. Seen far too much of what had happened; he had seen it over and over again in his mind ever since. He woke up in the night and Corry asked if he was having a bad dream. "You was groanin' and moanin' like a cow with bloat," she said.

"Sure, kid, I'll be over in a little." There had been something in Carter's voice, a hard kind of edge, that made him uncomfortable. The fish would be there tomorrow, and it was true he could get the pads off the horse today as well as any time.

He was picking up the first hind foot and getting ready to cut the protective leather piece from inside the shoe when Carter cleared his throat close beside him. "Bud," he whispered, "Bud, can a horseshoe explode? Can it just blow up by itself?"

307

Bud put the foot back on the ground. "What do you mean, a shoe explode?" He picked one up from the back of the truck. "Look, it's solid iron, you know what it's like, it's just metal. Nothin' there to explode—" He handed the shoe to Carter.

"It has holes in it," Carter pointed out. "There are holes all around it," he went on, running his finger around the shoe, following the groove on the bottom. "Something could be in the holes that could explode, couldn't it?"

"Nothin' in the holes but nails." Bud picked up the horse's foot again. "How about you hand me that knife, son? Nope, nothin' in the holes could explode."

"What if something was wrong with the nails?"

"Can't be nothin' wrong with nails," Bud said. "They all come right out of this same box—" He stopped, mid-sentence. What he was thinking was too crazy to waste thought on. Still, his mind wouldn't let go of it—the nails in Beau's feet were the ones Watson had given him; it was part of that promotion he told him about, the guy from England with the fancy ideas. They weren't out of the same box as any other nails, they were the same kind he'd nailed the shoes on Townsend's horse with. Well, then, nothing had happened to the Ghost, did it? He'd better get hold of his imagination and get back to work. He began to cut the tough leather with a sharp, curved knife.

Carter eyed him, cannily. "Those special nails weren't out of the same box, were they? You said—"

"Come on, Carter," Bud looked up. "Where'd

308

you get this idee anyways? Who told you anything about shoes blowing up? Who told you that?"

When Carter finished telling about his trip to Oak Hill, Bud put his knife down on the truck. "Let's us leave the pads on front a while. Let's see if your mom's home and tell her about it, like you told me." They walked up the path together and Bud was surprised to find Carter's hand in his as they walked. The poor little kid was really shook up.

Adrian was unloading the Jeep. "Tell her about it, Carter. See what she thinks."

It took a long time for Adrian to sort out the jumble of words. "Honey," she said, "are you sure this is what they told you? Maybe they were just kidding you. Dad was sure it was something they didn't get cleaned up from the old base. It was a target range, after all—" She turned to Bud. "What's that about the President's nails? Were they different, or what? Talk slow and let me get it through my head."

Bud explained to her how he thought for fun he'd bring these nails to Carter; they seemed to him like any other nails, but Watson had been so excited by the idea of making some money on promoting them, he'd humored him and gone ahead and used them on Townsend's horse and brought the leftovers out here.

The more they talked to Adrian, the more Bud began to feel like a fool for taking any stock in the whole exploding nail theory. She talked such good sense to him that finally they were both trying to convince Carter to forget the whole story. The little boy walked with him back to the barn.

"I don't care what Mom says." Carter picked up a handful of nails. "They could have something, something we can't even imagine, they could make the nail out of it and get you to put it in Grey Ghost's feet and they could *kill* the President." He looked up at Bud and his eyes were very big. "They could do it any day they wanted to, Bud, they could kill him and it'd be our fault, for knowing and not doing anything."

Bud took him by the shoulders and looked him in the eye. "Carter, listen. I can't go running down there and pull the Ghost's shoes and say it's a plot to kill the President. They'd make sure I was crazy. It'd get Watson in trouble, there ain't a way in the world to explain it to anyone. Carter, I just can't do it."

The eyes never changed. "How are you gonna feel when it happens, Bud? How are we all gonna feel? You better go and do it, Bud. Let me go with you?"

Bud loaded up his things and got in the truck. He still had time to catch a fish or two before supper. Carter hung over the window of the truck, just his hands and face visible to Bud. "Bud, please. I'm scared." The voice was small and a little shaky. Something about it was like a fingernail on the blackboard, and a shiver ran down Bud's back. The fish were going to have to wait. He took the key out of the ignition and opened the door. "OK, you talked me into it, I'll go down there now. I ain't gonna be able to sleep now you got me going on this, but one person that ain't comin' with me is

310

you, Carter Bedford. Your mom has got enough to worry her without you runnin' off, too. Just leave me use the phone in the barn and call Corry, and you scat up to the house." He got out of the truck and watched Carter start towards the house before he went in and dialed Corry.

"I gotta go in and do a horse at Quantico. Need anything from town on my way back?" Corry was not unused to these delays. The welfare of some horse's feet always seemed to get in the way of everyday life. She felt like saying, "Just pick up some supper on your way home, because yours will be long cold when you get here." But, instead, she told him to take his time, that she'd be there whenever he chose to come home. He hung the phone up and scratched his head. Fool kid, make up a story like that and get everyone all riled up over it. Best he just go down and pull the shoes, reset them, and dump the nails off the bridge on his way home. Danged if he would tell anyone what he was doing, but at least he wouldn't be kept awake all night waiting to hear the morning news, and find that Carter's story was not so crazy after all.

As soon as Bud went into the barn, Carter abruptly reversed direction, and, keeping the pickup between himself and the barn door, ran across the barnyard. The gray cat jumped up as he went past, and started for the barn. Carter threw himself on her and picked her up. "No, you don't go in there and make him look out here," he whispered and tucked her under his shirt.

He cut over to the side of the truck and climbed up onto the bed. Behind the anvil and the wooden

311

box that held Bud's tools, there was a heavy tarpaulin, covering boxes of shoes and nails. Carter slithered over the anvil and wedged his way under the tarp, between the boxes. The cat began to resent her confinement. Carter raised the tarp enough to let her out. "OK, go ahead, he can't see me now." He gave her a push.

"Cat, git out of my truck," Bud called, coming out of the barn. Carter held his breath. He heard the truck door open and Bud crank up the motor. He stretched out, luxurious, under the tarp, and the truck bounced down the lane.

"Carter," Adrian called. "Carter, come on in!" Her voice echoed softly across the rolling hills.

Chapter Eighteen

Washington, D.C., May 6, 1989

It was after four o'clock and Henry was at his desk, staring out the window. He'd been going over and over in his head the tangle of information that had come into his office since he'd gotten there a little after nine this morning. There hadn't been much time to think about Adrian, or even poor Carter, desolated by yesterday's disaster. He wondered if they had found out what really happened, and what Adrian was going to do with the shambles of the first Oak Hill International Event.

The telephone interrupted his thoughts. He supposed it would be the report from the lab on what they had found in old Vlascki's basement. With so much on his agenda for getting the President off safely to New York, he was sick to death of the reports on the old defector.

He got the first wind of it right after lunch, but it had started early in the day. The Park Police had answered a call to Rock Creek, where a suicide had jumped from the Calvert Street Bridge, landing on the parkway. He had narrowly missed landing on top of an early commuter who was enjoying the beauties of Rock Creek Park at daybreak in an open convertible. Clearly, it had been a mistake to listen to the city government, which recently had demanded removal of the high guard rails erected in the early eighties, designed to prevent exactly this sort of activity. This was the second person in two months to seek death on the pavement almost a hundred feet below the high stone arch of the bridge.

When the police got to the scene, traffic was stacked up for five miles on the parkway. The driver of the convertible was in the road, trying to get cars funneled into one lane, around the body of the old man, where it lay crumpled and twisted on the pavement. The man was plainly shaken from being so narrowly missed by a falling human being, and the woman, still sitting in the car, had buried her face in the morning paper, finding the reported disasters less upsetting than the real one at her feet. Two more squad cars arrived and took over traffic control while the first policeman questioned the driver. All he could tell them was, "I was just driving along when suddenly, splat! — I thought I was going to hit him. Oh, my God, officer — " He sank back into the seat of his car while the officer finished the report.

There was no way to identify the old man. His wallet held nothing but a few dollars; no credit cards, no driver's license, and no employee's ID card. His clothes were neat and clean, certainly not the rags of a derelict. Yet there was something outdated about the way he looked; or perhaps it was foreign, a sort of Middle European look. The expression of serene resignation that was frozen on his grey face reminded Sergeant Kowolski of his Polish grandfather.

He was fingerprinted and delivered to the morgue. The fingerprints turned up an identity. He was Jurek

Vlascki, ten years in the United States, a defector from Moscow. No record of residence or occupation. He had seemed to drop from sight right after his naturalization in 1984. At 10:15, as a matter of routine procedure, notification went to the CIA and to National Security, where the information was put on file. When the report went to National Security it was brought to Bedford's attention, where it was put on hold. Nothing about it pointed in the direction Henry was looking; he could deal with it after New York was secure. In any event, the press would get hold of it soon enough, and the papers would be retelling, in every sentimental detail, the story of Vlascki's dramatic exit from the Soviet Union, and his arrival in the United States a little more than ten years ago.

Then, about one o'clock a call came to the Seventh Precinct in Georgetown. A woman called to say that she was worried about the old man who lived downstairs in her duplex. Her children had been after her for a couple of days because he seemed to have gone and left his little dog in the basement and they could hear it crying. They couldn't raise a sound in the house, and they thought someone should check on the old man. Could someone come out to Burlieth?

The lieutenant thanked her for the information and said he would send a squad car over. Probably another of those calls that enliven a police officer's day—a break-in that didn't happen, a missing child that turned up hiding under the bed, or a vicious dog that was found to be a chihuahua, but still he'd better check it out. When Officer Williams and Officer Hansen stopped at the corner of 37th and Tunlaw

Road a woman ran out to meet them. "Oh, thank goodness you've come," she said. "We're really worried about him—"

She made them follow her around the end of the row of houses into the alley, and down the alley to the third backyard where there seemed to be a disastrous nursery school picnic in progress. Two little girls clung to the mother, crying, three other children sat on the fence, staring at the house, and one little boy was being pulled away from the window he was trying to look into.

Hansen stepped through the gate and got out his pad. "Who made the complaint? I need your name and address."

The first woman interrupted him. "Look, Officer, can't you just help us get in and see what's wrong. These children are driving me crazy, they haven't let me alone since last night. Listen, you can hear the dog—"

He listened, and he could hear some plaintive yelps and whines coming from the basement. "OK, lady, we'll see what we can do, but first I gotta make the report." He resumed his questions, and Williams sat down on the back steps. One little girl, her awe of the uniform overcome by curiosity, came up and took his large black hand in her small one.

"Come get Boris," she commanded. Her face was wet with recent tears, and she had to sniff a couple of times before she could go on. "He's afraid, and Mr. Bronski isn't here."

Her mother picked her up. "Janet honey, if Mr. B. went away and left Boris, I'm sure he left him food and water. Let the nice policeman alone; he'll go in and look. We have to be sure Mr. Bronski is all right, too." The child regarded her mother with distrust and wriggled down. She sat on the step with Williams again until Hansen had finished.

"Doesn't anyone have a key?" he asked.

"Of course we don't, or we'd have gone in," the woman snapped. "He'd never have given us a key to his house, he was too private. No one ever went into his house except my Billy and Janet," she went on. "They used to play with his dog."

"Well, let's see what we can do, then," Hansen said, and the two policemen climbed the cement steps up to the back door. When it had been a single-family house this had been the sun room, and the door was made with twelve panes of glass to let in light. They tried the knob and it wouldn't give. Williams said, "Y'all stand back, now," and smashed one pane with the butt of his revolver. He reached through with a gloved hand and opened the door.

The sound of shattering glass startled everyone, and a little boy whispered, "It's a real gun!" One of the women shooed the children off the steps and began picking up the splinters of glass. They could hear, through the open door, the sound of Boris's sorrowful cries, rising for a moment and then fading into silence, as though he lacked the strength even to call for help.

Both officers went into the kitchen where they stopped, to listen for the dog's cries. At first it was so quiet they thought he must be dead, but then a small wail came up through the door to the basement. This door opened easily enough and they cautiously descended the stairs, Hansen in the lead. Feeling his way in the dark, Hansen bumped into a door at the bottom of the steps. "I can't find a knob," he said. "Give me a light."

The flashlight shone on a heavy steel door that looked like the door to a vault. There was no knob, just a combination lock. "Jesus, what have we got here?" Hansen breathed. Williams peered over his shoulder and shrugged. "Maybe we can get in from the outside," he suggested. When they came out the back door without any rescued little dog in their arms, fresh tears greeted them, and they were some time explaining that they had to find another entrance or they wouldn't be able to get him out at all.

A skinny little boy showed them down a narrow stairway to the outside basement door. This door opened easily. It wasn't even locked, and Williams grinned sheepishly at Hansen. They shrugged and went in, only to find themselves shut in a little hallway. "No wonder it wasn't locked," said Hansen. They were facing another vault door.

They called the precinct and were given reluctant authorization to call a locksmith. By the time he arrived on the scene an hour later, the knot of children and mothers had mostly sunk down under the mimosa tree, and a couple of the smallest children were asleep. They couldn't hear the dog anymore at all, and Hansen and Williams were resigned to a wasted afternoon. The man looked at the lock, muttered an obscenity, and brought more tools from his car. It took him forty-five minutes of sweaty work, kneeling on the floor of the basement. At last, he heard a smooth click-click inside the heavy steal of the door and, when he gave it a gentle push, the door moved silently inward.

Hansen stepped past him and looked into the room. On the floor, a crumpled ball of fur moved slightly, and a whimper reached his ears. He picked up the almost weightless little animal and handed it to Williams. "He's alive," he said. "Take him out to the ladies." Williams looked at him and said, "What about the old guy? I thought we came here to find him—" He held the dog in one of his huge hands

318

and carried it up the stairs.

"Here's your dog," Williams said, and a little girl held out her arms for it. Her mother picked her up as she hugged the poor animal and kissed its rank fur. "We'll take him up and give him some water," the mother said. "And if he's not OK, we'll take him to the vet when Daddy's home—"

"Joe," Hansen hollered up from the basement. "You better check upstairs for the old boy. I'll take another look down here." He turned and went into the room. He immediately felt a blast of cool air, and heard the air conditioner running. He found a switch and when he flipped it, he blinked his eyes in a glare of light that blazed from the ceiling. The chill he felt wasn't entirely from the air-conditioning. His spine tingled unaccountably and he looked around the room in disbelief. In front of him was a workbench that held, instead of Harry-Home-Owner tools, an incredible array of scientific apparatus, an immense computer, some dish-shaped antennae, and a gleaming rack of tiny, useless-looking tools. A jewelers' loupe lay on the table and pages of finely written equations were spread beside it. The walls were lined with books, and in one corner there was a row of little doors, like safes. Red warning lights flashed above each safe, and Hansen could hear another sound besides the hum of the air conditioner.

Over the sound, he could hear them above him, faintly, calling, "Mr. Bronski, are you here? Are you OK?"

He found Williams upstairs. "Any luck?" he asked. Williams shook his head. "Not here," he said. "A few days' mail in the hall, nothing personal. I guess he split." He shrugged. "Anything down there?"

"Come look," Hansen invited him. They studied

the room again. "What the hell do you s'pose—?" Hansen scratched his head.

"Joe, you better stay here and keep it sealed off. I'm going back to the lieutenant with this. It gives me the creeps."

The lieutenant listened to his report. Then he called Headquarters to see if the disappearance could link with the suicide in Rock Creek Park. He decided then to pass the word on to Langley and the FBI. The old guy could have been up to any kind of funny business from what Hansen had told him. Headquarters called back and said they were sending a crew of specialists out to see what the stuff in the basement was.

It was four-thirty when the FBI called Henry. "We think you'd better know about this," the agent said. "We identified a suicide this morning; it was Vlascki, you remember, the defector in the seventies? The Einstein on the Volga? He came here, got citizenship, and then vanished. Your people have our report on that." He paused and Henry told him he'd been rather busy with the New York thing and hadn't felt the need of any action of Vlascki. "Well, of course you haven't," the agent said. "No reason you should have. That's why I'm calling you now. We've had a report from the DC police that sheds more light on Vlascki. They had a missing person call, and, you guessed it, it was the old boy himself. Neighbors called in that an old man in Burlieth hadn't been seen for a couple of days and his dog was locked in. When they got in the house, he was gone, all right—they matched up the prints and sure enough, it was him, but, good God, what they found in his basement could blow up the Kennedy Center!

You knew that was his field—?"

Henry interrupted. "They identify anything he was working on? Anything we ought to know about?"

"Our people are down there now, checking it out. You'll be hearing if they pick up anything useful—" Henry thanked him, and hung up.

It didn't sound related, but it kept nagging at him, like the missing piece of a puzzle. He picked up the red phone and dialed the White House. "Bedford," he said. "Look, I'm hearing things I don't like. Can we reschedule *Air Force One?* Let's get him out of here tonight, say seven o'clock? Tell him I think it's urgent." Of course the flight time tomorrow hadn't been announced, but you could be sure that it was known exactly where it shouldn't be.

"Negative," the voice said. "He's not here."

"Not here? What do you mean, not here?" Henry snapped. He felt cold, and his hand gripping the phone was shaking.

"Gone riding. At Quantico. Clements is with him. You know how it is—he does what he wants to."

"Raise him on the radio. Get busy. Get him back to the White House." Henry hung up. This was all he needed. Whatever was building up, it was definitely unfriendly, and he wanted his man where he could keep an eye on him.

Then the report came through on his screen from the old man's laboratory. Definitely some very heavy radioactive material was there, a basket of shredded paper, some schematics for electronic chips, high-powered optical equipment, and a handful of horse shoe nails! These had mystified the research team; evidently none of them knew what they were until the girl at the analysis lab identified them, and upon analysis found them to be perfectly ordinary nails, made from an alloy of nickel and lead. Henry was staring at the report on the screen when his secretary rang him. "Mrs. Bedford is on the phone," she murmured, and then Adrian's voice came through.

"Henry, I hate to call you, but I don't know what to do. Maybe you ought to know this, but then again I feel silly even bothering you with it."

"Shoot, hon, what's on your mind?" A domestic difficulty would be welcome relief, Henry thought.

"Well, I told you, it's silly," she said. "I got home from Oak Hill and Carter came running in dragging Bud Fleming. He'd called him, himself. Oh, first he went to Oak Hill . . . Yes, he walked there through Big Woods . . . I know I told him to stay with Bob at the barn—"

"Well, don't be too hard on him; he's had a rough couple of days—"

"Oh, it isn't that; it's what he told me. He talked to a couple of GI's there, and they told him—I know this sounds silly, but they told him Beau exploded himself, that one of his shoes exploded. It got Bud all upset, then, because it seemed like there were some nails he'd used on Ed Townsend's horse and he saved some out to use on Beau—for good luck, he told Carter. It just sounds crazy. I think those men thought they were being funny with Carter, but then, I wasn't sure what to think—I guess I thought you'd want to know." And the missing piece of the puzzle fell into Henry's lap.

Chapter Nineteen

Quantico, May 6, 1989

Bancroft was worried. It was the middle of the morning, on Monday, when he got the call. He couldn't imagine what they wanted from him; there wasn't anything else he could do. He understood that his job would be over when he got the nails to the farrier, so what did they want from him now? He didn't like meeting at the Iwo Jima, even at lunchtime, and he couldn't figure out why Orlov had planned it that way.

The bartender knew him now, and if Watson came in and found him with Orlov—Orlov, whose rendering of the English language sounded like a comedian playing a Russian peasant—he might get the wind up. It had been three weeks since he'd seen Watson, and the man might be getting suspicious, wondering about the heavy cash he was supposed to get from the sales. Watson had called him twice and left a message, but he hadn't returned the calls. He had better get the phone disconnected before Watson caused trouble.

He parked around the corner from the Iwo Jima, and sat a few minutes in the car. The place opened at eleven, and he didn't want to be the first customer. Better let it fill up a little and then find a table in the corner. Orlov was coming at quarter after; he was supposed to find a table and watch for him.

At five after, he put out his cigarette and got out of the car. He looked both ways down the street before he pocketed the keys. He left the door unlocked in case there was a need to leave in haste. Then he sauntered along the hot sidewalk; the sun felt like high summer in this shabby suburb. There were few trees to shade the sidewalk, and the one-story, World War II houses that lined the street offered little protection. The area was a bedroom community for families of enlisted Marines, stringing along beside Interstate 95, and the constant roar of traffic from the six lanes leading north to Washington rang in his ears as he turned the corner in front of the Iwo Jima.

It was dark in the bar, and cool. Already some Marines had found tables and were ordering sandwiches. A pretty girl came to the door and hesitated till a young man caught sight of her and went to bring her to his table. Bancroft nodded at the bartender and smiled, without speaking. He hoped he wouldn't recognize him, wouldn't remember when he had seen him before.

The corner booth was empty, and he hung his hat on the hook by the bench. Luck was with him; a waitress came to take his order, and the bartender didn't even look his way. "Thank you, young lady," he smiled at her, "I think I shall wait for my friend before I order. We shall be having lunch —"

"Can I bring you a drink while you wait, sir." Her

324

teeth were dingy grey, looking out of place under the bright lipstick and certainly offering no competition for her startling gold hair. He was about to answer, when, looking past her, he saw Orlov outlined against the door. He was not alone. His burly form pushed through the door, almost eclipsing the slight figure beside him. He hesitated and peered into the dim interior of the room. Apparently his eyes were adjusting slowly to the relative darkness. Bancroft leaped to his feet. "Excuse me, dear," he murmured to the waitress. "I see my friend." He got up and started for the door. Orlov saw him and crossed the room.

"Will that be three for lunch?" the waitress asked. Bancroft nodded. "I'll just get your menus and be right back," she said.

Like a big bear, Orlov settled himself in the booth before he spoke, or so much as acknowledged Bancroft's presence. The young man with him slid in beside Bancroft as Orlov almost entirely filled one side of the booth. Then Orlov spoke. "Good, you have come," he growled. "What can you tell me? Does it go well? Or have you, as they say, dropped the ball once more?"

Bancroft froze inside. Christ, he'd got the fucking nails, he'd had the fake boxes made and he'd had old Watson eating his story like Christmas cookies. Why was Orlov bringing up the other time? It had been the last time they'd used Vlascki, five or six years ago, and Bancroft had been the leg man. He'd almost got caught, his cover nearly blown, and after that he had been kept on ice until now. They'd brought him back because he was the one who could get to Vlascki, and they needed him.

The waitress came, and they ordered. Orlov looked at him again. "So, tell us," he said.

"Well, you know I found Vlascki for you, and you must have seen his work. "The old boy is a genius; we've always known that. It should go — "and he smiled ingratiatingly, "if you forgive the pun, it should go like clockwork."

Orlov didn't smile, and the young man — Bancroft could see now that he was dressed in the fatigues of an enlisted Marine — simply looked puzzled. He hadn't spoken, and now he was sitting beside Bancroft, staring morosely at the Coors ad on the wall. Once in a while he chewed on his thumbnail, or what was left of it. His nails were the nails of the perennial nail-biter; they were a quarter of an inch shorter than his fingers. Just looking at them made the hair rise on the back of Bancroft's neck, like the sound of chalk on a blackboard.

Orlov broke the silence. "Vlascki is dead," he announced. "A regrettable incident. He seems, inadvisedly, to have jumped, to have thrown himself, perhaps, from a bridge, onto the paving below." He smiled, and Bancroft thought of a crocodile. "Our old friend found himself unable to fly; he found that even geniuses have no more wings than others have . . ." he chuckled.

Bancroft's face was white. "Why?" he asked, and he knew the answer before the question was out of his mouth. Vlascki knew too much, that was his crime. Vlascki had obeyed orders, and this was his reward. He knew what he had done, and that knowledge had been his death warrant. Bancroft forced himself to look at Orlov. He seemed to hear a watch ticking, and it was marking the hours of his life. His voice was thin when he spoke.

"What if they find who he is?"

Orlov glanced over his shoulder and his eyes signaled silence. The waitress was setting down a heavy tray behind them. None of the three men spoke while she placed the food in front of them. "Be anything else, sir?" the girl asked Orlov, and he shook his head. "Y'awl enjoy your lunch, then," she said and was gone, lost in the shadows of the now crowded room.

"They won't find out soon enough. Schoolchildren, these Americans! Days it will take to find who our Vlascki was, and then our job is already done! Poof! He is gone, and with him the only other, besides us and the fool Henderson, who know. Henderson is a coward, that is why he is ours, why he cannot leave us or betray us. Then only you and I, and our friend Albert, here." He waved a huge hand at the Marine, who managed a weak smile in return for the recognition.

Bancroft was silent. Albert nodded at Orlov, and turned to Bancroft. "It's only us three, and they can never find us."

Bancroft nodded agreement and picked up his fork. His mouth was dry, and, though he chewed the fish until it was mush, it was still hard to swallow. He washed it down with the beer, and it lay in his stomach like a rock. "Only us three," Albert had said. Nobody had mentioned Clements at all, and he was certainly going to know. He choked down another bite and looked across at Orlov, who was wolfing down his food like a man without a care in the world. He didn't want to bring it up, but he needed to know. Clements would have the answer when he got to the barn that afternoon. His instructions would be waiting for him; the guards at the gate already had an envelope to give him when he arrived at five o'clock. Then he would know, too.

"Clements will know," he finally said. "When he finds out what he has to do, he will know." He studied the pale piece of fish growing cold on his plate. It was better than looking at the self-satisfied face and the dangerous little eyes across the table.

"You are stupid, my friend," Orlov murmured. "Do you think that we have thought of nothing?" He drank deeply from a thick mug of beer. "Of course he won't know! The idiot believes he gives a signal only. He thinks he signals that Sharovsky shall meet him in the woods. Of the nails, or their purpose, he knows nothing. Even Henderson knew at once that we had overestimated the man."

He paused. "He is scared now, and will not hesitate. But, no, he knows nothing of Vlascki, nothing of us. He believes Henderson, who, though a coward, is not a fool. We sent friends to give him the watch, and they convinced him he had no choice. Very gently, they convinced him, so gently that he believed they were his friends, and Vlascki's watch he accepted as his own." He sighed. "Ah, Vlascki, your greatest work, you shall never see it. Is pity." He shrugged, and pulled a pipe from his pocket. Deliberately he stuffed the tobacco in, and, with long, steady breaths, he drew it alight. His small, slanted eyes were fixed on Bancroft.

"Is pity," he continued, not shifting his gaze, "is pity only we three shall live to know victory, to see Townsend dead." Bancroft felt cold sweat dripping under his arms. He looked at the man sitting beside him, then questioningly back to Orlov. Why were there three of them? One of the first principles of the trade has always been to use the least number of people possible in any operation. Every additional pair of eyes, every extra pair of ears, and every added mouth constituted one more chance of discovery, one more factor of risk for them all.

"Albert here, you wonder?" Orlov grunted. Bancroft gave the slightest nod of his head.

"Spetsnaz, you know? You have heard who they are?" Orlov smiled. "There Albert was trained." He turned to the Marine. "Tell him what you do now, no?"

Albert smiled. "I work on the base. This is my third year in the corps, but it's my fifth year working for Orlov. For six weeks I've been assigned to yard duty around the barn. I've been a good Marine, dumb and obedient, and when I asked for duty at the barn, it came through. Nobody really wants to shovel shit and swat fucking flies all summer. They were glad to assign me—" He sat back and inhaled deeply on a thin, dark cigarette.

"I don't get it," Bancroft said. "If you're in the barn, why fool with Clements?" With one perfectly good man right there, it was insane to bring in another, and, in Bancroft's view, an untrustworthy one at that.

"You know more about their security than that, fella," Albert continued. "No one sees the big boy at the barn. No way. They fly him in by helicopter; they land back on the preserve and only Watson can take his horse to meet him. I tried that; I asked if I could. It almost lost me my job down there. Don't ask, they said. Boy, mind your own business and move that shit. I couldn't get near him." He drew on the cigarette again.

He went on. "Clements is the fair-haired boy around Townsend. He can ride with him any time. He's got the radio in his car, in that Porsche the sonabitch drives. They call him on it and say where to meet him, and it's hi-ho, Silver." He yawned. "It ain't a job I want, no way. When she blows, everything with her blows, and it's nitey-night for Clements."

"He's not coming back, either, you mean?" Bancroft chewed silently on the cold, pale fish. "You mean there are only three of us who will know?"

Albert nodded and Orlov growled again. "Can I bring you gentlemen some coffee, or how about a nice piece of apple pie?" Bancroft jumped at the sound of the girl's voice, and then shook his head. "Nope, I've had plenty, thanks," he said.

Orlov ordered pie with ice cream and black coffee. He handed the waitress his empty plate and looked over at Bancroft's almost untouched food. "Lost your appetite, my friend? Don't be afraid; this isn't the last meal of the condemned." He chuckled and sucked on his pipe. His evil little eyes glinted under the black brows. Bancroft shrugged his shoulders and attempted a smile.

Another thought occurred to him, and it was not a reassuring one. Supposing Clements didn't blow up with Townsend, if he somehow set the charge off from too far away? The blast would occur, and from a safe distance, Clements could see what happened. He would know, then, what he had done and they would all be in danger; the radio in his car was a direct channel. All he had to do was ride back to the barn and get to his car. He could report within minutes.

Albert must have read his thoughts. "And what do you think old Albert is doing, shoveling shit? Having a Sunday school picnic? No siree, Albert is there to see that the boy never gets to his car. He never gets near that radio. Watson goes to mess while Clements rides with Townsend. He leaves good ole Albert to watch the barn. Clements is dead as soon as he starts for the car." He was watching Bancroft's face. "Not to worry; he doesn't get away. If Vlascki's toy doesn't get him, Albert will." He patted a bulge in the baggy pocket on the leg of his fatigues. "You're as safe as in church, man. Relax."

In his apartment in Georgetown, George was pulling on a pair of brown field boots. He thought the leather smelled of everything that had been good in his life, and he stopped with one boot on and the other in his hand and sat on the edge of his bed, remembering. He remembered the smell on a Christmas morning in Wyoming, when there was a new saddle for the spotted pony, and he remembered how his first pair of hunting boots smelled when he would get up in the dark and polish them, listening, as he worked, to the hounds in the kennel across the valley where they waited, awake and eager, for the sound of the horn across the hills. Then he remembered the smell of clean tack and boots in the riding hall in Prague, and the major's voice, barking commands in the arena, and his mind hurried on to remember the summer evenings in Lincoln. There was the blessed coolness of the stone barn, and Joey, with her funny wide grin, coming into the tackroom, hiding something behind her back. She'd kissed him and wished him happy second anniversary, and showed him the boots. She had saved money from her riding lessons, and sent to England for them, a fortune in brown field boots, paid for with days of standing in a dusty ring, telling children to sit down, keep their hands quiet, keep their heels down, and get their hands out of their laps when they jumped. He knew how hard she worked when she taught, and how long it must have taken to save enough for the boots; he had held her in his arms and they had kissed and laughed. They were so happy, then.

Now he held the boot in his hand, and he found he could think of Joey without pain, at last. The memory was sweet now; he could take it out and think of it without the sadness. He could polish it like a precious stone and hold it in his hand, just as he held the boot, and remember the love and the childlike joy of it.

Then he caught sight of the clock across the room, and the moment was over. He jumped to his feet and pulled the boot on. The past was gone and the reality of the day pressed in on him; as he leaned over to fasten his spurs, his head throbbed, and the leathery smell seemed bitter now, and fear hovered in the back of his consciousness, crowding out the remembrance of joy. He had been in the apartment all day, and he had spent a large part of his time trying to reach Henderson on the phone. The only answer he got was from the mechanical voice on tape, and all it told him was that Mr. Henderson was unable to answer the phone just now. The last time it told him that, he had slammed the receiver down so hard that his phone skidded off onto the floor. Where was the damn man?

Henderson's vanishing act was probably what worried him the most. It gave him a sense of isolation; he was all alone in centerfield, without a glove, and god damn Henderson was gone. He tried to think rationally, to find a scenario he could be satisfied with, and he couldn't come up with much. There was the possibility that Henderson had to arrange things at the other end, had to leave town to do it. And, of course, there was security to think about; probably no one could get through to the people involved with this thing, now that it was in motion. God, it was a short day! When you don't want something to happen, time goes by so fast you can't see it. He realized he was wishing that five o'clock would never come, and here it was three-thirty. Just time to get dressed and start fighting the traffic on 95.

In spite of the fear and uncertainty, there was the other side of the coin. George had known for years that the one desire of Ed Townsend's life was to put an end to the growing cycle of terrorist attacks on the free world. If this meeting was necessary to that purpose, then George knew it was what Townsend wanted, and he ought to be glad to be a part of it. Still, he couldn't help wishing it was over, and that they were cantering back to the barn together in the light of the setting sun, with Sharovsky's promise securing the success of the New York summit.

Then, Townsend could dream dreams of peace, and he could call Cissy and tell her he loved her. His body wouldn't hurt any more, and the throbbing pain in his head would be gone. He would drive through the night, down the lane beneath the fragrant apple blossoms, and he would find her sitting in the swing, waiting for him.

He pulled a sweater over his head as he ran down the steps. Still running, he crossed the street. He vaulted into the open car, clamped his seat belt, and turned the radio on. WETA gave him a Vivaldi quartet that helped his thoughts to leapfrog over the next few hours; as he spun across the bridge, oblivious to the noise and traffic around him, he saw, instead, the long shadow of the mountain across a field where fireflies winked like a million stars and a breeze from the valley moved through the trees with the sound of a sigh.

Last night when he and Cissy had sat in the swing, the same little breeze had brought the fragrance of the blooming apple trees to them up the hill. "Even if they smell better," Cis had said, "I still like dogwood time the best. At night, the ones in the valley look like fluffy clouds, and in the daytime, the Judas trees look like flowers in the snow." She leaned back and moved the swing with her feet. George was glad to hear her talk about trees; anything except the awful afternoon. He wanted her to be able to forget it, at least for tonight.

"Why do you call them Judas trees," he asked. "I always called them red buds."

"Oh, it's what Berry told us," she said. "It's a story they have in the mountains."

"Tell me," he said. "Tell me a story from the mountains—"

She leaned against him and put her hand in his. Her voice was soft and it sounded to George like music. "They tell it in their Sunday school," she said. "How the red bud was once a big tall tree, and it only had leaves, no flowers. Then, after Judas betrayed Christ, he went out and hanged himself from one of its branches, and ever after that it had blossoms of Christ's blood, and it got to be a little twisty tree because it was sorry and never wanted to hang anyone again. She used to tell it to us at Easter when we were little and I think we really believed it." When she stopped talking she looked up at him, and in the dark, he could see her great pale eyes, wide open, as though the child who believed was still inside her.

"I don't see why the tree was sorry to hang him," George said. "After all, he was a traitor, wasn't he? He sold Christ to his death for the thirty lousy pieces of silver. It should have been glad to hang him." He wanted her to keep on talking; he could have listened to her voice all night, sitting in the creaking swing and holding her cool hand in his, while she told him bedtime stories so that she could forget, for a while, the little boy crying himself to sleep upstairs, and he could forget the boat, waiting offshore near the Chopawamsic.

"Well," Cissy said smartly. "That's the whole point. Berry says he thought he was doing the right thing. That's what they teach them in their Sunday school. The point is, there was this prophecy, you know, the Old Testament thing. One of them *had* to do it, like, to fulfill the prophecy. It was supposed to be the way it was done, the only way Jesus could die and save us, so poor old Judas thought he had to do it. After all, Jesus picked him out himself and said he was the one. So he did it, even though he hated it, and that's why he hung himself after, and that's why the tree was sorry for him." Now her voice was quiet and there was only the creak of the swing as it swayed in the light air.

Then, from another world, the scream of the telephone had recalled him to reality, and he had left Cissy, sitting alone in the swing, her dress pale in the moonlight, and her eyes big and solemn.

Well, he was going back tonight, when it was all over. The Porsche inched along behind a stinking eighteen-wheeler bearing an admonition to Drive Safely and spewing out clouds of diesel fumes as it crept south on 95. At last, the turn off to the base, and a winding road through the trees.

The two men on the gate knew him and waved him on with a crisp salute. He hesitated, remembering the instructions, and one of the two ran over to the car. "Wait up, Mr. Clements," he called. "Got a letter for you."

It was on State Department stationery, probably from Henderson's office, he thought. "Thanks, fellas," he said, and was astounded at the nonchalance in his own voice. He had been afraid the trembling in his hands would translate into a nervous stutter when he spoke. Without opening it, he folded it casually, and stuck it in his shirt pocket.

He drove on till he was out of their line of vision, and slowed down. He stopped the Porsche by the side of the road and he took out the envelope. Now he would at least know what he was supposed to do. The message was typed in capital letters and bore no signature. The initials B.H. were typed at the bottom.

"AT YOUR DESTINATION START STOP-WATCH MECHANISM ON YOUR WATCH. AFTER ONE MINUTE AND BEFORE TWO, STOP MECHANISM. SIGNAL WILL REACH VESSEL OFFSHORE. STAY WHERE YOU ARE TILL CONTACT IS MADE."

He read it over again and studied his watch. It was his same old sports watch, the one he had so often timed himself with on cross-country or checked his speed on training rides. It had been to Czechoslovakia with him when he was fifteen, a new watch, a present from his father. It had been through a lot with him. As he studied it, wondering what in hell the message meant, he found himself looking for the dent on the bezel, near ten o'clock, a dent that had been there since the time he had crashed in the steeplechase and broken his wrist against the timber of the fence.

Funny, he hadn't noticed before; the dent wasn't there. It was his own watch in every detail, worn with age, crystal scratched, everything to seem like his own. He remembered waking Saturday morning and feeling the band. True, it had been far from his first priority then, but he remembered wondering why it was loose. He thought his wrist ought to have been swollen after the working over they had given him.

Now he viewed the watch with loathing. It was as though his own watch had betrayed him. He'd been wearing some crazy sci-fi machine ever since Saturday morning, and never even noticed. He wondered idly whether he was ever going to get his own old faithful watch back, and pulled his sleeve down to cover the imposter on his wrist. It was almost five; he accelerated and screeched into the yard. Watson was there, and he had Chester tacked and ready to go. "Thanks, Sergeant." George smiled at him, and took the reins. "Tell me where he is?"

It was like any other day, the comforting sounds of the horses in their stalls at feeding time, and the sweet smell of leather and of summer hay and of the skin of clean horses—except that he could hear the insistent ticking of his watch that wasn't his watch, and it was turning his blood to water. It didn't make sense. Henderson could have given him the damn watch, or whatever it needed to send the signal. Why did these spooks have to play like children? They must get their ideas from prime-time TV— Watson's voice startled him. "Down the Jeep trail to the power line—you can pick him up there. I'm goin' over to the mess while you're here," he said. "Albert'll finish up here—but I'll be back before you and the Boss git done. Take good care now, you hear?" He pulled the baseball cap low over his forehead and ambled across the yard to where his old Chevy was parked. George waved to him as he left, and then he was alone, except for Albert.

He reached up to unhook the cross-ties that held Chester in the aisle and his watch was caught in a ray of light slanting through the barn. No, not his watch—*their* watch. The watch he was wearing yesterday, timing Carter's ride just before the— He heard the sound in his head and felt the nausea tearing at his guts. He remembered Cissy's eyes as she held Carter in her arms, and he remembered reaching for the watch on his wrist to stop it from ticking off the useless minutes.

Chapter Twenty

May 6, 1989

Bud cut through the back way to pick up Ox Road, going south from Fairfax. He was driving too fast, and he plugged in the fuzz-buster. He kept telling himself he was out of his mind to believe the kid. The story was crazy; he'd driven those nails in himself. He could still see the box they came from—no, they didn't come from the box with Queen Elizabeth on it. Watson brought these to him another time. They weren't out of the box he'd been using. They were only in Grey Ghost's feet and in Beau's.

He mashed down on the accelerator, trying to make time before he hit the Interstate. It was almost four-thirty, and traffic leaving the city was beginning to be heavy. He hoped he wouldn't have trouble at the gate because it wasn't the right time of day; he always came in the morning. When he passed Lorton he slowed down. The radar detector was sounding off, probably in response to security at the prison, but the last thing he wanted was to get pulled over for doing sixty-five in a forty-five-mile zone. He saw that his hands were sweating as they gripped the steering wheel, and he was holding

339

it as if he thought it was trying to get away from him. It was a spooky story, all right, that the kid had told him. He wished he'd never listened to Watson and his crazy English nail idea in the first place.

Thinking these thoughts he sped across the new four-lane bridge at Occoquan, and he fell in behind the southbound traffic on 95 by four-thirty. The radio played country music, and he chewed in time to its rhythms. Bud always chewed, a fact which seemed to fascinate Carter, who would watch wide-eyed when he spat, as he was able to do, accurately, a distance of six feet through a gap in the fence straight into the manure pile.

His chewing slowed as the music became a commercial for Koons Ford and Lincoln at Tyson's Corner. He waited for the music to start, but instead, "the latest news from the nation's capital" was announced. Thinking his own thoughts, Bud let the voice drift past him: "—the upcoming summit meeting in New York. Security has been strengthened around the UN building and the White House has declared a news blackout surrounding the President's departure. *The Washington Post* has reported that, according to reliable sources in the Pentagon, the President will leave Washington tonight, while *Air Force One* will make its scheduled morning flight without him. White House Press Secretary Brian Donnelly denies knowledge of—"

Jesus, it gave him the creeps! Bud swore at the driver of a small Toyota pickup that cut into his lane, and he spat expertly out the window. He'd be glad when he got there and got those shoes off. Damned if he'd tell anyone why he was doing it; they'd think he'd lost his marbles, for sure; he might even lose his contract if they thought he was crazy. Suppose he went in there and said, "Hey, I just

340

think I'll pull these shoes before they explode." How would that look, anyhow?

Henry sat with his hand on the phone after Adrian's call. The winking numbers on the digital clock mocked him, relentlessly displaying the advance of time. He watched 4:58 and 4:59 blink past while Adrian's voice echoed in his ears. "Carter said they told him the pony's shoes exploded—can you believe that?" Three hours ago he couldn't have believed it, but there were the horseshoe nails, lying in the middle of old Vlascki's shop; and there was old Vlascki himself, dead on the pavement in Rock Creek Park. Adrian was right, it didn't make sense, no sense at all unless you suspected that in less than a quarter of an hour the President would be riding on the horse that had his feet full of nails straight from Vlascki's laboratory. The clock winked again and it was 5:00. Henry picked up the phone and dialed the radio-phone operator at the White House.

She put him through to the helicopter crew, who picked up immediately. "Is he with you?" he asked, almost before they could answer. "Is he still with you?"

There was a crackling on the line, but over the static he could hear the answer. "Negative, sir—left in the Jeep ten minutes ago."

Henry's face was white. "Raise the Jeep for me then," he almost barked into the receiver. While they were trying to make the connection he picked up the other phone. "Get security at Quantico—cover the barn area. Yes, I mean now. We have to pull him in—it may be for real." A voice reached him from the two men in the Jeep. They were on their way back to the heli-pad. The President and Johnny were on the horses, had picked them up five minutes before.

The air in his office felt cold, and chilled Henry's back where sweat was soaking through his shirt. He snapped at the man in the Jeep. "Get Grimes. Get Townsend off the horse and away from it . . . I don't care, just do it *now!*" The White House man with Townsend should be able to be reached — well, they'd better be able to reach him. What in hell could the old boy have put in those nails? And what made it go off? He remembered the sound that shattered the air at Oak Hill and he saw the look on the faces of the men who had been there when it happened. He remembered George, smudged and blackened from the smoke, his face showing white beneath the grime, bringing Cissy and poor little Carter up to the trailer.

A buzz on his desk interrupted this moment of contemplation. The crackle of the radio phone, then a voice, tense and hurried. "We don't read Grimes, sir. We aren't getting through — there must be some interference." The radio man on the Jeep sounded almost frantic. "Keep trying, damn it," Henry snapped. The system so studiously planned to protect the man was only as reliable as the men who administered it — where in hell was Grimes? Was he even with the President? Henry was drawing little squares on his desk pad while he waited word from Quantico security, or from Grimes, damn him. From a corner of his mind, like the annoying hum of a mosquito in a dark room, he heard George's voice. "Oh, lots of times he doesn't let Johnny come — he wants a good gallop now and then." Damn, he thought, we're lucky if he's anywhere near his escort, or his communications.

One half mile behind Bud, a car from the Secret Service worked its way south along I95. As the driver worried through the traffic, the other man in the car put on a head set and began calling the security number at Quantico. He, too, was trying to raise Johnny Grimes.

"Come in, Equus Two," he called. "Come in, Equus Two." The set crackled and there was no answer. "Step on it," he said to the driver, and the black car began weaving in and out of the dense mass of southbound vehicles. He tried again to raise Johnny. At last, across the static, a voice came through. "Equus Two here. What's up?"

Never taking his eyes from the road, the driver said, "Just tell him to keep the man away from the horse, Ed; that's all they told us." When this information was relayed, Johnny's voice wavered through to them again. It was hard to hear over the interference, but it sounded as though he said the President was already riding the horse. "Well, get him the hell off! Get back to the 'copter," Ed snapped into his phone.

"I don't read you." Johnny's voice was clearer, but it sounded like the voice of a man under a terrible strain; panic was very close to the surface. Ed shouted, "Get him off the godddamn horse! *Now!*" and Johnny heard him.

"Roger, I read you," Johnny's reply came faintly over the air.

Deep in the woods, he looked the little palomino in the eye as he stood beside her. "Please be good, horse," he said. "Stand still, for God's sake." Trembling, he led her to a stump, and managed to heave his fat ass onto her back. He surveyed the two forks in the trail and wondered which way he should go.

343

Bud reached the gate to the stable area. An extra car was there, meaning the President was on the grounds, and Bud pulled to a stop to show his clearance ID. He'd never come at this time of day before, and he didn't recognize the guards on duty.

They took his ID inside and ran it through the computer. His skin felt clammy while he waited. Maybe they wouldn't let him in; it wasn't his regular day, and certainly five o'clock wasn't his regular time. The guard brought his card back. "It looks OK, Mr. Fleming. Go ahead in." He looked about sixteen years old and smiled a smile so polite that it would have made his mother proud of him. Bud saw no need to volunteer his reasons for coming at this hour of the day.

"Thanks," he said. "I'll be out in about an hour." He was going to have to reshoe the horse before he could leave. Jesus, he wouldn't be home before seven-thirty. All because of that crazy kid's story. He wished he was home now, having a beer on the porch, while Corry fixed supper and his boys shagged a ball around the backyard.

The boy went to the car by the gate. "It's the blacksmith," he told them. "He checks out OK; he comes every two weeks." The man behind the wheel of the car nodded and waved him on.

He could see the Porsche as soon as he rounded the corner. He wondered who else was here; the car certainly didn't belong to Watson, or to any of the other guys who worked at the barn. It was feeding time, and someone was bound to be there, but not in a silver Porsche! He could see the silhouette of a man and a horse against the light coming through the hall of the barn. A man in fatigues was near the door, sweeping the dirt floor.

Bud stopped the truck and opened his door to get out. From the corner of his eye he saw the tarp in the back begin to move, and then he saw Carter slither over the tailgate and streak towards the barn. The boy's feet kicked up puffs of dust as he ran, and Bud stood where he was as though mesmerized, half in and half out of the truck. How had the kid got in the truck, for God's sake? Mrs. Bedford would be all done in with worry, the way she cared about that boy.

Carter was yelling as he ran. "George, George, wait! Don't don't—" He stumbled and fell to one knee. Bud ran towards him, but Carter was up and in the barn before Bud was halfway across the yard.

Coming around the corner into the relative dark of the barn, Bud could see, at the far end of the long aisle, Carter flinging himself headlong at the man beside the horse, still yelling, almost sobbing. "It was the nails, George—the *nails!* They'll kill the President like they did Beau!" He had to catch his breath. "We got to stop them, George—Where's Grey Ghost? Bud has to pull the shoes!" He was tugging at George's arm with one hand and wiping his nose with the other sleeve. He didn't seem to know he was crying, and he didn't even notice Bud running up to them.

George took him by the shoulders and held him still. "Hey, buddy, how'd you get here?" he said. His face was white under the tan, and Bud could see little beads of sweat forming on his lip. "Calm down and run that by me again—"

"He sneaked up on me," Bud said. "I never meant to bring him here—"

"Tell him, Bud, tell him what we found out." Carter's voice was small but carried a weight of authority now. The sobbing breath had stopped and the tears hung on the lower lids of his eyes.

"I guess you're goin' to think we're crazy," Bud began. "See, I had these nails that some joker was tryin' to sell Watson. We put 'em in the Ghost's feet—an, well, I had some over so I just put 'em in Beau's feet for Carter. I dunno, I thought he'd feel good about it, you know how kids—"

George's blue eyes were cold and hard as crystals of ice and his voice was unsteady. "What about the nails—? What in hell—?" He didn't finish and Bud swallowed some spit, coughed, and started to tell him. Carter interrupted.

"The Army men told me, George. They said it was Beau's *shoe* that blew up and killed him and it had to be the nails, nothing else can blow up about a shoe, can it?" He paused. "So Bud has to get them off the Ghost. Where is he, George—where?"

There wasn't a sound in the barn except the slow, grinding clink that Chester made, chewing his bit in boredom as he stood tied beside them in the aisle. It seemed to Bud then that they had all frozen to the spot where they were standing. George didn't move, he just looked at Carter with eyes that had gone blank. Then, under his breath, so they could hardly hear him, he said, "He's riding him."

He pushed past Bud and Carter and ran for his car. "The radio," he shouted over his shoulder as he ran. Bud started after him down the aisle, but before he got out of the barn he saw the Marine put down his wheelbarrow and race after George. The man sprang like a panther and threw George to the ground where they rolled briefly, struggling in the dust. The Marine saw Bud coming, and rammed his right hand into George's chest. Before Bud could get to them, he saw George fall limply back to the ground. The Marine knelt by him briefly and ripped the watch off his wrist. Bud made a flying tackle, but the man was slippery as a river carp lying in the mud and was up and running for the barn while Bud felt the dust of the barnyard in his teeth.

Whoever he was and whatever the hell he was doing, he'd better be stopped. As he scrambled to his feet and set off after the man, Bud tried to think what he could be up to. If he wanted to get to the President for some reason, he could run right through the barn and out onto the trails. Or he could untie Chester, hop on him, and ride off to lose himself in the woods or find Townsend, alone on the horse, the horse with twenty-eight of the nails in his feet!

Then he remembered Carter, still in the barn. My God, the idiot was heading straight for where they'd left Carter, alone with the tethered horse! Bud rounded the corner into the barn at a dead run. His heart raced and anger rushed through him like a brush fire in the wind. He could see the man now, in the aisle of the barn, running towards the light at the other end. Then he saw Carter and the horse, and for a minute his breath caught in his chest. The horse was crashing from side to side in the cross-ties, panicked by the excitement, and it looked as though Carter was trying to quiet him down. The little boy was at the frantic horse's head where he could be thrown against the wall or fall under the animal's feet as they pounded the floor in frustration.

The man was close to them now and slowing his pace. *"Run,* Carter!" Bud yelled with all the breath he had left as he raced towards him. But Carter wasn't running. He was at the horse's head, struggling to undo the snaps. Suddenly the horse was free. Carter dodged behind it, yelling and whacking it across the rump. The animal sprang forward and thundered down the narrow aisle in sheer panic. It didn't even see the figure of the man trying to get out of its way. The great hooves pounded flesh and bone into the dust and, leaping over the prostrate form, the horse came panting out into the light. It pulled up, heaving and sweaty, a few feet away.

Bud ran past the animal to where Carter was standing over the crushed form of the Marine, who lay with his neck twisted oddly to the back and one leg bent beneath his body. The gun was still in his hand.

"Are you OK—?" Bud's breath was dry in his throat and his voice was harsh and rasping.

"Sure, I'm OK," Carter said. "Did you see him, Bud? Did you see old Chester? He ran right over this guy like he wasn't there! Shit, I just gave him a whack. I knew how he'd go out of here if I got him loose!" He knelt on the ground, surveying his handiwork with apparent satisfaction.

Bud leaned down and started to pull Carter to his feet. "You were great, buddy—that was just great—" he said.

The boy interrupted him. "Look," he said, pointing over the motionless body of the Marine to where a shining object lay in the dirt on the floor. "Look, Chester smashed G-George's wonderful w-watch!" He leaned over and picked up the twisted piece of metal and broken glass. He held it in his hand staring at the ruined mechanism as though it might spring to life through the sheer power of his will. Then, before Bud could stop him, he ran to where George still lay in the yard.

He fell to his knees and shook George's shoulder. "I'm sorry, George, I'm sorry! It's my fault—I'm sorry—" Then Bud saw the dark stain spreading on the ground and a small red spot staining the white material of George's shirt. He saw Carter's eyes widen as he stared, watching the red circle as it grew and began to run down to join the pool of blood on the ground. He pulled the boy to his feet and held the disheveled head against him. He could feel the boy's shoulders shaking, but when Carter looked up, his eyes were dry, startling dark circles in his ashy face. He dropped the broken watch into his pocket and buried his face against Bud's chest. "He said I could have it," he murmured into Bud's shirt. "But I didn't want it like this—"

The air around them was suddenly so still that Bud could hear his own heart beating. Carter's little snuffling noises had stopped. They stood there, unmoving, as though time was suspended for them while the rest of the world rushed past unnoticed. "Carter, look," Bud said. "Just always remember that George was brave and good and he didn't die for nothin'." His voice seemed to come from far away and from another person. His throat ached. Against his chest he felt Carter's small nod of assent.

The sound that broke the stillness didn't reach his consciousness until Carter pulled away and fell on the ground by George's body. "Bud, he said something! George said something—!" His voice was a husky whisper, close to George's face. "George—George, it's me—Carter. Don't be dead, please—" Carter was holding George's hand in both of his and staring at it as if he had never seen a hand before. "Bud, he can feel me! He isn't dead, is he—is he, Bud?" Oh, God, he wasn't. We got to get help, Bud thought, got to stop the blood. He was ripping off his shirt when he heard the siren's lonely howl. "He's awake!" Carter said. "He can hear the ambulance—"

Bud leaned over. "It's OK," he said. "You're gonna be OK—"

He couldn't make out what George said. It was just one word, "Eleni?"

A half mile away, Ed Townsend trotted along the spongy, soft earth of the path by the creek. He should meet George any moment now, and they would have a good gallop together. On a day like this it was easy to believe in the future, and the President of the United States felt confident. The meetings next week wouldn't fail and one day the world would know the blessings of peace. He wondered why George was late and then, echoing through the woods, he heard the faroff wail of a siren.

THE FINEST IN SUSPENSE!

THE URSA ULTIMATUM (2130, $3.95)
by Terry Baxter

In the dead of night, twelve nuclear warheads are smuggled north across the Mexican border to be detonated simultaneously in major cities throughout the U.S. And only a small-town desert lawman stands between a face-less Russian superspy and World War Three!

THE LAST ASSASSIN (1989, $3.95)
by Daniel Easterman

From New York City to the Middle East, the devastating flames of revolution and terrorism sweep across a world gone mad . . . as the most terrifying conspiracy in the history of mankind is born!

FLOWERS FROM BERLIN (2060, $4.50)
by Noel Hynd

With the Earth on the brink of World War Two, the Third Reich's deadliest professional killer is dispatched on the most heinous assignment of his murderous career: the assassination of Franklin Delano Roosevelt!

THE BIG NEEDLE (1921, $2.95)
by Ken Follett

All across Europe, innocent people are being terrorized, homes are destroyed, and dead bodies have become an unnervingly common sight. And the horrors will continue until the most powerful organization on Earth finds Chadwell Carstairs—and kills him!

DOMINATOR (2118, $3.95)
by James Follett

Two extraordinary men, each driven by dangerously ambiguous loyalties, play out the ultimate nuclear endgame miles above the helpless planet—aboard a hijacked space shuttle called DOMINATOR!

Available wherever paperbacks are sold, or order direct from the Publisher. Send cover price plus 50¢ per copy for mailing and handling to Zebra Books, Dept. 2681, 475 Park Avenue South, New York, N.Y. 10016. Residents of New York, New Jersey and Pennsylvania must include sales tax. DO NOT SEND CASH.